DEATH BLOW

HOMICIDE DETECTIVE VERANDA CRUZ TAKES
ON THE MOST RUTHLESS MEMBER OF THE
VILLALOBOS CARTEL IN THIS FAST-PACED
FOLLOW-UP TO PHOENIX BURNING

ISABELLA MALDONADO

MIDNIGHT INK
WOODBURY, MINNESOTA

First Edition
First Printing, 2019

Book format by Bob Gaul
Cover design by Shira Atakpu
Cover illustration by Dominick Finelle / The July Group
Editing by Nicole Nugent

Midnight Ink, an imprint of Llewellyn Worldwide Ltd.

This is a work of fiction. Names, characters, places, and incidents are either the product of the author's imagination or are used fictitiously, and any resemblance to actual persons living or dead, business establishments, events, or locales is entirely coincidental.

Library of Congress Cataloging-in-Publication Data
Names: Maldonado, Isabella, author.
Title: Death blow : a Veranda Cruz mystery / Isabella Maldonado.
Description: First edition. | Woodbury, Minnesota : Midnight Ink, [2019] |
    Series: A Veranda Cruz mystery ; #3.
Identifiers: LCCN 2018041425 (print) | LCCN 2018042603 (ebook) | ISBN
    9780738755601 (ebook) | ISBN 9780738751030 (alk. paper)
Subjects: | GSAFD: Mystery fiction. | Suspense fiction.
Classification: LCC PS3613.A434 (ebook) | LCC PS3613.A434 D43 2019 (print) |
    DDC 813 / .6—dc23
LC record available at https: / /lccn.loc.gov / 2018041425

Midnight Ink
Llewellyn Worldwide Ltd.
2143 Wooddale Drive
Woodbury, MN 55125-2989
www.midnightinkbooks.com

Printed in the United States of America

For women in law enforcement everywhere,
my sisters in crime.

CAREFUL TO HIDE her suspicions, Detective Veranda Cruz bent to examine the dead man bound to a metal folding chair in the center of the open self-storage unit. The distinctive scent of charred human flesh permeated the early morning air as she scrutinized the image of a wolf's head seared into the victim's chest. Light from a pair of buzzing fluorescent tubes ten feet above her head spotlighted the gruesome tableau, reinforcing her growing sense that the scene had been staged specifically for her. To draw her in.

Hands sweating inside tight latex gloves, she pointed to the outer ridge of burned skin. "The brand is fresh," she said, turning to her partner.

Sam Stark, senior detective in the Phoenix Police Department Homicide Unit, stroked his thick silvery mustache. "Is it legit?"

She straightened, pushed a loose tendril of hair behind her ear, and gave him a curt nod. "Villalobos cartel."

More than two years spent chasing the Mexican criminal organization at its North American base of operations in Phoenix had made her a subject matter expert. And a target.

Her thoughts raced. The cartel would never have left a victim on display without a reason. She knew of no connection between Desert Bloom EZ Storage and the Villalobos family or any of its front companies. So why here? Why now? Missing facts compelled and frustrated her in equal parts.

Lieutenant Richard Diaz ducked under the perimeter crime scene tape and shouldered his way past the Crime Scene techs clustered at the entrance to the unit. She wasn't happy to see the Homicide lieutenant. The tenuous alliance forged between them during a recent crisis had settled into an uneasy ceasefire over the past month and a half.

She felt the weight of Diaz's dark stare when he addressed her. "What have you got so far?"

By directing his question to her when Sam was the senior detective at the scene, Diaz underscored her lead status on the case. Her first lead detective assignment since the last cartel-related killing seven weeks ago.

She gestured up and down the victim's nude body and delivered a rapid-fire summary of her observations. "Unknown Hispanic male. Single gunshot to the forehead, no exit wound. Likely small caliber. Fresh brand in the shape of a wolf's head on his upper left chest."

At Diaz's nod, she supplied further details. "Subject has no clothing, ID, or personal effects. Tattoos on his arms indicate he served in the Mexican military. Lividity and blanching look like he's been dead in that chair at least a couple hours."

The ME would provide a more accurate time of death, but Veranda could tell by the presence of lividity, which purpled the extremities, that the man's blood had stopped flowing a while ago. Without the heart pumping it through the system, gravity caused blood to pool at the body's lowest points. Whiteness of the skin under the cords binding him showed the pressure used to restrain him, referred to as blanching.

Diaz was all business. "Who found him?"

Her eyes flicked from her wristwatch to her notebook. "An employee discovered the body fifty-two minutes ago. Tyler Kendall. He's worked at Desert Bloom EZ Storage for about six months. No criminal record. No prior contacts."

"Where's Kendall now?"

"According to the paramedics who showed up, he's still freaked." She tipped her head toward the main building. "He's in the front office sucking on an oxygen mask."

"You think he's involved?"

She exchanged glances with Sam before answering her lieutenant. "Marci and Tony are interviewing him now, but he doesn't look good for it."

She had designated two of her Homicide squad members, Marci Blane and Tony Sanchez, to take Kendall through the start of his day. Before Diaz arrived, Marci had texted a brief but colorful description of Kendall's borderline hysterical reaction to the grisly discovery.

When her lieutenant raised an eyebrow, she added, "According to Marci, Kendall got an anonymous call complaining of an odor coming from one of the units, went to investigate, crapped his *chonies*, and called nine-one-one."

"The ambulance crew had to break out the smelling salts," Sam said. "Still looks a bit green under the oxygen mask."

Her partner's comment jarred her memory. "We got lucky with the paramedics this time. They didn't mess with the body."

She understood that EMTs had a duty to render aid, but she'd seen them compromise a few crime scenes where the victim was what the

3

Homicide squad called DRT, dead right there. Despite obvious signs of death, occasionally paramedics would drag a body across the room, plop equipment on every available surface not trampled by their boots, and leave a blizzard of sterile gauze, white adhesive tape, and other medical debris strewn all over. This time, thankfully, they hadn't gone through the motions.

Diaz scanned the bare cinder block walls around them. "Who's renting this unit?"

The remaining members of her squad, Steven "Doc" Malloy and Frank Fujiyama, were running down the rental history. The PPD Homicide Unit consisted of ten squads, each with five to ten detectives. Veranda's squad had six, usually working in three pairs. As the newest member of the team, she partnered with Sam, who'd been working murder cases when she graduated from the police academy.

"The site manager showed about ten minutes ago," she said. "Doc and Frank are with him in the back office digging through their records, but they got a tentative ID."

Beside her, Sam peered down at his notebook through half-moon reading glasses. "A subject named Federico Davila rented it out two weeks ago. Every way Doc and Frank run the name leads to a dead end. The only photo is the copy of the Arizona driver's license attached to the rental agreement—fake for sure." He stashed the pad in his back pocket. "They're reviewing video surveillance of the lot now."

Veranda signaled one of the Crime Scene techs opening a reinforced plastic carrying case. "You guys ready to move him?"

He glanced at her through clear plastic goggles. "I'll cut the zip ties." He stooped to pull a flex-cuff cutter from a compartment in the bulky case and moved behind the chair. The tech reached down to fasten the yellow-handled tool onto the black nylon restraints binding the man's swollen wrists together behind his back.

The naked corpse shifted, and something red caught Veranda's eye. Squatting, she focused on the smooth metal surface of the chair beneath the man's crotch. The job had taught her there was no dignity in death. Only the attempt to bring whoever had caused it to justice.

At first, she assumed the speck of crimson was a trickle of blood. A moment later, she realized the shade of red was too bright. The storage facility employee had discovered the body close to an hour ago. Blood would have oxidized after exposure to air and darkened to maroon by now. A distant memory tugged at the back of her mind, bringing with it a ripple of unease. She had seen this before, but where?

A moment later, recognition jolted through her like an electric current. "Everyone out." She sprang to her feet and whirled to face the others. "Now."

Sam stepped toward her, craning his neck to see over her shoulder. "What's going on?"

Without answering, she turned to the tech, who stood transfixed behind the chair, poised to cut. "Don't touch him," she said.

Eyes widening behind the clear protective glasses, he turned to the highest-ranking official present for direction. "Lieutenant Diaz?"

"Nobody move," Diaz said, then shifted his eyes to her. "Explain yourself, Cruz."

She responded with a single word. "Bomb!"

Spreading her arms, she plowed into Sam, forcing him backward. Thrown off balance, he staggered into Diaz. Veranda lowered her center of gravity and used her legs to push, driving them toward the open bay door of the storage unit. She darted a glance over her shoulder, checking to make sure the tech had followed. He sprinted past her to the parking lot.

Sam grunted as she shoved him again. "What the hell, Veranda?"

She latched onto the sleeve of the remaining Crime Scene tech and yanked him along with her as she crossed the threshold onto the asphalt.

Diaz recovered his footing and glared at her. "Where did you see a bomb?"

She huffed out a breath. He wasn't getting it. "We need to get farther away."

Diaz became an unmovable wall. "I asked you to explain yourself, Detective."

She stifled a curse, aware that her tendency to operate from instinct, skirt rules, and rush headlong into her investigations had caused this. Diaz, always uneasy with her methods, demanded clarification before following her instructions. She knew he would probably have acted immediately to anyone else's order to evacuate, but she had given him too many reasons to question her actions in the past.

Instinctively, she positioned her back to the entrance, using her body to shield the others while she squared off with her supervisor. Unable to move him any farther physically, she had to convince Diaz she'd recognized a cartel booby trap.

"I saw a red wire sticking out of his...body." She stopped short of using the anatomically correct word. "I've seen it before in my background research into the Villalobos cartel. They do it in Mexico, but not in the US." She paused. "Until now." Without time to be delicate, she got to the point. "They shove an IED inside a corpse, then use a remote detonator when police show up to investigate."

Diaz narrowed his eyes. "Then why aren't they scraping pieces of us off the storage unit walls?"

She blew out an exasperated huff of air. "Maybe it didn't work. Maybe they put it on a timer instead. Maybe the signal didn't transmit." Her temper ratcheted up with every moment of delay. "How should I know?"

"Are you sure you saw a wire?" Diaz asked, completely unruffled. "You said it was red. Could it have been a trickle of blood?"

She gritted her teeth. "I know what I saw. We need to clear the area and get a bomb tech out here."

He considered her for a long moment. "Before I set off the buzzers and bells, I'll see for myself." He started to walk around her.

She grabbed his arm. "No, Lieutenant."

His gaze traveled down to her fingers clutching his forearm. "Take your hand off me, Detective." His voice was deadly calm. "That's an order."

"No." She matched his tone. "Sir."

Their eyes locked.

"Cruz, this is insubordina—"

An explosion cut off Diaz's words. The force of the blast hit Veranda in the back, propelling her forward into Diaz and Sam. Her body barreled into both men, knocking them off their feet. They tumbled in a tangle of arms and legs, her head landing on Sam's chest and her legs on Diaz's lap.

Ears ringing, she blinked to clear her vision and saw the rest of the team sprawled on the asphalt nearby. She extricated herself and shouted over the buzzing in her ears to ask Sam if he was okay. When he gave her a thumbs-up, she turned to Diaz, who had his portable radio to his mouth, barking orders at the dispatcher. She heard the words *rescue* and *bomb squad*, but couldn't make out the rest.

Gradually, sound began to return. She lurched to her feet and staggered to the Crime Scene tech who'd been ready to cut the zip ties.

Still sitting on the ground, he let out a stream of expletives. "All my equipment was inside that storage unit."

That meant every scrap of evidence he'd collected had blown up as well. She extended a hand to pull him up. "You hurt?"

He grasped her hand and got to his feet. "I'm fine." He turned to stare at the unit.

She followed his gaze. The explosion had peeled back the metal edges of the bay door, leaving jagged shards protruding outward. Inside, black streaks of char snaked across the cement floor. Remains of the folding chair lay twisted in a heap. There wasn't much left of the man who had occupied it, and she steeled herself for the next part of the crime scene investigation. Instead of examining a corpse in a relatively empty area, she would help the Crime Scene techs hunt for chunks and pieces peppering the walls, floor, and ceiling.

Sam gently touched her elbow, startling her. "You were closest to the blast." He looked her up and down. "You okay?"

"I'm fine."

"She's not fine." Diaz's sharp voice came from behind her. "She's bleeding."

She spun to face him. "What are you talking about?" Even as she asked the question, the top of her left shoulder began to throb.

Concern wrinkled Diaz's brow. "The back of your shirt is scorched and torn. Your skin is exposed, and there's blood." He drew in a breath. "Looks like a piece of shrapnel cut you."

Sam, now behind her after she turned to confront Diaz, concurred. "Lieutenant's right," he said. "The EMTs are here, best let 'em check it out."

The paramedics who had been treating the overwrought employee were still in the main office when the bomb went off. Triage bags in hand, they had rushed toward the storage unit after the explosion, the rest of the Homicide squad on their heels.

Veranda pivoted so her back faced away from both men. "We have more important things to do than worry about a scratch."

Ignoring her, Diaz beckoned the EMTs over. "Treat her first."

She raised her voice. "I don't need a medic. I need you to listen."

He turned to her. "I hear you, Detective, but it's my call. You will submit to an examination. Now."

She balled her hands into fists to prevent herself from using them to strangle her supervisor. "Lieutenant, the cartel uses a remote detonator to set off these devices. That means the bomber is nearby. Maybe even watching us right now. Instead of wasting time with Band-Aids and antiseptic, we should be checking the area."

"I've already taken care of that." He jerked his thumb at a phalanx of black-and-whites at the far end of the parking lot. "The patrol sergeant is forming a grid search pattern. The air unit will be overhead any minute. The bomb squad and the mobile command bus are on the way." His expression hardened. "Don't tell me how to do my job."

Before she could respond, the taller EMT distracted her, snapping on light blue latex gloves. "Let's have a look at your back, ma'am."

She crossed her arms. "I'm fine. Why don't you check on the others?"

"I've already done that," Diaz said. "You're the only one with an injury."

The second EMT circled around behind her and she felt him tug at the fabric of her blouse. His voice carried a clinical tone. "The laceration doesn't look too deep, but it stretches up onto your shoulder. That's as much as I can see right now. Come over to the wagon and let's get a better look."

Diaz's withering stare killed her protest before it began. She trailed the paramedics, acknowledging Sam's sympathetic look with a roll of her eyes in the general direction of her boss.

The taller paramedic gestured toward the ambulance. "Climb up and sit inside. We'll need to cut your shirt to clean and treat the injury here because I'm assuming you'll refuse transport."

Diaz had followed her. "Not sure I'm going to let her refuse."

She contemplated how many years in prison she would get for the justifiable homicide of a supervisor. "You can't force me to go to the hospital."

"But I can make you leave this crime scene, which will happen if I think you need the hospital."

Sheer annoyance at the waste of valuable time forced a groan from her. "Fine. Go ahead and take care of it here. Then let me get back to work."

The taller EMT slid a pair of shears from his equipment belt and deftly sliced her blouse straight across the top of the left shoulder seam. Once the collar had been cut, the silky fabric fell away on both sides, revealing her bra strap and several inches of skin down to her shoulder blade in back and past her collarbone in front.

Everyone froze. Shock reflected in their eyes.

Was her injury worse than she thought? She glanced down, concerned she might see a shard of metal sticking out of her body. Instead, she saw what had caused the reaction.

A black wolf's head tattoo covering the left side of her chest just above the lace of her bra stood out in sharp relief against her caramel skin. The beast's lips curled back over razor sharp fangs in a predatory snarl. Above the design, a crimson letter V had been inked in bold calligraphy.

The paramedic tore his gaze away from the tattoo to scan her face. A spark of recognition ignited. "You must be ..."

She longed to snatch the tattered edge of her top and yank it up a few inches to cover the ugly ink, but restrained herself. She couldn't hide who she was.

"Yes." She lifted her chin. "I'm Veranda Cruz."

The EMTs exchanged a look she recognized well.

Revulsion.

"And yes, that's a cartel tattoo," she continued. "With the Villalobos family mark above it." Heart pounding beneath the indelible mark that proclaimed her heritage to the world, she gave voice to the tacit judgment both men had failed to conceal. "Because Hector Villalobos is my father."

2

DARIA VILLALOBOS BRIEFLY closed her eyes and inhaled, breathing in the heady blend of primal male musk, sweat, and fear. Her designer boots stirred tiny puffs of dust from the compacted dirt floor as she took measured steps behind the circle of men. Her men. She had ordered them to what she referred to as "the pit building" to teach them the consequences of failure. She intended today's lesson to fill their every waking moment with dread. And haunt their dreams.

Under her guidance, twelve of her men had recently constructed the barn-sized prefabricated building on a vast plot of scrub-covered desert at the foot of South Mountain on the outskirts of Phoenix. Heavily sound-proofed and situated beside a nature preserve, outsiders seldom came near the area. Barbed wire fencing and dense chaparral kept wayward hikers away.

When designing the building, Daria had included a service door at the back to vent fumes or make a fast exit. Equal parts science lab, demolition site, and personal fortress, the functional external structure hadn't been her focus. What lay inside, however, had taken a great deal of time and money over the past few weeks.

No one reported any disturbances when the men used her specially designed explosives and jackhammers to blast through the rock-hard layers of caliche just below the desert floor. Created by thousands of years of calcium carbonate deposits, the caliche around the mountain was particularly dense, but she had ordered them to dig a deep pit to her exact specifications.

Now her men stood in silence around the perimeter of the hole they had toiled to create. She stopped circling behind them and drew near enough to lay a hand on the nape of a damp neck, a smile curling her lips when the man flinched. She addressed him in Spanish. "You were too slow, Pedro."

When the bomb in the storage unit failed to explode, she had turned to Pedro for the backup detonator to the device. While the idiot fumbled through a box of equipment, Veranda Cruz had managed to push everyone out to safety. Two hours later, Daria's anger hadn't cooled in the slightest.

Pedro began to turn his head toward her, then appeared to recall himself and returned his gaze to the dirt floor. "I could not find it, Señorita Daria."

She gave him a slight nudge, and the treads of his worn leather work boots scraped the ground, sliding forward. The scuffed toes were now only inches from the edge of the pit. He sucked in a horrified gasp.

"You should have been prepared for emergencies. That bitch would be dead right now if you had done your job." She said nothing for several awkward moments, aware that silence could terrify more than words. She finally spoke again, allowing anger to sharpen her words. "But you are not the only one to blame."

Dropping her hand, she moved on. Eighteen of her men surrounded the pit. Over twelve feet deep and just as wide across, she had designed it for a specific purpose. Now one of them would be the first to test her new invention.

She paused behind another man's back. "Julio, where were you when I examined the wires?"

"By your side, Señorita, double checking. Everything was good."

"And yet … no boom." She reached out to stroke his quivering shoulder blade before moving on to the next man. "Which leads me to you, Guillermo." She watched a trickle of perspiration course down from under his dark ponytail to disappear inside the collar of his damp shirt.

"I did as you told me, Señorita," he said, voice thick with strain.

"And what was that, Guillermo?"

"I put the bomb inside Oscar after he was dead."

She twisted the smooth hair of his ponytail around her fingers, relishing the terror permeating the open area surrounding the yawning hole in the ground. She could drag this out all morning, and probably would have, but the pit beckoned. Curiosity spurred her decision.

She let the man's hair slide from her grasp and used her index finger to trail a leisurely path down his spine. "Did you push it in hard, Guillermo?"

His voice elevated an octave. "I had to … to get it deep enough inside not to fall out."

She kept her finger moving down until she reached his belt. "Perhaps a wire came loose with all that shoving." She rotated her hand and placed it gently on his back pocket. "You have to be careful when you push." She cupped his bottom. "Especially here."

His legs shook violently. "Please, Señorita Daria."

She lowered her voice to a whisper. "But you weren't careful, were you?" His rising panic intoxicated her. "You pushed too hard." She gave his backside a shove that toppled him forward. "Like that."

He pitched forward over the edge, arms windmilling in desperate circles. His guttural shriek ended with a thud.

Daria leaned over to peer down at him, hoping the fall hadn't knocked him unconscious. That wouldn't do. Relief rushed through her when he scrambled to his feet on the pit's earthen floor. She ordered her men to watch Guillermo scamper in a circle, picking his way around the pressure plates surrounding the metal pole in the center. He cast pleading eyes upward and placed his hands against the curved wall of reinforced cement that lined the pit's sides.

Daria spared Guillermo another glance before scanning the stunned faces of the men surrounding the hole. They didn't like her, didn't respect her, but they feared her. She had made sure of that.

Born into her father's patriarchy, she'd carved out a place for herself among her three older brothers. Their status as leaders in the family business was their birthright, but hers had come at a very steep price. Hector Villalobos had been upset that his youngest child wished to play what he thought was a man's game. He had devised a brutal test before allowing her into the inner sanctum. Only fifteen years old, her victory had surprised everyone. And irrevocably changed her.

A rueful smile twisted her lush mouth. Her trial by fire had ended more than ten years ago, but she'd been forced to prove her mettle every day since. Guillermo's punishment would ensure the remaining seventeen men would follow her orders without hesitation.

She cleared her throat, and even Guillermo stopped his frantic scrabbling. All eyes turned to her. "Guillermo will be the first to test my newest invention." She crossed her arms. "For those of you who weren't part of the construction crew at this site, I'll explain."

The men watched in rapt silence as she continued. "The pole in the center is an upgrade to the classic Claymore mine. Instead of targeting one direction, my version launches a shower of nails and ball bearings in a three-sixty spread." She warmed to her subject. "If I've designed it right, a bit of C-4 will detonate, sending shrapnel in every direction." She stopped and looked down. "There's nowhere to hide when you've disappointed me."

She drank in the stark horror on Guillermo's face as he wrung his hands. He took a step toward the metal pole, extending his arm as if he intended to disconnect the multicolored wires sticking out at odd angles.

Did he really believe she hadn't thought of that? "You can't get near the device without stepping on the metal plates," she called down to him. "Which will detonate it instantly."

The front of Guillermo's jeans darkened as urine leaked from his pant legs, soaking into the dirt at his feet.

She looked past him at the digital display timer mounted near the top of the pole for all to see. "Twelve seconds left. Any last words?"

"Please, Señorita Daria. I swear it will never happen again!"

"No, Guillermo." She signaled the men to back away from the pit and jammed an index finger into each ear. "It won't."

The explosion shook the building, vibrating through every part of her body from the soles of her feet to the fillings in her teeth. The pit's mouth vomited up a plume of pebbled cement. In the eerie stillness that followed, the men crept to the edge, waving away curling clouds of dust and squinting down. When several of them retched, she knew Guillermo's death had served its purpose.

"Scrub down the inside wall and wash the smaller pieces down the drain," she said, pointing to a circular metal grate the size of a manhole cover that concealed a waste disposal chute.

Daria reflected on the lessons gleaned from her father about disciplining subordinates. *El Lobo* extracted maximum value from every death sentence he ordered, selecting each participant with care and purpose. The condemned, the executioner, and the person who disposed of the body carried meaning and significance.

Her gaze locked on one of her men, singling him out. "Pedro, bag what's left of Guillermo and dispose of it on the other side of town. I don't want anyone tying the remains back to this location."

Pedro might have joined Guillermo in the pit. Mopping up bits and pieces of his friend would drive that point home as nothing else could.

Trembling, Pedro inclined his head. *"Sí, Señorita."*

She strode from the building, reassessing her predicament. Determined to find a way to salvage this morning's disaster, her feet hurried toward a nearby Jeep waiting in the barren dirt lot next to the building.

She wrenched open the driver's door and slid onto the utilitarian vinyl seat. The weight of impending judgment settled on her shoulders as she recalled the meeting in her father's office at their family compound in Mexico seven weeks ago, when the course of her life had changed for the second time.

Because she was female, her father had given her rightful place in the family business to Salazar, his trusted fixer and right-hand man. When she objected, he promised to reconsider if she eliminated Cruz. *El Lobo* didn't specify the method, but the kill order had to be carried out personally. Expecting quick results, he hadn't understood why Daria insisted on a bomb rather than a bullet.

Any idiot could pull a trigger, but she'd engineered the pit, a thing of beauty designed to carry out her personal agenda. She had kept her reasons to herself, letting her father believe a fondness for explosives drove her choice of method.

The Jeep's engine sputtered awake at the second twist of her key in the ignition, pulling her thoughts back to her present situation. Her father's impatience had forced her hand. He had called yesterday threatening to send Salazar to carry out her assignment if she didn't act this morning. Her men worked through the night, but the pit wasn't ready until an hour ago, well after her deadline. The storage unit bomb had been her backup plan.

As she drove out of the lot, the beginnings of an idea slipped into her awareness. She had taken pains to frame Salazar for Cruz's death. Now that Cruz had survived, the planted evidence took on a new role. While the police chased Salazar, occupying his time and theirs, Daria would be free to implement the alternative plan uncoiling in her mind like a viper preparing to strike.

3

VERANDA WATCHED THE range of emotions flicker through her mother's hazel eyes. Fear, anger, and sorrow finally resolved into an expression of deep pain. A single tear escaped, wrenching Veranda's heart.

After Lieutenant Diaz sent everyone home to eat and get cleaned up, she'd changed clothes at her small two-room bungalow house downtown before coming to see her mother at the family's food truck. While her uncles took orders and cooked, Veranda had ushered her mother to the driver's seat, squatting beside her to tell her about the explosion. It hadn't gone well.

She reached out to sweep the droplet away with her thumb. "I'm okay, Mamá. It's barely a scratch."

"This time," Lorena said, a slight Mexican accent lacing her words. "What about the next time?"

Her mother knew, better than anyone, how relentless the Villalobos family could be. And how dangerous. Hector had brutalized her, and his son Bartolo was the reason she toiled in a cramped food truck every day.

Lorena Cruz-Gomez had started a family restaurant with her younger siblings soon after arriving in Phoenix over thirty years ago. After Bartolo burned the restaurant down last summer, Lorena had accepted an offer from her youngest brothers to share their food truck. They had stationed the brightly colored vehicle in the former restaurant's parking lot to keep existing customers coming during reconstruction. The new building was almost finished, and the family planned to throw a grand reopening celebration.

Veranda took pride in her family and dreaded bringing more suffering to their door because of her job. The moisture on the pad of her thumb from her mother's tear told her that was exactly what she'd done.

She bent her head. "I'll be careful, Mamá." The words came out hollow, even she could hear their empty promise.

Lorena stood and smoothed her white apron. "I must help them." She inclined her head toward Veranda's uncles, who were struggling to keep pace with the lunch rush.

She wanted to say more to her mother, find a way to make things right, but she knew Lorena preferred to work through her troubles. Over the years, she had observed her mother in the kitchen. Chopping, cooking, and plating were a kind of meditation. Feeding others fed her mother's soul.

Her tío Rico gave her a nod when she followed her mother into the food prep area of the truck. "Chuy's waiting for you," he said, pointing a serving spoon at three heaping paper plates sitting on the tiny metal counter. "He already ordered."

Chuy, her favorite cousin, had asked her to meet for lunch. The third plate meant he must have brought Tiffany, his girlfriend, along.

Stomach growling, she inhaled the mingled scents of onion, cumin, and cilantro as she threaded her way through the cluster of sun-bleached card tables and weathered folding chairs. Snatches of conversations in Spanish and English reached her ears from diners enjoying an al fresco meal in the fine late-October Arizona weather.

Plunking the plates down, she quirked a brow at Chuy, who sat next to Tiffany at the farthest table from the food truck.

"You had to pick the farthest table?"

Chuy slid a calloused hand over his shaved and tattooed scalp. "Yeah, I want to talk serious shit, so I'm sitting where folks can't listen in." His dark eyes swept the area like an inmate checking a prison yard for threats, a tactic he was intimately familiar with. "Especially our *tíos* and *tías*."

She grinned and pulled out a folding chair. "And people say you don't have manners."

"I know, right?" He reached a muscular arm out to slide his plate closer. "I'm a considerate fuckin' guy."

She sat down, pushed Tiffany's enchiladas toward her, and considered the couple. Extensive elaborate body art set them apart from the midday business crowd. While Tiffany's ink consisted of brightly colored animals and flowers, Chuy's tended toward dark biker-style Gothic symbols and intricate Mesoamerican tribal patterns. Over the past five years Chuy had converted his crude prison tatts into professional designs. Once he got out, opened a car repair shop in an old garage, and began making legitimate money, he'd forged a new direction for his life. After he got clean and sober, he'd fallen for Tiffany, whose bleached-blonde locks, custom Harley Softail, and mostly spandex wardrobe reminded Veranda of Barbie. If Barbie ditched Ken for a badass Chicano biker.

She handed them plastic forks. "What's up, Chuy?"

Never one to mince words, her cousin got right to the point. "I'm glad you came to talk to your mom in person. Would have been much worse for her to see it on the news."

Veranda winced inwardly at the memory of her mother's stricken expression when she told her about the bomb. She recalled an incident years ago when one of her fellow officers had been shot. Despite his pain, he'd clutched her arm as paramedics lifted his gurney to load him into an ambulance. He had one request: "No one calls my wife except me."

She understood that the officer wanted to reassure his wife by letting her hear his voice. Every police spouse dreads a phone call or a visit from department officials when their husband or wife is late coming off shift. She had been present when the wife of a member of her first patrol squad was notified of his line-of-duty death. The woman had opened her front door, gazed up at the duty commander, and collapsed into his arms before he could say a word.

Veranda looked back at Chuy. "I knew Mamá should hear about it from me in person. That way she could see me, touch me, know I'm okay." She shook her head. "Still, I thought she'd pass out when I told her what happened."

"*Ay*, Lorena must've crossed herself twenty-seven times," Chuy said, using her mother's first name as he usually did.

She picked up her burrito, careful to hold it together so the spicy green chile sauce wouldn't ooze out and drip on her beige slacks. "Why did you want to see me?"

Chuy took a swig of lemonade. "Lorena checked out that cut on your shoulder, didn't she?"

As soon as she heard about the injury, her mother had insisted on pushing aside the collar of her replacement shirt to inspect beneath the bandages.

Veranda paused before taking a bite. "Don't worry, Mamá gave me the magic ointment."

Tiffany's brow wrinkled. "Magic ointment?"

Chuy grew serious. "Didn't you know Mexicans have a traditional medicine that heals everything?" At Tiffany's shake of the head, he continued. "It's a secret recipe we keep to ourselves. Handed down through our grandmothers for generations."

Tiffany lowered her voice. "What's in it?"

Chuy blew out a dramatic sigh. "I don't know if I can tell you, *mamacita*. This is kinda … sacred to our people."

Veranda gave his arm a smack. "Quit messing with her, Chuy."

He spread his hands. "Am I lying?"

Veranda rolled her eyes and turned to Tiffany. "It's Vick's VapoRub."

Tiffany wrinkled her nose. "That smelly goop that comes in a blue jar?"

Veranda nodded. "We use it for everything from a head cold to a sucking chest wound."

Tiffany smacked Chuy's other arm. "Sacred to our people. Please."

He winked at her and turned to Veranda, his mood shifting. "Seriously though, we need to talk."

His tone made her wary. "About what?"

"About you. And Lorena." He hesitated, choosing his words. "My dad told me what happened when your mother saw your tatt. He said you were both real upset."

Her stomach tightened into a knot and she put down the burrito. Uncle Rico had been watching when Lorena's gentle hands had pulled her shirt collar aside, exposing the top of the letter V tattooed below her collarbone. Her mother had sucked in a breath, and Veranda knew the sight of it pained her.

She pretended not to understand. "What about it?"

Chuy waited a long moment before speaking. "This might come as a surprise, but I know a few tattoo artists."

She lifted her head to make an exaggerated study of his extensive body art. "Really?"

"The best one in Phoenix owes me a favor." When she narrowed her eyes, he dropped his plastic fork and raised his hand, palm out. "I didn't do nothing illegal, *mi'jita*, don't worry." He picked up the fork. "He could rework that ink for you free of charge. Make it into something different."

Though she was certain he hadn't meant them to, Chuy's words cut to the bone. She had not asked for the tattoo, which, like her unusual first name, had been given to her by a parent. Her mother had named her Veranda to express her love. Her father's family had marked her as a Villalobos to humiliate her.

Every morning, the vivid reminder of her origins confronted her in the bathroom mirror when she stepped out of the shower. Not only was she the daughter of a notorious criminal, but his brutal assault on her mother had brought Veranda into this world.

She realized her mind had wandered when Chuy paused, a forkful of *arroz con pollo* halfway to his mouth.

"Where you at, Veranda?" he asked, concern creasing the pointed tip of the dark tattoo that formed a widow's peak on his forehead.

"It's not something I like to think about," she said. "I've had the tattoo for seven weeks and I still don't know what to do about it. I hate the damn thing and what it stands for, but I need time to figure out what works for me."

"You want to get it lasered off? I know a guy who can do that too." He shrugged. "Hurts like hell, takes a bunch of visits, but I can make it happen."

She rolled her eyes. "You know a guy for everything."

"That's what it's all about, *mi'jita*. Knowing the right people."

"No, Chuy." She shook her head. "It's about knowing what you want. Which I don't right now."

"We'll talk later, here comes your mom." Chuy lowered his voice. "And she still looks angry. I don't want her mad at me too."

Veranda suppressed a grin. Her tough, ex-con cousin was afraid of a middle-aged woman half his size. Of course, Lorena could be formidable. Especially when it came to her eldest daughter's personal life, safety, or career.

She glanced up to see her mother bearing down on them, brandishing a wooden spoon. "Mamá worries about me too much. She lets it get to her."

"She's not a fan of your job." Chuy raised both pierced brows. "Too dangerous."

"She's not a fan of anything that doesn't involve me getting married and producing grandchildren for her to spoil."

Lorena's dark expression cleared as she halted in front of the table. "What did I hear about grandchildren?"

Veranda groaned. "Nothing, Mamá. There aren't any grandchildren on the way." She cut her eyes to Chuy. "See what you started?"

Chuy chuckled.

Her mother latched onto the subject closest to her heart. "And there never will be as long as you keep—"

"My life is too hectic for kids, a dog, and a white picket fence."

Lorena put a hand on her hip. "White picket fence, bah! You will build another casita on our family property."

Over twenty years ago, when land in the city was cheaper, her mother had used proceeds from the family restaurant to buy three acres on a corner lot in South Phoenix. As her younger siblings—Veranda's aunts and uncles—got married, they built their own homes on the land. Now, five houses were grouped around an open space in the center of the family property. Only her mother's youngest sister,

Maria, had left the area, moving to Sedona to open up a New Age tea shop.

Her mother obviously expected Veranda to sell her mid-century bungalow downtown and move to the property with the rest of the family. This was the first time her mother had mentioned these plans, and Veranda found the idea both comforting and disturbing.

She didn't want to argue. "Those dreams will have to wait."

"*Ay, mi'ja*, don't wait too long." Lorena looked wistful. "You are already past thirty. When will you start a family?"

"When it's safe."

Chuy jabbed a plastic fork in her direction. "It's never going to be safe. Not totally."

She leveled a death stare at her favorite cousin. "Stay out of it, Chuy, I don't see you pushing a stroller around."

Tiffany giggled.

Lorena became tenacious when she got on the subject of grandchildren. "Hector Villalobos has already taken too much from me. Don't let him take your chance at happiness, *mi'ja*."

Her mother's perseverance in the face of such pain and grief only sharpened Veranda's determination to solve the storage unit murder. Certain the cartel was behind it, she suspected Daria, who procured their weapons and explosives. Daria was the only Villalobos family member left who could operate freely in the US. Bartolo and Carlos were dead, and Adolfo had multiple outstanding warrants. *El Lobo*'s chief enforcer, Salazar, was wanted for murder in seven countries. Taking down Daria would inflict serious damage to their organization.

Veranda changed the subject to the only topic guaranteed to divert Lorena's attention. "What are we doing for *Día de los Muertos* this year?"

Her mother's excited expression made her regret her tactic. She didn't plan to attend, which wouldn't go down well with the family.

She blew out a sigh. At least the inevitable argument would distract Lorena from the explosion.

Tiffany's blue eyes widened. "Wait, is it *Día de Muertos* or *Día de los Muertos*?"

"People say it both ways," Veranda said. "But in our family, we leave in the *los*."

Lorena shrugged. "That's how I was raised to call it."

"I've seen pictures of people at the parties," Tiffany said, turning to Chuy. "I'm going to dress up. Wait till you see my outfit."

Since Chuy and Tiffany had been dating less than a year, his girlfriend had never attended their annual Day of the Dead celebration. Everything Tiffany owned consisted mostly of Lycra. What she might wear for the occasion was anyone's guess, especially if she used internet photos as a party fashion guide.

Chuy, apparently borrowing Veranda's distraction technique, spoke around a mouthful of rice when Lorena looked alarmed at Tiffany's comments. "Are we doing a party on the family property like usual this year?" he asked.

Lorena nodded. "After we visit the cemetery. The celebration will be on November first in the evening, that's this Wednesday." She directed her next words at Veranda. "The day after tomorrow, *mi'ja*. We'll close the food truck an hour early."

She squirmed. Better start to lay the groundwork now. "I'm not sure I can make it this year."

Her mother acted as if she hadn't spoken. "Come by tomorrow evening. You will help me prepare the decorations. And the *Pan de Muertos*."

"Mamá, I'm going to be very busy." She made a show of looking at her watch. "In fact, I have to head back to headquarters now. Lieutenant Diaz ordered everyone to the briefing room and I'll be late if I don't get going."

The sparkle in her mother's eyes activated Veranda's internal alarm system.

"Ah, Richard Diaz," Lorena said, pressing the wooden spoon to her chest. "Such a good man. He will come to the party too."

She cursed herself for mentioning Diaz in front of her mother. Lorena adored him. "*Ay*, please no, Mamá. Not Diaz."

"But Anita Diaz will be there," her mother said, frowning. "Of course her son must come."

Anita Diaz was Lorena's best friend. Recently reunited, the two women had formed an unholy alliance, waging a not-so-secret campaign to march their offspring down the aisle together. The department's rules against supervisors fraternizing with subordinates were of no consequence to two Latina mothers on a mission.

At times she suspected her boss might be colluding with them, but then she would put a toe over the line at work. He'd swoop down on her like a hawk on a desert mouse, quoting regulations at her until she couldn't imagine he viewed her as anything other than a problem employee.

Chuy look offended. "What's wrong with Diaz?"

Instead of answering her cousin, she shot his girlfriend an imploring look. "A little help here, Tiff?"

"Not from me." Tiffany gave Chuy's hand a squeeze. "I owe a lot to your lieutenant. If it weren't for him, Chuy and I wouldn't be together."

Diaz had helped Chuy start a new life after his last stretch in prison ended five years ago. That almost—but not quite—made up for the fact that Diaz had put Chuy in jail in the first place. Her cousin had made it plain he felt differently than she did about the arrest, and he now treated Diaz like a respected older brother.

Clearly outnumbered, she crossed her arms. "If any of you had to answer to him, you'd know what a pain in the ass he is."

"I've had to answer to him." Chuy leaned forward. "How do you think he kept me from going back to jail? It's because he's a pain in the ass that I'm here, *mi'jita*."

Her mother scowled at Veranda. "Don't you talk about Richard like that. He's a good man with a good heart. He is coming to the party and you will be there too. No arguments."

How could she make her mother understand why she didn't want to go? Diaz was only one reason. Her reluctance had far deeper roots.

Every year, her family honored the memory of the departed souls dearest to them. In addition to her parents and grandparents, Lorena grieved the loss of her first husband, Ernesto Hidalgo. She also mourned her son, Bobby, a high school student who overdosed on drugs sold by a cartel dealer.

This would be the first time Veranda celebrated the holiday after learning about her past. Two of the people they would honor had been killed by her biological father; one directly, the other indirectly. Either way, Hector Villalobos had their blood on his hands. She felt tainted, undeserving of a place among her father's victims.

Chuy gave her a knowing look. "We all want you there, *mi'jita*."

"The party will be *muy grande* this year," her mother said. "We will have a band, costumes, face painting, and dancers. Father Ramirez announced it at mass last Sunday. Everyone is coming." She looked at Chuy. "Of course Veranda will be there."

Veranda accepted defeat. She would have better luck changing the path of a tornado than changing her mother's mind.

"Yes, Mamá," she said. "I'll be there."

4

TWENTY MINUTES LATER, Veranda took her customary seat beside Sam at the government-issue modular table in the Violent Crimes Bureau conference room. Known as the War Room by VCB detectives and supervisors, the large room occupied the center of the second floor. Detectives from all units in the bureau gathered to share information, coordinate investigations, and hold briefings.

VCB Commander Nathan Webster sat at the head of the long rectangular table, scanning the group over smudged drugstore reading glasses with black plastic frames. "I heard from Sergeant Jackson's wife early this morning. The appendectomy went well. He'll recover at home until next week."

Veranda and Sam exchanged looks. After their squad sergeant's appendicitis attack yesterday, Commander Webster had designated Lieutenant Diaz to step into the breach. In addition to overseeing all ten squads in the Homicide Unit, Diaz would respond to scenes with Veranda's team while Jackson recuperated.

"Sergeant Jackson's a healthy guy," Veranda said. "Maybe he'll get back on his feet sooner." She tried not to sound too hopeful.

Across from her, Detective Doc Malloy cleared his throat, drawing everyone's attention. Doc had earned his nickname. A Homicide detective for eight years, he was her squad's unofficial medical expert.

"Sometimes complications set in during recovery," Doc said, always eager to discuss medical conditions, the grimmer the better. "Surgery is nothing to fool around with. He should stay home until released by his surgeon." Shifting in his chair, he pointed a pale finger at her shoulder.

She grimaced, knowing what was coming.

"Actually, Veranda, I'm concerned about your injury too," Doc said. "That laceration could get infected. Are you taking antibiotics?"

Doc had attended more autopsies than anyone but the ME. So much time spent focused on death and disease had given him an understanding of human anatomy. And more than a touch of hypochondria. Some people who died violently also had illnesses and conditions. Doc observed the conditions, learned about the illnesses that brought them on, then began to manifest the symptoms himself.

"Got it covered." She waved his comment away. "Dab on Vick's VapoRub morning and night."

Doc scribbled a note on his pad, no doubt intending to do research later. She cast her eyes around the room to see if anyone picked up on the reference. Only Lieutenant Diaz gave her a wry smile.

Marci Blane had no patience for her fellow detective's drama. "Doc, you've got to stop going to autopsies."

"Moving on," Commander Webster said, cutting the banter short. "We have visitors." He indicated the two men sitting to his right. "This is Detective Malcolm Jones of the Bomb Squad. And you all know Detective Tye Kim from the lab."

31

The bomb tech wore a black nylon golf shirt with a gold PPD Bomb Squad emblem embroidered on the left upper chest. The design featured a phoenix bird clutching a fragmentation bomb and two jagged lightning bolts.

"Call me Mac." His smile displayed straight white teeth, contrasting with his dark skin. When he glanced around the table, his balding scalp gleamed under the florescent lights.

"What have you determined about the explosion so far?" Webster asked.

"At this point, it looks a type of pipe bomb," Mac said. "Remote detonation setup. Probably programmed to receive a signal from a cell phone." He frowned. "My supervisor reached out to the local ATF Field Division. I'm sure they'll want in."

Aware the Bureau of Alcohol, Tobacco and Firearms maintained records about bombings nationwide, Veranda wasn't surprised they would be involved. She had worked with them on arms smuggling cases in her task force days. The location of their Phoenix Field Division a few blocks down the street from police headquarters made collaboration easy, but occasionally politics created unnecessary challenges.

Sam turned to Webster. "Are we about to be swimming in a sea of dark suits?"

The commander nodded. "Special Agent Nicholas Flag from DHS is flying in from Washington DC tomorrow. He's bringing an ATF agent with him." He shrugged. "Not sure why Flag isn't working with our local ATF division."

Veranda had met Agent Flag with the Department of Homeland Security when he participated in a Phoenix-based task force recently. Sam had speculated Flag was affiliated with one of the various US intelligence agencies despite what he claimed, and Veranda had come to agree with her partner.

Curious to know how he would respond, she put the question directly to her commander. "Why does Flag care?"

"We'll hear from Crime Scene next," Webster said. "Detective Kim will answer your question."

"Wait." Mac looked confused. "Can someone loop me in?" He looked around. "I know the Villalobos cartel is involved, and I've seen news reports about them like everyone else, but more details would help my investigation."

All eyes turned to Veranda, the subject matter expert. Taking the silent cue, she kept her response brief. "The Villalobos cartel is the largest criminal organization in Mexico, and they're into narcotics, computer hacking, financial crime, weapons smuggling, human trafficking, and the sex trade among other things. The leader, Hector Villalobos, has four adult children. Two of them are dead. The two left standing are Adolfo, who failed when he tried to take over their North American operation seven weeks ago, and Daria, who specializes in weapons and explosives."

Mac grinned. "My kind of woman."

"If you're into sociopaths."

He lifted a shoulder. "Nobody's perfect."

"I've studied the Villalobos cartel too," Diaz said. "Haven't found a case where they used bombs inside the US against law enforcement."

Veranda had also been disturbed by the new threat. "I'm guessing this is Daria's move to show she's ready to step up and take over."

Mac looked intrigued. "What do you mean, step up?"

She outlined the crime boss and his family structure. "Hector Villalobos goes by *El Lobo*, which means 'the wolf.' His children—named in alphabetical order—are his retirement plan. In order to do that, he needs an heir who can run the whole organization. In the past, he'd divided areas of responsibility between his kids. One of them has to step up and consolidate power."

"How is it divided?" Mac asked.

"His firstborn son, Adolfo, is the cartel's CFO. He handles financial crime and keeps the books. The next in line, Bartolo, *comandante* in charge of narcotics, died in a shootout in July."

Mac leaned back. "I remember that fiasco."

Rather than rehash one of the department's greatest embarrassments, Veranda plowed on. "*El Lobo*'s third son, Carlos, used to manage the coyotes, who run human trafficking operations across the border and maintain sex slave rings. Carlos … got in the way of a bullet recently."

Mac snorted. "Yeah, I heard something about that. On every news channel. Every day. For a solid week."

His remark reminded her just how public her run-ins with the cartel had been. She let out a long breath and continued. "His youngest is Daria. Supposedly, she has a munitions-manufacturing plant somewhere near their compound in Mexico. Satellite images are inconclusive, and the *federales* haven't had any success sending an operative inside. The intel we get is mostly from people they arrest shortly before the cartel manages to shut them up. Permanently."

At the far end of the table Marci spoke up. "So Daria's trying to take over then?"

She considered the question. "A female leader of a cartel is rare, but not unheard of. I don't know how *El Lobo* feels about women, but some of these guys are full-on sexists. Daria will have to prove herself if she wants the top spot."

"I don't understand," Mac said. "If Adolfo's the firstborn son, why isn't he in charge?"

Diaz provided the answer. "He's viewed as weak, both inside and outside the cartel. Everyone thinks he's brainy but lacks the killer instinct. His father gave him a shot at the throne recently. Rival criminal organizations moved in on cartel territory, resulting in that turf war last month."

Tony Sanchez, another member of her Homicide squad, weighed in. His heavy Brooklyn accent carried through the room. "They're still digging rounds out of the sides of buildings downtown."

Mac turned to Veranda. "The murder this morning involved an unknown subject burned with a branding iron. How does that fit in with the cartel's MO?"

"The cartel brands their property," she said. "It's a sign of owner-ship. They put their mark on packages of narcotics, prisoners, and sometimes, sex slaves." She fought to keep the anger out of her voice. "Because they consider them property."

Marci muttered an expletive under her breath that drew a glare from their commander.

Veranda caught her eye in tacit agreement before she continued the briefing. "They also use the brand to terrorize and punish enemies and traitors. The hot iron burns the outline of a wolf's head on the upper left chest over the heart."

She schooled her features to hide her feelings about the next part, drawing a deep breath before proceeding. "A *tattoo* of a black wolf's head in the same place, on the other hand, is seen as an honor re-served for those loyal to the Villalobos family. It's something you have to earn."

She felt everyone's gaze on her and hoped no one noticed how she'd kept her voice flat and her eyes on the table as she added, "Ex-cept in my case."

Her comment met with silence. The fact that everyone knew why she bore the tattoo didn't ease the awkwardness of the moment. Or the sting of her humiliation.

"You mentioned they also branded traitors," Doc said. "Could the subject in the storage unit have been part of the cartel?"

She welcomed the distraction of the question. "Not possible. I got a good look before the bomb went off, and the guy only had a Mexican army tattoo. If he'd been a cartel member, the brand would have gone directly on top of the wolf tatt. The idea is that the ink didn't sink in far enough, so the cartel's mark is burned into the flesh to make a deeper impression. Normally, this is followed by immediate execution. Once in a while, the person is given a second chance to prove himself."

Doc winced. "These people are barbarians."

Marci gestured to Tony. "Hey, Tony here happens to be a Barbarian-American. Don't disparage him by comparing him to those assholes."

"Detective Blaine," Webster began, a note of censure in his voice.

Marci held up a hand in apology. "Excuse me, Commander." She leaned toward Veranda and lowered her voice. "What's the word in Spanish?"

Before Veranda could answer, Marci straightened. "Wait, I remember it now. I meant to say don't compare him to those *pendejos*." She feigned a look of innocence that deceived no one. "It's okay if I say it in Spanish, right?"

As usual, Marci had managed to ease the tension in the room. She'd also taken the focus away from Veranda and her unwanted tattoo. Marci's wink told her she'd done it on purpose.

"No, Detective," Lieutenant Diaz said over the sound of chuckling around the table. "It's not."

The trace of a grin lifted the lieutenant's lips before he turned to the man sitting to Mac's right. "Let's hear from the Laboratory Services Bureau. Detective Kim, you mentioned a report that will explain why Agent Flag from DHS is involved?"

Veranda had worked with Tye Kim before. As detective liaison, he ran interference between the forensics lab and hundreds of detectives constantly pressuring the scientists to push their evidence to the front of the line for examination. She had heard Tye describe his job as triage on a tight rope, and he did it well.

Tye bent down to reach inside a black leather satchel slouching at his feet on the factory-grade blue carpet. "I've got a bit of information you might find interesting." He pulled out a manila folder and a letter-sized brown envelope. Every eye followed Tye's deft movements as he unclasped the envelope slid a lab report out with a flourish.

Though he said nothing, Commander Webster's knowing look indicated he'd already been briefed.

"What is that?" Diaz asked, apparently not in the loop.

A satisfied smile lit up Tye's face. "The identity of the bomber."

5

VERANDA'S BREATH CAUGHT in her throat. Tye's announcement had shocked the War Room into silence. Then everyone started talking at once. Commander Webster held up both hands. "Before we get to the suspect, Detective Kim, could you please ID the victim? Your findings will make more sense."

Tye reddened. "Sorry, Commander." Straightening, he addressed the group. "I'm glad everyone already took a lunch break, because the details of this one are … unpleasant." He reached for the manila folder resting on the table in front of him beneath the opened envelope. "The bomb destroyed the evidence collected at the scene before it detonated." He scanned the page. "Photographs, measurements, and samples. All gone. We had to go back in after the explosion and collect what we could."

Veranda suppressed a shudder as she recalled walking back inside the storage unit after it had been deemed safe to enter. She'd never forget the sight of a Crime Scene tech scraping bits of flesh from the walls.

Tye looked up from his notes. "As Commander Webster mentioned, we made a positive ID off three good fingerprints and two partials from what was left of his hands. We ran them through the United States AFIS first and struck out. We resubmitted through I-24/7 to Interpol's AFIS and got a hit. The victim's full name is Oscar Cristóbal Flores-Cabrera. Went by Oscar Cabrera."

Veranda had used Interpol's I-24/7 system to run prints of foreign nationals when she worked narcotics. The "I" stood for Interpol, and the "24/7" indicated its continuous availability. In an effort to track fugitives across borders, Interpol had established their own Automated Fingerprint Identification System, or AFIS, so local law enforcement agencies worldwide could access various databases. While not all-inclusive, the system had proven useful when she'd investigated citizens of other countries.

"Turns out Mr. Cabrera has been a guest of the Mexican prison system on several occasions," Tye said. "I requested a photo and rap sheet through Interpol. Should have it later today."

Commander Webster cut in. "Detective Cruz, you mentioned a Mexican military tattoo on the subject's arm." He arched a thick, sandy brow. "Since we don't have any photos of the victim before the explosion, could you elaborate?"

"Sometimes cartels recruit former military personnel," she said. "They can acquire trained men at low cost." She slid a paper out from a file folder and held it up. "I sketched what I saw from memory."

Diaz squinted at her pencil drawing. "Are those knives?"

She shook her head. "I'm no artist. They're supposed to be a pair of swords." She pointed at the page. "I only know about these tatts because they've been catalogued in the prison and arrest records of other offenders over the years. Most of the tattoos have a unit number and a flag. The ones showing crossed swords are for the Mexican special forces."

Doc's eyebrows shot up. "You mean this guy was like a Ranger or a SEAL or something?"

She put the paper down. "Not necessarily. Anyone can get the ink. Doesn't prove anything."

In typical down-to-earth language, Tony posed the question plaguing her since she'd first laid eyes on the tattoo. "What the hell was he doing in the US and how did he piss off the cartel?"

Commander Webster took off his readers and laid them on the table. "Which brings us to Detective Kim's earlier announcement." He gave Tye a nod.

Tye took the cue. "The techs found fragments of a plastic water bottle at the scene in the back corner of the storage unit." He paused. "Part of the bottlecap survived the blast." He looked around, apparently waiting for them to catch up. When no one reacted, he leaned forward to emphasize his next words. "That section of the cap was still screwed onto a piece of threaded nozzle from the bottle."

She had seen forensic experts gather trace evidence from tiny pieces of detonated bomb material. Partial fingerprints, DNA, and origin codes had been successfully recovered in terrorism investigations even after a sizable bombing attack. The device at the storage unit wasn't an enormous fertilizer bomb, but a relatively small IED. Pieces of a bottle tucked into a corner several yards away from the detonation point could yield usable evidence.

Veranda's pulse kicked up a notch as she took a logical leap. "There was DNA under the cap?"

"Bingo," Tye said, unable to hide his excitement. "The heat from the explosion melted the mouth of the bottle to its cap, forming an airtight seal around a droplet of saliva, trapping it between the piece of cap and a fragment of plastic."

Sam grinned under this mustache. "Did you get a DNA hit?"

"Not yet," Tye said. "We'll run it through CODIS if the sample turns out to be viable. But in the meantime, we got something else just as good."

Everyone traded bewildered glances.

"Quit playing around," Sam said. "What the hell did you find, Tye?"

"A partial fingerprint," he said, slightly abashed. "And we got a definitive hit."

Veranda didn't understand. "Daria Villalobos doesn't have prints on file. She's never been arrested. How could you get a hit?"

"You're right. Daria hasn't been arrested," Tye said. "But Adelmo Salazar has."

The name sent a shockwave through her body. "But Salazar's in Mexico. He couldn't have ..."

Tye tapped the lab sheet with his pen. "A partial print matching his left index finger was on a shard of clear plastic lying next to the piece of bottle cap in the corner of the storage unit." He dragged the pen's tip down and poked the paper again. "Both pieces of evidence were found in the same location inside the storage unit. Those are the only two points we can prove. Everything else is speculation."

"But Daria's the explosives expert," Veranda said, almost to herself. "She has to be behind this."

"Wait," Mac said. "Who's Salazar?" The Bomb Squad tech looked from one end of the table to the other in confusion.

His question snapped her out of her reverie. "The cartel's fixer. He goes by *El Matador*." A realization sparked. "And he was in the Mexican Army's special forces." She turned to Commander Webster. "That's the connection, isn't it?"

Webster steepled his fingers. "Agent Flag seems to think so. He's meeting with an alphabet soup of US agencies now. Once word spread about the fingerprint hit, the Mexican government got interested. They think Salazar's in Phoenix and they want him extradited if we catch him."

"This Salazar sounds high profile," Mac said.

"He's a stone-cold killer," Sam said. "Specializes in taking out cops, judges, and anyone else in law enforcement who gets in the way."

"And he's targeted Detective Cruz before," Diaz said, drawing everyone's attention to Veranda.

Her heart pounded under the cartel tattoo on her chest. The mark Salazar had put there. Her mind dredged up an image of his pitiless black eyes boring into hers as his powerful hands wrapped around her neck, slowly squeezing until darkness overtook her. She had barely survived their last encounter. Now he'd come back to finish what he'd started.

6

VERANDA CAUGHT THE smile playing across Cole Anderson's lips. She put down her glass. "What?"

The sun had set hours ago, casting her small kitchen table in a warm glow from the overhead light, softening the planes and angles of her boyfriend's features. He looked into her eyes. "Don't tell your mother I said this, but your enchiladas taste just as good as hers."

She tilted her head back and laughed. "Oh, I am so telling her."

"I'll deny it."

"Chicken."

"Yeah, I like them with shredded chicken too."

Veranda had dated Cole off and on for more than three months. Probably a record. Long enough for her Homicide squad to quit teasing her about getting involved with a fireman. Long enough for her mother to start entertaining hopes. Too many failed attempts at fix-ups with every eligible Latino north of Yuma had left her mother considering the tall, blond *gringo* her best option. Or perhaps just the last man standing. As long as she and Cole were together, Richard Diaz would remain her mother's backup plan.

They had both gotten off their shifts late and opted for a home-cooked dinner at her house. Already past ten o'clock, she had just enough energy to do the dishes and head for bed. So much the better if her hunky fireman decided to join her.

She pushed back from the table and stood. "Let me have your plate." She scooped up her earthenware dish and held out a hand for his.

He gathered the glasses and silverware after she took his plate.

She carried the dishes to the sink and put them in. Cole sauntered up behind her, setting two amber-colored drinking glasses down on the counter before reaching around her to place the flatware in the oversized sink. He pressed his chest against her back, nuzzling the top of her head with his jaw. He slid his left hand along her arm, gliding it up to her shoulder. She winced when he squeezed.

"Oh, crap." His hand stilled. "I forgot."

She pushed down the stopper and turned the faucet on. "It's okay. Just a nick."

"Let me see."

She squirted a dab of dishwashing liquid into the running water. "You're an arson investigator, Captain Anderson, not a paramedic."

She heard the smile in his voice as he spoke from behind her. "Some of my best friends are paramedics. I've learned a thing or two from going to fires over the years." His tone grew serious. "I want a look."

Why did everyone insist on checking her injury? She thought about refusing, then decided it wasn't worth another argument. Heaving a sigh, she swept her thick mane of hair to one side, exposing her left shoulder.

He kissed her ear, then gently pulled the scooped neck of her T-shirt aside and peered down. She felt the hitch in his breath and knew he had spotted the upper edge of her tattoo.

She'd only let Cole see all of it once. Standing before him in her bedroom, she had held her breath and peeled off her shirt, letting it drop to the floor. His fleeting look of disgust, quickly concealed, had confirmed her worst fears. He viewed her differently. After that, she'd insisted on complete darkness whenever they were intimate.

Before he could tug at the bandage, she stepped away from him, released her hair to spill down her back again, and plunged her hands into the warm soapy water filling the sink.

"There's nothing to see." She kept her voice light.

He pressed closer, resting a palm on the counter on either side of her. "Veranda, we need to talk."

Their position should have been intimate, but it made her feel trapped.

She turned off the faucet. "The EMT told me the laceration was fairly superficial."

"About the tattoo."

"I can probably take the bandage off tomorrow."

"About what it means."

"I'll keep putting the Vick's on until it closes completely after that."

He lifted his hands and wrapped them around her waist, pulling her tight against him. "Dammit, Veranda, you know I'm not talking about that cut."

She groped around in the water for the sponge. "You made your feelings clear a long time ago."

"So, we're back to that again?"

She picked up a plate and scrubbed it with unnecessary force. "You said the entire Villalobos family came from a defective gene pool." She spoke around a lump that had congealed in her throat. "Which makes me defective in your eyes."

"I didn't know you were Hector Villalobos's daughter when I said that. Hell, no one knew." His tone hardened a fraction. "Except you."

"What is that supposed to mean?"

"You could've told me when you first found out. Instead, you tried to hide it."

"With good reason." Her temper went from simmer to low boil. "Everyone treats me differently now. They look at me like I'm infected with something contagious."

"I'm still here."

"Are you really?"

He looked hurt. "I wish you had trusted me enough to tell me yourself. I found out from watching the news like everybody else."

"What if you discovered your father headed one of the most brutal criminal organizations in the world?" She didn't wait for his response. "You'd take the secret to your grave if you could."

"Like you almost did." He spoke the words softly, eyes filled with remorse. "I nearly lost you, Veranda."

Her cell phone buzzed on the countertop nearby.

Cole eyed her hands, up to the elbows in dishwater, and snatched it up. Glancing down at the caller ID screen, his face reddened. "It's your son-of-a-bitch lieutenant."

Her nerves, already worn from her spat with Cole, frayed. If Diaz was calling, she'd be going out to the scene of a homicide. Probably for the rest of the night. She and Cole wouldn't be able to sort out their problems. To make matters worse, Cole and Diaz despised each other.

Cole tapped the screen and put the phone to his ear. "What do you want, Diaz?"

Hands dripping, she leaned over to grab a dishtowel.

Cole put his free hand on his hip. "We're kind of in the middle of something. She might need a few minutes to … get dressed."

She threw the towel down and snatched the phone from Cole before he could continue peeing in his proverbial corner. Cole had made it clear he viewed Diaz as a rival. No matter how many times she explained she couldn't, and wouldn't, have anything to do with her supervisor.

"Lieutenant Diaz." She tried to sound professional. "Whatever it is, I can respond to the scene immediately. I'm already dressed, I just need to change from jeans and a T-shirt to something more suitable."

She was even more annoyed for feeling the need to explain herself to Diaz. Her personal affairs were none of his business.

"I'm glad to hear that, Detective." Diaz sounded irritated before reverting to his usual detached supervisory manner. "A dog walker noticed a garbage bag floating in one of the canals downtown. His dog latched on and pulled it onto the sidewalk. The dog's teeth split the bag open, spilling body parts all over the place."

She grimaced. "I'm guessing there was no ID in the bag with the body parts?"

"The guy didn't look. Too busy tossing his cookies."

"I don't understand why you're calling me. I'm not at bat, Lieutenant."

Since her team caught this morning's case, another squad should have been assigned to handle the next one.

"I'm calling you because what was left in the bag looked fresh and showed signs of an explosion."

"What the hell's going on?" Her mind raced. "Two cartel hits within twenty-four hours?"

"That's why I want you there, Detective. You know them better than anyone. I'll text you the location. Sergeant Jackson's still out. I'll respond to the scene personally."

"On my way, sir." She disconnected and fixed an icy glare on Cole, who stared right back. She refused to be intimidated. "What was that bullshit about me not having any clothes on?"

He crossed his arms.

She jabbed a finger at him. "You made it sound like we were in bed. And you did it on purpose. You're so damned jealous of him that you take every opportunity to rub his nose in the fact that we're together."

"You may not understand how he looks at you, but I do." Cole's voice dropped to a low rasp. "He wants you."

"I don't have time for this." She spun toward her room.

"I'm not going to stay here all night waiting for you." His words sounded harsh, but she could hear the hurt beneath them.

She stopped and looked over her shoulder. "I probably won't be back before dawn." Aware they had only delayed the argument, she softened her tone. "We'll talk later."

"I want this to work, Veranda." He went to the front door, jerked it open, and paused on the threshold. "You know how to find me when you're ready to get serious."

Was he resentful about her getting called out, leaving their argument unsettled, or spending a night that should have been theirs at a crime scene with Diaz?

As she struggled for the right thing to say, he shut the door behind him.

7

VERANDA'S BOOTS KICKED up clouds of dust on the bank next to the cement canal. She paced in and out of the glow of illuminated circles cascading down from six portable lights on stands surrounding the scene. Well within the barrier of the crime scene tape, she zipped her jacket up to her throat. At night, the desert air nipped in late October. Though she'd been at the scene for over an hour, she still didn't have a firm grasp on what had happened.

Sam slid his thumb and forefinger along his oversized gray mustache. Over the past three months since they'd become partners, Sam's characteristic gestures and the thought patterns they represented had become familiar. Mustache stroking signaled contemplation.

"These body parts look too much like what was left of Oscar Cabrera for coincidence," he said, watching the forensic techs move back and forth in a kind of crime scene ballet. "The two killings are connected."

Experience investigating violent death had kept Veranda's dinner in her stomach when she first laid eyes on the torn black plastic garbage bag, its grisly contents spread across the sidewalk. She agreed with Sam's assessment. The remains looked disturbingly similar to the carnage in the storage unit.

The sound of pumps clacking on pavement interrupted her thoughts. Marci halted at the far edge of the sidewalk, her Jimmy Choos safe from the dusty canal bank and the puddle of coagulated blood.

"Tony and I finished interviewing the dog walker," Marci said, tipping her blonde head toward one of the nearby marked cars. "He's with his pooch in the back of that patrol unit."

Veranda faced her squad mate. "What's your take?"

"I doubt he has anything to do with this," Marci said. "But Tony's making a few phone calls to check out his story."

Behind Marci, Tony glanced down at his notepad as he spoke into his cell phone.

Lieutenant Diaz joined the group and shot Marci a questioning look. "Why is this guy out walking his dog along the canal at this time of night?"

"Claims he works the graveyard shift," Marci said. "Says if he doesn't walk his dog before he leaves for work, his apartment will be destroyed by the time he gets home in the morning. His dog's a beagle, and they're known for their noses." She grimaced. "Snoopy caught the scent pretty quickly. The owner said his dog jumped in, clamped his teeth on the bag, and wouldn't continue with the walk until he'd dragged it out onto the sidewalk."

Tony slipped his cell phone into his pocket and plodded over to them. "The dog walker's story checks out. His boss verified the guy supervises an overnight office cleaning crew downtown. I got his ID and contact info." He looked at Veranda. "Ready to cut him loose unless there's anything else."

She dismissed the witness with a wave of her hand in the general direction of the patrol car. "Let him go. We know where to find him if we need him."

While Tony shuffled off to carry out her instructions, she scanned the area. "I can't see any from here, but we'll need to check for security cameras nearby."

Diaz rested a hand on the gold badge clipped to his belt. "Which reminds me," he said to Marci. "Did you and Detective Sanchez have any luck with the traffic cameras or video surveillance from the storage lot case this morning?"

Marci sighed. "Couldn't catch a break. We had no suspect or vehicle to work from, so we searched through the videos for people matching Salazar's description or acting suspiciously." She rolled her eyes. "Which includes just about everyone in that part of town."

Veranda followed up with a question of her own. "What about the anonymous call to the storage facility about the foul smell coming from the unit?"

Marci shook her head. "Originated in Phoenix, but untraceable. Caller probably used a burner phone."

Veranda remembered a comment the Bomb tech made in the War Room earlier. "Mac said bombers usually like to have a visual on their target when it detonates." The dispute with her lieutenant in the storage unit parking lot still fresh in her mind, she rounded on Diaz. "You said patrol had the area locked down tight. Why didn't we catch anyone?"

Diaz straightened. "We can discuss critical incident scene management strategies later. Right now, we have more important things to deal with."

The Crime Scene van's rear bay doors slammed shut, drawing Veranda's attention to the tech striding toward her team.

She gave the man dressed in a Tyvek suit a quick lift of her chin in recognition. "And here I thought the dayshift guys would get all the action today."

"We take turns." The tech spread his hands. "That way, everybody gets to share the fun."

A tone sounded. Diaz tugged his cell phone out of his pocket, brows knitting as he glanced at the display. "Wonder what dispatch wants." He tapped the screen and put it to his ear.

She turned back to the tech. "Will you be transporting the remains to the ME's office?"

He nodded. "We're wrapping up now."

"Find anything interesting?"

"Nothing conclusive yet. We'll take what we have back to the lab and—"

"When did it happen?" Diaz's sharp tone attracted everyone's attention. "Was anybody inside?" he said into his phone. "Get the Arson Investigation Unit and the Bomb Squad out there. I'll notify Detective Cruz. She's with me now." He disconnected.

She had never seen Diaz act like this. Why had he mentioned her name to the dispatcher? "What's going on?"

The color drained from his face. "Veranda, I..."

She could count the times he'd used her first name on one hand. All of them in bad circumstances. She stepped closer to him. "Lieutenant?"

He closed his eyes briefly, then met her gaze. "An explosion."

"Why are you looking at me like that?" Dread gathered inside her like a storm about to break. "What blew up?"

Voice thick with strain, two words escaped his lips. "Your house."

8

VERANDA HAD BEEN to many fire scenes in her career. She had witnessed families huddled together in a ragged circle beyond the yellow perimeter tape. Shell-shocked and disheveled, they squeezed each other tight while their house, their possessions, and their memories were reduced to cinders before their eyes.

She'd never imagined herself in the role of displaced homeowner, helpless against the flames consuming her modest bungalow as curious neighbors gathered around the block to bear witness to her personal tragedy.

After the phone call from dispatch, Lieutenant Diaz had turned the canal crime scene over to Sam, then followed in his car as Veranda drove to her house. She had badged her way past the patrol car posted at the outer perimeter and screeched her Tahoe to a stop behind an idling hook-and-ladder truck, Diaz nosing his unmarked supervisor's car in behind her.

Red and blue lights sliced the night sky as she flung her door wide and leaped out. Deaf to Diaz's shouts to wait for him, she sprinted past the firefighters and their hulking vehicles until she reached the corner lot and her footsteps pounded to a halt. Where her house once stood, only a smoldering husk remained.

Her hand flew to her mouth, and she choked back a sob, refusing to give voice to the howl of anguish trapped in her throat. She would not allow herself to go to pieces. Not in front of everyone. A firm hand gripped her shoulder. She spoke no words and offered no resistance when Diaz pulled her to him. So much devastation. So much loss. She stared wordlessly at her ruined home and sagged against her supervisor's chest.

"Get your hands off her."

Her head snapped up at the sound of a gruff male voice to see Cole in his beige turnout glowering at Diaz. She should have realized he would be the one to respond from the fire department's Arson Investigation Unit. The last time the two men had been within an arm's reach, they'd come to blows.

Diaz tightened his hold on her shoulder. "I don't take orders from you."

She was in no mood for their bullshit. "My house just exploded." She pivoted out of Diaz's grasp. "Can you two dial it back for five minutes?"

Cole directed his response at Diaz. "We're investigating this as a possible gas leak, so it's a fire department scene right now." He brought himself up to his full height. "And I don't take orders from any police lieutenant."

Diaz straightened. "It's a joint investigation until we know what caused it. If it's a gas leak, you guys handle it. If it's a bomb, it's ours."

"A bomb?" Cole's icy blue gaze slid away from Diaz to settle on her. "Who the hell would blow up your house?"

She saw the moment his jumbled thoughts converged on the only logical conclusion. As his angular features hardened into a mask of fury, Veranda seized on the possible alternate explanation he had offered.

"Maybe this was a gas leak," she said, looking at Diaz and Cole in turn. "Maybe a weird coincidence. Maybe ..."

The words died on her lips. She'd heard victims and witnesses say *maybe* over the years and recognized what it represented.

Denial. An indulgence she couldn't afford.

Cole took her by the elbow and pulled her aside. Angling his head down, he dropped his voice to a rough whisper. "We both know this was no gas leak, Veranda." He jerked a thumb at her house. "That fucking cartel did this, and they damn near blew us both to bits."

A wave of remorse washed over her. She understood the realization that he had almost died in her house bubbled beneath the surface of his anger.

She covered his hand with her own. "I never meant to put you at risk."

A muscle in Cole's jaw bunched. "Promise me you'll stop this insane vendetta with the Villalobos family." His voice shook with barely contained emotion. "Look where your decision to fight them has gotten you."

She took her hand away. "I had no choice."

"You went after Hector Villalobos because of what he did to your mother thirty years ago. Now he knows who you are." He swallowed hard. "That you're his daughter."

"Hector never paid for his crimes. I'm a cop, Cole. I put bad guys in jail."

"You act like you're the only one who can. And that's a choice." He reached out to touch her face, then slipped his finger under her chin, forcing her to meet his intense gaze. "I'm asking you to choose me instead, Veranda. Turn the investigation over to someone else."

He had put it on the table. A condition for their continued relationship. She recalled that Diaz was close enough to overhear their exchange and held her emotions in check. "You know I can't," she whispered.

He let his hand fall to his side. "Can't or won't?"

Without another word, he turned away and trudged toward the charred remains of her house.

She watched Cole's retreating back as Diaz's deep voice came from behind her. "I can't stand that *pinche* fireman, but he has a point."

She whirled to face him. "If you weren't my supervisor, I'd punch you in the mouth." Seething, she itched to vent her frustration on Diaz. "Hell, I might do it anyway. It'd be worth the suspension."

He softened his tone. "*Cálmate.*" He approached her again, raising an arm as if to put it around her shoulders.

She narrowed her eyes at him.

He held up both hands, palms out, in surrender. "I know you're going through hell right now, Veranda, but try to focus on the investigation so we can arrest whoever is responsible."

The fact that Diaz was right irritated her further. "I'll get to work right away," she said.

He nodded. "I'll have one of the other squads take over. You can give them a complete briefing. For the lead investigator, I'll pick a senior detective who's—"

Not only was he about to pull her off the case, he intended to reassign it to a completely different squad.

"I'm the best one to investigate this, Lieutenant. And you know it."

He sighed. "You can't investigate a case where you're the victim."

She scrambled to counter his argument. "Then put Sam on point. I promise to follow his lead."

"But it's *your* squad. *Your* people."

"Exactly my point," she said, willing him to see her perspective.

Diaz's obsessive rule following would set the investigation back. She had to make him see beyond the regs.

"My team knows all the background." She flung her hands up in the air. "What are we going to do? Turn our case files over to another squad and get them up to speed while the trail goes cold?"

Diaz dragged a hand through his thick, close-cropped hair. Looking into his dark eyes, she saw an inner battle raging. Aware silence was the best option, she opted not to answer, giving him time to consider.

Finally, he spoke. "I'd lock you away in a safe house, but we both know how that would end." This time he did touch her, grasping both of her arms. "You disregard orders. You go rogue." He released her with a slight shove. "You're impossible to supervise."

Sensing his crumbling resolve, she took advantage. "Lieutenant, you almost died this morning because you didn't listen to me." He opened his mouth as if to argue, but she forged ahead, softening her tone. "Don't make that mistake again."

He closed his eyes and let out a stream of Spanish expletives.

She held her breath and waited.

His eyes opened, fastening on hers. "Your squad will continue to investigate. But Detective Stark will have the lead." He jabbed a finger at her. "Not you."

She inclined her head to show her agreement, unwilling to betray her thoughts with words. Silently, she turned to look at what had been her house. She easily spotted Cole, his white arson investigator's helmet contrasting with the yellow ones worn by the firefighters.

Her chest tightened. Not only had she lost her home, she might have lost her man. Unbidden, a stray thought filtered up from the dark recesses of her mind. *Cole is better off without me.* If he had stayed behind to wait for her, he'd be dead now. Because he'd fallen for a woman with a target on her back. And a certain tattoo on her chest.

Anyone I love is at risk. Something else occurred to her. Something truly horrific. Her head snapped back to Diaz. "My family," she said, anxiety rocketing through her. What if this hadn't been the only explosion tonight? "I have to check on them."

Diaz's voice became soothing again. "I called your mother on the way here. Everyone's fine. I sent a South Mountain precinct patrol unit to the family property to keep watch for the night."

A wave of relief washed through her, followed quickly by remorse. She should have thought of her family's safety before Diaz did.

"Thank you, Lieutenant. That was very thoughtful."

He drew nearer. "I take care of my own."

She'd heard the sentiment from supervisors before when referring to their subordinates, but Diaz made the expression sound intimate. She considered asking him what he meant but decided to let it go and focus on the clear and present danger.

She thought about her kickboxing lessons. Jake, her instructor, had taught her two critical things every fighter must do before entering the ring. First, be ruthlessly honest with yourself. Identify any weaknesses. Second, eliminate those weaknesses. Failing that, minimize them.

She couldn't help having a family, but she could prevent a man from being in her life. Until her personal war ended, she couldn't allow anyone to get close to her. She had dared to take on the Villalobos cartel. And they had detected her greatest vulnerability even before she did.

Her heart.

9

Villalobos family
compound, Mexico

DARIA SAT FORWARD, perched on the plush leather chair facing her father's elaborate mahogany desk. Finished delivering her report, she gripped the overstuffed arms with knuckle-whitening force and gazed through the tall mullioned window. The morning sun painted the landscape with soft pastel hues in stark contrast to the dark sense of foreboding seeping through her as she waited for *El Lobo*'s judgment.

When her father learned of the second failed attempt, he had summoned her to appear before him immediately. Such a directive from Hector Villalobos required instant compliance, even from his daughter.

Still edgy and exhausted after her predawn flight to the family compound, she was far from prepared to defend herself. She'd longed for sleep during the journey, but the prisoner's constant wails and pleas for mercy had interrupted her nap. Even after duct-taping Pedro's mouth, the prospect of facing *El Lobo* upon arriving in Mexico had prevented her from getting any rest.

Unnerved by her father's silence, she watched him reposition the pieces of his ivory desk set with infinite care, still not looking at her. His meticulous movements and placid expression spiked her adrenalin. Unlike men who yelled and broke things when angered, her father always grew calmer and quieter.

"Adolfo and Salazar are here for a reason," Hector said.

She swallowed. Her father preferred an audience when he doled out punishments. She cut her eyes to the right, where her older brother, Adolfo, stood ramrod straight with his back against the wall, refusing to meet her gaze. Not good.

She swiveled her head to the left and felt a rush of pure hatred. Salazar occupied the chair next to hers as if he belonged there. She caught a fleeting expression of ice cold fury on his face before he schooled his features into his customary inscrutable mask. Also not good.

Smoothing her slacks with nervous fingers, she faced her father. "What is it, Papá?"

He placed the letter opener down on the blotter and deigned to look at her for the first time since her arrival. Her father spoke in formal, elegant Spanish. His crisp white suit, perfectly barbered goatee, and manicured nails belied the squalor of the Mexico City barrio where he grew up in abject poverty. Many people had died because of *El Lobo*'s determination to distance himself from his humble beginnings.

"Your explanations sound like excuses to me, *mi'ja*."

After gesturing for her to take a seat, her father had listened without interruption while she justified her actions over the past twenty-four hours. She had spoken to his profile as he steepled his fingers and leaned back in his leather swivel chair gazing up at the ceiling. Despite her detailed account of events, he'd concluded she was at fault.

"But how would I know that bitch detective would leave her house at night?" She tried to keep any sign of pleading out of her voice. "Cruz was at home with her lover. Why would she leave?"

Daria had seen surveillance pictures of the fireman. If he had been in her bed, she would have kept him busy until dawn.

Her father lowered his voice to a dangerous whisper. "*Your* man dumped Guillermo Pequeño's body where someone would find it."

His emphasis on the word *your* laid the blame squarely on her shoulders.

"The police were called for a body that had been blown up, just like Oscar Cabrera was earlier the same morning," Hector continued. "You should have known they would assign Cruz to investigate."

Her father had made it clear he considered avoiding responsibility a sign of weak leadership. A true leader readily accepted praise or blame. Still, she tried to lessen the damage. "I ordered Pedro to dispose of the body far away from my South Mountain facility. I had no idea he would throw it in a downtown canal."

Salazar broke his silence. "Then Pedro was either too stupid to weigh the bag down, or too lazy to drive it out into the desert for the buzzards." He lifted a sardonic brow at her. "Your instructions weren't good enough."

Daria's blood boiled. The bastard had her father's ear, and he continued to undermine her at every opportunity. She rounded on him. "How dare you criticize me?"

"We are far beyond criticism, Daria." Salazar's flared nostrils betrayed the anger raging beneath his calm exterior. "I am here to accuse you."

She made a pretext of innocence, rearing back in her seat. "Of what?"

Salazar cut his eyes to Hector, who nodded. The silent communication told Daria her troubles were exponentially worse than she'd believed. Her father had granted permission for this attack in advance.

Like a panther, Salazar slowly rose from his chair to glare down at her. "You planted evidence for the police to find. Evidence against me."

She shot to her feet, figuring a strong offense was her best strategy. "Bullshit."

He stepped closer, invading her personal space. "We intercepted an alert through Interpol early this morning." His hot breath fanned her face. "The police found pieces of a plastic water bottle in the storage unit where Oscar Cabrera's body exploded. My fingerprints were on some of the fragments, which is interesting." He tilted his head in mock confusion. "Because I haven't been in Phoenix for weeks and the last place I drank a bottle of water was at your home."

She'd prepared for this. Her father had forced her to take Salazar in when he traveled to Phoenix recently. A wanted fugitive, Salazar's options had been limited.

"My men work at my house. They reuse plastic bottles often." She tried not to sound too rehearsed. "They half fill them to freeze so they can have cold water for hours."

This would have the ring of truth. Salazar had seen them do it. Saving one of Salazar's used bottles had been a stroke of genius.

Her accuser didn't look appeased. "What about the prisoner you chose? Why Oscar Cabrera?"

She sensed the trap. Salazar and Cabrera had been in the same special forces unit in the military. They'd been close. Until Cabrera took a job with a rival cartel.

"The *cabrón* had it coming." She flung out a hand in a show of exasperation. "I wanted to draw Cruz to the scene. I picked the best target to make sure she came." She lifted her chin. "And it worked."

"You could have used a different prisoner. Our brand seared onto any man's chest would have brought Cruz." He shook his head. "But no. You chose Cabrera because of my past association with him. Another way to link me to the crime."

She stole a glance at her father, wondering if he agreed with Salazar's assessment. As usual, *El Lobo*'s expression revealed nothing. She doubled down. "I did what I had to." She jabbed a finger into Salazar's broad chest. "And I don't answer to you."

He caught her wrist. "Never touch me again." He tightened his grip, forcing a gasp from her lips. "You are a liar, Daria."

Hot tears of pain and humiliation stung her eyes. She jerked her wrist, trying to pull free, but he only squeezed harder. "Let me go, you bast—"

"Daria, stop!" Speaking for the first time, Adolfo pushed away from the office wall to stand next to her. "Not another word." He cleared his throat and turned to their father. "Salazar is already a wanted man. Another warrant won't make a difference. But Daria can still operate freely in the US because no one suspects her."

She seldom valued anything Adolfo had to say, but she appreciated his intervention this time. She had almost crossed a line.

Hector inclined his head toward Salazar. "Let her go." He gave her a shrewd look. "I have made my decision."

Daria forced herself not to moan with relief when Salazar released his bone-crushing hold. She rubbed her wrist and shot him a glare that promised retribution before searching *El Lobo*'s rugged face, where she found no fatherly compassion whatsoever. "What decision?"

"In a moment." Hector glanced at Adolfo. "First, where is Pedro?"

"In the dungeon awaiting your verdict, as ordered," Adolfo said.

Daria pictured Pedro shackled to a wall in the dank underground chamber. She couldn't muster any sympathy for him. His incompetence had cost her dearly.

"I will see to him later," Hector said, then aimed his next remark at Daria. "You will prepare something for Pedro before you go back to Phoenix."

Every muscle in her body went rigid. Hector had selected her to play a role in the punishment, which meant he had convicted her along with Pedro. She held her tongue and waited.

"That makes twice you have failed me, *mi'ja*." Hector smoothed his lapel. "My terms haven't changed."

Daria sensed one of her father's overblown speeches coming. He did not disappoint.

"Clearly, I was correct in my assessment that you are not ready to lead this organization." Hector paused, as if weighing his next words. "It's not merely because you are a woman, *mi'ja*." He jerked his chin at Adolfo, who had resumed his previous stance against the wall. "Your older brother is a man, but he has no *cojones*."

Adolfo remained silent, a muscle twitch in his jaw the only visible reaction to his father's cutting remark.

Pride lit her father's features as his gaze turned to the man next to her. "But fate has smiled upon me and given me Salazar."

As usual, Salazar showed no emotion. He had proven himself to be ruthless and bold, making him a deadly instrument for Hector to wield as he consolidated power over the years. Everyone feared Salazar, *El Matador*. But no one outside of this room knew his secret.

Daria involuntarily touched the small scar on her cheek. She would not make the mistake of declaring open warfare against Salazar again. Instead, she would get rid of him. Permanently.

Salazar had made a mortal enemy when he maneuvered himself into her position in the family hierarchy. She had plotted her revenge for weeks, devising a scheme to eliminate Cruz and frame Salazar at the same time. But things hadn't gone to plan, and Salazar was once again capitalizing on the opportunity to enhance his status with *El Lobo*.

Hector turned back to her. "You had your chance. I am out of patience."

She resorted to begging, hating herself for doing so. "Please, Papá, I need—"

Hector didn't wait for her to finish. "I'm putting Salazar in charge of your part of the operation. He will stay here for the *Día de los Muertos* celebration, then go to Phoenix with some of our coyotes."

Daria fought the despair threatening to overwhelm her. A surge of righteous anger emboldened her. "I can take care of my business."

"I have made up my mind." He gave her his back, addressing Salazar. "After you leave for Phoenix, I will oversee your duties here in your absence."

Her father's callous dismissal wounded her to the core. He wouldn't listen to her arguments. Wouldn't accept her explanation. Wouldn't show her basic respect. The ground had shifted beneath her, leaving her standing alone, irrelevant, invisible to the men in the room.

Adolfo took a step forward from the shadows, eyes locked on his father. "I can help you."

The deck had been reshuffled, and her dear brother wanted new cards.

Hector shook his head, a slight curl to his upper lip. "Salazar has almost completed the factory here in Mexico, I can oversee the final construction when he leaves for the US."

Daria blinked in shock at Salazar's latest incursion. She had been the one to foresee the burgeoning opioid market and propose a transition to a hybrid operation. Her research had shown they could refit their manufacturing plant to double their profits if they could establish a foothold in the US. She'd begun the redesign, ordered parts, and bribed the appropriate officials. She'd returned to Phoenix assuming her father or Adolfo would finish the project, but apparently Salazar had taken over. Now her father seemed to believe the plan was his idea in the first place.

She was the one with vision. She should have been named successor to the family business. But she was a woman, so her father had turned to Salazar, and the bastard had stolen her future.

She composed herself, refusing to let her pain show, and addressed her father. "What am I supposed to do?"

He turned as if he'd forgotten she was there, then tapped the silver stripe in the middle of his dark goatee with his forefinger as he regarded her. "You still have the kill order for Veranda Cruz, but Salazar must approve your plan next time. As of now, you answer to him."

She bit back a scream of rage. "If that's all, I'll go to my suite until the plane is ready to fly back to Phoenix."

All three men exchanged meaningful looks. She knew they disapproved of her private activities, and she didn't care.

Her father gave her a curt nod.

She stalked to the office door, flung it open, and strode out. Three of her guards stood at attention outside the closed door, as she had ordered. Their apprehension at her sudden appearance pleased her. These were her men. Under her control. And they knew it. She tapped her chin in a parody of her father, looking them up and down. The one on the left was pure eye candy and the one on the right had the stamina of a bull. The ugly brute in the middle, however, desperately needed a shower.

She pointed to the left and the right. "José and Umberto, follow me."

The man in the middle cast a pitying look at his two comrades.

She whirled and got right up in his pock-marked face. "Do you have something to say, Manuel?"

Eyes wide, he swallowed audibly. "No, Señorita."

The fear in his voice spiked her arousal. He would pay for his insolence. She slid her tongue along her teeth. "On second thought, you come too."

She sashayed down the empty hall, three pairs of booted footsteps thudding in her wake.

"You've just volunteered to try out my new equipment," she said over her shoulder. "I've got to break the leather in properly."

The answering gasps from behind her brought a hot flush of excitement to her cheeks.

10

VERANDA'S IDEA OF haute couture involved ballistic nylon in chic tactical black. Overriding her objections, Marci had cajoled her into a charcoal gray Chanel suit hanging in her closet, pairing it with a white silk blouse. Then she'd foisted three other ensembles on her, insisting they were all second-hand from a Scottsdale boutique specializing in vintage fashion. Since last night, Marci had done everything conceivable to lift her spirits, but she should have foregone the wardrobe overhaul. Veranda glanced down at her Ferragamo-clad feet and sighed, yearning for her Hi-Tec boots.

Marci stuck her head around Veranda's cubicle. "Let's go, chica." Veranda stood to peer at the wall clock above the warren of fabric-covered partitions spanning the Violent Crimes Bureau. Five minutes until the eight o'clock meeting in the War Room. Cole had texted her to say he would attend to represent the Fire Department, but he hadn't stopped by her desk on his way in. What did that mean?

She pushed the thought aside and joined her squad mate in the passageway between cubicles. "Thank you again," she said to Marci. "But you really shouldn't have loaned me your designer outfits. I can be hard on clothes."

Veranda's squad had come to the housefire late last night after clearing the canal homicide scene. They had supported her through the shock and grief of losing everything she owned. Then Marci had insisted Veranda spend what was left of the night at her apartment. Sleep had only come in fragmented pieces, but at least she had showered and slurped down some coffee before driving to headquarters this morning.

Marci planted a hand on her hip. "Are you kidding? You rock that Chanel."

Before she allowed Veranda to leave the apartment, Marci had handed her a grocery bag filled with makeup samples and toiletries.

"I could have dug my go-bag out of the trunk of my car. There's always an emergency outfit inside."

"Let me guess," Marci said. "Hi-Tec boots, black BDUs, and an UnderArmour shirt, right?"

"Think of it as cop couture."

Marci gestured at her partner, Tony, who had shuffled past them on his way to the conference room. "You have to look professional. There's a prime example of what happens when you let yourself go." She called out to him. "Hey, Sanchez, pick your knuckles up when you walk. You're leaving wear marks in the carpet."

Tony flipped her the bird over his shoulder and continued toward the War Room door without comment.

"You're not fooling anyone," Veranda said as Marci chuckled. "When Tony retires, you'll miss him the most."

Marci let out a theatrical groan. "He says he's going back to New York, but I don't believe it."

"He complains about the heat from April to November. Why wouldn't he go back?"

"The desert's gotten into his blood," Marci said. "He's gone native."

They continued toward the conference room. Marci and Tony's ongoing verbal battle returned Veranda to a sense of normalcy. Throughout her career, she'd learned to recognize the banter between squad members for the bonding ritual it was. Often, the ones who teased each other most were closest. Cops don't gush about their deep emotional attachment to each other. Not when biting sarcasm, elaborate pranks, and trading barbs communicate the point just as effectively.

Marci's hard exterior hid a compassionate heart, which she had just proven by giving Veranda the clothes off her back without being asked. Had any of her other teammates been female, they would have done the same.

When they entered the packed War Room, Veranda was reminded of the gravity of her current situation. Commander Webster, Lieutenant Diaz, and the rest of her Homicide team milled around in loose groups sipping rot-gut VCB coffee from Styrofoam cups or stained ceramic mugs. Agent Flag listened attentively to a man she didn't recognize in the far corner of the room. The sight of Cole chatting with Detective Kim from the lab and Detective Jones from the Bomb squad unsettled her. Their last conversation had ended badly.

"Nice threads," Sam said, startling her from thoughts of her troubled relationship.

Sam's remark turned several heads in her direction.

Tye Kim did a double take. "You look great, Veranda." A moment after the words left his mouth, he tried to take them back. He flicked a glance at Commander Webster before holding his hand up, palm facing her. "I mean, you look, uh, very professional, Detective Cruz." A red scald crept up his neck as he put his other hand up. "Not to say you don't always look professional, that is, um—"

Webster's frown silenced his babbling.

Tye's awkwardness magnified her discomfort at the unwanted attention. The room had gone quiet, all eyes on her. Cole's jaw dropped, Flag gave her a nod, and Diaz did a slow perusal.

"She's been Marci-fied," Tony said, his Brooklyn accent making the invented word funnier, ending the awkward moment.

Her eyes found Cole's but slid away from his penetrating gaze. She would talk to him later.

Commander Webster cleared his throat. "Take a seat. We have a lot to cover."

She claimed the chair next to Sam's.

"We have two more guests today," Webster said, lifting a hand to indicate Flag and the other man in the corner, who took the last unoccupied seats. "Most of you remember Special Agent Nicholas Flag with the Department of Homeland Security."

Mumbled greetings went around the table.

"He's accompanied by Agent Javier Ortiz with the Bureau of Alcohol, Tobacco and Firearms." Webster yielded the floor to Flag, who elaborated.

"Agent Ortiz works out of the ATF's Washington Field Division," Flag said. "I requested him for this investigation because we've worked closely together on international cases." He inclined his head toward Ortiz. "He speaks fluent Spanish, understands cartel culture, and has traveled extensively in Central and South America."

Ortiz's hooded eyes scanned the room without comment. Veranda thought his rugged features and stocky form made him look like a rugby player in a business suit.

"Thank you, Agent Flag," Webster said, turning to Lieutenant Diaz. "Let's get started."

"The first order of business is a change in the lead detective." Diaz gestured to Sam. "Detective Stark is on point now. Any and all supervisory decisions still go through me."

No one asked for the reason behind the abrupt change, which meant everyone was aware of her new status as victim.

Diaz glanced at Mac. "Any updates from the Bomb squad?"

"I've confirmed that a man-made device caused the explosion at Detective Cruz's residence," Mac said. "Once we ruled out a gas leak, the fire department turned the scene over to us."

"Then we won't need to include the Arson Investigation Unit going forward. Any objections, Captain Anderson?" Diaz posed the question in a neutral tone.

Heads swiveled to Cole. "This will be my last briefing." His voice sounded strained. "I've submitted my report and will be available for any fire-related questions."

Both men's faces were carefully blank, their demeanor completely professional. If she didn't know they loathed each other, this exchange wouldn't have clued her in. She studied Cole's handsome Nordic features and felt the emptiness of impending loss. She forced her attention back to the briefing when she realized Mac had started his report.

"Trace evidence from fragments of bomb materials recovered at both scenes proves the devices at the storage unit and Detective Cruz's house were manufactured at the same location," Mac said.

Agent Ortiz from ATF spoke for the first time. "I've made arrangements to send the bomb remnants to our Walnut Creek lab."

Commander Webster forestalled any debate. "I approved the transition to their California facility. ATF labs have state-of-the-art equipment." He shot a rueful look at Tye. "Our lab is excellent, but they specialize in explosive materials and have access to worldwide databases."

Veranda read between the lines. Ortiz was putting his size elevens smack in the middle of this case.

"Will that delay DNA results from the piece of water bottle cap?" she asked.

"Not at all." Ortiz waved the question away. "We're only taking bomb fragments. Your lab will keep the rest of the evidence. Besides, partial prints from Salazar have already been recovered, right? The DNA will only confirm what we already know—he's behind this."

The ATF agent had drawn a conclusion she didn't share. Time to offer an alternate view. She prepared to perform the dance local police sometimes did with Feds, each leading in turn while avoiding toes.

She opened with a statement of fact before getting to her theory. "Salazar isn't a bomber and isn't sloppy. He wouldn't leave incriminating evidence behind." She paused to let that sink in, waiting for a few slow nods and thoughtful expressions, before continuing. "I like Daria Villalobos for both explosions. Unfortunately, she's never been arrested, so we don't have her prints or DNA on file for comparison."

"What are you getting at, Detective?" Lieutenant Diaz asked her.

"If either lab finds unknown samples, we should get a search warrant for Daria's DNA."

"Your PC?" Diaz pressed.

Her boss wanted to hear her probable cause. The question was reasonable, but the intent behind it grated on her, as if Diaz didn't believe she could convince a superior court judge to sign a warrant.

When she paused to consider her best argument, Sam's rumbling baritone filled the gap. "You'll have my affidavit in support of a search warrant on your desk tomorrow morning, Lieutenant."

That settled the matter. As lead detective, Sam could call that play, and as one of the most renowned detectives on the department, his opinion carried serious weight. Weight he had just thrown behind her.

After giving Sam a grateful smile, she focused on Agent Ortiz again. "If Daria's DNA is found under the piece of bottle cap or on the explosive materials, we'll have her."

"I'm familiar with Salazar," Ortiz said, veering away from a discussion about Daria. "I agree he's not sloppy. Have you considered that he might have believed the explosion would destroy the bottle? Or that he left it behind on purpose? The cartel may have wanted to put US law enforcement on notice."

She countered both ideas, beginning with the first. "Even though it's not his preferred method of killing, Salazar's dealt with explosives in his line of work, so he'd know forensic evidence could survive a blast." She waited a beat before moving on. "I can't accept that Salazar would deliberately incriminate himself to make a point either. The cartel sent their message by branding the murder victim before blowing him up."

Ortiz pounced. "The brand on the victim brought *you* to the scene, Detective Cruz." He placed both hands on the table and leaned forward. "Exactly as it was intended to do."

She had blundered straight into Ortiz's trap. The snare clamped down tight. Her eyes drifted to Cole, who looked like he wanted to hit something, no doubt still angry about the bullseye on her back. The ATF agent's remark would make everyone else in the room question why she still had any part in the investigation. Ortiz was about to get her thrown off the case.

"Your point is well taken," Commander Webster said to Ortiz before looking at the others. "I had intended to have a private conversation with Lieutenant Diaz about this, but now that the elephant's in the room ..."

She barely managed to contain herself. This conversation should take place behind closed doors, but Ortiz had challenged her in the middle of a briefing, guaranteeing an audience. What the hell was he up to?

Webster put his elbow on the table. "I have three major concerns." He raised his index finger. "Detective Cruz is under direct threat." A second finger went up. "Everyone around her is in danger." A third finger completed the count. "And she has ties to the suspects." He lowered his hand and turned to Veranda. "I have to reconsider your involvement in the investigation."

Webster sat through a barrage of objections flying at him from every direction before offering a response. "Five people under my command came within seconds of dying yesterday morning." His voice thickened. "Last night, Detective Cruz and Captain Anderson were almost killed." A vein pulsed along his temple. "On my watch."

No one moved. No one spoke. Tension expanded with each passing moment, crackling through the air around them. Veranda had never considered the weight of responsibility that burdened her commander.

Sam broke the silence. "I've been on the job more than thirty years," he said, somber gray eyes drilling into Webster. "I've taken my share of beatings and a couple of bullets along the way. There were times I thought I wouldn't make it home to my wife. She doesn't like it, but she accepts that it's part of the job." His dark bushy brows knitted. "With all due respect, Commander, risk goes with the territory."

Webster's back stiffened. "With all due respect to you, Detective, I'm in charge." He jerked a thumb at his chest. "Whatever happens is on me. I have to answer for my decisions." The ruddy tinge climbing his face stood out in sharp contrast to his sandy gray hair. "And I'm not talking about my career either. Fuck promotion. I'm talking about my detectives. It's been nine years since I've had to bury a detective under my command, and I never want to do it again. Especially if I can prevent it." He leaned into his next words, aiming them directly at Sam. "Who do you think would have done the death notification if you hadn't made it out of that storage unit? Who would have sat next to your widow at the funeral?"

"I'd have retired a long time ago if safety was my top priority," Sam said, unfazed. Decades with a badge had given him an air of steady resolve. "If I die on the job, then at least I'll die doing something I believe in. Something that matters."

She had never heard her commander and her partner at odds before. And she was at the center of their dispute.

"You didn't order me into that storage unit yesterday," she said to Webster. "I went in because it's my job. A job I freely chose." She narrowed her eyes. "But I didn't choose my father. He's gunning for me and I need my department to back me up, not shut me out."

Webster's flush deepened to a shade of maroon. He opened his mouth to shoot back what Veranda was sure would be a scathing reply when Marci inserted herself into the debate.

"Our Kevlar vests aren't fashion accessories," Marci said. "We all understood the risks when we were sworn in."

Tony followed suit. "We're gonna have to investigate these cases one way or another. Why bench our best player?" He shrugged. "Just sayin'."

Doc cleared his throat. "Statistically, police have a much better chance of dying from heart disease than a bullet." He grimaced. "If you ask me, a bullet would be far less painful."

Her squad had spoken. The commander felt responsible, but the detectives were the ones physically in harm's way. She hoped their unanimous support would convince Webster, but doubt clouded her mind. What more could she add? She studied the commander, trying to read his body language, when he turned to Diaz for input.

She tensed, prepared to hear a litany of reasons why she should stay away from any case involving the cartel, when her lieutenant's response stunned her.

"Cruz can't take point on this investigation, so I reassigned the lead to Stark," Diaz said. "But there's no specific policy preventing her from assisting." He gave a small shake of his head. "Truth is, Commander, we can't keep her away from the case. The cartel killed a man to draw her in. They've gone after her twice since. They're not going to stop." He spread his hands in a gesture of resignation. "She's in, whether we like it or not."

Veranda caught Sam's eye and raised her brows. He returned her bemused expression. She glanced at her squad mates, reading the same mix of confusion and surprise on their faces.

Webster shook his head. "This squad has no supervisor at the moment. Sergeant Jackson's still recovering from his appendectomy and I don't have another sergeant to spare." He took off his reading glasses and rubbed the bridge of his nose with his thumb and forefinger. Without looking up, he said, "I'm pulling another lieutenant to cover the Homicide Unit on a temporary assignment." After a long pause, he raised his head and leveled a weary gaze at Diaz. "You will work exclusively with this squad until Jackson's back on full duty. I expect daily reports and constant oversight." His red-rimmed eyes found Veranda. "Especially where Detective Cruz is concerned."

Her victory felt more like defeat. The same skills that gave her the edge as a narc made her a liability everywhere else on the force. Quick-thinking, flexible with the truth, and adaptable to most environments, she'd relied on a combination of brains, bravado, and bullshit to stay one step ahead of her quarry in the past.

Now her supervisors viewed her approach to investigations with more than a hint of skepticism. She had colored outside the lines too many times, and Commander Webster seemed to think she would go rogue if given half a chance. Deep inside, she knew her reputation for what she thought of as creative thinking and Lieutenant Diaz called a complete disregard for the rules was well-deserved, but her commander's last comment irked her anyway.

Diaz's dark eyes bored into hers as he responded to Webster. "I take full responsibility for Detective Cruz. I'll keep her close and monitor her activities at all times."

She had extricated herself from Ortiz's trap only to land squarely in Diaz's with her very next step. *Nice going, Cruz.*

11

VERANDA WATCHED HER mother's hazel eyes widen in shock.

"You could have died, *mi'ja*." Lorena clutched a corner of her apron. "You could have blown up into a million pieces. You could have—"

She stopped her mother's downward spiral into panic. "Mamá, I'm fine. I wasn't anywhere near my house when it happened." She deliberately avoided using words like *explosion* or *bomb*.

When Veranda arrived at the cluster of casitas on the Cruz family property minutes ago, her relatives were chopping food, arranging tables, and decorating every available surface. Aunt Juana had directed her to the kitchen in the main house to find her mother.

"I know you were not inside your house because Richard Diaz called me last night—before you did." Lorena's nostrils flared. "My own daughter did not call me until an hour after her house blew up." She crossed herself. "*Gracias a Dios* that Richard thought of me right away."

Her mother had foregone the spoon to dish out the guilt with a ladle. And, true to form, Lieutenant Diaz had managed to make her situation worse. Veranda always found it odd when her mother referred to her supervisor by his first name. In recent weeks, Diaz's friendship with her favorite cousin and her mother made her increasingly uncomfortable. Why on earth did they like him? Of course, they didn't have to work for him, so he probably didn't get in their business. Or order them around. Or question their every move.

She did a quick assessment of her mother's body language. From childhood, she'd learned to gauge Lorena's anger level from the position of her arms. If her arms were crossed, she was annoyed. If her hands were on her hips, she was exasperated. If her hands were clenched at her sides, look out.

Continuously balling the apron's hem in her fist, Lorena had gone way past livid, right up to the edge of hysterical. Veranda looked around for an ally. Aunt Juana and Uncles Juan, Felipe, and Rico had come to the kitchen to support their older sister. They stood shoulder to shoulder, flanking Lorena, with crossed arms and matching scowls. No help there. In desperation, she turned to Chuy, who had parked himself at the small dining table, and threw him a pleading look.

Chuy took the hint and stood. "Listen everybody, it's not like there's anything new going on here," he said. "Veranda's at war with the Villalobos family, and that's not about to change."

She did a mental head slap, belatedly recalling that Chuy specialized in causing fear, not easing it.

"Thanks a lot, Chuy." She threw her hands up in frustration. "Huge help."

Chuy ambled over to her and slung a tattooed arm around her shoulders. "I don't blow smoke, *mi'jita*. And I'm not saying anything they don't already know." He gave her a meaningful look. "Sometimes, you can't walk away from a situation. The odds are stacked against you, so you do whatever it takes to survive." He dropped his voice. "Whatever it takes, *mi'jita.*"

Only the soft bubbling of *molé* sauce simmering on the stove broke the silence. Chuy's expression had gone flat, his eyes, cold. His words were those of a man who had walked the prison yard in years past. A man who understood what it was to fight for survival against ruthless enemies. To sleep with one eye open every night.

Choking back a sob, Lorena darted forward and threw her arms around Veranda and Chuy. "*Ay, mi'ja,*" she said. "I am so scared I will lose you."

Veranda longed to promise her mother she would always be okay. But the words lodged in her throat. She could make no such vow. And even if she did, no one would believe it.

Chuy wiped a tear from her mother's cheek with a tattooed knuckle. "There's no time for that now," he said with surprising gentleness. "You have a party to plan. Didn't I hear you say two hundred people were coming here tomorrow night?"

Veranda marveled at the effect of her cousin's words. Galvanized into action, Lorena straightened and began barking orders at everyone in sight.

Veranda took up her post at a makeshift food prep station at the kitchen table with Chuy. They each pulled vegetables from the pile heaped on an enormous earthenware platter in the center of the table and started chopping.

Chuy's knife was a blur, the steel blade slicing through an onion in a series of staccato thumps on the thick wooden cutting board. He kept his eyes on his hands as he spoke. "Where are you staying?"

She lopped the top off a bell pepper. "Don't know yet."

"You could move in with me." Chuy lifted a muscular shoulder crisscrossed with an elaborate black spider web design. "It's small, but there's room enough."

Her cousin lived in an apartment directly over his auto repair shop. Tiffany had moved in with him, apparently preferring the scent of motor oil and engine grease to her place.

"Thanks, but I can't take you up on it." She had refused her co-workers, her boyfriend, and her family. No one else would get hurt because of her. "And you know why."

Thoughts of Cole reminded her of their brief phone conversation while she drove to her mother's house. She'd asked him to join her, but he'd begged off. Then she asked him about dinner, and he said he wouldn't be off shift until tomorrow. She wondered when she would see him again.

Chuy grabbed another onion. "I won't let you sleep in your car."

"Spoke to a claims adjuster from my insurance company this morning. They'll pay for a hotel until I can find a place."

"We're family. We take care of each other."

"I know you're a badass and all, Chuy, but I can't put you in harm's way, it's not—"

"I got it." His grin exposed a silver tooth. "I crash with Tiffany, then you can stay at my place by yourself."

"I couldn't impose."

Extending his index finger, Chuy put her on hold, plunked down his knife, and left the kitchen without another word.

She shrugged and continued dicing, her thoughts meandering over the case. She was certain she'd missed something important, but what? Lieutenant Diaz had been right to assign the lead to Sam. The turmoil in her personal life made her feel as if she stood on shifting sand, unable to gain purchase.

Chuy returned and picked up his knife. "It's done."

She didn't like the determined set of his jaw. "What's done?"

"Just got off the phone with Tiffany. I remembered her saying she used to live in a trailer before she moved in with me six months ago.

I've never seen it, but I'm sure it's big enough for two. Tiff and I can stay there for as long as you need."

She splayed her palms on the table and speared Chuy with her darkest glare. "No."

Chuy snorted. "You mad-dogging me, *mi'jita*? You got to do better than that."

"You're not listening to me."

"Tiff's right down the street getting her nails done. She's coming straight here in about ten minutes." He tilted his head in thought. "We're both on bikes, so you'll have to take us to my apartment in your Tahoe. We'll grab some stuff, then you can drive us over to her trailer and give us a ride back here for our bikes."

The plan sounded convoluted, but she knew her cousin. She could argue with him all day and then give in, or she could accept the inevitable and get on with it. She decided to be gracious. "Thank you." She reached out to squeeze his shoulder. "I'll find a different place as soon as I can."

Her mother strolled over to check on their progress. Queen of the kitchen, Lorena insisted on inspecting everyone's work when it came to her food. She peered at the pile of chopped vegetables. "Looks like you're almost finished."

"We'll be done soon," Chuy said. "And then Veranda's moving into my apartment."

Her mother's brow creased. "But I thought she would stay here in my house."

Chuy gave Veranda an *I told you so* look before facing Lorena. "We decided she should crash at my place. I'm going to Tiffany's."

Veranda could practically see the gears turning in her mother's mind. When Lorena's lips pursed, she knew her mother had read the subtext. Her oldest daughter should live alone for everyone else's safety.

Lorena smoothed her apron, took a deep breath, and eyed Veranda. "But you are coming to the party, yes?"

"Of course, Mamá."

Lorena relaxed. "And your *capitán,* the fireman, he will come too?"

Veranda stifled a groan. How could she explain that her relationship with Cole was probably over? "I don't think so. We're going through ... a rough patch."

Her mother gave her an accusatory look. "He's a nice man. He has a good job. What happened?"

She wasn't surprised when her mother asked about her love life. When it came to Veranda, personal boundaries did not exist. For years, the entire family had done their best to find her a husband, the level of urgency increasing with each year. Now that she was on the wrong side of thirty, she figured they were at DEFCON 1.

Before she could come up with a response, Lorena pressed a hand to her chest. "No, don't tell me. I can guess. Something to do with that horrible cartel."

Veranda studied her shoes.

"I came to the United States to get away from Hector Villalobos." Lorena motioned around the room at the rest of the family. "To get all of us away. Now we are Americans. We are free. But you are not."

When Veranda raised a brow, Lorena wrung her hands. "*Ay,* I don't know how to say it right in English."

Her mother turned to the group and switched to Spanish, something she only did when she wanted to be perfectly clear.

"I've kept secrets for most of my life, and it's time to let them go," Lorena said. "I never planned to tell a soul, but the truth came out anyway." Her eyes slid to the floor. "Except for the reason I called my daughter *Veranda.*"

Everyone stilled at the abrupt shift in the conversation. Veranda remembered every detail of the day last July when her mother had confided her most painful secrets. Including the one she was about to reveal to the rest of the family.

Thirty-two years ago, Lorena was a young bride, married to Ernesto Hidalgo, in Mexico City. When she spurned his advances, *El Lobo* murdered her husband and raped her. Lorena became pregnant and kept the baby without knowing whether her dead husband or his killer had fathered her child. But recently, Veranda's true lineage became public when the Villalobos cartel leaked a paternity test to the media, devastating her mother in the process.

"Everyone may know how Veranda was conceived." Lorena looked up to meet her eldest daughter's eyes. "But only she knows how her name gave me strength while I raised her." Voice thick with emotion, Lorena turned back to the family. "I combined the words *ver* and *la andadura* to remind me that my daughter's choices would reveal her true nature."

Veranda saw recognition dawn on the faces around her. Roughly translated, *ver* meant "see" and *la andadura* referred to a "path," or a "journey." Her mother had given her a name that would serve as a constant reminder that Veranda's own actions created her destiny, not her bloodline. Lorena would wait and see which path her daughter took.

"I used to believe Veranda became a police officer because Ernesto was her father." Sorrow tinged Lorena's words. "Before I learned the truth."

Veranda's heart ached for her mother. Lorena had raised Veranda with an open heart, no doubt convincing herself over the years that her late husband lived on through her child. Then, as he had taken everything else, Hector Villalobos had stolen her last vestige of hope when Veranda's paternity had been revealed.

Lorena reached out to clasp Veranda's hand. "It doesn't matter who your father is, *mi'ja*," she said, taking her other hand. "I have watched you seek your own path." The tears that had gathered in her eyes began to spill down Lorena's cheeks. "And I am proud to call you my daughter."

"*Ay*, Mamá, I'm proud of you too." Veranda felt her own eyes moisten. "You're so strong."

"You both are," Uncle Rico said, putting his arms around them.

The rest of the family began to press in, gathering into a group hug. The only one with dry eyes, Chuy kissed the top of Veranda's head. She wished the moment could have lasted longer, but her mother wasn't finished.

"That's what I was trying to say before," Lorena continued in her native tongue. "Our life is here now. *El Lobo* is part of your past, but he will ruin your future if you let him. That's why you must stop, *mi'ja*. Leave him alone."

First Cole, then Commander Webster, now her mother. Three times today she'd been given a cease and desist order regarding the Villalobos family. As if she had a choice.

She raised her head and caught Chuy's nod of support. As an unspoken understanding passed between them, her cousin's words floated back to her.

Sometimes, you can't walk away from a situation. The odds are stacked against you, so you do whatever it takes to survive.

12

Villalobos family compound, Mexico

SALAZAR CLUTCHED A metal briefcase in the subterranean anteroom, eyes adjusting to the gloom. The rough-hewn stone of the cylindrical wall surrounding him could have been in a medieval fortress.

Hector Villalobos spoke in his customary refined Spanish. "I had this dungeon built to my specifications after much research." He reached out to trace a finger along a paper-thin crevice between two stones. "Only the best workmanship."

Salazar had seen all sorts of punishments meted out in the dark chambers that held *El Lobo*'s prisoners. Most who entered left in a bag. Those who survived were never the same, physically or mentally. He would dearly love to see Daria dragged into one of the cells.

He broached the subject of Daria's betrayal with surgical precision, as he did everything. "The *federales* in Mexico City are working with US law enforcement now. They will run the DNA from the water bottle through our system." He paused for emphasis, treading carefully. "When they get a match, they will know. Everyone will know."

Hector lowered his hand. "Secrets from the past eventually find their way to the surface no matter how far down they are buried. Maybe it's time the world knew about yours."

He chose his next words for maximum impact. "*You* would have revealed my secret at a time of your choosing. If ever. Instead, Daria decided for you."

Hector's expression darkened. "I am not pleased with her behavior."

Direct hit. The reaction cued him to double down. "She planted that bottle. Set me up."

He waited to see if he'd gone too far.

Finally, Hector's jet-black eyes locked with his. "Yes."

Without further comment, Hector strode to the heavy wooden door and seized the wrought iron bolt. He threw it back with a grunt and tugged the handle. The door creaked open. Hector stepped over the threshold, stopped short, and spun around.

Close on his heels, Salazar nearly collided with him, barely managing to jerk the briefcase out of the way before it hit Hector's thigh.

"You will fly to Phoenix and relieve Daria of her command," Hector said. "I will still permit her to kill Veranda Cruz as I promised her earlier, but only on your orders and according to your plan."

He had to change Hector's mind. "I want the kill order transferred to me as well as Daria's part of the operation."

Hector gave him an appraising look. "You are aware of what that means?"

Three months ago, Hector told Adolfo he could not become heir apparent to the family empire until he eliminated Veranda Cruz. By his own hand. When Adolfo failed, the order passed to Daria to prove she could take the reins. Killing Cruz had become inextricably linked with assuming control of the cartel.

And Salazar intended to do both.

"I know what it means." He spoke the words that had been in his heart for years. "You know that I am the one to lead our organization."

He'd said it. Now he waited an interminable minute while *El Lobo* regarded him with fathomless lupine eyes. Had he moved too quickly? Did naked ambition demonstrate his determination, or expose him as an opportunist?

Salazar couldn't read the emotion behind Hector's austere features as his boss studied him with a fierce intensity. In that moment, Hector reminded him of the *generales* he had served during his time in the Army. Without conscious thought, he reverted to his military training. His entire body stiffened until he stood at attention, ready for inspection.

With slow, deliberate movements, Hector circled behind him. "As of this moment, the kill order is transferred to you," he said into Salazar's ear.

He remained rooted to the spot as Hector continued around to face him once again. The next words out of *El Lobo*'s mouth meant victory or defeat. He kept his face completely blank as he waited for the decision.

Hector raised both arms and pulled Salazar against him in an *abrazo*. "And so is the prize that comes with it," he said, breaking the embrace after kissing him on both cheeks.

Salazar suppressed any outward display of excitement. "I will leave at once."

"Stay here until after our *Día de los Muertos* celebration tomorrow night. You will participate with us this year. You can notify Daria about the change in plans tomorrow."

"As you wish."

"Also, I will tell you who the Rook is."

Salazar was surprised. For years, Hector had unsuccessfully tried to recruit someone he referred to only as "the Rook." He would only divulge that the man was in law enforcement and could provide unprecedented access.

"Do you have him, then?"

"Not yet," Hector said. "But I want to put more effort in because of Daria. Her actions will make it harder for you to do your job on both sides of the border."

"That never stopped me before. I know how to travel undetected."

"A good chess player always thinks several moves ahead. I am creating a backup plan, and the Rook is a critical piece on my board." Hector pivoted to continue down the passage.

Salazar switched the briefcase to his other hand and fell into step beside him. "Isn't the hacking program providing intelligence?"

"The reinforced security on the police servers has slowed progress. The computer tech firm I am purchasing will speed things up."

The passage opened to two rows of prison cells separated by a cement floor the width of a city sidewalk. All cells stood empty except the one in front of them.

"Good afternoon, Pedro."

Hector's greeting was met with a whimper from the far corner of the cage.

"Come forward so I can see you."

Pedro stumbled toward them, clutching the iron bars as if he feared he would fall. "P-please, Señor Villalobos, I—"

Hector held up a hand. "I come bearing a gift." He smiled. "You will be an honored guest at our *Día de los Muertos* celebration tomorrow night. You must wear this."

At Hector's signal, Salazar bent to lay the steel briefcase on the ground and popped open the latches. He lifted the top and reached inside. Taking care to avoid touching any wires, he picked up the locking metal neck shackle and straightened.

"Show Pedro what he will wear to the party, Salazar."

He extended his arms toward Pedro, who squinted in confusion. "W-what is that?"

"It is a special kind of collar," Hector said, baring his teeth in a feral smile. "The last one you will ever put on."

Pedro sank to his knees and sobbed.

13

VERANDA HAD OBSERVED many suspects concoct stories, and Chuy's girlfriend was exhibiting classic signs of deception. Fed up, Veranda steered the Tahoe to the side of the road. Thrusting the gear shift lever into park, she twisted in her seat to face Tiffany. "I'm not driving one inch farther until you tell me where we're going." She narrowed her eyes. "The truth this time."

Veranda had spent the last hour helping her cousin and his girl-friend pack enough clothing and other essentials to last a month in Tiffany's trailer. After loading everything into the back, Chuy had climbed in amid the bulging green garbage bags.

Tiffany stopped her incessant texting. Her thumbs had been fever-ishly tapping the screen since they'd left Chuy's apartment above his auto repair garage. She flung her phone into her open handbag and looked up with wide, innocent eyes and a smile as believable as her platinum dye-job.

Veranda lifted a brow. "You can't bullshit me, Tiff. Whatever story you're thinking up won't work."

Chuy poked his head between the two front seats. "I don't know what you're hiding, *mamacita*," he said to his girlfriend. "But you better come clean."

Tiffany crossed her arms, a defiant expression on her pretty face. "I was checking to see if we could stay with any of my other friends. But no one's got room."

Chuy's pierced black brows came together. "I thought you had a trailer."

Tiffany slapped a hand over her eyes and grimaced. "I lied."

Tiff had been dating Chuy for almost a year. She'd moved in with him six months ago, explaining that her single-wide needed a lot of work. Chuy had offered to fix it, but Tiffany had declined. Now Veranda knew why.

"You never had a trailer at all, did you?" Veranda said.

Tiffany separated her fingers a fraction to peek out at Veranda. "No."

"Then why have I been driving around for the past twenty minutes going nowhere?"

"I thought I could keep you driving in circles until I came up with a way out." Tiffany yanked her hand away from her face. "But I can't."

Veranda didn't like the edge of hysteria creeping into Tiffany's voice. "A way out of what?"

With a look of deep regret, Tiffany turned to Chuy. "We'll have to stay with my parents."

"That's not so bad." Chuy's finger traced the edge of a purple butterfly tattoo at the base of her neck. "I've had to crash at my dad's place now and then. Nothing wrong with that."

Tiffany groaned. "You don't understand. My parents' house is not the kind of place you'd want to be. Not even on a bet."

Chuy moved his hand from Tiffany's neck to cup her chin, forcing her to meet his gaze. "This is only for a little while, babe. Veranda doesn't have time to hunt for an apartment because of her case. Besides, it's better if her name isn't on a lease. Makes her harder to find."

Veranda's frustration at Tiffany for misleading her drained away. Chuy's girlfriend was obviously deeply ashamed of where her parents lived. Chuy's tiny apartment over the garage was far from palatial, so Tiffany shouldn't feel uncomfortable showing them where she came from.

Veranda tried to lighten the mood. "Don't worry about the living arrangements," she said, pointing at herself and her cousin. "It's hard to scare either one of us."

Tiffany rounded on her. "You have no idea. This is the house I grew up in. It's horrible. And my parents…" She covered her mouth with her hand. "I haven't visited them since I left six months ago to move in with Chuy."

Veranda pictured a rundown shack on the outskirts of the city. In her mind's eye, a grizzled older man in a sweat-stained wife-beater undershirt and boxers sat on a porch sofa next to an older version of Tiffany wearing a saggy tube top and too much lip gloss. Tiffany shouldn't be embarrassed. Veranda and Chuy had grown up in a low-cost housing complex before their parents had pooled resources to buy land for the casitas.

Chuy seemed to have come to the same conclusion about Tiffany's upbringing. He ran calloused fingers through her hair. "Before I got my apartment above the garage, the last place I lived had a warden and a cell mate called Oso. That's Spanish for 'bear.' The sonofabitch stood six-foot-five and weighed about three bills. I couldn't turn around without bumping into him. And don't get me started about his bathroom habits." Chuy shuddered. "There's not many places worse than that."

"Fine." Tiffany lifted her chin. "You want to meet my parents? You want to see the old homestead? You want to stay there with me?" She crossed her arms and glared straight ahead. "Then let's go."

Veranda put the Tahoe in gear. "Where am I heading?"

Tiffany didn't look at her. "Paradise Valley."

Veranda and Chuy exchanged glances. Paradise Valley was among the wealthiest suburbs of Phoenix. With its sprawling mansions, lush palm trees, and mountain views, PV was home to the rich and famous.

"Babe, what are you talking ab—" Chuy began.

Tiffany cut him off with an icy glare. "I'm done talking. You'll find out when we get there. And don't say I didn't warn you."

Fifteen minutes later, following Tiffany's directions, Veranda pulled up to a set of massive scrolled iron gates in front of a long cobblestone driveway. She stopped at a keypad with a camera mounted above it and punched in the number Tiffany provided.

The gate swung open and she cruised the lengthy driveway, lined on either side by towering royal palms, until she reached a portico in front of a mid-century Frank Lloyd Wright–style estate.

While Chuy fired off a few choice words describing the expansive home, Veranda focused on the man standing in front of the towering bright-red double doors leading inside, barring their entry. Over seven feet tall and built like a Clydesdale, the man could only be described as hired muscle. With his black tactical outfit, dark shades, and a curling mic wire leading into his ear, he looked like a secret service agent who guarded the president of the underworld.

He approached the open driver's door window and bent low to peer inside. His gaze locked on Tiffany. "You have guests, Miss Durant?"

She nodded. "I brought bags too." Her manner had undergone a complete transformation. "Put them in the guest house." Her tone was borderline haughty. "We'll show ourselves inside."

Stunned, Veranda got out of the Tahoe to stand next to Tiffany and Chuy.

The guard hadn't moved to unload the heaps of garbage bags. Instead, he leveled a hard stare at Chuy, who reciprocated in kind.

Tiffany stepped between the men and tilted her head back to give the guard a stern look. "I texted my father. We're authorized."

The Clydesdale didn't budge. "I'll need to search these two."

Veranda put a hand on her hip. "You'll find a .45-caliber Glock on me, and probably a few knives on my cousin, but you're not taking them."

The guard's head snapped toward her and he reached for the holster on his hip.

"Stand down," Tiffany said. "She's a cop." When the guard turned his gaze back to Chuy, she added, "And he's … my boyfriend." Silence stretched between them. "You have your orders. Move aside."

The guard turned and opened the massive double front doors. Without another word, Tiffany flounced inside. Veranda noted that the guard trailed them as they made their way through a wide hall toward the back of the house.

Tiffany continued through a lavish family room, where an open glass wall led to the lanai. A distinguished-looking couple sat at a small round table covered in a crisp white linen cloth. They both rose to greet the new arrivals. Judging by the shock on their faces, Veranda concluded they were Tiffany's parents, and that their daughter had drastically altered her appearance in the past six months.

Tiffany's halter top revealed brightly colored sleeves of tattoos decorating both arms from wrist to shoulder. Her atomic-blonde locks contrasted with dark brows pierced with silver barbell studs that matched Chuy's.

A teaspoon clattered to a china plate, breaking the silence. Tiffany's mother, dressed in a casually elegant linen ensemble, seemed unaware that she'd dropped the utensil. Eyes fixed on her daughter, her mouth opened and closed several times before she managed a complete sentence. "Tiffany, what happened to you?"

"I got a life, Mom. I'm twenty-four. About time, don't you think?"

"Your hair. Your clothes." Her mother flapped her manicured hands in distress. "Your... tattoos."

"Your boyfriend." Tiffany's father spoke for the first time. While her mother had focused on their daughter's appearance, her father had zeroed in on Chuy.

Veranda had to give Tiffany credit. She straightened her shoulders and responded in a determined voice. "Dad, this is Chuy."

Tiffany's father's eyes drifted up and down her cousin. Veranda followed his gaze, trying to see Chuy from the perspective of a concerned parent. The black leather vest over his bare chest, faded jeans encased in chaps, and jagged scar on his cheek were the only interruptions in a solid tapestry of biker tattoos traversing every inch of exposed skin on his body. The wall-to-wall ink capped his shaved head, ending in a widow's peak at the top of his forehead. Yeah, Veranda thought to herself, Tiffany's parents probably weren't trying to decide whether he was a Harvard or a Yale man.

Bristling under the disdainful scrutiny, Chuy pulled himself up to his full height. Jaw rigid, muscles flexed, and eyes narrowed, he met the unspoken challenge.

Now Veranda understood what Tiffany had wanted to avoid. Her parents turned their attention to Veranda, who felt their judgment shift to her. Their combined gazes rested on the clothing she'd borrowed from Marci, and a visible flicker of relief registered. Naturally, they recognized a Chanel suit. Perhaps perceiving her as one of their tribe, Tiffany's mother gave Chuy a wide berth to approach Veranda.

She extended a hand. "Jacqueline Durant." She inclined her head toward Tiffany's father. "And this is my husband, Sebastian. But everyone calls him Baz."

Jaqueline didn't actually say *at the club* at the end of her sentence, but Veranda heard the words as if Tiffany's mother had shouted them.

"Veranda Cruz." Shaking hands, she decided to have some fun. "And this is my cousin, Jesús. But everyone calls him Chuy." She barely stopped herself from adding *at the pen.*

Baz turned to Chuy. Neither man proffered a hand. Nor did they say anything in greeting. Veranda saw her cousin's spine stiffen as his eyes went hard, flat, and cold. She recognized his posturing as something he would have used in the prison yard to intimidate other inmates. But Baz didn't seem to be intimidated. Instead, his baleful expression became calculating.

Jacqueline wedged a knuckle between her front teeth, briefly closing her eyes before nervously glancing at each man in turn. After a moment, her face cleared. She pivoted to give Chuy an overly bright smile. "Have you been in our country long, Mr. ah … Chuy?"

When Chuy merely stared at her, Jacqueline turned to her daughter. "Does he speak English?"

Tiffany whirled on her mother. "Stop that!" Clearly mortified, she turned back to the man she loved. "This is why I didn't want to bring you here. To my parents, Latinos are cooks, landscapers, or cleaning ladies who come here illegally." She marched over to Chuy and wrapped her hands around his bare arm. "He speaks English. And he might even answer your questions if you show him some respect."

Veranda glanced at Chuy, afraid of how he might respond. Then she remembered the guard, who had remained mutely behind them. The situation had all the earmarks of an impending disaster. She was planning a hasty exit when Chuy threw his head back and let out a full-throated belly laugh.

Recovering himself, Chuy gave Tiffany a wry grin. "You shouldn't have been worried about taking me to meet your parents, babe. I've dealt with people like them my whole life."

Jacqueline let out an indignant huff and stomped into the house.

Baz watched her go, apparently deep in thought. After a long pause, he faced his daughter. "Sorry, about that, honey." He gestured to Chuy. "But he does look a bit … rough."

"Don't talk about him like he's not here," Tiffany said. "And he *is* rough." She gazed up at Chuy with admiring eyes. "Like an uncut diamond."

"Of course." Baz seemed hard-pressed to see any diamond-like potential in his daughter's boyfriend. He gave Chuy a curt nod. "You're welcome to stay with Tiffany in the guest house. There's plenty of space and a separate garage."

Tiffany beamed. "That's perfect. Veranda's going to give us a ride back to South Phoenix to pick up our bikes. Your neighbors will have to get used to loud pipes."

Baz looked like he could use an antacid. "How long will you two be here?"

Tiffany tilted her head. "Only until Veranda finds a place to stay or takes down the Villalobos cartel."

The color drained from her father's face. "The Villalobos cartel?"

Veranda suppressed an urge to smack her forehead. Tiffany could have talked all day without those words passing her lips. Why had she mentioned the damned cartel?

"That's who blew up her house, Dad." Tiffany spoke with a matter-of-fact air, as if being targeted by one of the most dangerous criminal organizations in the world was no big deal. "It's all over the news. She needs a place to stay, so she's moving into Chuy's apartment."

"A Mexican drug cartel is after her?" Baz's face went from pale to puce as he slowly swiveled his head toward Veranda. "That was your house on the news? And you hang around with Tiffany?"

Baz had apparently concluded Veranda posed an even greater threat to his daughter than Chuy did, which was true.

She rushed to answer before Tiffany tried to help her again. "Don't concern yourself, Mr. Durant." She shot Tiffany a repressive look. "I hardly ever see your daughter, and Chuy has nothing to do with the cartel at all. That's why I can't stay with him. They'll both be safe here with you."

"You're right about that." Baz gave his daughter a sympathetic look. "Honey, you can stay here as long as you like." His glance at Chuy seemed like an afterthought. "And you too."

Veranda was satisfied that at least Tiffany and Chuy would be out of danger. And quite comfortable. She imagined Chuy sitting poolside ordering drinks from the domestic staff. The Durants' palatial estate would never be the same.

She owed them both. Chuy, a proud man, was prepared to deal with constant humiliation for however long it took for her to find a new place to live. And Tiffany had revealed a secret she'd been hiding for months because she knew her parents' racist attitudes would cause pain. They had sacrificed for her, and she could never repay them.

She regarded Chuy's girlfriend, who had held his scarred, oil-stained, and work-worn hand while fiercely defending him. She would never give Tiffany a hard time about her wardrobe again.

14

VERANDA GRASPED HER ankle and slowly pulled it back, lengthening her quadriceps and testing the limits of Tiffany's form-fitting hot pink Lycra shorts as she stretched. She had just released her grip when a rough male voice catcalled from across the street, interrupting the final phase of her warmup.

"*Hola, morrita!*"

She turned to see who had called her a hottie. A man in his twenties, dressed in baggy jeans and a sweat-stained undershirt, grabbed his crotch and grunted at her. Charming.

"Why don't you come over here and get some of this, *mami?*" Baggy Jeans said, rubbing his hand up and down his front zipper.

Raising her index finger, she yelled back to him. "Hold on a sec." She patted herself down as if searching for something. "Damn, didn't bring my magnifying glass and tweezers." She gave him a palms-up shrug. "You should've told me you'd be here."

"Bitch!" He flipped her off and slouched away, muttering profanities in two languages. Impressive.

She shook her head, already regretting her vow not to give Tiffany a hard time about her wardrobe. If the shorts didn't garner unwanted attention during her run, the matching midriff-baring crop-top definitely would.

She'd changed into the outfit at the Durant family's guest house after Tiffany spotted her yanking off Marci's designer pumps and rubbing her feet. Tiffany had rooted around in one of the plastic bags, dug out a handful of workout gear, and thrust it at her. After several refusals, Veranda had caved when Tiffany dangled a pair of Nikes by their shoelaces.

Diaz had ordered her to take time off to relocate, and her meeting with Sam wasn't until that evening. With a long afternoon ahead of her, she'd appreciated the chance to get comfortable. Once she wriggled into the clingy outfit, however, she realized that Tiffany's athletic wear could be mistaken for lingerie.

After dropping Chuy and Tiffany off at her mother's house to pick up their motorcycles, Veranda had used her cell to call Cole on the drive to Chuy's apartment. It had been her first opportunity to have a serious conversation with him since the meeting in the War Room. Cole had sounded busy, explaining that he was finishing his report on the fire investigation and couldn't talk.

Frustration whipped through her. She needed an outlet. When she found herself driving too fast, gripping the wheel too hard, and getting too angry, she'd pulled into a vacant lot down the street from Chuy's place to go for a run.

Warmup now finished, she scanned for Baggy Jeans. Nowhere in sight. She zipped her cell phone into a hidden pocket at the back of her waist and launched into a trot heading west on Southern Avenue.

102

Moving to South Phoenix meant finding a new route for her regular runs. These were her childhood stomping grounds, so she knew this part of the city well. She'd already figured out what streets she could take to arrive back at Chuy's garage after about four or five miles.

Instinctively, she kept an eye out for Baggy Jeans, who she'd begun to think of as BJ. No self-respecting Latino male would stand for such an insult to his manhood. Her taunt could come back to haunt her. Unfortunately, she'd locked her gun in the Tahoe's glove compartment. Tiffany's outfit had no place to hide a Glock. She made a mental note to carry pepper spray on her next outing in case BJ tried to take it to the next level.

Her feet found a steady rhythm as she pounded along the sidewalk on Southern. She passed squat buildings lining the street that had been there since she was a child. Many storefronts were abandoned, their boarded-up windows put the lie to the promised revitalization that never reached South Phoenix.

The day's stress gradually released its hold, easing the tension from her limbs. She turned north on Montezuma and kept going. A sheen of perspiration glistened on her coppery skin. She felt free. Energized. Late October offered the perfect weather for outdoor pursuits. Still warm and sunny, but without the blistering heat of the summer months. The scenery, featuring chain link fences, broken windows, and colorful graffiti, wouldn't get a spread in *Arizona Highways* magazine, but she felt right at home.

The screech of tires killed her runner's high. Glancing over her shoulder, she saw a dark van with blacked-out windows swerve to the curb a few yards behind her. Reverting to cop mode, she performed a quick threat assessment. The van had stopped between intersections without any other cars around, so traffic hadn't caused the sudden maneuver. No pedestrians in sight meant the driver wasn't avoiding a jaywalker either. She came to the only logical conclusion at the same moment the van's side panel slid open.

BJ leaped to the sidewalk behind her, the silver blade of a knife glinting in his hand. Weaponless, she opted for flight and kicked on the afterburners, sprinting away from him. Eyes darting in a fruitless search for help, she pelted across the deserted avenue, turning down a street that would take her toward the Tahoe. She had to reach the vehicle before he caught up.

Heavy footsteps thudded behind her, matching the wild banging of her heart. She had already run more than three miles, but BJ was fresh. Despite her adrenalin-fueled dash, he was steadily gaining ground.

"I'm gonna fuck you up, bitch!" BJ rasped the threat between breaths as he chased her down, a cheetah on the heels of a gazelle.

Arms and legs pumping, she had no hope of pulling her cell phone from its zippered pocket, much less making a call. She tried shouting, but her burning lungs barely produced a hoarse yelp. She had to conserve oxygen to feed her brain and sustain her fatigued muscles.

She considered using the last of her energy for an all-out sprint until she either reached the Tahoe or collapsed. But if he caught her, she'd have no reserves left to fight him. BJ would gut her with his knife. She discarded the idea in favor of attack, her only remaining option. Her rapidly forming plan hinged on precise timing, the right location, and the element of surprise.

She chanced another look over her shoulder. He was about twenty feet behind, closing in fast. Now or never.

She left the sidewalk to make a beeline for Southern Avenue, cutting between two abandoned buildings. She would come out within thirty yards of the Tahoe, but getting to her vehicle would do no good if BJ got there with her. She needed time to unlock the door, jump inside, and lock it shut. Her plan would buy her at least fifteen seconds.

Rounding the first corner of the building, her eyes locked on the boarded-up windows. She knew what lay around the next corner and put on a final burst of speed to reach it quickly.

Veranda had been in many foot chases during her time in patrol. The most dangerous times were when the suspect left her line of sight. He could double back and strike, catching her off guard.

She used her experience to set BJ up by running around the first corner and going straight. He was now conditioned to follow her blindly around the edge of a building. When she disappeared again, he would barrel after her without thinking.

She raced around the second corner, planted her foot, and snatched the edge of the plywood she'd seen on her first pass down Southern Avenue dangling by one nail from a broken window. She wrenched it free from the sash and grasped one edge in each hand. In one fluid movement, she hoisted the poster-sized plank and spun toward the sound of BJ's approaching feet.

He whipped around the corner at top speed, oblivious to the wide wooden board coming straight at him with all the force she could muster. His face smashed into its flat side with a sickening crunch. Veranda loosened her grip a split second before impact to avoid injuring her hands.

BJ's feet flew out from under him. His back slammed to the ground, the loud *oof* telling her the wind had been knocked out of him. While he lay gasping, she took off. Seconds later, she was tearing down the sidewalk paralleling Southern Avenue as fast as her feet would carry her. The Tahoe was in sight, but farther away than she'd estimated.

BJ shouted something from behind her, but she ignored him, completely focused on her goal. She was going to make it to her car. She was going to—

A second man, tall and wiry, stepped into her path and took up a shooter's stance, the barrel of his gun aimed squarely at her.

"On your knees, *puta*," the gunman said.

15

SHE SKIDDED TO a halt, eyes scanning wildly for an escape route. Confronted with two attackers, one behind her wielding a knife, the other brandishing a gun at her face, she was out of options.

As she began to drop to her knees, hoping the gunman would come close enough for her to disarm him, the welcome sound of approaching traffic reached her ears. Maybe someone would see what was going on and call 9-1-1. The engine noise grew louder, and she realized it came from a lone motorcycle. *Damn.* Whoever it was would have to pull over to use a cell phone. Probably drive to a safer location before parking the bike. She didn't have that kind of time.

"Now, bitch." The gunman gestured in a downward motion with the muzzle.

She complied, pebbles on the rough pavement digging into her knees. She prepared to go for his gun if he was stupid enough to get close.

He wasn't.

The gunman kept the muzzle trained on her while BJ grabbed a fistful of her hair from behind and jerked her head back. As he bent over her, droplets of blood fell from the tip of his shattered nose, plopping onto her cheek.

"You gonna come with us, *puta*." He waggled the knife in front of her face. "And you gonna wish you was dead before we get done with you."

The motorcycle got closer, the growl of its drilled-out baffles rumbled through the deserted street like thunder.

BJ and the gunman both turned toward the racket. Taking full advantage of their momentary distraction, she clasped both hands around BJ's and drove the point of his knife into his thigh.

Shrieking, he stumbled backward and wrenched the blade out. A dark stain blossomed around the slit in his jeans. She rolled away, coming up to a crouch.

The gunman set his sights on her again. "Back on your knees!"

She straightened and squared her shoulders. "No."

Moments ago, she had knelt as a ploy to get his weapon. She refused to do it as an act of obedience. Time stopped. The roar of the motorcycle, the stream of expletives spewing from BJ, the sound of her own breathing, all receded. In the stillness, an unmistakable *snick-snick* froze her insides. The gunman had thumbed the hammer back, cocking it as a final warning.

BJ clutched his upper leg, blood oozing between his fingers. "Just fuckin' shoot her, man."

She forced her gaze from the barrel pointing at her to meet the gunman's eyes a split second before a thick metal chain bashed against the side of his head, knocking him to the ground. She glanced up from his crumpled form to see Chuy, a look of cold fury on his scarred face and a chain wrapped around his clenched fist.

The gunman groaned, sat up, and raised his weapon. Veranda lashed out with her sneakered foot, landing a blow to his right forearm. The pistol clattered to the pavement.

Chuy bent to scoop it up, but BJ had quietly circled around to jump him from behind.

"He's got a knife," she warned her cousin before diving on the gunman, who had started crawling toward his weapon.

Chuy hadn't been trained in defensive tactics or disarming techniques at the police academy. He'd learned both skills in the prison yard, where they played for keeps. She'd never witnessed her cousin in an actual fight, and he was something to behold. She watched him from the corner of her eye, guarding his back as she would a fellow officer's, while she grappled with the gunman.

Chuy's eyes went dark as he went into battle, feet planted wide for stability, knees bent to lower his center of gravity. His arm was in constant motion, swinging the chain in a vicious arc, repeatedly whipping the heavy links around to lash BJ's ribs, arms, and legs. Chuy's relentless onslaught never allowed his adversary close enough to use his knife.

Satisfied her cousin was holding his own, she concentrated on putting the other man down. The gunman lurched to his feet, and she hammered his face with a series of elbow strikes before he could fully straighten. He sank to his knees and she prepared to deliver a kick to his jaw designed to knock him out.

The blast of a nearby car horn drew everyone's attention to the street. The driver of the black van laid on the horn a second time. He gestured frantically at the open side door, signaling the two attackers to get inside.

Veranda processed the new information. What had at first appeared to be a random encounter with a foul-mouthed moron, then seemed to morph into a revenge attack with his friend, had actually been a coordinated ambush all along. As she considered the implications, the gunman took the opportunity to bolt toward the idling van.

She started to give chase when Chuy's warning shout halted her. Instinctively, she ducked and spun away as a flash of silver flew past. If she hadn't moved, BJ's knife would have plunged into the middle of her back.

Seeing his cohorts about to abandon him, BJ had distracted Chuy and Veranda by hurling his blade at her. While Chuy rushed to her side, BJ pelted to the van, diving through the open side door as the driver peeled out in a plume of exhaust and smoking tires.

Chests heaving, Veranda and Chuy watched the fleeing vehicle fishtail down the street, disappearing around a corner. Even if she sprinted to the Tahoe, she'd never catch up before the van reached the I-17 interchange.

Cursing, she tugged her cell from its zippered pocket at her waist. To her relief, the phone was intact. She tapped the screen and hesitated, considering her best move. The South Mountain Precinct was close, but by the time patrol units responded, got her story, and started searching, the van would be on one of several possible freeways. The Air Unit wouldn't have much to work with, even if the helicopter happened to be on this side of the 500-square-mile city. She pictured herself answering questions, filling out forms, and looking at mug books for hours on end.

Chuy watched her deliberation with an amused expression. "You're not gonna catch them," he said. "Besides, do you really want Diaz here?"

Shit. She pictured her lieutenant in full rant after learning about the attack. He'd review the reports and discover that she'd gone for a jog with no gun, no radio, no pepper spray, nothing but a cell phone. After the aneurism that would surely follow, he would frog-march her to the nearest safe house and sleep on the bed next to her.

Nope. This little incident would stay between her and Chuy.

She turned to her cousin. "Tell you what. I won't say anything if you don't." She eyed him. "Especially not to Diaz. I don't care how tight you two are." She put her hands on her hips. "I'm serious, Chuy."

"Deal." He chuckled. "Besides, if this ever got to court, there's not a prosecutor in the city that would put me on the witness stand."

"I hear you." Now that her main dilemma was resolved, she turned her attention to another nagging question. "How did you know I was in trouble? How did you find me?"

"I didn't." Chuy shook his tattooed head. "I was coming back to the garage to work on a car. The owner said he needed it tomorrow."

Good thing she'd doubled back to Southern Avenue. Chuy would never have seen her on a side street like Montezuma. "And where did you get that chain?"

Chuy held a chain heavy enough to do a lumberjack proud. He'd wrapped the solid steel links around his wrist twice and clutched them in his fist, letting the remaining length dangle to the ground.

"The law says a convicted felon can't carry a gun," Chuy said, links clanking as he shrugged. "Nothing about carrying a chain, though. I hide one of these on all my bikes." His eyes widened in mock realization. "Sabes qué? There's some scary motherfuckers out there."

She laughed. "Then you must be the head motherfucker who keeps all the other motherfuckers in line."

"Damn straight." He inclined his head in agreement. "I got to ask you something, mi'jita." He grew serious again. "Yesterday, the Villalobos cartel tried to kill you. Today they try to grab you right off the street. What's up?"

Reeling as if she'd been hit with Chuy's chain, she saw her cousin in a new light. Not only did he spot the wolf logo on the back of the van, he also recognized the symbol. In addition, he understood that BJ and the gunman weren't trying to kill her outright.

Snatching pedestrians from sidewalks in a blitz-style attack was a hallmark of criminal organizations around the world, and the Villalobos cartel was no different. In a matter of seconds, the unsuspecting victim was ambushed and hustled into a waiting van, whisked away before anyone could react. Never to be seen again.

She didn't insult Chuy's intelligence by denying it. "I don't know why, but something changed. Someone in the cartel wants to capture me alive now."

Chuy scrubbed a hand over his face. "Not gonna lie to you, *mi'jita*. I don't like this. Those dudes weren't playing. Maybe you should tell Diaz so he can watch your back."

"Not just no." She crossed her arms. "But hell no."

His scowl reminded her forcibly of the lieutenant in question. "How did they find you? Do they know you're at my place now?"

She'd already thought of that. "They didn't see where I'm staying. I'm sure of it."

"How?"

Now Chuy even grilled her like Diaz. She dredged up the glare normally reserved for her supervisor and directed it at her cousin. "I stopped here on the way home from *Mamá's* house. I haven't been to your apartment since this morning. There's no way they tailed me to Paradise Valley and back without me noticing." She hated to admit the next part. "They must have followed me from the family property just now." Recalling her brief, frustrating conversation with Cole, she cursed herself for being too distracted to notice the black van in her rearview.

"Or they could have stuck a tracker on your ride," Chuy said.

She pursed her lips. "Doubtful."

"Let's go to my garage." He turned toward his bike. "I'll check it out."

She waited behind the wheel of her Tahoe while Chuy tucked the chain into a hidden compartment under the seat of his customized Fat Boy. Through the slight haze of dust on the windshield, the dark tattoos rippling over his bronze skin gave him a sinister appearance. Like many in law enforcement, Veranda often wore a Saint Michael pendant to honor the Archangel warrior who battled evil. Her cousin, more sinner than saint, looked like Michael's hellish counterpart, an unholy avenging angel.

Following the Harley down the street, she recalled the way Chuy fought, revealing a level of brutality she hadn't known he was capable of. There was nothing out of bounds, nothing off limits. When he wasn't thrashing BJ with the chain, Chuy jammed a thumb in his eye, kicked him in the balls, and punched him with a massive silver skull ring that split the man's face. She had no doubt Chuy would have resorted to biting him if he had to. Veranda gained a new understanding of how years behind bars with the worst humanity had to offer had changed her cousin.

She also realized Chuy had shown her how to fight the cartel. While her department's regulations held her in check, Hector Villalobos had a distinct advantage. *El Lobo* had no mercy, answered to no one, played by his own rules. Perhaps she should borrow from her cousin's playbook. She knew the cartel would come after her again. Before they did, she'd have to learn to fight dirty too.

16

VERANDA FORCED OUT a fake laugh. "Guess I'll tell Jake to go a little easier on me next time." Covertly eyeing Sam to see if he bought her story, she pretended to admire the extensive collection of reference books crowding the tall maple shelves that lined the walls of his home office.

She'd come up with the perfect explanation for her cuts and bruises. Sam had seen her many times after her weekly training sessions with Jake, her kickboxing instructor. She'd often sported marks from sparring.

"Try a different flavor." Sam's gray eyes bored into her. "'Cause I'm not swallowing that steaming pile of coyote cookies. Your session with Jake is scheduled for tomorrow, not today."

In a vain attempt to conceal her injuries, she nestled deeper into the cushioned armchair across the desk from Sam as his gaze roved over her skinned elbows, scraped knuckles, and cut lip.

"I've been around long enough to tell you've been in a street fight." His expression darkened. "And you're trying to hide it."

She'd showered, changed into one of Marci's outfits, and put on extra makeup before arriving at her partner's house an hour ago. Sam had invited her to a working dinner, offering a home-cooked meal while they wrote the affidavit he'd promised the lieutenant first thing in the morning.

All through dinner, Sam had eyed her suspiciously while she made small talk with his wife, Sarah, in between trick-or-treaters ringing the doorbell. As soon as they cleared the plates, Sam had ushered her to his home office to grill her about her injuries. And he hadn't bought a word of her well-crafted story.

Gaze still focused on her, Sam lapsed into silence, his bushy black brows raised expectantly.

She recognized the interrogation technique. The urge to fill the gap in conversation, to satisfy Sam's questioning look with an answer, almost overwhelmed her. Time spent working undercover in her last position had made her good at spinning a tale, but she'd been no match for Sam. More than thirty years on the job, a deep understanding of human nature, and a fine-tuned bullshit detector had gifted him with unparalleled skills.

One card remained in her deck. "I'm protecting you," she said. "I didn't exactly follow protocol and you'll go down with me if Diaz finds out."

Sam gave her a sardonic look. "What's he going to do, charge me with Accessory After the Fact for violating policy?" He rolled his eyes. "We're supposed to be partners, have each other's backs. After everything we've been through, I should have earned your trust by now."

She did trust him. Since their first case three months ago, he'd guarded her every secret, sometimes putting his career on the line. As her resolve crumbled, she lowered her gaze, dropped her shoulders, and tilted forward in the distressed leather chair. To her amazement, she realized her body had assumed the textbook position of a suspect about to confess.

Certain Sam had picked up on her inadvertent body language, she prepared for him to go at her hard. When he softened his approach instead, she experienced firsthand what made him a great interrogator. He sensed when to keep silent, when to move in close, and when to make physical contact.

He reached out to rest his fingertips on her forearm. "Tell me what happened, Veranda."

His words, delivered in his characteristic rich baritone, compelled her to speak. She blew out a sigh. "Three cartel goons tried to stuff me into a van this afternoon."

His eyes widened a fraction before a look of calm acceptance replaced the fleeting expression of surprise. Every detective learned to hide any sign of disbelief, dismay, or disgust when listening to a confession. The suspect had to feel comfortable relaying every detail of the crime. Nothing stopped an interview faster than overt judgment on the part of the interrogator.

"Why don't you start from the beginning?" he said.

She took her partner through the entire incident, leaving nothing out. Sam leaned back in the swivel chair behind his well-used desk, listening intently until she finished.

"I decided it would be a waste to call dispatch," she said, concluding her account. "The van would be long gone before patrol set up a perimeter and I couldn't provide a direction of travel to the Air Unit. I'm sure they were at the interchange in minutes." She felt the urge to justify her actions. "Hell, they could have switched vehicles twice by the time the first officer arrived on the scene."

Sam waved a dismissive hand. "I don't care whether you followed procedures to the letter. I care that the cartel may know where you're at." Lines of concern creased his forehead. "You said your cousin didn't find a tracking device on your city car?"

She nodded. "He practically crawled inside the engine. The Tahoe's clean."

"Then they tailed you somehow. Maybe from your cousin's apartment."

She recalled her conversation with Chuy, who had wondered the same thing. "I haven't been anywhere near the apartment since this morning. I drove to Paradise Valley, then to my mother's, then pulled over on Southern to go for a run." She dragged a hand through her thick, dark mane. "My head couldn't have been so far up my ass that I didn't see a car following me all over the valley."

"Then where did they latch on to you?"

She summarized her current theory. "I have two choke points. They'd pick the softer target."

She used a term Sam would understand. Police are trained to identify choke points—in short, any place an adversary can pinpoint an officer's location ahead of time and lie in wait.

Sam made a circling motion with his hand, encouraging her to continue.

"My family and my job. In that order. Everyone in the cartel knows they're the two most important things to me. They wouldn't risk staking out police headquarters, so that left the family property. They could have easily waited nearby to tail me when I drove away." She twisted her hands in her lap. "Thanks to me, everyone in the cartel also knows where most of my relatives live."

Sam shook his head. "Stop kicking yourself over what happened."

Her heart ached. "You know the expression about sleeping dogs? Well, I woke up a sleeping wolf." She tapped her chest. "I'm the one who took on *El Lobo*. Not my family. Now they all live in fear again." She swallowed. "Because of me."

Sam's rugged face conveyed compassion. "It's not like you can stop now."

"No," she said. "I can't."

"For what it's worth, the cartel seems to have you in their sights instead of your family. And they want you alive now. Any idea why?"

"Been running through scenarios for hours." She spread her hands. "I've got *nada*."

They both sat in silence, Veranda felt certain Sam's thoughts moved through the same maze hers did, ran into the same dead ends, then turned back only to find more blocked passages.

"I can't figure out what they're up to either," Sam said on a heavy sigh. "Let's table that for now. Got to bring you up to speed before we work on the affidavit."

"You won't share anything about the attempted abduction with Diaz, then?"

His face clouded. "There's nothing to be gained and one hell of a lot to lose by coming out with it now."

"Diaz would have my ass." She lowered her voice and scowled, doing her best impression of their lieutenant. "*Departmental regulations require any officer involved in a criminal incident, whether on or off duty, to report said incident forthwith. Failure to comply will result in disciplinary action.*"

"Sounds just like him," Sam said.

"Wait, I can also do the face that goes with it." She snapped her brows together, jutted out her jaw, and narrowed her eyes. "Looks like his *chonies* are chafing him, right?"

Sam laughed. "Speaking of Diaz, he called me a couple of hours ago while you were tag-teaming with your cousin in South Phoenix. I'll loop you in before we start on the affidavit." He glanced at his watch. "I don't want to be up all night."

"Just give me an overview," she said. "Your Geritol's probably wearing off about now and I don't want you falling asleep in your chair."

"No respect," he muttered, mustache twitching. He shunted one of the teetering stacks of papers on his desk to the side and got down to business. "Flag and Ortiz flew to Mexico City this afternoon."

She wondered why agents from DHS and ATF would have any business in a foreign capital. "They felt like sightseeing?"

"They're meeting with the *federales* at their headquarters." Concentration crinkled the corners of his eyes. "What are the *federales* really called again?"

"The PFM. Stands for *Policía Federal Ministerial*. They're like the Mexican FBI."

"According to Flag, Salazar is *numero uno* on Mexico's most-wanted list. The Mexicans want boots on the ground here since we have reason to believe he's in Phoenix."

"I don't understand," she said. "They can extradite him if we arrest him. Why do they want in at this stage in the game?"

"Flag wouldn't tell us much. Kept saying the info was *classified*." Sam accompanied his annoyed expression with air quotes. "He did let on that muckety-mucks in both governments are working on a special arrangement if we lay hands on Salazar."

"Wish I could have gone with Flag and Ortiz. I'd love the chance to peek at Mexican law enforcement files on the cartel."

"You don't think the *federales* share?"

"They share what they think is important, or what we request, but I bet there's a lot more. For instance, I'd like to know what they have on Daria. There's not much reliable intel on her in our databases. The woman's personal life is a complete mystery and she's always surrounded by guards."

Sam looked puzzled. "Why Daria?"

"I'm still convinced she's behind the two bombings." She spoke quickly to forestall his objection. "I know we found Salazar's prints at the scene, but explosives are in Daria's wheelhouse. I can't seem to let it go."

"Here's what I've got so far for the affidavit for Daria's DNA." Sam handed her a manila folder. "Don't get your hopes up. The lieutenant thinks we don't have a shot at convincing a judge. To be honest, I agree with Diaz on this one." He sent her a rueful grin. "But we have enough to try, so that's what we'll do."

She took the folder. "If this doesn't work, I'll find another way."

He folded his hands in his lap, regarding her thoughtfully. "What's your end game, Veranda?"

Her partner wanted to know how far she would go. Whether there was a line she refused to cross. He deserved an honest answer. "I won't stop until the whole cartel goes down," she said, borrowing a line from her cousin, she added, "whatever it takes."

"Hector Villalobos will make an example out of you." His voice held a note of warning.

"Worth it."

"To show everyone in law enforcement what tangling with *El Lobo* brings to their door."

She crossed her arms. "Still worth it."

He hesitated a beat. "Because of what happened to your family?"

Sam had hit the mark. The rest of the world knew the broad brushstrokes of her story, but he had been by her side through every painful moment as family secrets buried for decades came to light. He knew details she shared with no one else but the man who had become her partner, mentor, and friend.

"The Villalobos cartel has systematically terrorized everyone I care about," she said. "They silence their enemies through fear. Burning my mother's restaurant to the ground, taking Gabby, blowing up my house, almost killing Cole ... they're not going to stop."

"Sounds like you've got a score to settle."

"What if I do?"

"There's getting justice, and there's getting payback." He gave her a moment to consider his words before hitting her with the hard question. "Which are you after?"

Unwilling to examine her motives too closely, she avoided a direct answer. "Someone has to hold them accountable."

"And that someone has to be you because ..." He cocked his head, waiting for her response.

"Because this is a cage fight," she said. "Now that we've each drawn blood, the match isn't over until one of us submits or dies. Hector's not the type to submit." She reluctantly acknowledged the sheer bloody-mindedness that could only have been inherited from her father. "And neither am I."

She met Sam's eyes and knew that he understood. In the end, either Veranda or her biological father would die.

17

Policía Federal Ministerial headquarters, Mexico City

AGENT NICHOLAS FLAG surveyed the cramped governmental office that could have been in Chicago, Copenhagen, or Beijing. Regardless of his assignment, he'd found the culture of law enforcement—and the unadorned spaces where those in management toiled—to be similar in every corner of the world. The men around him at PFM headquarters also bore a striking resemblance to officials he'd encountered in many countries. This time, however, Flag had a distinct advantage. On the flight into Mexico, he and Agent Ortiz had devised a strategy to use it.

After fifteen years married to a Puerto Rican woman, Flag spoke fluent Spanish, a fact very few people knew. He marveled at the intelligence gleaned from overt observation when his subjects believed they could speak openly in front of him. As planned, Agent Ortiz had excused himself to go to the men's room. Predictably, the *federales* used the opportunity to have a private discussion in their native tongue.

Flag drew his brows together to project confusion as the debate between the three *federales* grew heated. Comandante Raul Espinoza, head of the PFM's Mexico City bureau, wore the harried look of a law enforcement executive burdened with too many obligations and not enough funds to meet them. Flag followed their rapid-fire Spanish without difficulty.

"You can't both go to Phoenix," Comandante Espinoza said. "We're understaffed as it is."

Flag recognized the supervisory style. Espinoza had probably chosen a career in public service early on, trading the trappings of wealth for the chance at power and influence. Anxious to reach the highest echelons of the organization, he would be apt to second-guess every decision.

Agent Esteban Lopez responded to his boss. "At least one of us has to go, Comandante."

Flag had met Lopez a few weeks back on a task force in Phoenix. In his fifties, his silver-white hair and goatee stood out against his dark brown skin. Doubtless thicker around the middle than when he began his career, Lopez still had the bearing of a man of action.

Next to Lopez, Agent Manuel Rios fidgeted in the cracked vinyl chair. Rios had worked on the Phoenix task force as well. In his early thirties, Rios had a fighter's build. Flag's trained eye spotted the definition of dense muscles bunching beneath the thin fabric of his off-the-rack suit as he moved.

"I should be the one to go," Rios said.

Flag wondered why Rios seemed so determined. Then he remembered how the younger *federale* had looked at Detective Cruz during his stint on the task force. Perhaps he craved a reunion. Interesting.

He tucked the observation away for future reference and continued listening.

Espinoza thumped his chest. "I decide who goes. Not you." He cut his eyes to Flag as if to make sure he couldn't understand them. Flag tilted his head like a befuddled Cocker Spaniel.

Apparently satisfied, Espinoza addressed his two compatriots. "The Americans won't turn Salazar over to us if they capture him alive. He has committed felonies in the US, but not murder. They'll throw him in one of their prisons for twenty years and then extradite him to a country with the death penalty. They can take their pick—Salazar has outstanding murder warrants all over Central and South America."

"How can we stop that, sir?" Rios asked.

Lopez's upper lip curled. "More to the point, *why* would we stop it?" He shrugged. "Let the sonofabitch die."

Blotchy spots of color climbed up from Espinoza's starched white collar as he glared at Lopez. "Mexico does not execute prisoners. Nor do we support the execution of our citizens overseas. Besides, he should serve his time here, where he has committed the majority of his crimes."

Lopez pulled at his goatee. "I don't see how you can—"

"Of course you don't," Espinoza cut in, his tone impatient. "Discussions are underway through diplomatic channels between the two governments. The American president is coming for an official state visit at the end of the year to negotiate a new trade deal." His fleshy mouth curled into a grim smile. "Which gives us leverage."

Drawing on years of training and field work, Flag continued to stare blankly at the men as they spoke. He had uncovered their end game but wanted more. Why would their government expend political capital to fast track Salazar back to Mexico?

His ears pricked when the younger *federale* posed that very question. "There are hundreds of Mexican nationals rotting in US prisons," Rios said. "Why all the effort for one man?"

Espinoza crossed his arms over his chest. "That information is classified."

Unfortunately, Ortiz chose that moment to return from the men's room. Aware the American ATF agent spoke Spanish, the *federales* cut their conversation short.

After Ortiz took his seat, Espinoza switched to heavily accented English. "We were just discussing which of my agents will travel to Phoenix with you."

Lopez gave his younger partner an appraising look. "Perhaps Agent Rios should go. He is a former tactical officer and has more experience with Salazar."

Rios inclined his head to Lopez before turning hopeful eyes to his boss. Flag decided he would prefer to have Rios assist the team. Instinct told him he might use the man's obvious attraction to Veranda Cruz to his advantage. When Espinoza showed signs of consenting, Flag nudged him along.

"I couldn't understand what you three were saying while Agent Ortiz was gone," Flag began, maintaining the façade of ignorance. "But we need a decision." He gestured to Ortiz. "We're wheels up in two hours."

His comment had the desired effect.

Espinoza jabbed a beefy finger at Rios. "You will go." He turned to Flag. "Agent Rios will also assist with the extradition process if Salazar is arrested on US soil."

"I'm curious about your government's interest in Salazar." Flag tried for an offhanded tone. "Why so eager to drag him back before he does any time in the US?"

Espinoza's smile held no mirth. "I do not question my orders."

Flag pressed him. "We only have felony abduction and assault warrants out for Salazar. I'm aware your government is opposed to the death penalty, but those aren't capital offenses. Salazar can't get the needle." He shrugged. "There's no danger of us executing him before he's returned to you. So what's really going on? Why do you want Agent Rios to rush him back here?"

Espinoza dug a finger into his shirt collar. "He is wanted for murder in Mexico. I am not at liberty to say more, Agent Flag. I am sure you understand."

Flag did understand. He was being stonewalled. Something was going on at the highest levels of the Mexican government. Whatever the situation, it involved Salazar. Which meant that it involved Hector Villalobos and his cartel. Mind racing, he eased back in his chair to figure out his next move.

18

ANOTHER TEAR COURSED down Sofia Pacheco's cheek. She peered at the clock hanging from a nail in the wall. In seven minutes, at the stroke of midnight, her fifteenth birthday would arrive. For years, she and her twin sister had dreamed of their *quinceañera* party. The beautiful ceremony was a rite of passage many Latinas took for granted, as she once had.

Not anymore.

For the past month, she'd been a captive in the Villalobos cartel's West Phoenix armory, which also served as their main base, under the supervision of their computer expert, Ignacio. Others called him Nacho, but he made her call him "sir" to remind her of her place. She suspected he needed the reminder as much as she did. His lanky frame, boyish dimples, and side-swept hair gave him a youthful appearance, unlike the coyotes, whose thickset bodies spoke of manual labor and hard training. American born, Nacho had confided his true age to her last week. He was only nineteen.

He sat down next to her on the polished cement floor in the tiny workshop wedged in the corner of the building. "What's wrong?" Nacho's Spanish had a distinctly American accent. Concern filled his eyes as he wiped the teardrop from her face.

His unexpected kindness undid her, and she began to sob. "It's almost my b-birthday. I m-miss my sister."

Nacho stroked her hair. "Please don't cry, Sofia."

"Quit your sniveling and get back to work." The icy female voice ripped Sofia out of her misery and slammed her into pure terror. Dashing the remaining droplets from her eyes, she looked up to see Señorita Daria standing in the doorway.

Nacho shot to his feet. "She's got something in her eye."

Sofia scrambled to stand on shaky legs.

"Don't lie to me, Nacho. You should have hacked into the police server by now." She strode into the room, head swiveling, scanning their work space. "Instead of doing your job, I find you getting cozy with the prisoner who's supposed to assist you."

A film of sweat broke out on his upper lip. "They've amped up their security, but we're close."

Daria turned her venomous glare on Sofia. "Maybe you'd actually get through the firewall if you didn't have any distractions."

"She's helping me," Nacho said.

"Is she truly helping?" Daria strolled over to Sofia. "Or is she slowing you down?" She reached out to cup Sofia's quivering chin. Sofia flinched when Daria sank her lacquered nails into the soft flesh of her cheek.

Transfixed, Sofia looked into the beautiful face glowering down at her. She saw the sharp edge of cruelty lurking beneath the smooth surface. A whimper escaped her lips.

Still clutching Sofia, Daria gave Nacho a side-eyed glare. "You have twenty-four hours to hack into that server. If you aren't in by then, you will be punished." She dug her nails in harder. "Or perhaps your little protégé will. Would that bother you, Nacho? Have you become attached to her?"

Daria's harsh laugh sent a chill through Sofia.

"We breached the Mexican Federal Police server," Nacho blurted.

Daria dropped her hand and turned her full attention to him. "What have you learned?"

"They sent Agent Manuel Rios to Phoenix with two American Feds." His eyes darted to the clock. "Should've landed at Sky Harbor about two hours ago."

Daria tapped her foot. "When did you plan to tell me about this?"

"The next time I saw you."

Daria seemed to consider the new information. "Before you do anything else, forward all data to my secure account. I'll download it to my phone. Did you get his cell number?" At Nacho's nod, one corner of her mouth tipped up. "Track his movements and monitor his calls. If Agent Rios is in town, he'll work with Detective Cruz. Why put more of my men at risk when I can use technology to follow her?"

Nacho gestured to Sofia. "I'll need help."

When Daria bent to scrutinize her, Sofia fought the urge to cringe. She felt like a butterfly pinned to a board under the intense focus of those cold brown eyes.

Daria's shapely brows knitted in scorn. "Have you been crying?"

She tried to respond but only managed a squeak.

"She's upset," Nacho said. "It'll be her birthday at midnight."

A calculating expression replaced Daria's sneer. "How old?"

"Fifteen." Sofia's voice caught on the word.

Daria turned to Nacho. "Leave us."

Nacho shot her an apprehensive glance before closing the door behind him.

Sofia's fear bordered on panic. Alone in a cramped workshop with the most terrifying woman she'd ever met, her body began to tremble in earnest.

Daria regarded her thoughtfully before speaking. "You are feeling sorry for yourself because you can't have your *quinceañera*." She made it a statement. "Do you want to know how I spent my fifteenth birthday?"

The question caught her completely off guard. How should she answer? "Um, yes."

"I'm sure you think I wore a pretty dress. That my father danced with me and presented me with my first high-heeled shoes. That all the other girls were jealous." Daria let out a mirthless laugh. "Are you jealous, little one?"

Still unsure what to do, Sofia took her best guess and shook her head.

"Good," Daria said. "Because no ceremony at all is better than what I went through."

The last words came out in a bitter rush. She realized Daria was about to reveal something about her past and waited, holding her breath.

Daria began to pace. "I'm the youngest of my father's children and the only female." She snorted. "If you only count his legitimate children, anyway." She pivoted, turning her back to Sofia. "The night before my fifteenth birthday, my father called me to his office. He explained that I was about to become a woman in the eyes of my community. From the next day on, I would spend all of my free time with my mother, learning how to run a household. While my brothers learned to shoot, fight, and negotiate business deals, I would go to a beauty salon for a makeover. Once he deemed me compliant and pretty enough, he would begin looking for a suitable husband for me. Someone whose family could expand his business."

Sofia's mouth fell open and she snapped it shut. What century did *El Lobo* live in? He sounded medieval.

Still pacing, Daria continued her story. "I dared to argue for equal treatment with my brothers. My father explained why, in his opinion, women are not equal. They are smaller, softer, weaker than men. Their bodies are made for childbearing, not for fighting." She shook her head. "I told him I would fight for my place among the men."

Halting, Daria faced her. "He offered me a choice. To earn a stake in the family business like my brothers, I had to defeat one of his coyotes in hand-to-hand combat. There would be no weapons, only strength, skill, and cunning. And if I lost, he would allow the man to teach me what it was to be a woman." Her eyes locked with Sofia's. "My father had guarded my virginity until that day, but he would turn me over to one of his henchmen to keep me in my place."

A chill slid down Sofia's spine as she imagined herself in that situation. Daria had been raised by a monster. She struggled to identify the emotion tugging at her. Pity. Sofia had been born into poverty in a Mexico City barrio, yet she felt sorry for someone raised with everything wealth and prestige could offer. She would never again look back on her early years with disdain. Her family had little money, but an abundance of love.

"What did you do, Señorita Daria?"

Daria picked up a wrench from the dusty surface of a nearby workbench. "I agreed to my father's terms. He tried to change my mind. Reminded me of the comfortable life I would have as a woman under his protection." Her knuckles whitened as she gripped the hand tool. "But I stood by my choice."

Sofia couldn't believe her ears. What kind of teenaged girl willingly agrees to fight a grown man trained in combat? She recalled the times she'd been manhandled by the coyotes during her captivity over the past three months. They were burly, sweaty, smelly beasts. And they were strong.

Frown lines marred Daria's smooth skin. "The next day, instead of having a *quinceañera* party, I fought for my future." She laid the tool back down. "And I lost."

Sofia sucked in a gulp of air and listened in horror.

"The night I spent with that foul brute was worse than anything you can imagine." Daria's voice dropped to a whisper, her expression bleak. "He went on for hours. Did disgusting things. I was innocent, but he showed me no mercy."

Sofia's hand flew to her mouth as she imagined Daria at her age. "How did you survive?"

"Every moment of his abuse, I plotted revenge. Purpose guided me. Rage gave me strength." Daria's gaze grew distant. "After he tired himself out, I waited until the asshole fell asleep, and I slit his throat. When my father found out, he congratulated me and welcomed me into his inner circle with my brothers." She lifted her chin. "I had defeated my opponent after all."

"*Ay, dios mio.*" Sofia could hardly grasp what Daria had suffered at just fifteen years old.

Daria seemed to snap back to the present, giving her a cagey look. "You came to Phoenix on a scholarship, yes?"

Last May, at the end of term, Sofia had qualified for a grant for inner-city youth from Mexico City to study computer science in Phoenix beginning in August. Her father had died the year before, and she figured they wouldn't be able to afford the portion the families had to pay. By July, her mother had arranged the trip, taking her twin sister along.

Leery of the motive behind the abrupt change in subject, she kept her answer short. "*Sí, Señorita* Daria."

"When my brother learned you had computer skills, he assigned you to help Nacho hack, but I see more potential in you."

Resentment scorched her. Daria had glossed over the fact that she'd never been able to attend the promised advanced computer course. Snared by a Villalobos cartel trap, Sofia had been beaten, starved, and terrorized into serving them.

"One day, the Villalobos cartel will be mine," Daria went on, seemingly unconcerned with Sofia's suffering. "The organization is filled with stupid, arrogant bullies. In other words, men." She chuckled at her own wit. "But I have ways to keep them under control." She briefly closed her eyes and smiled. "Ways that bring me great pleasure."

Sofia bit her lip. She'd overheard comments and seen dark looks exchanged among the men. But why was Daria discussing this with her? "Let me give you an example." Daria tapped her chin with a slender finger. "I ordered three of my men to set up surveillance on a side road near Veranda Cruz's family property. I told them to stay in the van on eight-hour shifts around the clock. All they had to do was wait until the bitch came to visit her mother, follow her out, see where she's staying, and report back to me." Daria planted a fist on her hip. "Simple, right?"

Sofia swallowed a gasp at the mention of a woman who had become her hero. Veranda Cruz was brave, resourceful, and smart. If Sofia could be like that too, maybe she could get away. Seven weeks ago, Veranda rescued Sofia's sister and saved her mother from a horrible death. When Hector Villalobos found out what happened, he had punished Sofia for her sister's escape. For the rest of her life, her scars would bear witness to *El Lobo*'s brutality. As they were meant to.

"Do you know where I just came from?" Daria asked, cutting off the stream of dark memories that always flowed close to the surface. Without waiting for a response, she grabbed Sofia's wrist and tugged her to the closed door. "Come see."

Panic blossomed, crowding out reason as Sofia's heart pounded. Where was Daria taking her? What would happen when she got there?

She stumbled from the room, directing an anxious glance toward Nacho as Daria hauled her past him.

"You're not a child anymore," Daria said, pulling her past a group of men stacking crates in the vast storage area. The men paused, following their progress across the expanse of concrete floor.

"Get back to work." Daria's sharp command sent them scrambling back to their tasks.

After navigating a short passageway, Daria yanked her in front of a closed door. Sofia knew this was the section of the building where Daria slept, but she'd never been inside. She watched as Daria slipped a key from her pants pocket and twisted it in the lock.

Hand on the doorknob, Daria turned to her. "I could use a trustworthy woman as my assistant. Someone loyal only to me. Someone who won't fuck me." She raised a brow. "In any sense of the word."

Sofia wanted to say she'd rather die than willingly work for the cartel. Instead, she tried to appear tempted by the offer. "You are too kind, Señorita Daria. But I must return to my family."

"You're not going back, Sofia. Not ever." Daria turned the knob and opened the door but didn't enter, blocking Sofia's view of the room beyond. "This is your life now. Make the best of it." She picked up her conversation from the workshop. "The men I sent to tail Veranda Cruz didn't follow my orders. The idiots saw her get out of her car without her gun, threw a plan together, and tried to grab her." She sneered. "They got their asses kicked."

Sofia clasped her hands together to prevent her fist from pumping the air. She mentally promoted Veranda from hero to goddess.

Daria turned and stepped inside, beckoning her to follow. "This is what happens to men who fail me."

Sofia's mouth fell open in a soundless scream. At first, her mind refused to process what she saw. Her vision blurred, her teeth chattered, and a buzzing began in her ears. Gradually, the haze of shock lifted and she took in the scene in front of her.

Three naked men hung from chains stretching down from the ceiling to their shackled wrists. Apparently unconscious, the manacles held them upright as they slumped, knees buckled and heads lolled, forcing their purpled hands and upstretched arms to bear their weight. The long red stripes scoring their bare flesh brought her meager dinner to the back of her throat. Her own skin would forever bear the same marks. *El Lobo* had personally seen to that.

Sofia's hand clutched her mouth, muffling an agonized wail, and she wondered at what point Daria had become her own father.

Either unaware or uncaring that Sofia had begun to sway on her feet, Daria continued. "You have a choice to make," she said. "My father is in final negotiations on the purchase of a computer firm. Once he closes the deal, he'll have all the tech support he needs. Nacho will lead the new employees, but you will become—as they say in business—redundant. Without any necessary skills, you're just another woman."

Sofia tore her gaze from the grisly display to look at Daria. "If I'm not useful, why won't they just let me go?"

"I thought you were smart." Daria let out a derisive snort. "You can make money for the cartel by working in the brothels." She narrowed her eyes. "Don't you see?" She paused for emphasis. "That was always the plan for you after my father found enough tech support."

Sofia stood rooted to the spot. Snatches of overheard conversations, hungry gazes from the men, sympathetic glances from the women, clicked into place with sickening clarity.

Daria put a hand on each of Sofia's cheeks, framing her face. "You're a pretty girl. On the verge of womanhood. All the men are hot for you." She forced Sofia's eyes up to hers. "So why are you still a virgin?"

135

Her flaming face trapped in Daria's firm grasp, Sofia could only blink back fresh tears.

"Because you'll fetch a high price your first time out. That's why." Daria released her and stepped back. "Unless you work for me. Under my protection."

Sofia wrapped her arms around her gaunt body. Daria had laid out the options. Become her personal assistant or become a sex slave. Either way, she would belong to the cartel, body and soul, until the day she died.

Daria stooped to retrieve a length of braided leather coiled at her feet. "Which end of the whip would you prefer?" She jerked her chin toward the three men dangling from the chains. "That one?" Her hand tightened around the grip. "Or this one?" Fingers absently caressing the leather, she regarded Sofia. "In the cartel, you are either predator or prey. I made my choice on the day of my *quinceañera*, and so will you." She uncoiled the whip, sliding it through her outstretched hand and tracing the knotted end along Sofia's collarbone. "I'll expect your answer tomorrow night."

At a loss for words, Sofia gazed at Daria, unable to bridge the gap between them. At only fifteen years old, Daria had chosen power over security. She had gambled with her life, rewrote the rules, and come out on top in an organization where cruelty prevailed. Years spent fighting for dominance had hardened her heart into stone. In that moment, Sofia understood something about *El Lobo*'s daughter.

Daria Villalobos was even more dangerous than her father.

19

STANDING UNDER THE gargantuan mobile suspended above the two-story foyer of the Phoenix crime lab building, Veranda gazed up at its components. The morning sun reflected from beakers, petri dishes, scales, and other scientific paraphernalia dangling next to a double helix on wires in a wide circle above her head. Lieutenant Diaz had texted her to meet at the lab instead of the War Room at eight o'clock.

"I always liked that sculpture." Sam had pushed open the locked inner door accessing the offices and forensic area. "No time to admire the digs, though—everyone else is already here."

She glanced at her watch. Twelve minutes past. Her borrowed designer pumps clacked on the tile foyer floor as she hurried past Sam.

"I'm not used to the commute from South Phoenix," she offered in the way of an apology for her tardiness. "And then I had to walk over from the VCB lot because there's no damn parking at the lab." She lifted her foot and pointed at it. "In Marci's FMPs. How does she walk around in these things every day?"

"No worries," Sam said. "Everyone's on their second cup of coffee."

"Why are we meeting here, anyway?"

"Only a few of us are actually at the lab. The rest of the team's in the War Room."

"Why?"

Sam looked uncomfortable. "The forensic examiners found something. Tye's prepared a presentation for us, but he won't discuss it until we start. Should be interesting."

Veranda followed Sam inside the glass-paneled meeting room. Tye Kim stood next to Diaz at the far end of a long oval conference table next to a thermos and a stack of cups. Slipping in quietly to avoid drawing attention to herself, she found a chair.

Despite her effort to be inconspicuous, Lieutenant Diaz spotted her and took a seat at the head of the table. "Let's get started." The chatter died and everyone settled into a chair.

Scanning the table, she noticed Agents Flag and Ortiz flanking another man, then did a double take when she recognized Agent Manuel Rios of the Mexican federal police. Her internal thermostat spiked at the memory of their last contact. After his recent assignment in Phoenix, the *federale* had given her a very unexpected, very passionate kiss at the airport before boarding his flight back to Mexico City. None of her colleagues had witnessed the intimate moment, and she hadn't communicated with Rios in the seven weeks since.

Rios turned his head and caught her staring at him. A slow smile crept across his handsome face. Her cheeks flamed and she forced her focus back to the front of the room. Too late, she realized Diaz had witnessed her reaction.

As she felt her flush deepen, Diaz addressed the group. "Most of you have met our newest visitor. For those who haven't, we are joined by Agent Manuel Rios of the *Policía Federal Ministerial* in Mexico City."

Diaz belied the polite introduction when he aimed a look of pure loathing at Rios before turning to Agent Flag. "Would you brief us on your visit to the PFM?"

"It's classified," Flag said. "You don't have a security clearance."

She started to laugh, then realized Flag wasn't joking. "Agent Flag, we need information."

"I'll provide what I can on a need-to-know basis during the meeting." He spread his hands. "Look, I'll contribute what I can, but I won't provide a briefing."

She swept her hand in an arc around the table. "We are all on a need-to-know basis right now."

Stone-faced, Flag crossed his arms over his chest.

Diaz gave his head a small shake and started the report-outs with Sam. "Detective Stark, have you and Detective Cruz prepared the affidavit?"

"It's on your desk, as ordered," Sam said. "We pulled it together yesterday evening."

"I'll look it over when I get back," Diaz said. "Anything from ATF, Agent Ortiz?"

"The components of both devices are at our California lab," Ortiz said. "We confirmed the link the Phoenix lab found between the two bombs. Although constructed differently, some of the trace materials are identical. Independent verification from both forensic labs is enough to prove they were assembled at the same location."

Excited by the news, Veranda forgot her irritation with Flag. "So if we get a DNA hit on one bomb, we can show the suspect is good for the second one as well?"

Ortiz nodded. "That's about the size of it."

"Speaking of DNA evidence," Diaz said. "We're meeting here at the lab this morning because Detective Kim has developments to report."

Tye got to his feet. "The best way to explain this is with a visual aid." He crossed the room to stand next to a large screen extending down from a slot in the ceiling. He touched a control panel, and the lights dimmed.

Even in semidarkness, Veranda could read the eagerness on the detective liaison's features. Something had piqued his interest.

"You recall that we located Adelmo Salazar's latent fingerprints on the remnants of a plastic water bottle recovered from the storage unit scene." At everyone's murmured assent, he continued. "We also did a rush examination on the trace DNA trapped between what remained of the mouth of the water bottle and the cap." He clicked the remote, filling the screen with an array of horizontal rectangular bar graphs, each containing several spiked peaks in bright colors. "This is an electropherogram comparing that sample with the DNA profiles of Hector Villalobos and his deceased son, Bartolo. All three have a familial relationship, meaning they're all biologically related."

Tye paused to see that everyone followed his explanation. Taking in their nodding heads, he shot Veranda an apologetic look. "Sorry about this next part, Detective, but I had no other way to reach a conclusion."

Everyone's attention veered toward her before going back to Tye. Mouth suddenly dry, she licked her lips. She should have expected this. The lab would use every bit of information available to identify the unknown sample, and Hector had made sure everyone knew he was her father.

Tye cleared his throat. "Next, we used the previous DNA profiles to run another comparison. This time, including Detective Cruz in the analysis."

When Tye pressed the remote again, four graphs appeared, labeled HECTOR, BARTOLO, VERANDA, and UNKNOWN MALE.

"Her DNA shows that, like Bartolo, she's a child of Hector Villalobos. It also indicates a different mother."

She squinted at the screen, trying to make sense of the numbers, spikes, and colors in the rectangles. Glancing at Diaz, she caught him watching her, concern drawing his brows together before he directed a question at Tye.

"With all due respect," Diaz said. "We already knew this. Why are you bringing Detective Cruz's parentage up again?"

Tye smiled. "Here's where it gets interesting. Unlike Bartolo's DNA, the sample from the bottle is more like Veranda's profile. Same father, but different mother. It means the suspect is Bartolo's and Detective Cruz's half brother."

Veranda felt the blood drain from her face. "I have another half brother?"

Tye grimaced. "A half brother who has attempted to kill you. Twice."

"But the prints on the bottle belonged to Salazar," she said. "It doesn't make sense."

Sam stroked his mustache. "Perhaps Salazar let someone else drink from his bottle. Or maybe he screwed on someone else's cap. That could transfer DNA."

"We found no other DNA under the fragment of cap we had," Tye said.

She circled back to the issue making her pulse pound in her ears. "Bartolo and Carlos Villalobos are dead. The only brother left is Adolfo. Holy crap, did *El Lobo*'s wife step out on him?"

Tye shook his head. "Not possible. We also ran the samples for mitochondrial DNA analysis, which allows us to identify the matrilineal genetic line, and their mito DNA profiles are different."

"Pretend we all don't have advanced degrees in genetic science," Sam said through an exasperated sigh. "And give us the bottom line."

Tye turned to Veranda. "It means that you, the suspect, and Bartolo all share the same father, but different mothers."

Why should she be surprised? A man like Hector Villalobos probably slept with hundreds of women and thought nothing of it. Now another one of his offspring was at her throat. As waves of pity emanating from her colleagues swamped her, she put her game face on. Appearing flustered would get her reassigned for the duration of the investigation. She had to convince Lieutenant Diaz she could remain objective about the case. No matter where the evidence took her.

She drew a breath and focused on the *federale*. "Agent Rios, do you have any intel about mistresses Hector kept?"

"We don't." Rios seemed genuinely disappointed he couldn't help. "His women are very discreet, or they are very dead."

"We need a sample of Salazar's DNA to eliminate him," Tye said.

Agent Rios brightened. "We have Salazar's DNA from his military service. I can get it to you right away."

Tye shook his head. "The military doesn't allow us to use DNA samples from enlisted personnel unless it's to ID them in instances of death or injury."

"You're talking about the US military," Rios said, dimples creasing his cheeks. "Salazar served in the *Mexican* Army. I'll have what you need by the end of the day."

No one questioned Rios. Whether policies were different in Mexico or if he resorted to back channels to get the information, Veranda had no doubt he would deliver on his promise.

"This round of tests has already eliminated another suspect," Diaz said. "The DNA is from a male. That means we can't put Daria Villalobos at either scene." He looked at Sam. "Disregard the affidavit for Daria's DNA. No judge will sign a warrant for it now."

Diaz was right. And she'd been so sure Daria had been behind the bombings. No matter how she turned it in her mind, she couldn't argue with DNA science. Daria was in the clear. She glanced back up at the screen, a new concern uppermost in her mind. Who was the half brother who wanted her dead, and how did he fit into the Villalobos family hierarchy?

20

DARIA SMILED DOWN at José. "Perhaps you're not just a pretty face after all." She gave the glistening skin of his back a leisurely stroke, then lifted the tips of her fingers to her mouth and tasted his salty sweat. A bead of perspiration trickled between his shoulder blades. Well acquainted with the symptoms of pain, she knew when a man teetered on the edge of his tolerance. José couldn't take much more.

Her cell phone buzzed in her pocket. She slid it out, glanced at the screen, and cursed. "Stay exactly as you are," she said to José. "If you move so much as a centimeter..."

His muscles quivered with the effort of maintaining his position. "*Sí, Señorita.*"

She tapped the screen and lifted the phone to her ear. "What do you want?"

Salazar's harsh voice chafed her ears. "Are you at the Armory?"

"Yes."

"Is the new ammunition ready?"

"I said it would be ready, and it is."

"I'm flying to Phoenix in seventeen hours to take over your operation. You are to do nothing until then. Do you understand?"

The abrupt announcement jolted her. "Are you relieving me of my command?"

"Liars who plant evidence don't deserve to lead. I'm in charge now." Salazar drew out the proclamation. "You answer to me."

White hot rage shot through her. While she'd been in Phoenix, Salazar had used the opportunity to undermine her. "I won't take orders from you."

"Not only do I give the orders from now on, but I also take them away."

"What the hell are you talking about?"

"I've taken the kill order for Veranda Cruz," he said, not troubling to hide his contempt. "You will stand down."

With extreme effort, she steadied herself to ask the only question that mattered. "Did this come from *El Lobo* himself?"

"Straight from his mouth."

Everything she had built, all of her sacrifices, every drop of blood on her hands, had been in vain. Salazar had stolen her future.

A swelling wave of anger broke over her, leaving utter hatred for the person she held responsible in its wake. "I will never submit to a vile, manipulating—"

"You will show me respect when you speak to me. I'm not one of your servants or man toys," he said. "*El Lobo* made it official today."

"Made what official?"

"That I will succeed him."

She heard his disdain as clearly as his words. "You arrogant bastard!"

Salazar responded with quiet menace. "Call me that again, Daria."

Sensing she'd gone too far, she held her tongue. The silence stretched so long she wondered if he'd disconnected.

"*El Lobo* chose me to lead for a reason," Salazar finally said. "Your behavior is unstable, untruthful, and ... unnatural."

Far from keeping her proclivities secret, she'd made sure everyone knew what she did with her men behind closed doors. Still, his insult cut her. "How dare you judge me."

"When I take over tomorrow, I'll put a stop to that too."

"You're offended because I'm female. We all know what the coyotes do to the women they bring in and you've never said a word about it. Spare me your self-righteous attitude."

"Those women are easily replaced. They have no special skills nor any loyalty. Our men, on the other hand, are trained assets who routinely lay down their lives for us. There is no comparison."

"Women could be trained to—"

"This discussion is over. I called to check on the ammo and give you a direct order to leave Veranda Cruz to me. I have a plan to deal with her when I return tomorrow morning. Until then, you will follow orders." His tone sharpened. "Veranda Cruz is mine. Do I make myself clear?"

"Yes."

"Yes, what?"

She scrunched her eyelids shut. "Yes, sir."

"Good." He disconnected.

She spat out a stream of profanity and flung the phone onto a padded bench bolted to the floor. It landed next to a sheet of neon green paper.

She stalked over and bent to pick up the page José had brought her earlier. Heavy print scrawled across the top of the paper read *DÍA DE LOS MUERTOS*. An invitation to join the Cruz family for their annual celebration at their property in South Phoenix included an address, directions, and today's date.

Veranda Cruz would be at the party. Rios would probably go as well, thinking he could protect her. A check of the tracked GPS on his cell phone would let her know for sure.

She tightened her fist, crumpling the paper in her hand. To hell with Salazar's orders. Cruz was still hers. The party was her last chance to corner the bitch before Salazar flew in from Mexico. She had to act tonight. Her mind in turmoil, she began to pace.

To win her father's approval, this particular execution must have her stamp on it. Salazar would settle for a bullet to the brain, but she could do better. Her feet moved faster, as did her thoughts. An image of the pit surfaced, spreading a ripple of excitement through her. If handled properly, killing Cruz might change her father's mind about her.

Across the room, José groaned. She came to an abrupt stop, regarding him with cool detachment. He hadn't been one of the three who had tried to grab Cruz—a good thing, because he was too pretty for the kind of punishment she'd brought down on the others. As she considered how the three men could have succeeded, the seed of an idea found fertile soil in her mind.

The party invitation José had found was exactly what she needed. Smoothing the sheet, she perused it again. The seed took root, blossoming into a plan.

She strolled over to José, who still held his position. "How would you like a special assignment?"

"What do you want me to do?" he gasped, panting with strain.

"You're a very sexy man." She ran her fingers through his sweat-soaked hair. "I want you to get Veranda Cruz alone tonight at their *Día de los Muertos* party."

"Señorita, she arrested me two years ago. She knows who I am."

Despite the gravity of the situation, Daria laughed. Okay, so José was gorgeous. Just not too bright.

"There will be face painting, masks, and costumes," she said. "Cruz won't recognize you. Just get her to leave the party with you, and I'll take care of the rest. Can you do that for me?"

"*Sí, Señorita.*"

"Good boy." She slid her palm down his lithe flank. "Now you've earned a little reward."

21

VERANDA FEINTED LEFT, stepped right, and slammed her gloved fist into Jake's face.

Her kickboxing coach recovered quickly, landing a jab before she could dodge it. "What the hell's gotten into you today, Cruz?" he said around his mouth guard.

"I'm bringing the girl power." She planted a foot, pivoting into a roundhouse kick that nearly connected with his jaw.

He batted her leg away and countered with a foot strike of his own. "You seem angry."

Marci leaned on the ropes surrounding the sparring ring. "Of course she's angry. She just broke up with her boyfriend. As a member of the male species, you should be very afraid."

Like a lance to a blister, the comment pierced her, bringing the pain to the surface. After her morning meeting at the crime lab, she'd met Cole for lunch at their favorite sushi place. He explained how the bomb at her house had changed his perspective. Then he took her hand, looked at her with eyes full of longing, and gave her an ultimatum. Stop investigating the cartel or stop seeing him. As her heart broke, she gave him the only answer she could. When the check came, they parted as friends. She hoped.

Jake momentarily dropped his guard. "Shit, Veranda, I didn't know."

She would take his kicks and punches, but not his pity. Seizing the rare opening, she moved in with a speed combo that left her instructor reeling.

Marci's laugh echoed off the gym's cinder block walls. "She doesn't need a hug, Jake. She's here to blow off steam."

An hour ago, she'd been moping at her desk in the Violent Crimes Bureau. Marci had badgered her until she regurgitated every detail of the breakup, then marched her into Diaz's office to request time off to spar at her gym.

Jake's eyes narrowed. "You came here to work off pent-up frustration, Cruz?" He put his gloves back up. "A little angry with men right now?" His grin displayed a band of blue plastic covering his teeth. "Let's see what you've got."

With consummate skill, he began a relentless attack. The onslaught drove her back against the ropes. Under a torrent of blows, she had to resort to covering her head. Still, he didn't stop.

In the back of her mind, realization dawned. Jake was providing a way to channel her grief. He would pummel her until she gathered herself and did something about it.

Just like the cartel.

Grinding her teeth in the mouth guard, she forced her sluggish brain to focus. Jake had fought competitively. He'd won tournaments. Over six feet tall and heavily muscled, he was well beyond her level in the ring. She couldn't beat him in a fair fight. So why fight fair?

She allowed herself to slump. Her spine dragged along the ropes as she slid down to the mat and went limp.

Jake squatted beside her. "Veranda?"

"What did you do to her?" Marci lifted the rope and put one foot inside the ring.

Jake turned to answer Marci, and Veranda mustered all of her strength to deliver an uppercut straight to his oversized jaw. His head snapped back, and he fell to the mat in a heap.

Marci put a hand on her hip and peered down at Jake. "That doesn't count as a KO, Veranda. You cheated." She bent to pick up his wrist and laid her fingers over his pulse point. "He's alive."

Veranda tugged off her boxing gloves and leaned over her instructor's unconscious form. "He is so gonna kick my ass for this." She lightly patted his cheek and called his name.

Jake groaned and opened his eyes with rapid blinks. His pupils, initially dilated, constricted into pinpricks as he turned them on her. Nostrils flaring, he sat up and spat out his mouth guard. "You're going to pay for that, Cruz." He flicked a glance at Marci. "Get out of the ring. Cruz is done with her warm-up. The real session begins now."

She had never seen her instructor even slightly irritated. He was the master of self-control in mind and body. Clearly, her little stunt had crossed a line. Way past angry, Jake practically had steam billowing from his ears.

She held up a hand in a placating gesture. "I shouldn't have done that. I didn't—"

"Put your gloves back on." He lurched to his feet and steadied himself. "You think I was hard on you before?" He snorted. "I don't care if you just broke up with your boyfriend." He banged his gloves together. "This time, I won't hold back."

A male voice carried from the far side of the gym. "If you're looking for a fight, I'll give you one."

Veranda spun to see Diaz glaring at Jake. Agent Rios stood a few feet away, next to Agents Flag and Ortiz.

"Careful, Lieutenant," Marci said. "Your machismo is showing."

Ignoring Marci, Diaz kept his eyes on Jake as he advanced to the edge of the rope. "You will not use my detective for a punching bag."

His detective? What was her supervisor doing here, and how had he found her? She had asked Diaz for time off to spar, but how did he know where she would go? Then the last piece clicked into place. She'd seen Diaz here two months ago training boys in his at-risk youth program to box. He'd obviously noticed her too.

Jake pointed a gloved hand at Diaz. "*Your* detective knocked me out with a sucker punch."

Rios, who had edged forward to join Diaz, clutched the rope and leaned into the ring. "That's what happens when you let your guard down," Rios said to Jake. "Or was your mind on something besides training?"

"Whoa." Veranda held up a hand to calm the brewing testosterone storm and faced Jake. "This is my boss." She tipped her head toward Diaz. "I'm sure he had a good reason to track me down at my gym."

"We tried your phone, but you didn't answer," Flag said. "There's been a major development at the lab."

Diaz reverted to his default setting. All business. "You should hear this in person anyway." His dark eyes scanned the empty facility before coming back to Jake. "This is a police matter. We need privacy."

"I'm heading for the locker room," Jake said before turning to Veranda. "I'll have to decide if I want to keep coaching you."

Remorse gnawed at her as she watched him go. She'd deceived him. Violated her instructor's trust. She'd understand if he dropped her. But she hoped like hell he wouldn't.

After the door closed, Diaz beckoned Marci and Veranda, who climbed out of the ring to join the four men. "There's no easy way to say this," he said. "So, I'll be blunt. We've identified the DNA from the saliva on the piece of the water bottle from data supplied by Mexican authorities."

She didn't like the way Diaz shifted his feet. Her investigative training had taught her the movement represented a subconscious desire to flee. Every part of his body language screamed in protest at whatever he was about to say, but his face betrayed no emotion. She braced herself and waited.

He dragged a hand through his hair. "The DNA belongs to Salazar."

Marci's penciled brows tightened into a frown. "Well, the prints on the bottle were Salazar's. Why is this a surprise?"

"You weren't at the crime lab this morning," Diaz told her. "You don't understand what this means."

Marci put her hands on her hips. "Someone care to tell me?"

His attention on Veranda, Diaz didn't respond.

Flag frowned at Diaz, huffed out a sigh, and gave Marci an overview. "This morning, the lab verified a familial DNA match from the water bottle sample with known Villalobos family members. This afternoon, we got a definitive hit on Salazar from that sample."

All at once, Veranda grasped the implication with sickening clarity. She turned to Marci. "It means Salazar is Hector Villalobos's son. Adolfo and Daria's half brother." She swallowed a lump in her throat. "And my half brother too."

Marci's blue eyes widened. "Holy shit."

Shame and anger warred inside her. Of all people, she had to be related to Salazar. *El Matador.* Ruthless assassin. Cop killer. Cartel enforcer. How many times would another cold-blooded murderer show up in her bloodline?

Diaz's eyes never left her. "We'll need to reevaluate our investigation in light of this information."

Distracted by her inner turmoil, she hadn't fully processed the big picture. "If Salazar is *El Lobo*'s son, he's in the running for control of the cartel." She sucked in a breath. "Daria won't give up without a fight."

"There's no evidence against Daria," Agent Ortiz said. "Everything still points to Salazar."

"Which is why you're in more danger than ever," Diaz said. "You mentioned your family's annual *Día de los Muertos* celebration is tonight?" At Veranda's nod, he stabbed a finger at her. "Don't go."

She rolled her eyes. "If I don't show up, my mother will murder me before Salazar has a chance."

"That's not funny, Detective."

"I'm going. Deal with it." She crossed her arms. "Sir."

Diaz looked up at the ceiling as if searching for patience. He muttered a few choice obscenities in Spanish before glowering at Veranda. "I'll be there too. Stay close to me."

Rios gave Diaz a sidelong glance. "I'm coming with you."

Great. Just great. She would have an overbearing supervisor trying to guard her, a hot *federale* trying to entice her, and a Latina mother trying to marry her off—all at the same party tonight. The power-hungry psychopath trying to kill her was the least of her concerns.

22

VERANDA STOOD STILL, allowing Tiffany to unwrap the layers of black lace covering most of her upper body. Veranda had draped the filmy shawl over her head and shoulders during the somber graveside ceremony. To her, *Día de los Muertos* was meant to honor the dead respectfully. Now that everyone had arrived back at the family property, however, a more festive atmosphere had taken hold.

Tiffany, always ready to party, had dragged Veranda into her mother's bedroom for a mini-makeover. "You look like my grandma," she said, sliding the shawl away. "The one who died five years ago."

Mention of Tiffany's relatives reminded her to ask about Chuy while they were alone. "Speaking of your family, how's it going at your parents' house?"

"Dad and Chuy hit it off."

Veranda had expected disaster, mayhem, and possibly gunfire before the end of the week. "Wait. What?"

Tiffany giggled. "I know, right?" She worked the pins out of Veranda's updo. "Last night Chuy made margaritas. Dad said they were the best he's ever tasted. He and Chuy got into a discussion about aged tequila, and it went from there. They stayed up half the night drinking and chatting."

She imagined Chuy in a cloud of expensive cigar smoke deep in conversation with Baz. "No way. Chuy's sober."

"Chuy's margaritas were virgin, but he definitely put the tequila in Dad's," Tiff said. "It's turned into a bromance between those two. This afternoon they were behind closed doors in Dad's office for two hours. Chuy wouldn't tell me what they were talking about." She ran her fingers through Veranda's hair, pulling out the last pin. "They're both acting real secretive."

Veranda tossed her head and her dark mane cascaded halfway down her back. "What about your mom?"

Tiffany's shoulders drooped. "Mom had an extra lock installed on her jewelry cabinet. And she had one of the security guards bring us Taco Bell for lunch."

Veranda grimaced. "This party should take your mind off things."

"Point taken. Time to get out there." Tiffany stepped back to inspect her handiwork. "Much better," she said, turning Veranda to face her mother's full-length mirror. "What do you think?"

Veranda studied her reflection, taking in the black and white paint forming an artistic skull design covering her face. Her eyes traveled down to the clingy black dress trimmed in layers of bright red ruffles at the neck and skirt. The asymmetrical hemline reached to the middle of her thighs in front and angled down to skim her ankles in the back. Matching red stiletto pumps completed the ensemble.

She rolled her eyes. "I'm Halloween Barbie."

Tiffany frowned. "You're right. This is too cutesy." She snapped her fingers. "Got it." She tugged the elastic ruffled neckline down to the middle of Veranda's arms, exposing her bare shoulders. "How about now?"

"Halloween Barbie joins a cartel." She pointed at the Villalobos tattoos clearly visible above the lowered neckline. The red calligraphy V and the black wolf's head would cause her family pain. "I can't go out like this."

Tiffany scooped two tubes of body paint from the nearby dressing table. "No one will know you have any tatts when I'm finished."

As Tiffany began dabbing on a thick layer of black base, her blue eyes went to the shrapnel wound. Veranda had taken off the bandages to let it air. "That Vick's VapoRub stuff kicks ass. There's not much more than a scratch now."

The corners of her lips tipped up in response. The mystique of the ointment in the blue jar lived on.

After a few minutes, Tiffany straightened and stepped back. "Hmm." She tugged the neckline down a bit more. "Perfect."

Veranda quirked a brow. "Only you could find a way to cover my ink and reveal my cleavage at the same time."

Tiffany gave her arm a playful smack. "You've got a smoking hot bod. Own it. Your idea of sexy is opening an extra button on your oxford shirt." Her eyes widened. "Hey, you've got to buy new clothes anyway, come shopping with me and I'll find outfits that show off those Latina curves."

She side-eyed Tiffany's black spandex catsuit painted with a glowing white skeleton that matched her facial art. "I don't think so."

"You're no fun." Tiffany sent her a mock pout. "C'mon, let's go. I don't know what kind of costume your lieutenant changed into, but I'm sure he's looking for you."

With no place to tuck a gun, Veranda had resorted to a beaded purse slung over her shoulder on a decorative cord to conceal her duty weapon and cell phone. She opened her mother's bedroom door, stepped into the hallway, and stopped short.

Tiffany followed her downward gaze. "What's wrong with the shoes?"

"These heels are even higher than Marci's," she said. "Can't seem to walk in them without strutting like I'm on a catwalk."

"That's the point."

"I left my tactical boots in the car. I can go get—"

"I put that whole outfit together for you. The least you can do is wear it." Tiffany jutted out a spandex-clad hip. "You owe me."

She blew out a sigh. "I'll put my boots on in the car so I can drive home without killing myself."

She sashayed out to the front yard and forgot all about the formidable footwear. This year's party was bigger than ever. Guests decked out in every imaginable *Día de los Muertos* getup packed the common area between the five casitas. A mariachi band blasted festive music while partygoers ate, drank, and danced.

Tiffany peered at the throng. "I can't find Chuy. Looks like he'll have to find me."

She scanned for Diaz, but the darkness between the glowing outdoor lights and the sheer number of milling people around made it impossible to pick him out. She shrugged. Tiffany had the right idea. He was the worried one, let him find her.

Her skirt swished against her legs as she moved past tables festooned with candy skulls and heaped with platters of *pan de muerto*. She stopped at the *ofrenda*, an altar honoring the dead, which displayed tall glass-encased candles burned down by half and photographs of departed loved ones.

Veranda paid her respects to all of them but lingered over two. She kissed her fingertips and touched a frame holding a picture of Ernesto, Lorena's first husband, the man Veranda once believed was her father. She repeated the gesture and pressed a finger to the photo of Bobby, her young half brother, who had died from an overdose while still in high school. Both of them dead because of Hector Villalobos.

She caught movement out of the corner of her eye and turned to see a man in a skull mask and black frock coat with matching trousers and a top hat eyeing her. Without uttering a word, he held out a gloved hand, palm up. He smelled of sandalwood soap. She vaguely recognized the scent, but the spice-laden air with the aroma of food wafting through the open courtyard played havoc with her nose and she couldn't recall where she'd smelled it before.

Tiffany, who had followed her to the tables, elbowed her. "He's asking you to dance." She looked him up and down. "He looks yummy. You should go for it."

"I can't dance tonight," she said to Tiffany in a lowered voice. "Had to put my my cell phone and Glock inside this." The band had started a merengue, not ideal for carrying a heavy bag.

Tiffany held out her hand. "I'll hold your stuff while you're on the floor. Then we'll figure something out."

The music called to her Latin blood, but she hesitated. The aura of death from the ceremony at the cemetery and the cloud of sorrow surrounding the *ofrenda* weighed on her. Learning of her connection to Salazar had darkened her spirit further. She needed release to lighten her soul. If she surrendered to it, the dance would free her.

Tossing her bag to Tiffany, she grasped the man's outstretched hand. He led her onto the floor near the band. The beat thrummed like a pulse in her veins. He swung her in tight against his hard chest. A reckless impulse drove her to slide along his body before spinning away. Moving with the rhythm, he twirled her before catching her waist.

Her partner danced well. She felt the wildness in him matching her own. The music grew louder, and the crowd clapped as they whirled together, apart, then together again. Behind the mask, his dark eyes watched her every move. She felt alive again. Hot, vibrant as the red edging her dress, and untamed.

As the song ended, he pulled her close and bent his head down to hers. She felt his chest heave from the exertion of the dance. She moved a fraction closer, raised her hand to the edge of his mask, and began to pull it away. His voice came out as a harsh rasp. "Veranda, I—"

She sucked in a sharp breath, recognizing the voice. "Lieutenant Diaz." She yanked the top hat up with one hand and snatched the mask off with the other, flinging them to the floor. "What the hell?"

Infuriated by the deception, she turned to leave, nearly colliding with a man in traditional white pants and shirt with a red sash around his waist holding a single long-stemmed rose. His face was painted as a skull like hers, with black around his eye sockets and the rest in white pancake. He completed the outfit with an old-fashioned sombrero trimmed with a red fringe.

"Could I have the next dance?" he asked in formal Spanish, offering her the flower.

Veranda reached out to take it when a muscular arm circled her waist. She considered whether stomping his foot with her stiletto heel or jamming an elbow into his solar plexus would cause Diaz more pain. Before she could decide, the man behind her spoke. She knew the voice. And it wasn't her supervisor.

"The next dance is mine," Agent Rios responded in his native tongue. "And the one after that."

"Maybe she should decide for herself," the man in white said, lowering the rose. "And I don't think she wants you to hold her like that." He continued the exchange in Spanish. "Looks like she's trying to get away."

Lieutenant Diaz shouldered past the man in white and got in Rios's face. "Get your hands off her."

Veranda was sandwiched between two snorting bulls. The man in white melted into the crowd. She would have spent more time wondering if she would recognize him without the elaborate face paint and hat, but she was too busy plotting agonizing deaths for Rios and Diaz.

Rios grunted. "You're not my boss, Diaz."

Diaz made a fist. "I'm going to enjoy my time off after I break your nose, *cabrón*."

The *federale*'s arm was still securely fastened around her waist. "Let me go." She grabbed his wrist and tugged. No effect whatsoever. She lost her temper. "You will damn well listen to me, Rios." She slid her hand down his arm, wrapped her fingers around his pinkie, and prepared to dislocate it. "This is your last chance."

Both men looked down at her hand clutching Rios's little finger, their startled expressions telegraphing their understanding. Each man had enough close-quarters combat training to comprehend her maneuver. A fact she'd counted on. Diaz grinned. Rios cursed and released her.

She took a step to distance herself. "You two don't decide who I dance with or what I do on my time off. I'll say goodbye to my mother, then I'm leaving."

She found Tiffany standing with Chuy and retrieved her purse. Chuy told her Lorena was in the house getting more food. She worked her way around the yard making small talk with guests and entered the kitchen to find Diaz with her mother. What was he up to now? Even more frightening, what was Lorena up to?

"*Ay, mi'ja.*" Her mother's hazel eyes were full of concern. "Why are you and Richard arguing again?"

She always found it odd when her mother called the lieutenant by his first name. "Because he's an overbearing—"

"Stop." Lorena held up a hand. "I don't know why you will not see what I do." She looked up at Diaz. "He is a good man. A man any mother would be proud to have as a son-in-law."

Veranda briefly closed her eyes and wished for a hole to open in the floor and swallow her.

A ruddy scald crept into Diaz's cheeks. He gazed down at her mother. "Lorena, I've already explained. Your daughter and I cannot date. It's against the rules."

"Rules," Lorena said, scowling.

"I'm out of here," Veranda said. The reckless abandon during the dance had been replaced by a strong desire to bolt. She stalked from the kitchen as fast as Tiffany's heels would allow.

Maybe Cole had been right about Diaz being attracted to her. But the man who touted following the rules would never break such a basic one. Supervisors could not be romantically involved with someone within their chain of command. As long as they both stayed where they were, Diaz couldn't touch her, *gracias a Dios*.

Footfalls crunched on the gravel and soon Diaz fell into step beside her. "Where are you going?"

She quickened her pace. "Away."

"We should go somewhere and talk." When she made no response, he added, "At least let me walk you to your car."

She stopped in her tracks. "I don't need you to walk me to my car and I don't have anything to say to you. My personal life is not your business. My dance partners are not your concern." She crossed her arms. "Why did you dance with me anyway?"

"Why not?"

"And that move at the end. The way you held me. What was that about?" She instantly regretted the question.

"That's why we need to talk."

"Not going to happen. Good night, Lieutenant." She emphasized the last word in an effort to remind him she was forever out of bounds for him.

Lowering his head, he turned away and trudged back toward the party.

She reached the Tahoe parked at the far end of the long driveway and wrenched the door open. Sitting on the driver's seat, she snatched her boots from the front passenger's seat, trading them for the high-heeled pumps before swinging her legs inside and slamming the door shut. She tossed her purse onto the front seat where her boots had been. Still furious with Diaz, she crammed her key into the ignition. As soon as the engine caught, she executed a three-point turn, spewing gravel as she raced to the main street.

Muttering under her breath, she turned a corner and accelerated out of the neighborhood. Diaz still occupied her thoughts when she felt the muzzle of a pistol against her temple.

Two words came from the seat directly behind her. "Keep driving."

23

Villalobos family
compound, Mexico

ADOLFO VILLALOBOS PRESSED his fingertips to his lips and reached down to touch the gilded frame of his mother's picture on the *ofrenda*. Her love had been his sole refuge. As the only one who understood him, her death five years ago had left him without an ally among his family.

Salazar stood to his left, inscrutable as ever, and his father to his right, head inclined, lips moving in silent prayer. When he finished, Hector picked up the photograph and kissed the glass over his wife's face.

"She was everything a woman should be," Hector said, placing the picture down next to a burning candle. "Lovely to look at, capable in the house, responsive to my needs, and obedient at all times."

Adolfo bit back a retort. "I miss her every day."

"Of the four children your mother bore, only you and Daria are left." Hector reached out to rest a hand on Salazar's shoulder. "I am grateful to have produced another son." He squeezed. "One who is a fierce warrior like his father."

Salazar made no response. During their observance on the patio outside the main building, he placed no photographs on the altar, burned no candles for the departed, and no prayers left his lips. Adolfo wondered if Salazar had ever cared for anyone.

Adolfo had struggled in vain for years to win his father's approval. First, his younger brother Bartolo had undermined him, now Salazar had cheated him of his rightful place as *El Lobo*'s successor.

His hands balled into fists. "I'm a warrior too. I have fought for our business."

Hector responded in his customary overblown style. "You are my chief financial officer. Your tools are spreadsheets, computers, and crypto currency. Salazar wields weapons of battle. He has proven himself to be capable, intelligent, and, most importantly, fearless."

The last word delivered the punch to the gut he was certain his father had intended. Throughout the entire organization, everyone knew he abhorred violence. The sight of blood and gore made him retch. He called himself a man of intellect. Hector called him weak.

As Adolfo reeled from the verbal blow, Hector gazed up into the night sky. "The poverty and misery I suffered in my early life served me well. I craved wealth and power. That hunger drove me to create an empire out of nothing."

He'd heard his father's self-aggrandizing speeches before and tuned this one out until a phrase caught his ear.

"…and your secret is revealed," Hector was saying to Salazar. "The DNA results leave no doubt that you are my son. They have your date of birth, so they also know you are my firstborn."

Until a few weeks ago, Adolfo had been the eldest. Then his father admitted an affair with a married woman thirty-four years ago. The result of that union now stood between Adolfo and his birthright. Salazar was *not* a firstborn son. Salazar was—literally and figuratively—a bastard.

"Daria should not have planted that evidence," Salazar said.

Hector sighed. "I regret sending a woman to do a man's job. She has made a mess of our North American operations."

Salazar moved away from the altar. "I called her this morning to relieve her of command. She understands that I'm flying in tomorrow to take charge. I ordered her to stand down until my arrival." He withdrew a buzzing cell phone from his pocket and glanced at the screen. "One of the coyotes at the Phoenix main base armory. They are under orders to contact me for emergencies."

At Hector's urging, Salazar took the call. Spine stiff and face taut, he began to pace as he listened. In a rare display of anger, Salazar closed his eyes and gritted his teeth. "How long ago?" he asked, his tone measured. Adolfo and Hector exchanged uneasy looks while Salazar pressed for details. "Where is she now?" A brief pause. "Track her cell phone and go after her. I'll be there as soon as I can." He disconnected.

Hector raised his brows. "Well?"

Salazar crammed the phone back into his pocket. "Daria has disobeyed my direct order. She went to the Cruz family property to kidnap Veranda Cruz."

Adolfo couldn't imagine what his sister had been thinking. Not only had she defied Salazar, but she'd exposed herself by personally attacking an enemy on her home turf. An enemy who had already proven herself to be hard to kill. He watched his father, curious to see how he would react when one of his offspring betrayed another.

Hector rendered his verdict with the dispassionate finality of a judge. "I had hoped my blood in her veins would make Daria different from other women." His lip curled. "But like all the rest, she cannot handle power."

Salazar gave Hector a slight bow. "I will have the pilot ready the plane immediately."

"The men must understand that I will not tolerate disobedience from anyone, not even my own flesh and blood," Hector said. "Take Daria into custody. I want her brought before me in chains."

At first, Adolfo couldn't believe his father would degrade his own daughter in front of everyone. Then he glanced at his brother Bartolo's photo on the *ofrenda*. Hector had done much worse than merely embarrassing Bartolo. Apparently, Daria had not learned from her brother's mistake.

While Adolfo disliked his sister, he detested Salazar. Openly humiliating a member of the Villalobos family would only raise the bastard's status in the organization. And lower his own even more. He grasped for something, anything, to change his father's mind. "What if she succeeds in eliminating Cruz?"

Hector arched an imperious brow. "Then it will be the worse for her. I decide who has that right. And it is no longer Daria."

By the satisfied look on the bastard's face, Adolfo gathered Hector had transferred the kill order to him. The last vestiges of hope Adolfo had of following in his father's footsteps flickered and died.

El Lobo believed every detail of an execution warranted special attention. He selected the victim, the perpetrator, and the audience for specific reasons. Two months ago, when he proclaimed that Adolfo could never lead the family business while Veranda Cruz lived, Hector imbued more significance to her death than any other.

Hector turned back to Salazar. "Use extra care traveling inside the US. They already believe you are there and will be looking for you."

"Another reason for Daria to set me up," Salazar said. "She hopes to keep me away."

Hector ran a finger along his black and silver goatee. "We won't have any family inside the US when you bring Daria here. I must move faster to acquire the Rook."

Adolfo's ears pricked with interest. His father had recently mentioned intensifying his efforts to gain a new asset in law enforcement.

"I wanted more time to work on my plan," Hector said. "But Daria has forced my hand." He looked at Salazar. "Report to me when you apprehend her."

Dismissed, Salazar pivoted and strode inside the main house.

Determined to turn his rival's absence to his advantage, Adolfo stepped in front of his father. "I can help you recruit the Rook." He hoped his eagerness didn't show.

For years, Adolfo had tried to identify the target Hector had described as a prime asset. If he helped land the Rook, he could establish a relationship of mutual trust with him before his siblings had a chance.

His father regarded him. "You still believe you can run this organization, don't you?"

He straightened. "I do."

"Then I'm sure you won't mind attending to our guest of honor?" Hector reached into his pocket and removed what looked like a black plastic key fob.

Tonight's special guest, Pedro Carbajal, waited in the mini arena. Daria's incompetent lackey had been beaten and starved in the dungeon since his arrival on the plane with her yesterday morning. The time had come to carry out his sentence.

"He's already been fitted with the collar then?" Adolfo asked, relieved no hint of a tremor registered in his voice.

"Here is the detonator." Hector held out the fob-like device. "You will watch, and then you will dispose of the remains. Personally."

A hot blast of bile shot up to the back of Adolfo's throat. He had witnessed this particular punishment before. Pedro's head would explode, spewing brain matter and skull fragments in a wide radius around his decapitated body. Anticipation of the blood, the smell, the carnage, weakened his knees.

His father leaned closer, scrutinizing him. "Are you about to faint?"

Cold sweat pricked his scalp. "No." His vision blurred slightly. "Not at all." He took the detonator with clammy fingers.

Hector had orchestrated this execution as he always did, with all participants in mind. Had he originally intended Salazar to push the button? Perhaps, but once Adolfo tried to reassert himself, his father had seized the opportunity to demonstrate why he had chosen Salazar over him. Salazar would never flinch at the sight of blood, much less collapse.

His father looked at him with disdain. "You will not use latex gloves, goggles, or coveralls. Any man who presumes to wear my suit must also be prepared to wear the blood that spatters it." Turning away, he gave Adolfo a parting shot over his shoulder. "As Veranda Cruz will find out when Salazar arrives in Phoenix."

24

THE GUN'S MUZZLE pressed against Veranda's temple, pushing her head to the left. She glanced in the rearview mirror and caught the glimmer of an enormous gold tiger-striped .50-caliber Mark XIX Desert Eagle pistol. Only one person could be holding that weapon.

"Why don't you shove a little harder, Daria?" She deliberately used her captor's name. "Maybe you can force me off the road."

Daria leaned forward from her position directly behind the driver's seat to peer at Veranda's reflection in the rearview mirror. "Don't even think about driving off the road, *puta*. I'm watching your hands on the steering wheel."

"What do you want?" She kept her voice calm, but her mind kicked into overdrive. She had anticipated Salazar attacking her. He was behind the bombings according to the forensic evidence, not Daria. Was she acting on his orders? If so, why would he send her when he was such an efficient killer himself? Daria's terse response halted her spinning thoughts.

170

"Head east."

Veranda slowed as she drove, giving herself more time to plot an escape. Daria hadn't shot her yet. She assumed her stay of execution would only last until she'd driven out of the more populated areas. Once Daria had her away from the main thoroughfares, her death would be easier to cover up in the inky darkness of the vast desert at night.

"Keep a steady speed," Daria said. "Don't attract attention with your driving."

Veranda darted a glance at the front passenger seat where she'd tossed her purse. Her gun was still stashed inside the beaded bag along with her cell phone, the closure firmly snapped shut. Preparing to make a grab for the purse, she loosened her grip on the wheel and asked a question to keep Daria occupied.

"Were you behind those bombings?"

"What do you think?"

"You have the background, but Salazar's prints were at the scene." She didn't say where the latent prints were recovered, testing Daria's reaction.

"Because I left them there for you to find." Daria rapped her cheek with the gun's sight. "Put your hand back where it was. Take it off the wheel again and see what happens."

The Tahoe barreled through the darkness, bringing Veranda closer to whatever Daria had planned for her. Sparse streetlights contrasted with the impenetrable darkness of the surrounding desert. Aware her window of opportunity closed a fraction more with each mile they traveled, Veranda struggled to form a plan. Glancing down at the police radio mounted on a bracket stand bolted to the floor between the two front seats, she edged her right knee over to depress the mic button. *Damn.* Too far away.

"I am forever paying for my father's mistakes," Daria said after a brief silence.

Unsure what Daria was up to, she played along. "Paying for *El Lobo*'s mistakes?"

"The night he fucked your mother." Daria allowed a moment for the slur to sting. "Worst mistake he ever made."

She forced down all traces of anger, delivering a measured response. "Your father is a rapist."

"He wanted your mother, so he took her." Daria lifted her shoulder in a show of nonchalance. "After he killed her husband."

Heart pounding, she felt the pull of Daria's taunts sucking her in. Fighting for control, she gripped the wheel harder and said nothing.

"You are the product of a rape. Do you know what that means, Detective Cruz?" Daria moved so close her lips touched Veranda's ear. "It means nobody wanted you to be born." She leaned back and let out a throaty laugh. "Your mother only kept you because she thought you might be her dead husband's child. Then she discovers you are my father's bastard daughter." She heaved a theatrical sigh. "How she must suffer every time she sees your face. You're a constant reminder of the worst day of her life. The day she became a widow. The day her husband's murderer raped her."

Veranda's control stretched to the breaking point. She had let Daria slip in through her defenses, raining cruel words down on her like physical blows. A moment in her sparring session at the gym a few hours ago cut through the rage. Just as Jake had done, Daria had her against the ropes and would batter her relentlessly until she did something about it.

The thought calmed her, and two priorities emerged. First, change the subject. Second, find a weakness to exploit. Mentally scanning her accumulated research on the cartel, she settled on the most likely point of internal friction. "And what does your father think when he looks at you? Has he made you second-in-command?"

Daria's eyes narrowed to slits. "My father will put me in charge once he sees what I have done to you, *puta.*"

She'd scored a direct hit on both counts. The recent DNA results gave her more ammunition. "You call me a whore. Isn't that what *El Lobo* calls all women?" She probed the exposed soft spot. "Your father didn't pick you to take over the cartel when he retires, did he? I'll bet he chose Adolfo." She twisted the knife. "Or was it Salazar?"

"Adolfo had his chance." All traces of jeering superiority gone, Daria's anger seethed through every word. "And I'll take care of Salazar after I'm done with you."

Eager to keep her captor off balance, she pounced on the revelation of a power struggle. "So, Salazar's on point. Must be frustrating to watch him cut in line in front of you." Noting Daria's silence, she decided to use the new information. "Of course, Salazar *is* his first-born son."

Daria's eyes, locked with hers in the rearview mirror, widened with shock.

"We ran the DNA from the storage unit scene. I know about Salazar. Your father, being the progressive champion of women's rights that he is, will turn the cartel over to him. And you'll spend the rest of your life taking orders from your half brother. You should probably find out how he likes his coffee."

"Shut up." The command lacked conviction.

"You could turn this around, Daria. Testify against him. Make him pay. I can help you do it."

"What? Put me in one of those witness protection programs?"

"Have they shown you any loyalty? Any respect? Why go to prison for them? Save yourself and get even at the same time." She hesitated, then took a gamble. "Imagine Hector's shock when two women, who also happen to be his daughters, unite to take him down."

The moment the words left her mouth, she knew she'd overplayed her hand.

"You dare to call me family?" Daria slanted her body sideways to squeeze farther between the two front seats. "We may have the same father, but you are a bastard child. Just like Salazar. I would die before I joined forces with you."

Veranda noted Daria's position and realized she wasn't wearing a seatbelt. The lap and shoulder restraint wouldn't allow Daria to scoot so far forward in the roomy vehicle. She quickly hid the grin threatening to spread into a triumphant smile.

Daria had been carefully watching her hands, but not her feet. She pressed the accelerator gradually, hoping Daria wouldn't catch on.

As the Tahoe sped faster, Daria finally seemed to notice. "Slow down."

"Whatever you say." Veranda took her foot off the accelerator and stomped the brake pedal all the way to the floor. The Tahoe's tires shrieked in protest as the hood dipped down. Veranda's seatbelt caught her, holding her in place. Daria flew forward, her body sailing between the two front seats. Her momentum carried her headlong into the dashboard.

As soon as the Tahoe came to rest, Veranda pulled her hand back, made a fist, and punched Daria in the face. She prayed the impact with the dashboard combined with the blow to the head had knocked Daria out.

No such luck.

Blood streaming from her nose, Daria lay on her right side, gun in her right hand.

Veranda flicked a glance at the front passenger's seat. The purse, still containing her duty weapon, had catapulted forward when she slammed on the brakes. The beaded bag lay out of reach on the opposite floorboard. She unfastened her seatbelt, prepared to wrestle the Desert Eagle away from Daria. Still wedged between the front seats, Daria struggled to maneuver the massive pistol into firing position. Unable to get her hands on either gun, Veranda decided retreat was her best option.

Leaving the vehicle in drive, Veranda opened her door, took her foot off the brake, and rolled out of the car as it coasted forward, carrying Daria away from her.

She tumbled onto the pavement, scrambled to her feet, and raced toward the open desert, grateful she'd changed into her boots. The crescent moon barely disturbed the darkness that abetted her escape. If she could find a place to hide, Daria would be hard-pressed to find her.

The screech of the Tahoe's tires reached her ears as she crested a berm covered with chaparral. Daria had managed to stop the car. Would she drive off or get out and hunt for Veranda? The driver's door slammed as the engine idled, answering her unspoken question.

Eyes adjusting to the dark, Veranda spotted an enormous saguaro. She started toward the stately cactus, then paused. Daria would probably look there first. In this part of the desert, there weren't many natural features to use for cover or concealment. She spun, darted to a small outcropping of rocks and flattened herself on her belly seconds before Daria crested the hill. Silhouetted by the faint moonlight, Daria crept forward in a low crouch, the gun pointing in front of her.

Daria swiveled her head one way and the other, then picked her way among the scrub brush toward the saguaro. As she bent to check behind the cactus, a tiny movement on a far knoll seemed to catch her attention. She charged after it, giving Veranda an idea.

Lure Daria farther away, double back to the Tahoe, get her weapon, and use the police radio to call for backup. She picked up a stone about the size of a golf ball and hurled it in a different direction.

The moment Daria pelted off in pursuit, Veranda jumped to her feet and sprinted to the Tahoe, still idling in the middle of the road. She yanked the driver's door open and flung herself inside, sprawling across the seat. Her fumbling fingers searched the floorboard and found nothing. Daria had taken her purse as well as the gun and cell phone inside it. *Shit.* Her vision of slapping cuffs on Daria faded. She'd be lucky to survive.

Out of options, she sat upright in the driver's seat and closed the driver's door, prepared to make a fast escape. Belatedly, she realized the noise would alert Daria to her location. A .50-caliber round would tear right through a car door. A moment later Daria materialized at the top of the berm and took aim. Veranda threw the Tahoe into drive.

A bullet blasted through the side window, showering her with jagged shards. Most ammo would only make a hole in the tempered glass, but such a powerful round took out half of the window. She pinned the accelerator to the floor, fishtailing until the tires found enough traction to propel her forward. More shots hit the back of the SUV as she careened down the road.

She snatched the police radio's microphone from its holder and pressed the transmit button. "Charlie thirty-four, nine-nine-nine." She waited for the dispatcher to respond to her call for emergency backup. Silence. She lifted the mic to try again. The cord dangled, its end frayed. Daria had ripped it loose.

Unable to summon help, she would go and get it. The nearest police precinct was South Mountain. Catching Daria before one of her men retrieved her required a full-scale response with helicopter, K-9, and perimeter checkpoints. The duty commander, who might be on the far side of the city, would orchestrate the police response. But first, she'd have to convince the patrol units she wasn't a drunk party girl when she showed up with her face painted like a skeleton, wearing a torn, dirt-streaked *Calavera* costume.

Her shoulders slumped, bowing to the inevitable. Lieutenant Diaz was her best option. Gritting her teeth, she headed back to her mother's house. There wasn't enough Preparation H in all of Phoenix for the hemorrhoid he'd get once he got a look at her Tahoe.

25

VERANDA JERKED THE Tahoe to a stop in front of the other cars that lined the gravel drive. She jumped out and sprinted toward the central pavilion between the casitas. Rios and Tiffany sat at one of the tables near Diaz and Chuy, who stood next to one of the decorated altars, deep in conversation. She veered toward them, ignoring the blurted questions from startled guests as she blew by.

When she got close, Chuy thumped Diaz's shoulder and pointed. Diaz turned around to see her running straight at him. Rios and Tiffany glanced up at the same time. Rios pushed his chair back and got to his feet.

She saw Diaz's eyes widen, travel over her ripped clothes and disheveled hair, then narrow.

He caught her by the elbows. "What's wrong?"

"Daria Villalobos," she gasped. "Out in the desert by South Mountain. We need the air unit, K-9, patrol. Got to surround her. Hurry or she'll get away."

"Slow down," Diaz said. "Are you hurt?"

Rios joined them. "Did you say something about Daria Villalobos?"

"I'm okay," she said in answer to Diaz. "No time to explain." Still panting, she continued in short bursts. "Please get help now. Can't let her cross the border."

"Come with me." Keeping a firm grip on her arm, Diaz started toward his car, Rios a half step behind. "I'll use my radio," he said. "It'll be faster. But I'll need a lot more info to call out the cavalry. Start talking."

She rushed to keep up with his ground-eating strides as they hurried to the driveway. While they walked, she told both of them about her abduction and escape. "That's why I couldn't call," she finished. "Daria took my cell phone and disabled the car's radio."

"And your duty weapon," Diaz said. "With a full magazine."

She nodded. "Advise responding units she has at least two guns." She described Daria's Desert Eagle pistol.

Diaz tugged the door of his sedan open and reached inside to grab the microphone. He relayed the information to dispatch along with a request for support units. Pausing, he glanced at Veranda. "Where were you when you stopped?"

"Out past Caisson Road. Near the foot of the mountain. There aren't any good landmarks. I'll have to show you."

"How long did it take you to come back here after you left Daria?"

"Between fifteen and twenty minutes. She might have called someone to pick her up by now."

After Diaz gave the approximate location to the dispatcher, a gruff voice interrupted the radio traffic. "Car four, I'm ten-seventeen. ETA twenty minutes." The duty commander was on his way.

"Get in," Diaz said to her, motioning Rios toward the backseat. "I'm calling out Crime Scene techs to process your car. You're going to direct me to the scene."

She gestured at their costumes. "We can't go like this. Let me get my go-bag." Before he could argue, she rushed to the Tahoe, snatched the black nylon duffel from the rear cargo area and hurried back. Diaz barked orders into his cell phone as she slid into the front passenger seat. Rios buckled himself in behind her.

"I know it's after midnight," Diaz said into his phone. "I'll authorize the overtime. Put it in VCB's budget. Just get them on this right away." He disconnected and accelerated out of the driveway.

She knew Crime Scene wouldn't balk at responding to investigate in the middle of the night. Diaz must be working another angle. She turned toward her supervisor. "Who else were you calling out?"

"Computer Forensics. I want them to ping your cell phone to triangulate the location, then shut the damn thing down before they data mine it."

She sat back in her seat a moment, grudgingly impressed with Diaz. Her animosity toward him had blinded her to his intelligence and experience. He wore gold bars for a reason.

"My cell's password protected," she said. "But they'll break in sooner or later. There may be enough time for our guys to ping it first though. We have warrants out for Nacho, but he's still at large. Once he gets his hands on that device, we're cooked."

Diaz pulled onto a wide thoroughfare and gunned the engine. "This never would have happened if you let me walk to your car."

Was he seriously blaming her for getting abducted? Irritation replaced the momentary admiration she'd felt for her supervisor. "How could that possibly have made any difference?"

"I would have seen her hiding on the floor behind your seat."

She clutched the door handle as he swerved around a tractor trailer. "The Tahoe's windows are tinted. It's pitch black in my mother's driveway. How do you think I missed her?"

He gave her a sidelong glance. "Because your mind was on other things."

"The only thing on my mind was how annoyed I was with you." She shot a glare over her shoulder at the back seat. "And Rios."

Rios stared back at her, face hidden in shadow. He didn't join the debate.

"Maybe your friend with the rose distracted you?" Diaz said. "Did he show up in your car?"

"No." Now that Diaz mentioned it, she wondered if the man with the flower had been working with Daria.

"And there's another problem," Diaz went on in grim tones. "Your duty weapon and cell phone."

Her antennae went up. "What about them?"

"Officers are responsible for department-issued equipment."

As always, Diaz spotlighted her every misstep. Already angry at herself for losing the items, he piled on, adding his condemnation to her misery. "I didn't leave them lying around for anyone to take. I was the victim of a crime." Was she trying to convince Diaz, or herself?

"Your cell phone might provide information to the cartel," he said. "We've been careful since the last hack job, but something stored in your phone could compromise us again."

She hadn't thought about the phone's access to the server. Fighting for her life had been her only consideration. Now that she'd escaped, the full ramifications of her kidnapping weighed on her. They rode in silence until South Mountain loomed ahead.

"There." She spotted thick black skid marks on the road and pointed. "That's where I slammed on the brakes." Diaz pulled over and she used the radio to guide the others to the spot where she'd last seen Daria.

Within minutes, patrol vehicles of every shape and size converged. The duty officer, Commander Miller, arrived with the blue horde, taking charge immediately. Midnight shift units, accustomed to working in the dark, surrounded the scene with light. Officers hefted equipment from the larger vehicles and fanned out. Black boxes and tripods with long metal poles seemed to sprout from the desert floor. Clusters of LED lights flooded the area.

At Commander Miller's direction, the Mobile Command Bus lumbered to a halt, joining the ring of vehicles along the scene's perimeter. Circled like an Old West wagon train, the collection of cars, trucks, SUVs, and vans delineated a work space large enough to accommodate specific assignments.

Anxious to shed her costume and join the hunt, Veranda snatched up her go-bag and headed for the bus. When she pulled the door open, a tall figure standing inside blocked her path. She glanced up at the sergeant, who she didn't know, and he jolted in surprise.

Grasping the situation, she pointed at her head. "Face paint." Moving her hand down, she continued. "Costume." Then lifted her duffel with her other hand. "Go-bag." She smiled. "I'm a detective and I need to change into my gear. Can I use the bathroom in the bus?"

The sergeant looked dubious until Diaz stepped forward and swept his arm out to include Rios as well. "We all need to change," he said, holding up his gold shield.

After using the tiny sink to scrub her face, Veranda slipped into her black BDUs, UnderArmour top, and ballistic vest. Her fingers brushed the empty holster as she clasped the belt around her waist. Anger and regret surged in alternating waves. If anyone used her duty weapon to hurt someone or commit a crime, she would feel responsible.

She left the command bus to a cacophony of light and sound. Three K-9 handlers held Belgian Malinois dogs on tight leashes, their furry partners yelping with excitement at the prospect of a chase. The helicopter whirred overhead, gliding in ever-widening circles in search of heat signatures with its FLIR infrared camera. Commander Miller's voice crackled over the radio, organizing a grid search and coordinating check points on roads branching out in every direction.

Her department had deployed substantial resources. One of their own had been abducted, held at gunpoint, nearly killed. They would continue to devote time and energy until everyone was certain the suspect had evaded capture.

She worked steadily, checking in with each group, providing background information, doing anything she could to help. About an hour into the search, the Air Unit picked up a heat signature in the desert. She started toward the team heading out to investigate when a deep voice brought her up short.

"Where do you think you're going, Detective?" Diaz said, stepping in front of her.

"To check out the—"

"You don't have a weapon." He looked pointedly at her right hip. "You're not leaving the inner perimeter."

Frustration clawed at her, shredding her nerves. "I don't have my gun because that bitch stole it!" Aware shouting at her supervisor would only make her situation worse, she lowered the volume. "And I have to get it back."

"We'll deal with the gun later," he said. "Right now, we're focused on apprehending Daria. Commander Miller's covered all the bases, including notifying surrounding jurisdictions and Border Patrol. If she didn't get away before we locked it down, we'll find her."

A short time later, Veranda listened over the radio as the search team discovered that the Air Unit's infrared camera had detected a very large, very pissed off javelina. One by one, the other teams deployed throughout the area reported in with negative results. Her mood darkened with each broadcast.

After the exhaustive search spanned another hour with no results, Commander Miller shut down the command post. Daria Villalobos had escaped.

Drained, infuriated, and completely spent, Veranda trudged back to Diaz's car. She found him with Rios, leaning against the hood talking on his cell phone. He ended the call when she approached.

"Who was that?" She asked him.

"I updated Commander Webster. He insisted on keeping DHS and ATF apprised. He's calling Flag and Ortiz."

"Tell them I'll swear out a warrant for felony abduction against Daria. And this time, I'll get those search warrants. Daria can't operate in the open anymore. She'll go to ground like the rest of the cartel weasels."

Diaz opened his car door. "Did you get all of your stuff out of the Tahoe?"

She nodded. "Figured I wouldn't have access when you said Crime Scene would process it."

"Did Daria take your apartment keys and your creds?"

At least something had gone right. "I could only fit my gun and cell phone in that tiny purse. Stuffed everything else in my go-bag. In fact, can you drop me at my temporary place?"

"You mean Chuy's apartment." He made it a statement.

She rolled her eyes. "Chuy has got to stop telling you my business."

"I'm your boss." He was unapologetic. "Your safety *is* my business, which is why I'm not comfortable with you staying there alone and unarmed. Perhaps I should—"

"I'm not unarmed. My backup weapon is at the apartment," she said. "And I can manage for two or three hours without supervision."

"Can you?"

Too bone weary for a protracted argument, she blew out a sigh. "I'd appreciate a ride, that's all I need."

Diaz relented. "Wear your tactical gear tomorrow morning," he said. "Rios and I will pick you up at oh-six-hundred to take you to the range. You can qualify with a replacement gun. I'll have a new fleet car and cell phone issued to you. If we can't ping your old one, we'll brick it."

Briefly repressed thoughts of the missing Glock rushed back to her with a vengeance. She felt naked without its comforting weight at her side. "I still can't believe she took my damn gun."

Diaz didn't offer any sympathy. "You'll also have to give a statement to Professional Standards about the missing property. Don't give me that look, Detective. It's got to be documented and investigated."

"They would actually write me up for being a crime victim?"

"Disciplinary action from the department is the least of your problems," Diaz said. "No matter how it happened, your issued personal duty weapon is in the hands of the Villalobos cartel." His dark gaze met hers. "Trust me, this will come back to bite you."

26

A PAINFUL JAB to her thin ribs woke Sofia Pacheco from a fretful sleep. She groaned, rolled off the makeshift cot, and fell onto Nacho, who slept beside her. She blinked up at Daria, who kicked Nacho with the pointed toe of her boot and waited, hands on hips, looking down in overt disgust.

"Get up. You two have work to do."

Sofia struggled to her feet. The tiny workshop in the base building's armory was cold in the predawn hours. She had been up late working with Nacho, terrified to fail Daria. They'd been unable to hack into the police server, and Sofia had the sinking feeling that Daria's promised retribution was at hand. Today was her birthday. She would either join forces with Daria or suffer her punishment.

Nacho rubbed his eyes with his fists. "What happened last night? One of the men said you took José to get Veranda Cruz."

A red scald crept into Daria's beautiful face. "All you need to know is that I have her gun, and this." She lifted a hand, showing Nacho the slim rectangular device resting on her palm.

Nacho hesitated before he spoke. "Does Cruz know you've got her phone?"

"I just spent three hours hiding in the South Mountain facility before I could come here. I'm tired, thirsty, and in no mood for questions," Daria said on a weary sigh. "Yes, she knows."

Sofia shuddered. She had seen the building at the foot of the big brown mountain. Inside its soundproofed walls yawned a deep, dark hole that reminded her of the ones she'd learned about in science class. Hungry black holes from which nothing could escape. She never wanted to go anywhere near that place again.

"Is Cruz in the pit building?" Nacho asked, his voice cracking.

"She got away, but not before I took this." Daria held up a beaded purse in her other hand. "The cell phone is for you." Daria tossed it to him. "But this"—she pulled a blocky-looking matte black gun from the purse—"is mine." She gazed at the weapon, a gratified smirk curving her lips, and dropped the empty bag to the floor.

Nacho turned the mobile over, examining the back. "If the police know we have the phone, they might try to ping it."

Smile gone, her eyes snapped back to Nacho. "Which is why I turned it off. It's time you earned your pay. Start by disabling the GPS, then see what Cruz has been up to."

Nacho powered it up and tapped the screen. "Locked." He glanced up at Daria, who had released the gun's magazine and caught it in her left hand. "After the last security breach, they put more firewalls up to protect their server. I'm not surprised to see they've also added security on their cell phones. I'll have to be careful going in, but I should be able to unlock it."

Daria shoved the magazine back inside the grip, snicking it back into place. "*Should* is not an option."

"I'll get in," Nacho said, eyeing the pistol. "Then I can mine the unit. If she's downloaded stuff from the main server, I can backdoor my way in."

Daria looked mollified. "I'll grant you another twenty-four hours with your little assistant here to get into that system. But if you don't give me something by—"

The workshop door banged open, making Sofia jump. Framed in the doorway, Salazar surveyed the room. Legs wide, fists clenched, and teeth bared in a predatory snarl, his feral gaze swept the area, coming to rest on Daria. Sofia began to tremble. If *El Matador* ever looked at her like that, she would pass out from sheer terror.

Daria took a step back as Salazar advanced on her. The backs of her legs bumped against a workbench. Eyes locked on Salazar, she reached behind her, her fingers blindly groping along its dusty surface. Her shaking hands found a screwdriver and clutched it in a white-knuckled grip.

Sofia watched in horror as Salazar attacked. His hand shot out with the speed of a viper, clamping around Daria's slender neck. Daria swung the screwdriver up toward Salazar's face. His free hand snatched her wrist mid-strike, holding the tool's flat edge at bay. Powerful muscles rippled under his shirt as he raised his other arm enough to lift Daria to her toes. Daria dropped the screwdriver to claw Salazar's hand and kick him with the pointed toes of her boots.

Impervious to the counterattack, Salazar steadily raised his arm until Daria's feet left the floor. She thrashed frantically as he squeezed. Finally, face purpling, her eyes bulged and rolled back. When her body went limp, Salazar released her to crumple to the floor.

Sofia and Nacho traded petrified glances. Had Salazar murdered Daria right before their eyes in cold blood?

Sputtering and choking interrupted Sofia's racing thoughts. Daria sat upright, clutching her throat.

Salazar loomed over her. "I gave you an order. Did I not make myself clear?"

Daria tilted her head back to gaze up at him. She opened her mouth, but only managed a faint wheeze before she dissolved into a fit of coughing.

He knelt beside her. "I couldn't hear you. Let's try again. Did you understand my orders, Daria?"

She released a croak and nodded vigorously.

With a gentle touch, Salazar lifted her chin, angling Daria's face up to his, and slowly lowered his head. For a heart-stopping moment, Sofia thought he would kiss her, but he stopped just short of brushing his lips against hers.

He spoke with soft menace, every word filled with pure loathing. "After I finish cleaning up your mess here, I will drag you back to Mexico to face *El Lobo*'s judgment. I will convince him to disown you. Once you are not a Villalobos, you will become cartel property and join the other women working in the brothels." He gave her chin a shake. "Your first clients will be your own coyotes, who will treat you exactly as you have treated them." He shoved her away and stood.

Daria buried her face in her hands and sobbed. Tears leaked between her fingers.

Salazar curled his lip at her before turning to Nacho. "What are you working on?"

Nacho swallowed audibly. "I have Veranda Cruz's cell phone." He held up the device. "I'm using it to access their server."

Salazar's attention moved to Sofia, sending icy waves of panic down her spine. She'd been forced to watch Salazar brand her sister. Although she'd suffered the same punishment when *El Lobo* seared the cartel logo onto her own chest, her twin's screams tormented her more than any physical pain she'd endured. Since that day, Salazar's flat black gaze had haunted her waking moments and fueled her nightmares.

He regarded her in silence, watching her trembling grow into violent shaking that racked her frail body.

Nacho laid a hand on her shoulder. "She is helping me."

"Is she?"

Sofia heard the suspicion in Salazar's question as he moved to stand in front of her. She kept her eyes down, terrified he would somehow read her intentions. As he'd done with Daria, he used his index finger to lift her chin, forcing her eyes up to his. His raw power overwhelmed her, weakening her knees. She sent up a silent prayer. *Please don't let me faint.*

"You have shown yourself to be a liar and a sneak in the past," Salazar said. "I hope you've learned your lesson."

Somehow, she stayed on her feet. "Yes, sir."

Salazar dropped his hand and addressed Nacho. "She's your responsibility. You will answer for her behavior." He pivoted to Daria, who hadn't stirred from her position on the floor. "Get up."

When Daria didn't move, he strode to her and bent to grab a fistful of her long, glossy hair. He tugged her to her feet and she yelped, but offered no resistance. He marched her to the open doorway, his hand clenched against the back of her head.

Salazar paused before leaving the workshop and looked over his shoulder at Nacho. "I'm putting shackles on this one. Give me results, or you'll join her."

Nacho closed the door and leaned against it. "We can do this, Sofia," he breathed. "We have to." He pointed to the floor where Daria had fallen. "Hand me that screwdriver."

She noticed he had said *we*, and drew strength from it. They were a team. She retrieved the tool and held it out, plastic yellow handle toward him. He slid it from her grasp and began to pry open the back of the phone.

"What are you looking for? Wouldn't you disable the GPS using the screen menu?"

"I have to unlock the phone to use the menu. But first I'm checking for any kind of external tracking device hidden inside the shell. You never know, and I sure as hell don't want to make a mistake."

She watched Nacho pop the phone's back cover off and inspect the unit.

"It's clean." He snapped the cover back in place. "Now for the fun part." He turned the phone over in his hand and tapped the screen.

Tongue clamped between his teeth, Nacho worked feverishly. After several long minutes, his face split into a grin. "I've almost got it."

She peered over his shoulder, leaning closer to the phone. "Did you unlock it already?"

The screen lit up and the sound of a camera clicking came out of the phone's tiny speaker.

"Shit!" He looked at her, eyes wide.

"What just happened?"

"The fucking thing was equipped with an antitheft device." He swallowed audibly. "Some phones are set up so the owner can remotely access a system that takes a picture of whoever unlocks it. It's designed to get a snapshot and immediately transmit the image. I have no doubt someone on the Phoenix Police Department is looking at a picture of both of us right now." He leaned back and clutched at his thick dark hair. "We are so screwed."

Sofia tamped down her elation. Someone on the police department would know she was in the US, a prisoner of the cartel. If she managed to survive long enough, maybe they would rescue her. For the first time in months, hope blossomed in her heart.

"Maybe it's not what you think," she said, anxious to prevent him from sounding the alarm so Salazar wouldn't evacuate them before the police came. "I don't want to see you get in trouble. Just don't say anything. No one has to know. Besides, you might have just accidentally pushed the camera button."

He gave her a look. "I didn't accidentally push the camera button. I know what that was. I've got to report it."

"You saw what Señor Salazar did just now. There's no telling how he would react if you made him mad. They call him *El Matador* for a reason. It's not worth your life. Or mine."

Even though she couldn't convince him to let her escape, she sensed that Nacho had feelings for her. Time to see if she was right.

"You know Señor Salazar doesn't like me," she said. "One day, he'll kill me."

"Not if you continue to make yourself useful. And, of course, stay out of trouble." He got to his feet. "Which means I have to find him and report this."

"But Señor Salazar will—"

"Salazar will assess the situation and deal with it. Our only hope is to tell the truth and beg his forgiveness."

"My forgiveness doesn't come easily."

She whirled to see Salazar leaning against the doorjamb. Her mouth went dry. How long had he listened to their conversation?

27

VERANDA EXHALED SLOWLY, squeezing the trigger until the gun fired. The target was slightly out of focus and her sights were crystal clear. Perfect. She used the rhythm of the recoil to line up her sight picture for the next shot. A split second later, she leveled the barrel at center mass. Another squeeze. Another bang. The target swiveled away, and she holstered her replacement Glock.

The range master's voice sounded through the intercom from the tower. "Stand down for scoring."

Sam walked up behind her and squinted down range at the silhouette target, which had rotated back to face them. "Not bad."

Lieutenant Diaz stood at her other shoulder. "She threw one wide at the twenty-five-yard line."

She rested a hand on the butt of her gun and glared up at him. "Bullshit." When he raised a brow, she added, "Sir."

Sam's mustache twitched. "I think we're about to find out."

Veranda followed his gaze. The range instructor's tan polo shirt blocked their view of the target as he stood in front of it scrawling something in the upper right corner with a fat black Sharpie. She held her breath until he stepped aside.

"Two fifty," Sam said. "Perfect score."

She smiled up at Diaz with exaggerated sweetness. "What was that about dropping one, Lieutenant?"

"I stand corrected." He bowed his head in mock shame. "Let's get to the cleaning shed. Rios, Flag, and Ortiz are waiting."

Despite the early hour, the sun had already warmed the outdoor range. She was grateful to be here in early November with gorgeous weather. Qualifying with a duty weapon in the summer months could be brutal.

They trekked the short distance to the open-air shack topped with a terra cotta tiled roof. The two American federal agents, engrossed in conversation with their Mexican counterpart, continued their discussion as they drew near.

Rios rubbed the back of his neck. "I could never understand why Salazar left the army before, but now it makes sense."

"His loyalty was to his father, not his country," Flag said. "His sole reason for joining might have been free military training."

Ortiz looked at Flag. "What about that time in Colombia when Salazar showed up? We were—"

"That's classified." Flag glared him into silence.

Curiosity piqued, Veranda directed her question to Flag. "What would an agent with Homeland be doing in South America?" She paused a beat. "Why don't you just admit you're a spook, Flag? Everyone knows it."

For several seconds, nobody spoke.

Flag's features hardened into an opaque mask. "I work for DHS, Detective Cruz. That's all you need to know."

Irritation loosened her tongue. "Some Feds are like the kids in the sandbox who don't share toys, don't take turns, and don't play well with others." She tilted her head. "Nobody likes those kids."

Sam turned his laugh into a cough, fooling no one.

Ortiz jabbed a finger at her. "You should be grateful for the resources and expertise we bring to the table."

She opened her mouth to deliver a retort, but Diaz pointed at a nearby work bench. "Start cleaning your weapon, Detective." He turned to the others. "Let's go over last night's events."

As she dumped her magazine and cleared the chamber, Diaz began an impromptu meeting. "You've all heard Detective Cruz's debriefing. Daria Villalobos claimed responsibility for both bombings and implied she plans to take over the cartel in the future. How does this mesh with our intel?"

Ortiz spoke first. "I'm not buying it. Now that we know Salazar is *El Lobo*'s biological son, we can assume he's the shot-caller. He put Daria up to the kidnapping."

"Agent Ortiz has a point," Sam said. "But why would Salazar order her to do it? She was the only Villalobos family member without outstanding warrants in the States. Doesn't make sense."

"There's an important point we're avoiding." Ortiz gave her a considering look. "Why are they targeting Detective Cruz?" All eyes followed his gaze as he continued. "And why such elaborate plans? Two bombs and a kidnapping?" He shrugged. "Why not just tag her at a thousand yards with a sniper rifle and be done with it?"

A stricken look crossed Diaz's face before he recovered. "Thank you for that … assessment, Agent Ortiz." He hesitated. "Commander Webster and I have wondered the same thing. We've come up with a theory."

Veranda laid her gun on the cleaning table and gave Diaz her full attention.

"We believe *El Lobo* put a bounty on Detective Cruz." He held their questions with raised palm. "But only for someone in his bloodline. Maybe even for a designated individual." He flicked a glance at her before proceeding. "And if that's the case, then it would be the person who will take over the cartel when he retires."

"You're saying Hector tied inheriting control of the cartel to killing Veranda?" Sam asked.

Diaz nodded, but Flag shook his head. "That's a lot of supposition, Lieutenant. With nothing to back it up."

Diaz's over-protectiveness suddenly made sense. She needed to change the subject before the others got aboard his crazy train.

"Why is this even important?" she said. "What difference does it make?"

To her surprise, it was Rios who reached out to grasp her shoulder. "If it's true, you will always be in danger as long as any of the Villalobos family are alive." His grip tightened. "You need someone watching your six."

"Oh, no." She jerked away from him. "I can take care of myself." She turned from Rios to narrow her eyes at Diaz, who had opened his mouth to speak. "And no safe houses."

Rios looked at Diaz. "I can stay with her at her cousin's apartment."

Her jaw dropped. "What part of *no* don't you understand?"

Diaz fixed a murderous glare on the *federale*. "We can both move in with her."

Anger bubbled to the boiling point. She was choosing which profanities would best describe their behavior when Sam shot her a quelling look and intervened.

"Veranda's safe at the moment. The address isn't listed in any department databases and apparently you two are the only ones who know where it is." He shrugged. "Don't give away her location by parking police vehicles there."

Flag tipped his head toward Sam. "He's right."

An audible buzz sounded. Diaz pulled his phone from his pocket and tapped the screen. "It's marked urgent." He turned and put the phone to his ear.

She caught Sam's eye and mouthed *thank you*. His warm grin extended to his eyes. He had a way of wading in when her temper was about to override her judgment. Their bond as tight as any she'd had on the job, he could read her.

Diaz turned back to them, still on his phone. "I'm putting you on speaker." He touched the screen and held the phone out. "Detective Warner's with computer forensics," Diaz said by way of explanation. "Detective, please repeat what you told me."

"After we were hacked a few weeks ago, we set up additional safeguards on the server and some of our cell phones," Warner said. "When Lieutenant Diaz called us out last night, we initiated a process to triangulate the location of Detective Cruz's stolen phone. If we didn't get a hit in twenty-four hours, we'd brick the phone and call it done."

Diaz blew out an impatient sigh. "Get to the results."

Warner's words tumbled out in a rush. "We pinged the phone. Coordinates were in West Phoenix. A cross check of the location led us down a bunch of false trails. Eventually, we matched it to one of the Villalobos cartel front companies you provided for us earlier."

"Nice work," Veranda said.

"Hell yeah." Warner's enthusiasm carried over the mini speaker. "And it gets better. We also remotely accessed the phone's camera and set up a photo trap."

"What's that?" Sam asked.

"Antitheft device. When it's activated, the phone instantly sends us a photo of whoever unlocks it to Computer Forensics."

They exchanged grins as Warner continued. "The phone snapped a picture. I forwarded a text to Lieutenant Diaz with the image."

"Do you still have access to the phone?" Flag asked. "Can you activate the camera to take more photos or relay a live video feed?"

Warner responded without hesitation. "As soon as the photo came through, we remotely bricked the phone. Couldn't risk leaving it open for data mining or a Trojan horse from the cartel."

Diaz slid his thumb and index finger apart on the screen to expand the picture. She looked over his shoulder. Her heart raced when she recognized two faces squinting in concentration, their images captured as they peered down at the phone when it unlocked.

"Nacho and Sofia," she breathed.

Ortiz looked at her quizzically. "You know these two?"

"Nacho is a nickname for Ignacio," she told him. "He's the cartel's resident hacking expert and all-around computer geek. The girl is Sofia Pacheco." She shook her head in wonderment. "I can't believe she's here. The cartel's coyotes smuggled her across the border a couple of months ago. We managed to rescue her mother and sister, but she's still being held against her will. She has tech skills, so they force her to work for Nacho."

"We might have a problem." Warner's disembodied voice piped up from Diaz's hand. "Before we bricked Cruz's phone, they could have accessed a backdoor to the server through downloaded data on the device. If this Nacho is good at what he does, he might have even managed to clone the unit before we shut it down."

"What do you suggest?" Diaz asked.

"For a start, you should change the cell phone number for everyone in Detective Cruz's contact list."

She waved the comment off. "More than three hundred contacts are in that list. No way can we change all those numbers." She imagined the chaos such an overhaul in the PPD communication system would create. And she would be the cause of it.

Diaz weighed in. "Changing hundreds of phone numbers on the department's call lists isn't feasible while we're dealing with an imminent threat. Too risky. What else have you got?"

They waited while Warner consulted his fellow computer forensics detectives. After a lengthy discussion, he got back on the phone. "We can set up a notification system in our server's firewall to alert us the moment it's been breached. Best we can do."

"Do it." Diaz disconnected and faced the group. "Now that we have a location, I'll contact SAU. If we move fast, we might pin them down."

She'd worked with the Special Assignment Unit many times. The Phoenix Police tactical team was highly skilled. They could deploy on the fly if necessary, but storming a cartel stronghold involved too many unknowns. They needed an ops plan for this raid.

Sliding the phone in his pocket, Diaz turned to Sam. "Did you finalize the affidavits for Daria and her premises?"

Sam nodded. "As soon as the courthouse opens, I'm headed to a Superior Court judge to swear out warrants to arrest her and search the listed locations."

"I'll go with Sam," she said.

"You're the victim," Diaz said. "Detective Stark is the lead on this case and has no direct involvement with the suspects. His name goes on the documents."

As much as she wanted her name on the warrant and her cuffs on the future defendant, she accepted Diaz's logic. Police routinely obtained simple assault warrants against people who hit them, but this case rose to a completely different level. Felony abduction involving a blood relative who was part of a major investigation demanded bright lines between the arresting officer and the suspect.

"I'm calling SAU now. While we're in a holding pattern, they can use the time to get their teams briefed and prepped." Diaz checked his watch. "We'll meet at the SAU briefing room in two hours."

"There's a problem," Agent Flag said, looking at his phone. "Emergency weather bulletin. There's a massive haboob forming. Should hit here in about an hour."

Veranda groaned. The infamous desert dust storms could last over three hours and made it impossible to see clearly.

Diaz slid a finger down his phone's screen to scroll through the contact list. "I'll reach out to the air unit and ask them to take a look with the FLIR while they still can. They'll be grounded for at least a half hour before and after the storm window."

"Dammit," Sam said. "We can't execute the warrants until after the storm. We don't even have them in hand yet."

Still scrolling, Diaz responded without looking up. "SAU will have more time to evaluate whatever images the air unit comes up with and develop a plan. I'm changing the meeting time to four hours from now. Should put us at the tail end of the storm."

"Detective Cruz can get some rest before the operation," Rios added, looking at her. "You had a busy night."

She started to object, but exhaustion flooded through her. Her reaction time had to be sharp when they raided the cartel site. She was about to concede when her stomach growled loudly.

Everyone laughed. "And get something to eat, Detective," Diaz said. "There's no fleet car available, so I'll give you a ride. We can hit a drive-through on the way to the apartment."

Veranda decided only her mother's cooking would do. Plus, she should tell Lorena she was okay after her abrupt reappearance and departure the night before. "Lieutenant, you can just drop me at my mother's house and Chuy can drive me to his apartment after I eat. He's been stopping in for breakfast there before heading to his garage ever since he moved out."

Her family had shortened their food service hours since switching to the food truck. At this early hour, her mother would be at home with the family prepping food until lunchtime.

Diaz got that stubborn expression he always wore when she disagreed with him. "I'll take you there. Rios can come too. Then we'll drive to your apartment and check it out. You might think it's safe, but I won't take that chance."

Rios moved next to Diaz in tacit alliance. "Besides, I'd like to see your mother again," he said. "And I'm hungry too."

She scrunched her eyes shut and let out a groan. Her mother was bad enough with one eligible bachelor around. Two potential husbands for her oldest daughter at the same time would send her into matchmaking overdrive. Too exhausted to argue, Veranda accepted the inevitable and steeled herself for the breakfast from hell.

28

VERANDA SAT AT the scarred wooden table in her mother's kitchen. The scent of home cooking filled the house. Lorena put a heavy earthenware plate in front of her. She looked down to see *chorizo* and eggs. Her favorite breakfast. After sliding even larger helpings in front of Diaz and Rios, her *tío* Rico grabbed a round terra cotta warmer filled with freshly made tortillas.

Her cousin Chuy, who had arrived twenty minutes earlier, was steadily working his way through a second helping. "Paradise Valley's got the nice houses," he said around a mouthful of fluffy egg, "but South Phoenix is where the best food is at."

"And the best people," Veranda said, forking up a piece of *chorizo*. Parting her lips, she slid the spicy pork sausage onto her tongue. A moan of sheer pleasure escaped her as savory heat flooded her mouth.

"Damn, *mi'jita*." Chuy stopped shoveling to watch her. "Why do I feel like I should look away?"

Rios grinned. "I like a woman who enjoys her food."

Diaz reddened, indicating his plate. "You'd have to be dead not to enjoy this."

Lorena gave Diaz an approving nod. "Thank you, Richard." She gave him a coy smile. "I taught Veranda from the time she was little. She cooks real good too." She shifted her gaze to Rios. "My own recipes from Mexico City. For a man who is used to that kind of food."

Rios lifted the warmer's lid and pulled out a warm tortilla. "A man like me."

Diaz stabbed a piece of egg with unnecessary force. "A man like you who will be going back to Mexico City very soon." He paused. "Too bad it's so far away from here."

"Mamá," Veranda said, desperate to put a stop to her mother's blatant matchmaking. "We can't stay long. Thanks for breakfast, but we've got to leave as soon as we've finished."

"I'm sorry to hear it, *mi'ja*. Will you and your friends be coming back for dinner later?" Lorena looked at them hopefully as *tío* Rico brought more homemade hot sauce to the table.

"I doubt it. And you'll be at the food truck anyway."

Her mother didn't give up easily. "You could go there to eat."

She couldn't tell her mother about the upcoming operation, but she didn't want to get her hopes up about seeing them tonight. "We won't be finished until late."

Accepting defeat, her mother and uncle trudged back to the stove.

When Rios excused himself to visit the bathroom, Chuy lowered his voice. "I need to run something by you two, but it stays between us." He circled his finger to point at each of them in turn.

Disturbed by the reminder of her cousin's close friendship with her boss, she inclined her head. Diaz followed suit.

Chuy leaned in. "Tiffany's father, Baz Durant, wants to hire me for some part-time work."

She laid her fork on the table. "What does he do?"

"All that money he's got," Chuy said. "Turns out he made it from security work. His main office is in DC, but he winters here in Arizona. From what I understand, government agencies hire his company to do certain jobs."

Diaz's brows drew together. "He's a Beltway bandit."

Chuy cocked his head. "What the hell is that?"

"Sometimes federal agencies hire out certain jobs to private companies," Diaz said. "They're contracted as consultants for everything from white paper studies to covert operations."

"So, Baz is one of those 'security consultants'"—she air-quoted the term—"that crop up on the news doing stuff no one talks about. Stuff that never happened."

Diaz tensed as he regarded Chuy. "What does he want you to do for him?"

Chuy spread upturned palms. "He made the offer when he found out I'm a professional mechanic. Said something about having a couple of breakdowns on their last mission. I guess they can't wait around for Triple A."

When neither of them smiled, Chuy passed a hand over his smooth scalp. "See, Baz can't give me details because it's classified, and I can't get a clearance because of my record. He said I can go along with the team, but I won't know what the mission is and there may be certain things I can't see."

Her apprehension turned into confusion. "Then how can he expect you to—"

Chuy cut her off. "That's what I wanted to run by you. I'm interested, and the kind of money Baz is paying makes it worth my time—a few days here and there, I can work the shop's jobs around that—but I'm used to doing my own thing. And I'm not real good at following orders."

"Runs in the family," Diaz muttered.

She ignored the gibe, focusing on her cousin. "He must have something specific in mind. Something soon. Otherwise, he wouldn't have approached you so quickly."

"*Muy lista*," Chuy said, acknowledging her shrewd insight. "He just got a contract that will take his team across the border. They're all former commandos. Mostly clean-cut white guys. He needs someone who can speak Spanish and pass for a local." He lifted a shoulder. "And fix whatever kind of vehicles they drive."

The set of Diaz's jaw told her he didn't like what he was hearing any more than she did. She dug for more information. "Baz wants you to go to Mexico?"

"Mexico City, actually," Chuy said. "He mentioned the Secret Service."

She and Diaz looked at each other before turning back to Chuy. "The United States Secret Service?" Diaz asked before she could.

"Yeah. Why?" Chuy said, looking back and forth at their frozen faces.

Her sense of unease grew. "When's the mission, Chuy?"

"He didn't give me any dates. Just told me to be available in January."

Something she'd heard on the news registered. She turned to Diaz. "Isn't that when the presidents of the US and Mexico are having their summit meeting?"

Diaz nodded. "In Mexico City."

"What's in Mexico City?" Rios looked down at them, hands on hips.

Engrossed in their discussion, no one had seen him return from the bathroom.

She forced a bright smile. "We were just talking about the summit between our countries' presidents."

"Oh, that." Rios grunted. "Everyone in my agency is helping with planning and security. I'll have my orders as soon as I get back."

They spent the next twenty minutes eating and chatting about international politics. Rios kissed the back of her mother's hand on his way out, bringing a blush to Lorena's face that was as deep as the frown on Diaz's. Tension filled the confined space when they got into the lieutenant's sedan.

She sat in the front passenger seat next to Diaz while Rios rode in the back. At one point, Veranda thought she felt the *federale* touch a strand of her hair, but she wasn't sure. By the time they arrived at Chuy's garage, she'd gotten drowsy.

"Give me your key and wait here," Diaz said. "I'll clear the apartment."

She tugged out her key ring. "I'm going in with you." At his stubborn expression she added, "It'll be safer with two of us."

"Three of us," Rios added from behind them.

Diaz regarded him in the rearview mirror. "You don't have a gun."

"I was what you Americans call special ops in the Mexican Army before I became a tactical officer with the PFM," Rios said, a note of contempt in his voice. "I don't need a gun to kill someone."

Damn, Veranda thought. He was every bit the badass he looked.

Diaz grunted his consent. "Let's get this over with."

They got out of the car and climbed the steps to the apartment over the shop. Veranda drew out her new Glock, still surprised at how different it felt. She'd worked with armorers at the range, filing the grip's edge and smoothing the action until her previous piece suited her. She'd have to put another thousand rounds through the new pistol to bring it up to par.

Unlocking the door, she crouched and entered with her gun in low-ready position. Hundreds of hours spent training with her fellow officers enabled her to know what Diaz would do without verbal communication. Rios trailed her as Diaz split off to the far end of the main room and into the closet-sized bathroom. She checked the kitchen and bedroom. All clear.

She holstered her gun and plopped down on Chuy's worn sofa in the main room.

"The briefing at SAU starts in three hours," Diaz said. "Rios and I will pick you up on our way there." He pulled a phone from his pocket. "Here's your new cell. It's already charged. I put the number on the back with a sticky note. Memorize it."

"Thanks." She took it. "I've got another set of tactical gear. I'll grab a nap and change into fresh clothes." Fatigue beat at her. "I'm starting to crash."

"If you don't mind, I'll use your bathroom before we head out," Diaz said. "Too much coffee this morning."

She nodded and sank back against a sofa pillow. Rios sat beside her and scooted in close after Diaz left the room.

"You don't have to be so tough all the time," he said. "Lean on someone else for once." He reached behind her and gently pulled her toward him, laying her head on his shoulder.

After the adrenalin rush from her encounter with Daria, followed by one fitful hour of rest and then rich food at her mother's house, Veranda couldn't fight the debilitating exhaustion any longer. She wanted to relax for a minute, nothing more. Rios settled her back and stroked her hair. He whispered soothing words to her in Spanish and her weary eyes drooped. She released a deep sigh.

"What the hell are you doing, Rios?" Diaz had emerged from the bathroom. His harsh bellow brought her upright, bleary-eyed and blinking.

"Comforting her," Rios said. "She's had a difficult—"

"She doesn't need any comfort from you," Diaz said.

Rios stood. "What are you saying, *cabrón?*"

Embarrassed without knowing exactly why, Veranda stood up on unsteady feet. "You two need to leave." Utterly spent and fresh out of patience, she shoved them out the door and locked it behind them.

Their argument continued as they descended the stairs. She couldn't imagine how they were sharing a living space. Then she decided she didn't care and staggered to the bed, where she peeled off her clothes and fell on top of it, drifting off to sleep almost as soon as her head hit the pillow.

She dreamed of a snarling black wolf crouched low, ready to strike. A white wolf pounced on the black wolf's back. The two beasts savaged each other, rolling over and over until they melded into a single gray wolf. The lone wolf began to howl. She sensed it calling to her. The howl turned into a loud hum, and she awakened to the buzzing of her cell phone on the night stand next to the bed.

Head full of cobwebs, she picked up the phone and checked the screen. Only one hour had passed. She answered the call.

Diaz's voice cut through her mental fog. "I'm sending a patrol unit to pick you up in five minutes. The SAU briefing's been moved up."

They wouldn't shorten valuable prep time unless something had gone wrong. She heaved her sluggish body out of bed. "What happened?"

"The cartel breached the firewall," Diaz said. "They got into the server and downloaded our current files before we could stop them."

"Including the search warrant and the raid?"

"Yes. They know we're coming."

29

THE MANACLES CHAFED Daria's wrists as she eased herself down to sit on the cold cement floor. Craning her neck, she followed Salazar's movements across the open space inside the main building of the Phoenix armory. He paced like a caged panther, then halted to glare at Nacho.

"What the hell is a haboob?" Salazar asked him.

She strained to hear Nacho's answer. "Dust storm. They get pretty bad in this part of Arizona." Nacho raised a hand to indicate height. "A giant wall of dust—can be over a mile wide and five thousand feet high—rolls through the valley like a brown tidal wave. Visibility goes down to less than ten feet. Lasts three to four hours, give or take."

Salazar changed gears, demonstrating his tactical experience. "What's the exact time they're planning to execute the operation?"

Both of them acted as if she didn't exist. As if they didn't owe her their lives. She was the one who'd taken Cruz's phone, but Salazar had reaped the benefits when Nacho cloned it before the police shut it down. She'd been chained to the wall for hours when Nacho rushed out of the workshop, papers in hand, to show Salazar a printed copy of an operations plan. The police were preparing to raid their location.

Nacho shuffled through the pages. "They use military time. The memo says fourteen hundred hours. That's two o'clock." He looked back up at Salazar. "It's noon now, so we have a couple of hours to get out before they come."

Salazar slanted an irritated look at Nacho. "You don't understand operations. That wording means they'll deploy at fourteen hundred. They'll form a containment perimeter long before that." He lapsed into a pensive silence and resumed pacing.

As much as she despised the bastard, she appreciated his military expertise. His background in special forces gave him insight into the SWAT team's tactics. Studying their operations plan in advance, he might find a way to escape.

Salazar stopped in front of Nacho. "How long does it take to drive here from downtown Phoenix?"

"About twenty minutes without traffic."

Salazar ran his index finger along his goatee. "Then they'll leave their facility at thirteen hundred and begin staging around the perimeter thirty minutes later. We're down to one hour to avoid running into them. That's not enough time to empty the building." He swung out a hand to indicate the room around them. "We've consolidated most of our assets here, stockpiles of weapons, armor-piercing ammunition, computer equipment, and our last shipment of narcotics. We need several trucks to haul it away, but we only have three vans and a Jeep." He paused to glare in her direction.

Two days ago, Daria had dispersed their long-haul fleet, sending tractor-trailers loaded with contraband in every direction. They weren't due back for another week.

"Won't the dust storm keep the police from staging ahead of time?" Nacho asked, his voice tentative. "The front came in around ten o'clock this morning, so it won't be completely clear until two."

"The weather is in our favor. They would have already had a helicopter or drone monitoring our movements, but their operations plan says air support is grounded until thirty minutes after the storm passes." He frowned. "Unfortunately, the same weather traps us here."

Nacho straightened. "I just remembered something." He dug his phone from his baggy pocket and peered down at it. "I started a track on Agent Manuel Rios's cell phone when he arrived in Phoenix two days ago, he'll be—"

"He'll be with the group coming to get us," Salazar cut in, giving Nacho a rare smile. "We'll know when they approach, and from what direction. This may save us yet."

Daria felt her jaw drop open as hope sparked in her chest. She snapped her mouth shut before Salazar noticed her reaction. Nacho had sent the program to track Rios and contact files from the Mexican police server to her secure system, which she could access from her mobile device. That is, if Salazar hadn't confiscated it.

Nacho gazed at Salazar, his young face filled with reverence bordering on awe. "Thank you, sir. But we're still in danger." He paled. "You'll find a way out for us, um … that is, me and Sofia, we can come with you, right?"

"I have no choice." Salazar turned toward Daria. "Because of you."

She kept her composure under his withering glare. Once she remembered what was on her phone, the vague shape of a plan began to take form. She had to buy time for the idea to percolate.

"I can help." She lifted her chin. "I always have a backup plan." She started to stand, preferring to make her case on a more equal footing.

Salazar quickly closed the distance between them. "Stay where you are."

211

She had made it to her knees before he stopped her.

"Learn your place, *puta*." He waited a beat, extending her humiliation before getting back to business. "Your last backup plan is the reason we're in this mess."

Salazar had taken her dignity, her position, even her freedom, but she wouldn't let him take her future. The bastard would help her escape from the police, and then she would kill him. Personally. Painfully.

She swallowed her resentment. "We can go to my explosives facility at South Mountain."

"You seriously think I would listen to a single word you have to say?"

She blurted out her proposal before he could interrupt with another insult. "It's on the far side of the city. Nowhere near here. The police will expect us to make a run for the border. They'll have every major freeway and minor roadway watched. But we won't do what they assume. We'll hide out a while, then move when they're not looking." She tipped her head toward Nacho. "Thanks to him, we'll know what they're up to."

"Perhaps the rest of us should go there without you," Salazar said.

She'd anticipated this, and the lie slid easily from her lips. "I'm the only one who knows where the security devices are hidden and how to deactivate them. If you don't bring me along, the buzzards will pick at whatever's left of you." She held up her arms, chains clanking. "Take these off and I'll help pack."

"You'll try to escape."

"I'm a wanted fugitive. Where will I go?"

He regarded her for a long moment before he snatched the phone from his belt and tapped the screen.

Moments later, José entered through the rear service door. "You need me, Señor Salazar?" His eyes darted to her, widening in surprise.

Of all the coyotes, he'd summoned José, her favorite plaything, to see her on her knees. She bit back a shriek of impotent rage.

Salazar beckoned José to his side. "You're in charge of the prisoner." He pulled a gun from his waistband and handed it to him. "If she tries anything, shoot her."

Daria recognized the weapon. Veranda Cruz's Glock. The sonofabitch had stolen her prize.

Salazar signaled her to stand and began to unlock the shackles. "You and José will stay here and pack product. Do not touch any weapons." He turned to Nacho. "You and the girl gather up the computer equipment in the workshop." The chains rattled to the floor. "I'll be outside organizing the rest of the men to load the vehicles."

Salazar and Nacho left. She was alone with José. Eyes glittering with malice, he watched her rub her sore wrists, then ambled toward her, a lascivious smile curving his mouth. "You're mine now."

She redirected him. "I have to pee."

He pointed at a stack of cream-colored bundles the size of bread loaves with the barrel of his gun. "Señor Salazar expects those to be packed when he returns. There's no time to—"

"Please, José." She made a show of pressing her thighs together. "I only need a moment. You can come with me to make sure I'm not up to anything." She threw in a flirty wink for good measure.

He frowned in thought, trying to come to a decision.

Damn. The man had the chiseled bronze body of an Aztec warrior, but the brains of a *burro*. She jiggled up and down, giving him a show and selling her story.

"Okay." He motioned with the gun again, but this time toward the communal bathroom. "But I'm coming to watch you."

Exactly what she wanted. She knew what he liked, and how to distract him. When she entered the bathroom, he followed.

She turned to face him. "It's pretty tight in here. Why don't you wait outside?"

"I'm not letting you out of my sight."

Perfect. She would give him something to see. Sliding her hands to her waist, she undid the front of her snug pants and shimmied them down past her hips. Her black lacy panties followed.

She stood there, intentionally displaying herself for his perusal. "I don't think I can pee with a man watching me."

His pupils dilated as he stared down at her. She edged closer and laid a palm on his sculpted chest. Years of conditioning had rendered him responsive to her touch. She grinned to herself. Salazar was a fool. He'd summoned José to humiliate her, but had handed her a weapon instead.

José blinked. "What are you doing?"

When his eyes landed on her mouth, she ran her tongue across her teeth and bit her lip. She felt the rumble of his deep groan and tipped her head up in invitation. While he fought a losing battle with his self-control, she reached back with her free hand.

Her fingers found the smooth surface of the sink, sliding around its rim as José crushed his mouth against hers. Her pinkie bumped against the chipped ceramic mug that held the men's toothbrushes. She barely managed to snatch one out before José cupped her bare bottom and hauled her against him.

She writhed and moaned to cover the sound of the toothbrush head snapping off when she bent it with her thumb. The shiv she now held, crude but effective, changed everything. Within minutes, she'd have her weapons, her phone, and her freedom.

But first, she had to maneuver herself into position for the perfect strike. There would only be one chance. She planted her feet and made sure her arm had full range of motion. José's rough palm slid away from her backside and over her hip, plunging down between her legs. Feigning excitement, she bided her time. His ragged breaths filled her mouth. Tasting his desire on her tongue, she widened her stance as much as possible, allowing him better access. He pressed his body against hers as he accepted the implicit offer. His probing fingers pushed inside her. She broke the kiss, gazed into his lust-filled eyes, and drove the plastic handle's jagged tip deep into his neck.

30

VERANDA'S GAZE TRAVELED along the row of black-clad tactical personnel. Silent sentinels, they stood with their backs against the walls of the oversized Special Assignment Unit briefing room. Like most of the others in the room, she also wore black BDUs and a ballistic vest. Only the SAU team stood, everyone else sat at the conference table in the center of the room.

Her eyes found the wall clock. 12:15. Sergeant Grigg, every bit as massive as the room around him, wore a perturbed look on his rugged face. The team leader viewed the safety of his SAU operators as his personal responsibility. And this situation offered no safety whatsoever.

Grigg turned his cobalt blue eyes on her. "I should've known this would go to shit, Cruz. You're involved." She knew the sergeant harbored a soft spot for her under layers of ornery exterior.

"Not my bad." She held up her hands in surrender. "I don't control the weather or the cartel's hacking skills."

He grunted and turned his attention to Diaz and Rios, who sat at the conference table next to her. "What the hell happened to you two?"

Veranda wondered the same thing. After the patrol unit dropped her off, she'd walked into the briefing room to find her lieutenant and the *federale* sitting stone-faced with their swivel chairs angled away from each other. Both men looked like they'd gone a few rounds in the ring. Neither one would answer her questions about their cuts and bruises.

Diaz frowned at Grigg. "We were comparing use of force techniques. Rios was on the Mexican federal police SWAT team. He showed me some of their tactics and I showed him some South Phoenix moves." He waved a dismissive hand. "Call it an international training exercise."

Grigg guffawed. "Yeah, right. As long as you two are past it." He waited while both men nodded their assent. "We're good to go."

Sam, who stood on Veranda's other side, leaned down to whisper in her ear, "I'm sure their little fighting demo had nothing to do with you."

She shot him a quelling look. "Nothing at all." She ignored his snicker.

Commander Webster entered the room, trailed by Special Agents Flag and Ortiz, and the Tactical Support Bureau commander, Paul DeSoto. While the others took the remaining open seats at the head of the table, Flag remained in the doorway, speaking into his cell phone in an undertone. She could only make out the words, "in South America," before he disconnected and sat down. She didn't bother to ask, knowing he would simply claim the conversation was classified.

Worry and fatigue mingled in Webster's expression as he began the briefing. "We called everyone in early because the cartel hacked into our server, setting off the alert. Before computer forensics could quarantine the incursion, the hackers downloaded several files." He grimaced. "One of which contained the ops plan and copies of the warrants for this incident. Bottom line, they know we're coming."

DeSoto added to Webster's comments. "The ops plan says we hit at fourteen hundred hours, so we keep the element of surprise if we deploy early. It's our only play."

"What about the dust storm?" Sergeant Grigg said. "We had enough trouble driving here and this is downtown where tall buildings block some of the dust. It'll be a lot worse out on the west side where the target location is."

DeSoto bobbed his head in understanding. "It's what we've got to work with. If we don't move now, they'll pack up and head for the border. Taking their hostage with them."

Veranda's heart lurched when she thought about Sofia Pacheco. The girl had been in cartel hands for months now. How much longer could she last? "I agree," she said. "We have to go now. We'll work around the weather."

"Headlights will be useless," Grigg said. "They reflect off the sand particles. Same is true for flashlights." He looked around the room. "And before anyone asks, night vision doesn't work either. We'll have to put on clear goggles and do the best we can until we make entry into the building." He rested a meaty paw on the butt of his gun. "At least they'll be just as blind as we will."

Webster stepped forward, a folder in his hand. "The air unit is grounded until thirty minutes after the storm is over, but they got some FLIR images before the dust shelf rolled in." He spread a series of photo printouts on the table in the middle of the room. Everyone leaned in.

DeSoto took over, pointing at one of the pictures. "There are twenty-one people, three vans, and one Jeep at the facility. Topography looks like there are quite a few hills, which may help us with stealth deployment during our approach. If they have lookouts, they won't be able to see us in the dust."

"And we can't see them either," Sam muttered.

Grigg crossed his arms over his barrel chest. "True, but there are more of us than them." He jerked his chin at the men lining the room with their backs against the wall. "And we're good." He flashed a smile. "Very good."

Grigg wasn't bragging, Veranda thought, he was stating a fact. The PPD had several tactical teams, and they routinely won SWAT competitions. They were among the best in the nation.

Webster looked at Grigg. "Assume they're heavily armed."

Veranda couldn't let them go in unprepared. "And Daria Villalobos is an ordnance expert. She might have booby trapped the perimeter or planted a few mines. Especially if she knows we're coming."

Her comment met with silence, everyone apparently absorbing the ramifications.

"We'll use the robot," Grigg finally said. "We can send it ahead." He scrubbed his face with his palm. "I hate fuckin' bombs."

"Who owns the property?" Commander DeSoto directed the question at Sam.

"It's not associated with the cartel in any obvious way," Sam said, holding a sheet of paper out to him. "The land is owned by a construction company. They're supposed to store their equipment there. It's a pre-fab building, not too sturdy unless they've reinforced it."

DeSoto perused the proffered page. "Did you obtain warrants?"

Sam nodded. "We still have the outstanding warrant for Salazar from September, and I just got one for Daria, along with search warrants for her domicile and this location."

"Paperwork's good to go then." Grigg got to his feet. "Time to move out." The SWAT sergeant made it clear he preferred action to discussion.

DeSoto held up a hand. "One more order of business. I've already discussed this with Commander Webster. All Homicide detectives, federal agents, and international law enforcement personnel are to stage on the perimeter until SAU clears the building." He side-eyed Veranda. "I don't care how much experience anyone has working with SAU, there will be no exceptions."

Her reputation had obviously preceded her. DeSoto had quashed her objection before she could mount it. She gave him credit.

After waiting a beat, DeSoto gestured to the other brass and the Feds. "We'll ride to the perimeter in the command bus. It'll be difficult to position during the storm and we'll have to go slowly, but we need support apparatus and incident command on scene."

Grigg followed up. "Before I give out assignments, keep in mind what we're dealing with. They'll be heavily armed. There may be landmines or booby traps. They're holding a hostage. There will be no air support. Communications could be affected. Visibility sucks. And—in case that's not enough—they know we're coming." He raised an eyebrow at Veranda. "Am I leaving anything out?"

"The hostage," Veranda said. "Her name is Sofia Pacheco. She's fifteen years old."

She knew SAU members spoke to terrified captives using their first names to calm them when they could. She also wanted to personalize the victim.

"She's been held by the cartel for months now, so she could be experiencing Stockholm Syndrome." She had an obligation to prepare them for the worst. "I don't have any intel that it's the case, but I wanted you to be ready."

Grigg put his hands on his hips. "Well, ain't that the pickle on top of this shit sandwich."

31

VERANDA LICKED HER parched lips. After spitting fine particles of grit from between her teeth, she batted at her clothing. Dust rushed down her shirt collar, into her hair, even up her nose. The wind howled around her, coating everything in rusty-beige silt.

Forty minutes earlier, Veranda and her entire Homicide team had piled inside Marci's Tahoe to follow the command bus. Lieutenant Diaz traveled alone in his own car at the end of the procession. For over half an hour, the convoy of police vehicles had lumbered through the storm to reach the target location. The tactical team had gone ahead in their armored fleet of panic-inducing urban assault vehicles.

Veranda had arrived with the others a scant five minutes ago. While Commander Webster set up a command post on the perimeter, she'd clambered amidst the brush and cactus to reach a small hillcrest. The high ground, however, afforded no better view in the storm.

Marci stepped beside her, gesturing in the general direction of the target site. "I can see why you walked up here." Her tone oozed sarcasm. "This cloud of dust is way more interesting to look at than the cloud of dust where they parked the bus."

Veranda jerked a thumb over her shoulder at the idling diesel-powered behemoth. "At least we're not stuck in there." Inside the belly of the beast, command staff officers, supervisors, and federal agents were poring over maps and rosters.

Frank, Tony, and Sam joined them. "Why the hell did I bring these?" Sam tapped a pair of binoculars slung around his neck. "Useless."

She squinted at the group through her goggles as another gust of wind beat at her. "Where's Doc?"

"He needed some extra time to … what's the word? Accessorize." Tony's Brooklyn accent made the comment humorous. "Check him out."

She turned to look and rolled her eyes. "Are you serious?"

Doc had put on a hazmat suit. When he spoke, his words were muffled by the air filter over his mouth. "Dust particles can get in your lungs and do major damage." His eyes widened behind the clear face shield. "It's no joke."

She shook her head. "Our SAU team is about to assault a building filled with trained, well-armed criminals. Dust isn't my top priority."

Standing behind the scrub-covered ridge in relative safety, Veranda's frustration intensified. She wanted to be with the SAU operators making entry, not stuck on the perimeter. Given a choice, she always preferred action. Probably the reason she and Sergeant Grigg got along.

"What was that?" Doc asked, turning in circles to see through the face shield's limited window.

Veranda heard it too. "That was rifle fire. Full auto. The cartel's putting up a fight." More shots followed, this time single action in rapid succession. "And that would be Grigg and his band of merry men answering back."

She had full confidence in the SAU team, but they were going in under less than ideal conditions. Waiting through another barrage of gunfire stretched her patience to the breaking point. Though she expected radio silence during the assault, the lack of information over the shared frequency unnerved her. Every instinct urged her to rush over the hill to join the fray.

"Sounds like they're taking serious fire," Sam said.

As the rest of her Homicide team concentrated their attention on the volley of gunshots, Veranda heard a car engine approaching from the opposite direction of the firefight. Raising a hand to her brow above her goggles, she caught the movement of a vehicle cresting a nearby slope to her left.

"Hey," she said to get her squad's attention. "Someone's coming."

"Who the hell is that?" Marci said.

With visibility severely compromised, Veranda relied heavily on sound. As the vehicle drew closer and turned sideways, she made out the dust-covered boxy profile of a Jeep. A black square appeared near the front of the vehicle.

She pointed at the shape. "The front passenger window's opening."

Something wasn't right. Why would anyone inside a Jeep lower a window during a haboob, allowing grit and dust to blast them in the face and get all over the interior? She could only think of one reason.

She used her left hand to shove Sam behind her. "Get down!" As the others hit the deck, she drew her newly issued Glock with her right hand and stepped forward to cover her team.

A heartbeat later, several muzzle flashes erupted from the open window. Using the bright orange spots as a target, she took aim and fired repeatedly.

The sound of bullets pinging off the Jeep's metal frame reached her ears over the howling wind. Behind her, the others had begun to return fire from their prone positions. Her squad's suppressive fire provided an opportunity for a tactical reload. Never taking her eyes from the Jeep, she yanked open a pouch on her ballistic vest and tugged out a fresh magazine with her left hand. Working by feel, she used her right thumb to depress the release. She exchanged the two magazines with practiced speed, smacking the loaded one home with the heel of her palm. The maneuver took less than five seconds.

Dropping to the dirt next to Sam, she flattened herself on her belly and extended her arms in front of her. Planting her elbows on the ground marksman-style, she continued to shoot despite the absence of a clear target.

"I'll keep them busy," she said to Sam, eyes still fixed on the adversary. "You notify the command bus that we're taking fire. Advise we can only confirm one hostile."

Seconds stretched interminably. Weapon blasts rang in her ears. Was that why she didn't hear Sam's rumbling baritone over the portable radio mic clipped to her shirt collar?

She nudged his leg with her knee. "Sam?"

No response.

She flicked a glace down at Sam. He lay on his back, perfectly still. Blood seeped from beneath the edge of his ballistic vest to form a swiftly spreading crimson pool.

32

SQUINTING THROUGH THE swirling haze of dust, Daria watched one of the figures fall. A figure with a distinctly masculine shape. Definitely not Cruz. Cursing, she pulled the trigger again and again, sending the other cops diving to the ground. She lowered her front sight to shoot them as they lay on their stomachs. Her index finger tightened. No bang. She shifted her gaze to the slide. Locked back in the open position. Fired dry. *Shit.*

Daria had taken time before the ambush to load Cruz's Glock with special ammo. Manufactured in her own facility near the family compound in Mexico, they were called cop-killer rounds for a reason. Field tests in firefights with Mexican law enforcement had proven their ability to penetrate all standard-issue body armor.

A momentary calm between gusts had given her a clear shot at Cruz. She'd drawn a bead on her target as an eddy of dust blew grit into her face. She'd been forced to fire with her eyes closed, missing her target.

Tossing the Glock on the front passenger seat, she reached for her Desert Eagle, then hesitated. From the moment Daria held Cruz's Glock, she'd planned to shoot her with it. When Salazar took the weapon away, he'd ended her plans. Then she'd found herself plucking the gun from José's slackened hand as he lay dying on the bathroom floor.

She picked up the Glock again, considering it. As the return fire intensified, she realized she was outgunned, outnumbered, and outmatched. The police would soon close in. She'd squandered the second chance at Cruz fate had given her. She prepared to flee, shifting the Jeep into drive, when inspiration kept her foot on the brake pedal. Perhaps the gun could still hurt Cruz after all. Smiling, she pulled a bandana from the glove box, wiped her prints off the Glock, and hurled it out the open window.

Bullets ricocheted off the vehicle as Daria stomped her pointed boot down on the accelerator, stuffing the bandana into her pocket as the vehicle surged ahead. Careening through a fresh cloud of billowing dust, she barely managed to avoid plowing into a barrel cactus. She veered around it and bumped onto the roadway. Distant rapid-fire shots coming from the direction of the main building told her the coyotes were putting up a valiant fight. But the site would fall before long. If only Salazar would go down with it.

A light flashed from the top of the dashboard, catching her attention. She'd clamped her cell phone into a mounted holder to track Agent Rios using Nacho's program and now the screen's glow indicated an incoming call. Adolfo's code name appeared, bringing with it a frisson of dread. Her older brother almost never called. She tapped the display with a tentative touch.

"You're screwed." Adolfo spoke over a background filled with static. A result of the storm, no doubt.

"I'm a tad busy." Glancing at the console's compass, she corrected course to drive due east. "If that's all you have to say, I'm done talking." As long as she went in that general direction, she could find her explosives facility.

"I want to help you, Daria. We've never been close, but at least we're true family."

That got her attention. "What's going on?"

"I was in our father's office twenty minutes ago. Salazar called. He said you murdered one of the coyotes so you could run away and save yourself before the police came." Adolfo hesitated a beat. "He called you a coward."

She clenched the steering wheel. Salazar had taken precious time from his evacuation to stick another knife in her back. Maybe the delay had prevented his escape. She pictured the bastard's body jerking in a torrent of gunfire. "Was he captured or killed?"

"Neither. Our dear father ordered Salazar to have the men stay and fight while he chased you down."

"And he knows exactly where I'm headed." She had been the one to suggest they all hide out at her explosives facility at South Mountain.

"He said you don't have anywhere else to go."

Hope surged. "Wait, Salazar doesn't know how to get where I'm going."

"Nacho knows. That's why he took them."

She frowned. "Them?"

"Apparently Nacho wouldn't come without that girl."

"Oh, please."

"Listen, there's not much time. Salazar isn't far behind you. When he finds you he'll ..."

She checked the compass again, waiting for her brother to dislodge the words that had stuck in his throat. She groaned her frustration. "Spit it out for fuck's sake, Adolfo."

"*El Lobo* ... he ... he greenlighted you."

She was a dead woman. Even if she managed to evade the cartel's most notorious killer, her own father had ordered her execution. She had nothing to return to. Nowhere to go. No one who cared. Except —for some reason—Adolfo. Why would he ally himself with someone who couldn't possibly benefit him in any way?

No time for niceties. "Why are you telling me this?"

"I hate Salazar even more than you do," Adolfo said without hesitation. "I want the bastard gone. If you know he's coming, maybe you can surprise him with one of your ... creations."

So that was it. Adolfo wanted her to take Salazar out. If she failed, he lost nothing. If she succeeded, Salazar would be out of the way and she would still be ostracized, clearing a path for her brother to step into the top slot. He would be the heir to the family fortune. Clever.

She kept her tone measured. "Thank you for the information."

A sardonic smile lifted the corners of her mouth. At least she knew where everyone stood. Salazar had poisoned her father against her. Now he hunted her like the savage animal he was. Meanwhile, her brother had sucked her into a deadly game she had no hope of winning. He would use her to do his dirty work, then disavow her later.

"Blood has to stick together," Adolfo said and disconnected.

As the Jeep approached South Mountain, she contemplated how to take her life back. There would be nothing left of the Phoenix operation after the police stormed the main base armory. All of the men would be arrested or dead. If Salazar, Nacho, and the girl died too, she could return to her father as the sole survivor and explain how the bastard had lied to manipulate him. And if she also managed to kill Veranda Cruz ... so much the better. On the other hand, if everything went to shit, her backup plan was in place. No one knew about the overseas bank accounts, the villa, or the plastic surgeon on standby.

She examined the problem from every angle, turning it over in her mind, flipping its components around like a Rubik's Cube until a solution finally snapped into place. As her father had taught her, she devised a way to turn a desperate predicament to her advantage.

Her heart beat faster as she probed her plan for weaknesses and found none. There was only one way to beat them. She would play *their* game according to *her* rules. Anticipation thrummed through her body. The solution was not only perfect, it was elegant.

33

KNEELING ON THE hard earth floor of the pit building, Daria raised the heavy steel chisel above her head. Tensing her muscles, she slammed its sharp edge against a chunk of concrete, breaking it into brick-sized pieces. Rocking back on her heels, she swiped a hand across her damp forehead and surveyed her work.

Preferring to avoid a shootout that might accidentally detonate the pit device during construction, she'd had her men build a crude overhead door trap as a low-tech backup to the perimeter alarm. The mechanism required a load of rubble, and the pile she'd accumulated would be enough to drop an ox.

Satisfaction curved her full lips. Like most men, Salazar relied on brute strength and tactical skill. She would teach him to respect her superior intellect. Adolfo had given her the element of surprise. Her older brother might be a waste of donatable organs, but his information had served her well. Salazar was on her trail. And he would arrive soon.

She laid down the chisel to scoop the jumbled heap into the metal basket by her side. After pushing up to her feet, she tugged the rope through the pulley system. The basket rose to meet the arm overhead. Sweat trickled down her forehead from her hairline, stinging her eyes. She swiveled the arm to position the basket over the wooden shelf mounted to the wall above the rear service door. A flick of her thumb released the bottom of the basket, dropping the entire pile of broken concrete on top of the thick plank in a cacophonous rumble. As the last stray cement chunks fell to the ground, her cell phone buzzed. The silent alarm icon on the screen glowed red, indicating an outer perimeter breach. Salazar would be at the door in less than three minutes. Holding the remote activator in her hand, she tucked her lithe body into a dark corner to wait.

She checked her phone again. The system indicated a secondary activation near the back. Salazar's training had made him all too predictable. She knew he would use the rear service door rather than the front entrance because it was the safest approach.

The door whispered open a fraction. A sliver of sunlight sliced across the dirt floor. Anticipation spiked her adrenalin, preparing her for what was to come. A heartbeat later, the distinctive sound of a boot against a metal door sent it slamming against the interior wall. With a reverberating *clang*, it swung back toward the entrance. She would recognize the silhouetted shape of the man in the doorway anywhere.

Salazar's broad shoulders nearly brushed each side of the narrow entry as he inched over the threshold. Gun in hand, eyes sweeping the interior, he paused, a wolf scenting for prey.

Her thumb hovered above a button the size and shape of a pencil eraser. Impatience pricked her nerves. She willed the bastard to move inside a bit farther. Certain he couldn't see her, she had to stay still. To wait. She'd placed a red stone at the perfect spot. When his boot landed next to the marker, he would be in position.

Apparently not sensing any threat, Salazar crept forward. He took a tactical stance, crouching low as he moved with surprising stealth for such a large man.

The instant the edge of his boot nudged the red stone, she pressed the button. The spring-loaded wooden shelf collapsed above the door, raining concrete onto Salazar's head. The force of the cascade pummeled him until he fell to his knees, then face down in the dirt. A gray cloud of dust billowed up from his still form as the last of the chunks tumbled down to form a rugged peak covering his upper body.

Stiff muscles protesting, she pushed away from the corner and edged toward the rear service door. Waving away the shimmering particles of concrete dust floating under the fluorescent lights, she spotted the matte black Desert Eagle pistol in Salazar's slackened hand and bent to grab it. She checked his pulse, found it strong and steady, and shoved the barrel into the back of her waist.

After kicking the rubble away from Salazar, she grasped his wrists and pulled. Cursing and grunting, she dug in her heels and started to drag his dead weight across the three meters that separated him from the edge of the pit.

She thought about Veranda Cruz. A fellow cop had been shot with the detective's own gun. Everyone would despise her. With that kind of pressure on her, she'd take Daria's bait. She knew the one thing Cruz would not—could not—resist. She would offer the opportunity to avenge her comrade, and to ensure he hadn't died in vain.

Physically spent, she sat on the ground to catch her breath. Salazar groaned and rolled onto his stomach. Damn, what was the lummox's skull made of? She couldn't allow him to regain consciousness and overpower her. She could fight well, but he was more than she could handle.

Salazar opened his eyes. "What the fuck?"

Before he could gather his thoughts, she planted one foot on his hip and the other on his shoulder. With a massive effort, she straightened her legs, shoving him over the edge. She watched his arms flail a split second before he thudded to the ground below.

She peered down at Salazar. His fitted black T-shirt clearly showed his chest rising and falling, but he made no other movements. Working quickly, she strode to the rope ladder that dangled down from two steel rebars set into the cement at the edge of the pit. She slung a long coil of rope around her arm, hiking it up to rest on her slim shoulder.

She descended the ladder with practiced ease, rushing to Salazar's side before he woke again. Once she bound his wrists and ankles, she could take her time with the rest of the rope, making sure to position him in the most painful and degrading way possible.

After deftly securing him, she ran the tip of her finger along his swollen cheek. "Detective Cruz will join you soon."

34

VERANDA SAT ON a vinyl-covered chair in the trauma center waiting room at Phoenix General. No one occupied the seats on either side of her. Sam was in surgery, clinging to life. She checked her watch for the hundredth time. Six minutes past three in the afternoon. One hour and forty-eight minutes since her partner had been shot.

Circumstances had conspired against Sam. The air unit had been unable to medevac him due to the storm, and ground transportation had been perilous and slow, allowing more blood loss. She twisted her hands in her lap, recalling the ride in the ambulance, clutching Sam's hand as the paramedics worked frantically to stabilize him.

Doc appeared in front of her holding out a Styrofoam cup. "Coffee."

It was the first word anyone had spoken to her in over an hour. She'd noticed that none of her fellow police officers made direct eye contact with her as they huddled on the other side of the waiting room.

She took the steaming drink. "Any word from the doctors or nurses?" Doc had many friends and acquaintances in the medical profession, having been treated by most of them for countless real or imagined ailments over the years.

He shifted his feet. "Sam will be in surgery for a few more hours." He lowered his head. "Doesn't look good. He lost too much blood. Turns out he was hit twice." Doc pointed to his own chest. "Took one in the upper right quadrant of the thorax and one in the left bicep. His vest should've stopped the one to the chest."

"The cartel uses cop-killer rounds," she said in a hollow voice.

Doc's eyes widened. "Those are illegal."

She glared up at him without responding.

Doc winced. "Sorry, Veranda. Stupid comment." He took off his glasses and rubbed his eyes. "My mental bandwidth is down to fifty percent."

"Mine too." She heaved an exhausted sigh. "Did you hear the final update from SAU?" She resented having to pump information about the tactical assault from one of her Homicide squad members, but they were the only ones talking to her.

"No, I've been focused on the medical end here." He sipped from his cup.

"Right." Veranda stood and handed her untouched coffee back to Doc. She wouldn't sit by any longer to wait for crumbs. She strode to Lieutenant Diaz and Commander Webster, who had heads together in the far corner of the room.

Forgoing protocol—and even basic manners—she barged in on their private conversation. "What happened after Sam and I left in the ambulance? Did SAU take the building? Did anyone on the team get hurt?" She blurted the questions in rapid succession.

They turned to her, annoyed. Webster put a hand on his hip. "Yes, Detective, we killed five cartel members and took twelve into custody. Two of those are here with gunshot wounds. The remaining ten surrendered."

"And the SAU operators?"

"No injuries," Diaz said.

She released a breath she hadn't realized she'd been holding. Another police injury or death would devastate her completely. "What about Sofia Pacheco?"

"That's what we were discussing," Webster said. "Sofia, Daria, Salazar, and Nacho were not among those killed or injured. Looks like they escaped. We couldn't track them in the storm."

She straightened. "Are we searching for them now?"

Webster reddened. "I know my job, Detective. There's a BOLO and an APB out with a description of Sam's shooter's Jeep. We did an Amber Alert for Sofia too, but I'm not hopeful." He rubbed the back of his neck. "We reexamined helicopter photos from before the raid and discovered that a van is also unaccounted for."

Mention of the Jeep brought back the moments after the shooting. While she'd stanched Sam's wounds, the Jeep disappeared in the dust storm. Marci had raced to the Tahoe to give chase, only to find the windshield and two of its tires shredded by stray rounds. The multiton command bus wasn't an option for a car chase, and all other police vehicles at the scene were involved in the warrant service. With no air support available, they'd been forced to watch the shooter escape.

Diaz gave her a dark look. "Now that the storm is over, Professional Standards Bureau is at the scene. They're coming here next. You'll need to give a statement."

"Can it wait, Lieutenant? All I can think about is Sam." She heard the catch in her own voice. "My partner is on an operating table fighting for his life."

What would she do if Sam died? He had become more than her partner. He was a friend, a mentor, and a confidante. She had trusted him with her secrets. Her throat clogged, and she swallowed hard.

Diaz's expression thawed. "It can wait, but not too long."

Not trusting herself to reply, she turned and started for her chair. She stopped in her tracks at the sight of the police chief. Tall and distinguished in his crisp navy-blue Class A uniform, Chief Steven Tobias strode toward her, police hat tucked under his arm.

She felt the blood drain from her face. The chief only responded to the hospital when the situation was grave. And his formal attire meant he expected to make a statement to the media. Or console a grieving widow. His presence confirmed her worst fears.

She opened her mouth to acknowledge him as he drew nearer, but he walked right past her without so much as a glance. She stared after him as he joined her commander and lieutenant in the corner. He had seen her, she was sure of it, and had pointedly ignored her.

Face flaming, she whirled and plodded toward her empty chair. As she passed, some of her fellow officers gave her hard stares. A stream of harsh expletives emanated from a nearby corridor. She cocked her head. The voice sounded familiar. Following the sound, she peered around the corner to find Marci, nose-to-nose with a uniformed patrolman, telling him off.

Marci pivoted away from the man and locked eyes with Veranda. She made her way over, still muttering under her breath.

Veranda raised her brow. "What was that about?"

Marci's lip curled. "Rumor control."

She had a strange feeling this had something to do with her. The cold shoulder from the chief and the equally icy glares from other cops began to add up. Marci's comment could only mean one thing. She drew a deep breath and steeled herself. "What's everybody saying about me?"

Marci grabbed her elbow. "Let's go to the ladies' room."

Veranda wasn't surprised to find the women's bathroom empty when Marci propelled her inside. There were a lot more men than women on the PPD.

After the door swung shut, she leaned against the counter and faced Marci. "Well?"

Distress pinched Marci's features. "There's no way to be delicate about this, so I'll just say it."

Veranda watched while Marci gazed up at the bathroom ceiling as if the right words might appear in the air over her head.

Apparently finding no help from above, Marci's blue eyes dropped down to meet hers. "Crime Scene recovered your duty weapon at the scene. Word's out that the cartel used your gun on Sam." She cut off Veranda's protest. "I'm not done," Marci said. Now that she'd started, the words flowed freely. "And your partner is a legend on our department. He and Chief Tobias were booters together out of the academy. When someone like that gets shot on a case where he had to take over for you as lead detective, it doesn't sit well."

She knew there was more, and she had to hear it all. "What was that officer saying about me?"

Marci's nostrils flared. "In the absence of facts, people make shit up. The latest rumor is that you hid behind Sam when the bullets started flying."

Speechless, she worked her mouth, but nothing came out. She had been the target of speculation, suspicion, and gossip before, but no one had ever questioned her courage.

"I went off on that uniform for spreading bullshit," Marci said. "Told him I was there with you when it happened. If you hadn't warned us and pushed us out of the way, we all could have been shot. I also told him you were the first one to return fire, and that you stood in front of the rest of us."

Veranda deflated. When the cartel had put the tattoo on her skin, they might as well have made her wear it on her clothing. A scarlet letter so the world could see her shame and judge her. Would the rest of the department ever see her as one of them again? "It's because I'm related to *El Lobo*."

"It's not because of your heritage." Marci threw up her hands. "It's because you're a woman. Some of the troglodytes on the force still think women can't do this job, or that we'll panic and hide behind the big, strong men at the first sign of trouble." She cut her eyes to the door. "I might go back out there and kick that guy's ass so he understands what a woman can do."

"You're wrong," Veranda said quietly, aware that Marci was missing an important detail. "This is about me being a Villalobos. You remember when the Jeep was pulling away and something flew out of the window." At Marci's nod, she continued. "That was my duty weapon. The shooter left it behind so everyone would know."

Marci gasped. "Do you think the shooter was Salazar?"

Veranda nodded. "He's been in the military. He understands the bond between team members. When he failed to kill me with my own gun, he did something worse. He shot another cop."

Marci regarded her with sympathy.

"I've been through a lot," Veranda said. "But nothing like this."

Marci pulled her into a hug.

"Oh, shit, Marci. What did I do?"

"The best you could with what you had."

She refused to give in to the grief threatening to overwhelm her. "If I don't pull it together, they'll believe the rumors," she said, turning away. She went to the sink and splashed water on her face, washing away the last of the dust and grit. "A cop who would hide in the bathroom would also hide behind her partner. I've got to get out there and face them."

"Face who?"

"My accusers," she said. "The problem with gossip is that no one confronts you directly. Everyone talks behind your back, so there's no chance to set the record straight."

She pushed the swinging door open and strode down the corridor into the waiting room, prepared to speak her piece. The growing sea of blue stilled when she entered. Before she began, a heart-wrenching sob at the opposite entrance drew all eyes away from her. A uniformed officer entered the room with Sarah Stark, Sam's wife, leaning heavily on his arm.

Sarah's red-rimmed eyes found hers, and she headed for Veranda.

"I'm so sorry," Veranda whispered when Sarah stood in front of her. The words were hollow, wholly inadequate. She wanted to express her remorse, her pain, but didn't know what to say.

Sarah's body shook. "I begged Sam to retire. But he's not ready to leave yet." Her eyes narrowed. "Because of you."

Veranda was dumbfounded. "Me?"

"You can't leave the cartel alone, can you?" Sarah said, her tone strident. "You're supposed to be a Homicide detective, but you manage to make everything about that damned Villalobos family." She lowered her voice. "Your family."

Veranda sucked in a breath. The accusation thudded into her heart like an arrow finding its mark.

Sarah moved in close. "And now one of those ... those *animals* shot my husband." Her voice cracked.

The shooter wasn't here, so Veranda had become the target of Sarah's rage and fear. And she deserved all of it because her partner's wife was right. This was on her.

Unable to help Sam, she met Sarah's fiery gaze and offered the only solace she could. "I promise to do whatever it takes to bring the Villalobos cartel to justice."

Sarah slapped her full in the face, snapping her head to the side. "Don't you dare endanger another policeman's life with your personal battle. Those bullets were meant for you. And you should have taken them. Not my husband." Sarah collapsed into the patrol officer's arms, her body racked with sobs.

Everyone stared in shocked silence. Sam's wife had just assaulted a police officer in a room full of cops, but nobody made a move to detain her. A tacit understanding held the thin blue line in check.

Veranda had seen the blow coming and didn't flinch. Instead, she stood still to take the brunt of Sarah's wrath. Her cheek stinging, she remained silent as the officer guided Sarah past her.

"Veranda." Diaz's use of her first name distracted her from her self-recrimination. "Why don't you go home and wait for my call?" He held out a ring of keys. "Take my car. Agent Rios and I can catch a ride with one of the other detectives."

She understood the subtext of her supervisor's suggestion. The cartel had used her gun to shoot her partner, fellow officers had spread rumors about her, a woman who might be a widow very soon had just slapped her in the face, and the chief wouldn't make eye contact with her. Clearly, she was doing no good to anyone by staying at the hospital.

"I get it, Lieutenant," she said, taking the keys. "No one wants me around. I'm a disruption when everyone should be focused on Sam." She lowered her head. "I'll go. Just promise you'll call when there's news."

At his curt nod, she pivoted, passed through the automatic glass doors, and trudged down the hallway.

"Veranda," someone called out.

She turned to see Rios jogging to catch up with her.

"I told Diaz I'd come with you," he said. When she shook her head, he pressed her. "I'm useless here. This is not my department. I don't know the rank and file officers, or most of the command staff either. But I do know you. And I can be with you. On your side."

"Thanks, but no."

He continued walking with her. "I'm supposed to help apprehend Salazar, but who knows where he is right now? Until there's new information about where he went, I'm waiting. Like you. We can wait together."

She knew he meant they could wait for word on Sam's condition as well. And that he thought she shouldn't be alone if the news was bad, which seemed likely.

"Okay," she said on a sigh. "Diaz said his car was in the police parking zone. Shouldn't be hard to spot."

She led the way to the lot near the ER entrance and found Diaz's dust-covered Chrysler 300. The windshield appeared to have been hurriedly wiped clean. They got in and she drove toward the bridge leading into South Phoenix. Rios remained silent, giving her time to reflect while she steered the car on autopilot.

What if Sam died? She beat the thought back. That kind of speculation took her on a downward spiral. As long as he was alive, she would keep the faith.

She was almost to Chuy's garage when Rios's cell phone buzzed in his pocket. She read his shocked expression and knew he'd jumped to the same conclusion she had. They'd left the hospital less than twenty minutes ago. Sam was supposed to be in surgery for hours. Unless …

Fearing the worst, she pulled to the side of the road. If Diaz had called Rios, it meant he didn't want to notify Veranda while she was driving. She shifted the car into park as he slid the phone out.

"No number, just a question mark in the middle of the screen," he said. "Could be my *comandante*. Better take it." Lifting the phone to his ear, he answered in Spanish. "This is Agent Rios."

Curious, she listened in on the one-sided conversation.

242

He switched back to English, his tone harsh. "How did you get my number?"

Curiosity morphed into concern as she watched. He turned to her, the color draining from his face.

"I don't have to go and find her." He looked at Veranda. "She's sitting right next to me."

She gestured for him to give her the phone. Instead, he tapped the screen. "You're on speaker."

After a brief pause, she heard a frantic female voice. "P-please help me, Detective Cruz."

She stared at the phone a moment, trying to place the familiar voice. The caller's hysteria made her difficult to identify. She flicked through a mental list of female acquaintances before blinding realization struck. She gaped, trying to comprehend the incomprehensible, then finally spoke.

"What's going on, Daria?"

35

VERANDA WANTED ANSWERS. "And why the hell are you calling me on Agent Rios's phone?"

"Shut up and listen!" Daria sounded terrified. "Salazar trapped me in a building near South Mountain. He thought I lost my phone. I waited till he left to call you." She choked back a sob. "Something's happened to him. He's insane."

She struggled to catch up. "Salazar turned on you?"

"He took me prisoner at our armory in West Phoenix. I took out one of the guards and escaped. But he chased me down."

That would explain Daria and Salazar's absence during the raid. They were each driving to the other side of the city. Veranda was losing patience. "Let's have the rest of it, Daria."

"I'm running out of time." Urgency strained Daria's voice. "Salazar pushed me into a blast pit. I can't climb out. And ... and ... there's a bomb strapped to a pole in the middle."

Veranda and Rios traded wide-eyed glances. "A bomb?"

"Technically, two Claymore mines," Daria said in a rush. "On a timer."

"Slow down," Veranda said, her measured tone designed to stop Daria's babbling. "Tell me about the timer."

"Salazar set it for one hour. I waited until I was sure he was gone before calling you. The display says I've got forty-two minutes, thirty-eight seconds left."

Veranda checked her watch. 3:46 p.m. "Can you turn the thing off?"

"There are pressure plates surrounding the device. They'll detonate the bomb if I step on them." Daria sighed. "Look, the pit and the bomb are my prototypes. I designed them to be completely secure. I can't escape." She hesitated. "But I can be rescued."

Veranda glared at the phone as if Daria could see her exasperation. "How do you expect me to do that? And more to the point, why would I want to?"

"There's a kill switch inside the building. You can deactivate it if you're on ground level," Daria replied. "As for why you would want to … do you remember that deal you offered me?"

She snorted. "When you had a gun to my head? Yeah, protection in exchange for testifying against your father."

"I want the deal now," Daria said.

She tugged Rios's wrist, pulling the phone closer. "It's off the table. Everything's off the table. You assholes shot my partner."

"Salazar shot him before he caught up with me," Daria said. "Then he left your gun behind so everyone would know how you—"

Veranda cut her off. "I don't care about Salazar."

It was a lie. How could she not care when every cell in her body screamed for retribution? She would hunt Salazar down. Even if it took the rest of her career. The rest of her life. Rios's voice penetrated the wave of anger, drawing her attention back to the conversation.

"What about your men?" he asked Daria. "Why can't they help you?"

"I have no men left," Daria said. "My personal guards and all of the coyotes were arrested or killed at the main building. Salazar left me here to die and took off." Her voice took on a pleading note. "If you save me, I'll help you. We can work together to take down the cartel. You'll be the one to arrest Adelmo Salazar, the man who shot your partner. That's what you want, isn't it?"

It certainly was. "Where are you exactly?"

"The foot of South Mountain on the eastern side," Daria said. "In a building on twenty acres of land off a dirt road. I'll text Agent Rios the coordinates and you can use your GPS."

Rios mouthed an angry *no* and shook his head vehemently.

Veranda ignored him. "Stay on the phone. Let us know if any—"

"My battery's almost dead. I might not even have enough juice to send the text. Please hurry, Detective Cruz." Daria seemed on the verge of tears. "I'm down to forty minutes and fifty-two seconds." She disconnected.

Rios spewed a barrage of Spanish expletives.

She threw the car in drive and veered back onto the roadway. "I know roughly where she is. We're already in South Phoenix, so it'll take less than twenty minutes to get there. Forward the text to my cell when you get it." She gave him an apologetic look. "There's no time to drop you at a precinct. There's a fire station down the street. I'll let you out there."

Rios looked incredulous. "No."

"You can't come with me," she said. "I have to do this for Sam. And for my family, Cole, and everyone else I've put in danger. Sarah Stark is right. It's my battle, and I need to fight it. Alone."

"Daria's a liar." His phone vibrated with an incoming text message, but he kept his gaze on Veranda. "It's a trap. Daria and Salazar are laughing together while they wait for you to show up."

"I can handle myself." She pinned him with a glare before returning her gaze to the road. "Without any help from you."

Apparently unfazed by her patented death stare, he tapped the screen, silencing the buzz. He continued to gaze down at the phone in his hand as his expression became calculating. "Maybe I should call Lieutenant Diaz."

She couldn't believe he would stoop so low. "You're threatening me with Diaz?"

"Actually, why aren't you on the phone with him now? He's your supervisor, after all." His cunning smile widened as she struggled for a response that wouldn't make her position worse.

"You know damn well he'd tell me not to go," she said, going with the truth. "He'd insist on an ops plan and a SWAT team. There's no time for that."

"Let's see." Rios tapped his chin in mock concentration. "The woman who kidnapped you and claimed she blew up your house is next to a bomb. If we don't rush out to save her, she'll die." He frowned. "I say we wait and clean up the mess after the bomb goes off."

She gripped the steering wheel hard enough to leave her fingerprints in the molded vinyl that covered it. "I don't want to save her because she's a good person. I want her to testify against her father. And Salazar. She knows enough to help the Feds freeze their assets. Disrupt their markets. Root out their distributors." She pushed the car harder, anxious to get there. "Don't you get it? The cartel wouldn't survive."

"Do you actually believe anything that woman says? It could be a trap."

His calm demeanor maddened her. This was an unprecedented chance to strike at the heart of a vast criminal empire.

"Doesn't matter," she said. "Once I have her in custody, she's mine. She'll flip to save her own skin." She pictured Daria in an orange jumpsuit. "I don't see her taking one for the team."

He sat in quiet contemplation as they sped down the road. She felt his eyes on her for a long moment before he broke the silence. "If you're going to do this, I'm coming with you."

"The hell you are."

"I have the coordinates." Rios waggled the phone in his hand. "You think you can take this from me?"

She read his body language. The set of his jaw told her he wouldn't back down. Taut muscles indicated he was prepared to use brute strength. She considered her options. Pepper spray inside a moving vehicle would incapacitate both of them. Shooting him was tempting but might cause an international incident. She summed up her conclusion in one word. "Shit."

"You need backup and you need a plan." He hooked a thumb at his chest. "I'm a former tactical officer who's gone up against the cartel before."

Her resolve began to crack. "But you don't even have a gun. How can you back me up?"

"I've told you, I don't need a gun to kill someone."

Resigned to her circumstances, she relented. "Pull up the navigation on your phone while I check for gear."

She pulled to the side of the road again. Fingers crossed, she jogged to the back of the car and popped the trunk. Finally, something had gone her way. She seized Diaz's go-bag and angled herself back into the driver's seat. Tossing the duffel to Rios, she accelerated back onto the asphalt, tires spinning up a plume of dust.

Dimples creased Rios's cheeks. "Let's see what the *teniente* keeps in his bag."

He rifled through the duffel, plucking out Diaz's portable radio, flex cuffs, and handcuffs. "We'll need these." He dug deeper. "And this." He pulled out a military-style folding knife and flicked open a six-inch serrated blade.

"Do you see a backup gun?"

"Not even a Taser." He folded the knife again. "Diaz spends too much time behind a desk."

The insistent buzz of a vibrating cell phone had them both checking their devices. This time, her phone was the one receiving a call. Glancing down, she saw her lieutenant's name flashing from the console cup holder where she'd stashed it. Her thoughts immediately went to her partner. Heart aching, she nodded at Rios, who lifted the phone and tapped the speaker icon.

"Lieutenant, do you have news?" She choked out the question around the lump in her throat. "How is Sam?"

Diaz spoke as if every word pained him. "You should come back to the hospital right away. There may not be much time left."

36

VERANDA FOUGHT THROUGH the despair engulfing her. "I can't go to the hospital, Lieutenant." She wondered if her supervisor could hear her heart breaking on the other end of the phone. She blinked back the unshed tears that blurred her vision as she raced toward South Mountain.

"Why not?" Lieutenant Diaz went from grief-stricken to irritated in a nanosecond.

Her fellow officers would hate her for what she was about to do. It didn't matter that she did it for Sam. And for every other cop the cartel would murder in the future if she didn't stop them. They would see it as a betrayal. Her partner lay dying, but instead of rushing to his side, she rushed to save the sister of the man who pulled the trigger.

She owed Diaz the truth. "Because I'm on my way to rescue Daria Villalobos."

Agent Rios, sitting in the front passenger's seat next to her, mimed hanging himself.

"Excuse me?" Diaz said, irritation ratcheting up to anger.

She glanced at her watch and did a swift calculation. With less than thirty minutes until the device detonated, Diaz had no time to intervene. He wouldn't order regular patrol units to respond to a cartel stronghold; they weren't equipped. Sergeant Grigg and his SAU team were still on the far side of the city at the raid site. Another tactical team couldn't suit up and deploy fast enough.

She would make Diaz see that she was the only one who could respond. One of Rios's hands gripped the dash, the other held the phone for her as she outlined the situation while maneuvering through traffic.

Diaz waited until she finished before he brought the full weight of his authority down on her. "Let me make this crystal clear, Detective. Apprehending Daria Villalobos is not worth your life. I will not allow you to attempt this rescue by yourself. It's not—"

"She's not by herself," Rios said, interrupting Diaz mid-rant. "I'm her backup."

"Tell me something, Agent Rios." Diaz's tone grew wary. "How often do members of the Villalobos family call you?"

Rios reared back against the vinyl seat, indignation replacing shock on his expressive face. "Are you accusing me of working for the cartel?"

"How did Daria get your cell number?" Diaz demanded.

Veranda had asked Daria the same question. And never got an answer. She pulled her gaze from the roadway long enough to gauge the *federale*'s reaction.

Rios bellowed at the phone in his hand. "Remember Nacho, the hacker? Use your brain, *cabrón*. The cartel probably has a lot more than just my phone number."

"Even if you're telling the truth, you can't be her backup," Diaz said. "You don't have law enforcement powers in the United States. Or a gun."

Rios's response sounded like something he'd researched before coming to the States. "Officially, I can go as an observer. If necessary, I can take action to preserve life."

"I'll deal with you later, Rios." Diaz sounded angrier than Veranda had ever heard him. "Right now, I'm ending this suicide mission."

Why did Diaz thwart her at every turn? It always came down to a battle of wills between them. "You can't, Lieutenant." She took a moment to steel herself. "Because I'm not telling you where I'm headed."

Rios stared at her open-mouthed. A hot blush burned her cheeks, growing warmer with every second of silence that passed after her defiant words. She took another turn, pressing the gas pedal harder.

When Diaz responded, the chill carried through the phone. "There's a tracking device in my car, Detective. I'll get dispatch to find your location."

She knew patrol cars were tracked through dispatch, but not investigative supervisor vehicles. Diaz must have put in a special request to outfit his Chrysler. "You'll be too late," she said, trying not to sound belligerent. "We're almost there."

Diaz's voice grew eerily calm. He spoke slowly, enunciating each word. "Detective Cruz, I am giving you a direct order to stand down. Return to the hospital. Now."

She licked dry lips. Diaz had drawn a line. Crossing it could cost her badge. She paused to reconsider her options but came to only one conclusion. There would never be another opportunity like the one Daria offered her. She was prepared to sacrifice her position, her career, even her life, to destroy the cartel.

Heart pounding, she stepped over Diaz's line. "That's not going to happen, sir."

She disconnected before he could suspend her from duty over the phone. At least she was still acting under the color of law.

"Why did you tell him what we're doing?" Rios asked, exasperated. "He can't help, and he can't stop us either."

She couldn't save Sam, but she could avenge him. "I wanted someone on the department to know what I did and why I did it."

Rios gave her a shrewd look. "In case you don't make it back?"

He'd been straight with her, so she would do the same. "Yes."

Her phone buzzed in Rios's hand. He glanced down. "It's Diaz."

She kept her eyes on the road. "Turn it off."

He did as she asked, regarding her with deep concern. "What's going to happen to you?"

"I disobeyed a supervisor's lawful direct order." She continued to gaze straight ahead. "I'm well and truly fucked."

37

CLENCHING AND RELEASING her fists in rhythmic spasms, Daria paced across the blast pit's compacted dirt floor. She glanced up at the mirror high above her. How long would it take Veranda Cruz to arrive?

Salazar groaned and began to come around, bringing a smile to her lips.

She sauntered over to him and toed his ribs with the point of her boot. "Wake up." The command, delivered in sharp Spanish, bounced around the cement chamber.

She'd used a rope with large knots spaced at regular intervals to climb down after pushing Salazar's unconscious form into the pit. Skilled at restraining men, she'd expertly bound his wrists to his ankles behind his back before he regained consciousness. She'd taken care to leave enough slack for him to breathe properly, but not enough for him to move more than a few inches. Effectively hog-tied, the vaunted *El*

Matador lay at her feet. He had told her to learn her place. Now, he would learn his.

He stirred, muscular arms straining against the thick ropes.

As he thrashed, she admired him with a practiced eye. She considered herself a connoisseur of masculine beauty, and Salazar was a fine specimen, albeit a bit too brawny for her taste. Even though it had only been a few feet, dragging his dead weight to the pit had nearly exhausted her. He was built on a larger scale than most men, and she wondered idly if everything about him was oversized.

Salazar's eyes blinked open, scanned his surroundings, and fixed on her. "Let me go if you want to live, *puta*."

His comment drove more pleasant musings from her mind. "Let me bring you up to speed. Kicked your ass. Tied you up. Went outside to call Veranda Cruz. Told her you'd thrown me in the pit with a bomb. She's on her way to join you." She put a hand on her hip. "So don't threaten me. You'd be dead by now if I didn't want certain information."

That was a lie. He was still alive because she wanted him to suffer for humiliating her. And to share Cruz's fate. If she also extracted usable information from him, so much the better.

Beads of perspiration dotted Salazar's hairline, betraying the discomfort from his position and whatever injuries he had from the fall. "I am going to enjoy killing you, Daria."

She had expected him to be angry, humiliated, and afraid. Instead, he threatened her. His contorted position stressed joints and cramped muscles. Even the toughest man would break eventually. Salazar must have a high pain tolerance. She would have to accelerate the process.

She kneeled beside him. "Are you insane? Look where you are."

"I've gotten out of prisons with armed guards at every door," Salazar said, gasping. "I can escape from you."

So that was it. He'd fallen for her trap because he'd never been inside this building. Time to enlighten him. "Do you see that digital clock?" She jerked her chin at the metal pole in the center of the pit. "When it gets to zero, flying shrapnel will shred everything down here."

Salazar shifted his head to look at the timer and cursed.

She gestured to the knotted rope dangling down to the dirt floor a few feet away. "Or you can climb out before Cruz gets here." She waited for his gaze to swivel from the rope back to her. "If you answer two questions."

"What do you need to know so badly?"

He'd stopped berating her to see what she wanted. A good sign. She had no intention of letting him out of the pit, but maybe he thought she was stupid enough to untie him. Experience interrogating prisoners had taught her to begin with a smaller question.

"First, where is Nacho?"

"Nacho?" Salazar's brows shot up. "What the fuck do you care about him for?"

She would get to the important question next, but Nacho played a pivotal role in her future plans.

"I'm asking the questions." She grasped the length of rope between his wrists and ankles and gave it a sharp tug. "Not you."

Salazar jackknifed backward, spine arching as she drew his limbs closer together behind him. He gnashed his teeth, biting back a howl of agony.

She eased the tension long enough for him to catch his breath. "That overgrown schoolboy can access every part of our business." As Salazar gasped, she repeated the torment with each pronouncement. "Our finances." Tug. "Our distribution network." Tug. "Our facilities." Tug. "If they catch him, he'll cooperate." She released the rope. "And we're finished."

256

"Enough!" Salazar called out.

She crossed her arms and waited.

"I didn't want him killed or arrested at the armory," Salazar said, panting. "I sent him out to cross the border in one of the loaded vans while I came after you. He took the girl with him."

Anger roared through her. "You fool. Nacho will get caught."

Muscles along Salazar's entire body quivered spasmodically. When his watering eyes found hers, they did not display fear. They promised retribution.

Somewhat unnerved by this, she proceeded toward her objective. "Second question. Who is the Rook?"

Knowledge of the man's identity would give her considerable leverage. She might even form a secret alliance with him.

A slow smile spread across Salazar's strained features. "Do what you will, *puta*. You won't get his name out of me."

The bastard wouldn't tell her outright, but perhaps he would react if she guessed. "Is it the *federale*, Agent Manuel Rios?" She remained on her knees to study his face.

Not even a twitch.

"He's coming here with Cruz. Just the two of them. If he's the Rook, I won't kill him. He's an ally."

Salazar continued to stare at her.

Had she guessed correctly? Pointing to the ceiling, she made a final attempt to force his hand. "Look up." When he didn't move, she clutched a hank of his hair and pulled his head back to see the enormous convex mirror positioned at an angle above the pit.

Her men had bolted it to the rafters yesterday so she could supervise their work while she reset the explosives below. She'd been able to see her men carry cement mix in through the rear service door and patch the damage along the upper edge from her position at the bottom of the blast chamber.

"They'll enter through the back door like you did. I'll drop Rios first." She held up Salazar's matte black Desert Eagle. "With your gun. He won't survive, but I'll make sure Cruz does. She'll die in the pit… with you. Unless you tell me who the Rook is."

She sensed his implacable resolve. He wouldn't give up the name if she tortured him for hours. She glanced at the clock. There was still time to inflict other kinds of damage.

"You will die in the dirt on your belly like the worm you are." She gave him a moment to contemplate her words. "Putting me in chains earned your death sentence, but I assumed you'd been arrested in the raid and I wouldn't get to carry it out. I also gave up on my original plans for Cruz and tried to shoot her on the way here. Fortunately, I missed." She smoothed the deep furrows of confusion creasing his forehead with her fingertips. "When I heard you were chasing me, I wanted both of you here. You belong together."

He recoiled from her touch. "Who told you I came after you?"

"Figure it out." She stroked his cheek, relishing his revulsion at her continued contact. "Do you know what you and Cruz have in common?"

"A twisted, sadistic *puta* for a half sister."

Sick of being called a whore, she curled her fingers. Sharp nails sank into his face. "A tattoo you don't deserve." She raked down, gouging him from cheek to jaw. "Both of you are bastards, yet you bear the Villalobos family mark on your chests." She pulled her hand away and yanked a sock from her back pocket. "In less than twenty-seven minutes, those tattoos will be obliterated." Her fist tightened, wadding the sock into a ball.

His expression grew wary. "What are you—"

She punched his throat, forcing him to sputter and cough. When he opened his mouth to gulp air, she crammed the sock in. Holding the gag in place with one hand, she pulled the bandana she'd used on

258

Cruz's gun from her other pocket and wrapped it around his head, securing it with a knot.

"Can't have you warning Detective Cruz when she comes to rescue me." She stood, enjoying the sight of Salazar lying in the dirt. "My father transferred the kill order for Cruz to you." Bending down, she slid a finger under the taught rope between his ankles and wrists. "Well I'm taking it back." She raised her arm, relishing his agony. "Because Veranda Cruz is mine."

38

VERANDA SLID THE lieutenant's sedan to a stop behind a rocky outcropping and killed the engine, leaving the keys in the ignition for Rios. She'd agreed to let him back her up, but not to enter the building with her. He could be her eyes and ears on the perimeter.

Dreading the inevitable argument, she'd put off telling him she was going in alone. The mountainous desert landscape had proven helpful, allowing her to park nearby but far enough away to obscure them from view while they reconnoitered the site. She'd spotted the Jeep and a van parked out front and drove around to check out the back of the building.

Rios stepped out of the car with a pair of binoculars he'd appropriated from the go-bag. "Looks like we can approach from here using those bushes for cover."

She got out and joined him by the hood of the car and followed his line of sight. "Is there a rear access point?"

He twisted the outer ring around the lenses. "I can see a service door." He turned to her. "We'll make entry there."

She checked her watch. Just over twenty-five minutes to spare until detonation. Time to deliver the news. "Diaz won't send patrol units, and Grigg's SAU team is tied up on the west side. If the lieutenant called a fresh SAU team right away, it would still take at least thirty minutes for them to suit up and deploy. That doesn't factor in travel time from the Tactical Support Bureau building to this location. They won't make it before the clock runs out."

He lowered the binoculars. "What are you trying to tell me?"

"*I'll* make entry through the back," she said, bracing herself. "Alone."

"Bad tactics." He shook his head. "We shouldn't enter at different points with only two officers. It works with two teams in constant radio contact, but it can lead to a crossfire situation if I go in the front while you're going in the b—"

"You're not going in at all."

Her words floated in the air between them like dust particles after the storm.

He moved closer, invading her personal space. "*Pérdon.* I must have heard you wrong."

She recognized the move as an overt challenge to her authority and responded accordingly. Overriding the reflexive need to step back, she held her ground. "You're on my turf, Rios. I'm in charge. You will remain on the perimeter observing the building. Call or text me if you see any movement. If you spot Salazar, keep him in sight. If there's an explosion, stay outside and call Diaz." She lifted her chin. "Or you can sit in the car. Your choice."

Without waiting for a reply, she muted her phone and jammed it into a pouch on her ballistic vest. When she turned to start her approach toward the building, a firm hand landed heavily on her shoulder.

She spun out of his grasp to face him. "We don't have time for this." She tapped her watch. "We've wasted one whole minute arguing."

He exuded anger. "I thought we were a team."

"Exactly," she said. "If we both go in together, no one can help us. But if I go down, you've got my back." She had a strong urge to grab him by the vest and shake him. "Dammit, Rios, you're supposed to be my backup, so back me up."

He hooked his thumbs onto his belt loops and glanced at his shoes. After a long moment, the fight drained out of him. "Program my cell number for one-touch dialing."

She did as he asked and matched his cool tone. "I'll call if I need you."

"The rear service door opens inward," he said quietly. "You'll have a blind spot behind it. Look between the door and the frame when you go in." He held out the folding knife with the wicked-looking blade. "And take this."

She bent down to stuff it into the top of her tactical boot. "If Daria's information is correct, she's in there by herself." She held up both hands. "I know she might be lying. Or Salazar could have used her to lure me in. I'll watch my six." This time, she didn't get a chance to turn away before he reached out to her.

He clasped her hands in his, a torrent of emotion flooding his dark features. "Please be careful," he said to her in Spanish. "If anything happened to you …" He brought her knuckles to his lips, then released her.

What he had just done was about ninety-seven clicks past professional, but she let it slide. She would deal with the handsome *federale*, and whatever was happening between them, later. First, she had to come out of the building in one piece.

Using the shade from the red-brown boulders nearby, she picked her way around the cholla and barrel cactus to dart behind a saguaro. She leaned out, checking for signs of movement, cameras, or counter surveillance.

She noted the barn-sized building's lack of windows. Made sense if Daria routinely detonated explosives inside. To avoid attracting attention, Daria had probably installed soundproofing and blast-proofing as well. Filing these observations away, she raced forward and pressed her back against the rough exterior wall. When no one challenged her, she slipped around the corner to the back of the building.

She edged her way to the rear service door and considered the situation. Any structure containing explosive agents should include a secondary exit to evacuate people or fumes. Assuming the emergency exit would be unlocked, as it was in public buildings, she slowly twisted the metal doorknob. Relief rushed through her when it turned freely.

She inched the metal door open and peered through the opening. The interior lights seemed dim compared to the sun-washed desert outside. She placed a booted foot inside, paused, and scanned. She realized the door was designed to self-close, so she held it open with her shoulder. Looking to her right, she focused on the blind spot Rios had warned her about.

She'd been on enough tactical operations during her time in narcotics enforcement to have seen her share of nasty surprises lurking behind doors. Despite the best training, sometimes there was no good way to enter a room. Cops called them Fatal Funnels. Specific points where an officer was vulnerable to attack. Hallways, elevators, stairwells, alleys, and doorways topped the list. As part of an entry team, she would kick open the door, sending it crashing against the wall to clear the space behind it.

Working alone, she opted for stealth. A quiet entry gave her the advantage if she could get inside undetected. Aware of the danger posed by the door, she made her decision.

Drawing a deep breath, she eased her body over the threshold and entered the Fatal Funnel.

39

SALAZAR PRESSED HIS tongue against the sock wedged in his mouth. He felt a slight movement, but the saliva-soaked fabric slipped backward toward his throat, making him retch. He steadied himself. If he wasn't careful, the sock could unwind and suffocate him. He wondered if that would be a worse death than the one Daria had planned for him.

He might be dead already if he hadn't regained consciousness seconds before Daria shoved him into the hole. He'd twisted around to land on his feet, rolling onto his back and relaxing his muscles to prevent serious injury. After she climbed out, Daria had used a hatchet to cut the knotted rope into short, useless pieces. Even if he managed to untie himself, he couldn't escape. And if anyone came, they couldn't pull him up to safety without the rope. Daria had laughed at him as she tossed the chopped pieces into the pit.

Before that moment, self-mastery had been his greatest asset. Dispassionately dispensing *El Lobo*'s justice, he had killed countless times without a hint of remorse. But Daria Villalobos had burrowed into his psyche and unearthed hatred so strong it burned like acid. He realized he would gladly die if he could pull the *puta* down into the pit with him.

A thin shaft of light sliced into the building. Raging anger wouldn't help him think. He tamped it down and analyzed the situation. Cruz had probably entered through the rear service door as he had. The moment he crossed the threshold, Daria had sprung her trap. Someone had warned her he was coming. And he thought he knew who.

Pushing thoughts of Adolfo's betrayal aside, he tilted his head to gaze up at the convex mirror bracketed to the ceiling. Its curved surface distorted things a bit, but he could clearly make out the doorway. He spotted Daria hunkered on the hinged side of the service door, back to the wall, clutching his Desert Eagle with both hands.

The door gradually opened, revealing a lone figure silhouetted by the afternoon sun. He recognized the lean feminine form holding a Glock in low-ready position. Inhaling through his nostrils, he dragged air into his lungs and tried to force sound up from his throat. Only a faint murmur penetrated the gag.

He could do nothing as Cruz crept forward, her right shoulder against the metal door to hold it open. Eyes wide, he took in the scene playing out above him, Daria on one side of the door, Cruz on the other, both holding guns. The two women were separated by inches, unable to see one another through the barrier between them.

Salazar was struck by their similarities. Each had chosen a profession dominated by men, and managed to succeed. From what he'd learned about Cruz from a previous informant, she didn't follow orders any better than Daria did. Both women were beautiful, but Daria was cold-blooded while Cruz exuded fiery heat. They were two sides of the same coin, evenly matched, and he had no idea who would win this battle.

Gun in hand, Cruz put one foot inside, shifting her body weight forward.

Daria kicked the door, slamming it into Cruz's shoulder, knocking her to the ground and sending the Glock flying from her hand.

Daria brought the Desert Eagle up to take aim, but the door swung violently back toward her. She sidestepped to avoid it, giving Cruz time to scramble to her feet. Even in the mirror, Salazar could see the detective's shocked expression.

"That's right, bitch," Daria said, training her sights on Cruz. "It's me." She fired.

The Desert Eagle's report reverberated like a cannon blast through the cavernous building. Cruz's split-second dive and roll impressed Salazar, as did her decision to go on the offensive. When .50-caliber rounds were flying, nothing in the building offered real protection. Her only play was a full-frontal assault, and she obviously knew it.

Cruz popped up from her roll and launched her body straight at Daria. Daria stepped back to create distance for a better shot, but Cruz's momentum carried her forward. She juggernauted into Daria, driving her to the ground.

Salazar grinned under the bandana. He'd seen Cruz's ground fighting skills firsthand. No doubt she hoped to improve her chances by taking Daria to the floor. As the women wrestled for the gun, he willed Cruz to grab the slide, which would temporarily prevent it from firing.

The irony of his situation was not lost on Salazar as he sent fervent thoughts of encouragement to the woman he'd been sent to kill. Moments before, he'd recognized the similarities between the two women. Now he understood the key difference. Daria had no honor and therefore, no limitations. Cruz lived by a code. As he did. When the time came, he would grant her a merciful death. A warrior like himself, Veranda Cruz deserved that much.

Whatever his feelings about her, his survival depended on her success. He watched as Cruz wrapped both hands around the top of the pistol, holding the slide in place. She rolled Daria onto her back, pinning her. Salazar let out a grunt of approval when Cruz brought her knee up to deliver a vicious strike to Daria's thigh. Daria shrieked in pain, loosening her grip on the weapon. Cruz tried to wrench it away, but Daria pulled the gun closer. When it neared her face, she angled her head up and sank her teeth into Cruz's fingers.

Cruz let go of the gun and smashed her elbow into Daria's face, momentarily disorienting her. Under different circumstances, he would have paid good money to watch this fight. Cruz moved like a tigress. Lithe, focused, and relentless. Magnificent.

Blood streaming from her nose, Daria rolled away from Cruz and came up on one knee. She took aim, but Cruz was already in motion. She planted her left foot and executed a swift roundhouse kick, knocking the gun from Daria's hand.

Salazar watched his Desert Eagle spin though the air. He tore his gaze from the curved mirror to follow the massive pistol's trajectory as it plummeted to the ground inside the pit less than a meter from his face.

Daria and Cruz continued to fight hand-to-hand. As he lay listening to grunts and blows interspersed with obscenities, Salazar chanced working his tongue against the gag again. This time, he managed to move the entire sock to the front of his mouth. He widened his jaws and forced the wad against the back of his teeth, finally making enough space. He filled his lungs and let out a bellow.

Glancing up at the mirror, he saw Cruz turn her head toward the pit's opening. She had heard him. He redoubled his efforts to push the gag out, then froze, realizing what he had done. Daria, seizing upon Cruz's momentary distraction, rushed at her adversary, head butting her shoulder. Cruz stumbled sideways, arms flailing. Salazar shifted his gaze to the edge of the pit. He watched Cruz teeter on the brink, clawing the air, then plunge down as Daria's laugh echoed through the cavernous space.

Cruz thudded heavily to the ground next to Salazar, the gun between them. She tried to sit up, groaned, and flopped down on her back. Salazar heard her ragged breathing and knew she'd been winded from the fall. Her movements didn't indicate broken bones, but he couldn't be sure. The dirt floor had likely saved them both from catastrophic injuries when they hit the bottom of the pit.

Daria's face appeared over the edge. "I'm so glad you're alive." Her eyes moved to the clock on the pole. "At least, for the next fourteen minutes."

Cruz struggled to push her body up to a seated position. Salazar saw the moment her eyes landed on the Desert Eagle. Unfortunately, Daria had seen it too. As Cruz lunged for the weapon, Daria's head disappeared. He heard swift footfalls as she raced from the building.

He angled his head to see Cruz gripping his pistol in her bleeding hands.

Her eyes, glittering with fury, were riveted on him. "You shot my partner, you sonofabitch."

What lies had Daria told her? He tried to speak but only managed a muffled gurgle through the gag.

He found himself staring down the barrel of his own gun as Cruz leveled it at him and said, "This is for Sam."

40

VERANDA ALIGNED THE Desert Eagle's sites on Salazar's nose. She'd seen the kind of damage a .50-caliber round could do. Pulling the trigger at point-blank range would literally blow his head off his shoulders.

As she tightened her finger, Salazar's eyes beseeched her. He worked his jaw under the gag in a frantic struggle to communicate.

Was he begging for his life? Not *El Matador*. Was he cursing her? His desperate gaze said otherwise. She didn't see hate, but something raw and elemental.

Salazar rotated his head as far to the side as it would go. He groaned as he forced his shoulder blades together. Then he stilled his body, lifted his chin, and closed his eyes.

She stared down at him, baffled. The awkward position had to be excruciating. Why had he done it? She cocked her head and looked from a different angle. Then she saw it. He had exposed his throat to her. The stark gesture of surrender communicated his willingness to die by her hand.

An echo of Sam's rumbling baritone reverberated through her mind. *"There's getting justice, and there's getting payback. Which one are you after?"* Sam had questioned her motives. Challenged her to look inside herself. What would he say if he saw her preparing to kill a defenseless, unarmed suspect in cold blood?

Nothing else would have convinced her to lay down the pistol. She slid the folding knife from her boot and flicked it open.

Salazar's eyelids parted a fraction at the sound. His wary gaze focused on the serrated blade.

She crawled the short distance separating them and raised the knife's edge to his face.

He jerked his head away.

Apparently, he was willing to die, but not get carved up. She couldn't blame him. "Hold still." She used her free hand to gently angle his face back to her, then peered directly into his fierce black eyes. "I'm going to cut the gag off."

His whole body relaxed. She marveled that he trusted someone who had every intention of murdering him scant seconds ago. The knife's razor-sharp edge made short work of the bandana. She reached into his mouth, yanked out the slimy sock, and flung it aside.

"I didn't," Salazar said in Spanish, his voice raspy. He licked his chapped lips and tried again. "Didn't shoot your partner."

He clearly understood how important Sam was to her. His military background had instilled the same bonds between comrades who depended on each other for their lives, so the first thing out of his mouth was a denial rather than a plea for mercy. But was it an act?

"Don't lie to me, Salazar."

"Daria is the one who lied. She tried to shoot you." He coughed. "Against my orders. She's out of control."

"You're full of shit. No one goes rogue in the Villalobos cartel. Not even Daria."

He gave her a knowing look. "Have you ever gone against orders, Detective Cruz?"

Her skin prickled at the implication that he knew of her reputation for defiance. How much intel did the cartel have about her? "We're not talking about me," she said, ignoring the question. "Right now, I'm calling my backup to hit the kill switch and get us out of here." Still sitting on the ground, she pulled the cell phone from her vest pocket and hit the speed dial for Rios.

"You can't get a signal down here," Salazar said. "The building is shielded and soundproofed. We're at the bottom of a cement-lined blast pit four meters deep."

"But Daria called me from inside the pit when ..." The words died on her lips as she glanced at her phone. No signal. Daria had lied about being in the pit when she called.

"About the kill switch ..." Salazar began.

"Another lie?" At his nod, she closed her eyes and groaned.

She considered shouting out to Rios but dismissed the idea. Even if he heard her yells through the soundproofing, he couldn't stop the bomb or pull them out of the pit in time. She wouldn't summon him to his death.

She put her phone away and regarded Salazar. "We're going to die down here, aren't we?" She glanced at the timer. "In ten minutes and fifty-one seconds."

"You don't have to die," Salazar said. "Cut me loose and I'll lift you up. You can grab the edge and climb out."

She studied him for signs of deception but saw none. "You're a killer," she said. "How can I trust anything you say?"

"What could I gain by lying to you?"

She raised a brow. "What could you gain by saving me?"

He spoke with angry resolve. "Daria won't win."

"But you won't win either. Daria might not be the one to kill you, but you'll die all the same."

"I can accept that."

She read the resignation in his eyes. Either Salazar had just delivered an Academy Award–winning performance, or he was telling the truth. She weighed her options. Take the bindings off the most dangerous killer she had ever faced, or let a bomb blow her to smithereens. In the first scenario, she stood a chance at survival. In the second, not so much.

Despite the nagging feeling she might regret her decision, she scooted closer to examine his intricate bindings. She made contingency plans as she sawed back and forth, carefully avoiding his skin.

He shifted his bulk to give her better access. "Thank you. At least I can die on my feet like a man."

She pulled the last of the rope away. "You look pretty rough. Will you be able to lift me?"

His hand snaked out to scoop up the Desert Eagle. "You would be surprised what I can do."

She cursed her stupidity. First Daria, now Salazar. They had both played her. She should've known that, for anyone in the cartel, compassion was a weakness to be exploited. No more. She sized up his injuries to determine where she could strike to inflict the most damage.

Salazar tucked the pistol in the back of his waistband. "Did you think I would shoot you?" He got to his feet and extended a hand to her.

She scowled up at him. This man, a mortal enemy, would decide whether she lived or died. They both knew she could stand without his help. His offer was symbolic. He was asking for her trust.

She reached out to him, forging an alliance she would never have considered possible.

His large hand engulfed hers as he pulled her to her feet. "I am a man of my word."

"Give me the gun."

"I'm keeping my weapon ... for now." Still grasping her hand, he led her toward the pit's curved inner wall.

She turned her wrist to free herself from his grasp. Salazar tightened his fingers, refusing to relinquish his hold. He pivoted to lean his back against the smooth concrete surface and pulled her toward him.

"I will lift you up to climb out," he said. "On one condition."

She swallowed. What price would Salazar demand in exchange for saving her? Throat too tight to speak, she lifted a brow in inquiry.

"Once you get out, I'll toss my gun up to you." He brought her hand to his chest, eased her fingers apart, and pressed her palm over his heart, covering it with his. "And you will shoot me." He squeezed. "Here."

The steady pulse under her hand told her he was at peace with his decision. "No way," she said. "I'm not about to—"

He brought his free hand up to cover her mouth. "I die on my terms, not Daria's."

She pushed against his chest, trying to back away.

His voice grew rough. "And after I'm dead, you will kill Daria."

She froze.

"That's my price. Take it or leave it." He let go of her mouth but kept her hand against his chest.

She tilted her head back to meet his gaze. "You're asking me to murder two people. Your price is too high."

"You were ready to pull the trigger when you thought I'd killed your partner. What's the difference?"

"I laid down my weapon to free you even though I still thought you were the shooter."

"Daria's bomb will tear us to pieces and then she will escape across the border to live in luxury." He softened his tone. "You would sacrifice your life for hers? You would deny your partner justice?"

Her thoughts twisted into dark spirals. Salazar was right. It always came down to choices. He was asking her to choose her own life over Daria's. To choose vengeance for Sam. She thought of her promise to Sam's wife. Of every mistake she'd made leading up to the shooting. She refused to make another. If a pact with her enemy was the price of redemption, she would gladly pay it.

"I accept," she said quietly.

He nodded his agreement and released her hand. She could tell he'd read her perfectly. He knew she would keep her word.

And she knew she had made a deal with the Devil.

41

VERANDA PREPARED HERSELF as Salazar crouched down before her.

"Grab onto my shoulders," he said. When she complied, he laced his fingers together. "Put your right foot here, then step onto my left shoulder when I lift you."

She'd practiced this maneuver before in training, but never with such a high wall to scale. Drawing a breath, she placed her boot into the cup formed by his interlocking fingers. He hoisted her with a grunt and she planted her left foot squarely on his broad shoulder. She leaned forward, bracing herself against the wall, to avoid tipping backward.

He swung her right foot over to place it on his other shoulder. "Are you stable?"

She adjusted her feet. "I'm good."

He straightened to his full height. "You're more than halfway there. Step on my hands."

She glanced down to see his palms facing up. She carefully placed one foot on each open hand.

"On the count of three, I'll boost as high as I can, but you'll have to jump at the same time to grab the edge."

She would fall to the bottom if she didn't make it. "Got it." She bent her knees. "On your count."

He lowered himself again, and she understood that he would push up with his legs while simultaneously launching her with his arms, increasing the amount of lift he could provide. The sheer power such a move required was impressive. She hoped it would be enough.

"*Uno.*"

She raised her hands in preparation to grasp the ledge.

"*Dos.*"

Every muscle and sinew in her body tightened.

"*Tres!*"

She sprang up as his harsh guttural grunt sounded below her. She felt weightless for a moment, then her fingers latched onto the edge of the pit. She used her momentum to swing her feet up.

Her right boot caught, but her left leg dangled down.

"Get your right hand on the ground, Veranda!"

Salazar was correct. If she could get her right arm all the way out onto the flat surface, she would have enough leverage to get her hips up. She also knew that, as a woman, her center of gravity was at her midsection, unlike a man's, which was in his upper torso. She had to focus on maneuvering her legs, but she couldn't do that while clutching the edge with her fingertips.

She flung her arm out, scrabbling for a moment before her splayed hand found purchase. Using her powerful quadriceps, she pushed up with her left foot and pulled with her right. Every muscle protested as she forced her way up and out. She rolled over and lay gasping on her back.

"Veranda!"

The shout from below galvanized her. "Throw me the long piece of rope."

Before cutting him free, she'd examined the rope and discovered a way to salvage a piece about seven feet long. She watched him bend to pick it up.

He wore an unreadable expression when he carried it toward her. "You can't waste any more time." He looked at the display and she followed his gaze. It read 3:26.

"That wasn't our deal," he said, exasperated.

"There's time for me to try."

"I'll give you one chance." He flung the rope up to her. "Then I'm throwing you the gun."

She spotted a thick steel workbench nearby. Flattening herself on her stomach, she tossed one end of the rope over the edge.

"I can reach the end if I stand on my toes," he called up to her. "Ready?"

She hooked her foot around one of the table's legs and gripped the knot at her end of the rope. "Go."

The rope pulled taut. She skidded forward on the dirt floor, dragging the table with her. "How much do you weigh?" she groaned through gritted teeth.

"A hundred kilograms."

Her experience as a narcotics detective told her that was about two hundred twenty pounds. And her experience fighting with him told her he was solid muscle.

She strained to hold the grip in her sweaty hands. Her body slid closer to the edge of the pit. The table dragged behind her. Sweat beaded on her forehead and the rope burned her palms. Salazar was going to pull her and the table down into the hole with him. She got to the edge. Her arms went over. Still she held on. Her chest was on the precipice. A few more seconds and she would go down.

A tremendous weight landed on her back, crushing her into the dirt. Before she could register what was happening, strong arms reached around either side of her head and two large hands gripped the rope in front of hers.

"I don't know why you're trying to save this asshole," Rios said into her ear. "He doesn't deserve it." The *federale*'s weight, added to hers, counterbalanced Salazar's heavy frame and stopped her sliding. After much grunting and cursing, Salazar climbed up to the edge of the pit. As soon as he neared the top, Rios grabbed his wrist to hoist him out.

As Salazar pulled himself up, she canted her head to Rios. "Where is Daria?"

"Saw her run out, figured you rescued her." He panted with strain. "You didn't come out or call, so I decided to check on you."

Salazar used their combined weight to lever himself up to the surface and roll onto his feet. The two men sprinted toward the rear service door with Veranda on their heels. Salazar burst through the door and Rios barreled after him. As she neared the exit, a familiar shape caught her eye. She skidded to a halt, bent down and snatched her Glock from a pile of broken cement where it had landed just inside the threshold.

"Hurry, Veranda!" Rios was outside, holding the door open for her. "There's got to be less than a minute left."

She jammed the gun into her holster and sprinted for the opening. Legs pumping, she blew past Rios before coming to a halt several yards from the building. Winded, she planted her palms on her knees and sucked in gulps of fresh air.

The door shut behind her and she turned to see Rios walking toward her. "What were you doing in there?"

Before she could answer, Salazar pulled the massive Desert Eagle from his waistband, stepped behind Rios, and brought it down on the back of his head.

A sickening crack of metal on bone sounded as the *federale* slumped to the ground.

42

BY THE TIME Veranda's Glock cleared its holster, Salazar had dashed around the corner of the building without a backward glance. She realized Salazar had incapacitated Rios to sidetrack both of them. If he'd killed the *federale* outright, she wouldn't hesitate to pursue him, but gravely injuring him gave Salazar the chance to escape.

She rushed to Rios, dropping to her knees beside him. "Are you okay?"

He remained perfectly still.

Concern mounting, she laid two fingers on the side of his neck and found a pulse. His chest rose and fell. Rios was unconscious, not dead. Yet. She dragged him a safer distance from the building and prepared to stand guard over him until backup arrived. Couldn't be more than a few minutes longer.

A second later, the thunderous discharge of a Desert Eagle pistol coming from the far side of the building changed her plans. She pounded toward the sound, gun in hand, keeping tight to the outer wall until she reached the front side. She skidded to a stop and peeked around the corner.

The Jeep and van were both still parked in the makeshift gravel lot, but she saw no sign of Salazar or Daria. She shifted her gaze to the main entrance and spotted a fresh pool of blood sinking into the dirt. A crimson trail of spatters led inside the building. Salazar hadn't been bleeding before she heard the gunshot. He and Daria both had guns. One of them must have shot the other.

She crept to the door and kicked it open. As it swung inward, a woman's scream shrilled from somewhere inside, ending with an ominous thud.

She raised her weapon and started across the threshold when the Claymore inside the pit detonated. The entire structure reverberated with the shock wave. As she paused to steady herself in the doorway, Salazar charged straight toward her from inside the structure.

Dropping his shoulder, he caught her in the midsection, smashing into her like a battering ram. She flew backward, instinctively tucking her body before she hit the ground outside the building. She let the momentum roll her over, sprang to her feet, and leveled her gun at Salazar.

His pistol was already on target, its sight aimed center mass on her chest. He advanced on her.

She moved back, maintaining the distance between them. He continued forward. She realized he was stalking her like a predator, driving her in the direction of his choosing.

She halted. "What are you doing?"

"Moving us out of the blast zone. Daria wired the building for a secondary explosion. Remember?"

Salazar had bowled her over like a linebacker. He wasn't even breathing hard while she still gasped from the force of the blow. The fact that he also had the presence of mind to relocate their standoff grated on her.

He could have shot her before she recovered from his attack. Instead, he'd allowed her to engage him when he knew reinforcements were coming. She had no idea what he was up to, but decided to keep him talking until backup arrived.

"You threw Daria into the pit, didn't you?"

His cool expression didn't change.

A distant siren's wail drew their attention to the desert floor stretching away from the foot of the mountain. She watched a column of armored vehicles in a cloud of dust speeding along the narrow roadway that led to the building. Still many miles away, they looked like dark blue ants marching in line across a sand box. She knew every SAU team included a member cross-trained as a paramedic who could help Rios.

She turned back to Salazar. "You're under arrest. Lay down your weapon and lace your fingers behind your head."

A deafening explosion shook the earth beneath them as the building erupted into a towering fireball. Salazar flung himself onto her. They crashed to the ground, his large frame shielding her from chunks of debris raining down from the smoke-filled sky.

Salazar had effectively pinned her. From her current position, she had no hope of defeating a two-hundred-twenty-pound trained killer. At a complete disadvantage, she couldn't beat him in a fair fight. The thought brought back her recent sparring match with Jake.

Closing her eyes, she willed her body to relax and breathe shallow intakes, keeping the Glock in her slackened hand. Falling ash drifted around them. She felt Salazar raise his upper torso slightly. Assuming he would check her for injuries, she let her head loll to one side.

He pressed two fingers to her neck for several seconds. Then, with surprising gentleness, he cupped her chin and turned her face up to his. His ear touched her lips as he listened for breathing. She hoped he couldn't feel her heart pounding against his chest as she waited for an opportunity.

"I hope you can hear me, Veranda Cruz."

She felt his hand glide from her chin to the left side of her jaw.

"You have the heart of a wolf." He placed the other hand above her right ear, bracketing her head. "And a code of honor."

She sensed him watching her for a long moment.

"We are more alike than you might think."

When his mouth touched hers, she summoned every ounce of control to prevent a reaction.

"Because you have earned my respect," he murmured against her lips. "Your death will be swift and painless."

Her addled brain processed the last words. With dawning horror, she recognized the positioning of his hands as they gripped either side of her head.

Salazar was about to snap her neck.

Her trick had backfired. The instant she moved, Salazar would give her head a sharp twist. Surprise, speed, and accuracy were her only hope. Her hand tightened around her Glock. Tension flooded through her as she gathered her strength.

She swung her arm up, striking Salazar's temple with the butt of the gun. Without waiting to see if the blow had rendered him unconscious, she jerked her head from his grasp and slammed her weapon against the back of his head.

His body went limp.

First things first. She reached around behind him and slid her hands down until they found the Desert Eagle tucked into his waistband at the small of his back. She tugged it free and hurled it as far as she could.

The approaching sirens blared louder. Her sense of pride urged her to get out from under him and slap cuffs on him before help arrived. Her sense of survival told her he could come around at any moment full of rage and murderous intent.

She shoved him, barely budging his dead weight. "Get. Off. Me." Grunting with each word, pushing with her legs, and adding in a few choice expletives, she managed to roll to the side and push herself up to a seated position. Grateful he was on his stomach, she gave his bicep an experimental squeeze. It would take both hands to pull his beefy arms back to restrain him.

In her experience, heavily muscled men had difficulty putting their wrists together behind them. Elite athletes and body builders required two sets of handcuffs linked together to accommodate the breadth of their upper bodies.

Salazar looked like a two-cuffer. Did she dare put away her gun and get on with it, or should she wait for backup to help her? She regarded his inert form, unable to tell if he was faking. After a long moment, she holstered her Glock.

She'd singlehandedly captured one of the world's most wanted criminals. The only bracelets he would wear were hers. She slung a leg over Salazar's back, straddling him while she ripped open a Velcro pocket on her vest and pulled out two pairs of stainless steel Peerless handcuffs. She sat down on his ass and wedged her knees against his hips. Not that she had any illusion he couldn't buck her off if he woke up, but this position would give her more control.

Sirens drew her gaze to the property entrance a hundred yards away. An unmarked Crown Vic led a phalanx of SWAT vehicles crunching their way down the gravel road. She turned back to her task, intent on getting Salazar in custody before they reached her.

She lifted his left arm and ratcheted the handcuff around his wrist. He groaned when she tugged his right arm back, spurring her to work quickly. She picked up the second set of bracelets and deftly repeated the procedure, slapping one on his right wrist.

He let out a grunt and shifted under her. An open cuff sported a set of jagged steel teeth. With one attached to each wrist, he could slice her into fajita meat. If he got away from her now, he would wield a weapon in each hand.

Heart slamming against her ribs, she grabbed the two open cuffs and yanked them together. Her fingers curled around to ratchet them closed as he jerked his arms apart. The restraints held. Panting with the exertion, she sat up straight, a predator atop her prey.

When Salazar turned his head to regard her from the corner of his eye, she knew it would be her last chance to ask the question uppermost in her mind. "You want me dead, but you used your body to shield me from the blast. Why?"

He gave her a slow smile. "Because you are mine."

She must have hit him too hard. "You're not making sense."

"Were you conscious the whole time?"

She felt compelled to be honest. "I was."

"Then you heard what I said." He hesitated.

She nodded.

"I spoke the truth." His expression hardened into an unreadable mask. "I am going to kill you."

"The hell you are," Lieutenant Diaz interrupted before she could respond. "Because I'm going to kill her first."

43

SOFIA PACHECO TWISTED her hands in her lap, inadvertently rattling her chains. "I'm sorry, sir," she mumbled when Nacho glanced her way.

He frowned. "You don't need to call me 'sir' anymore." Turning back to his driving, he steered the top-heavy van around a curve.

She studied his profile. Slender and boyish, he didn't look like the other men. The coyotes had often leered at her as their lewd remarks peppered her from between brown teeth, their grease-stained hands forming crude gestures punctuated by grunts and laughter as she scurried by. The memory left a shudder in its wake. *Gracias a dios*, Nacho didn't act like them either, because she was in his custody. For now.

"Are we going to Mexico, si—" She blanched. "Um … do you want me to call you Ignacio?"

"Everyone calls me Nacho."

"All right … Nacho. Are we headed for Mexico?"

He nodded. "If our relays are still in place, we can make it past Border Patrol."

The mere mention of her country evoked distorted images that flickered through her mind as if streamed from a weak connection. She remembered making plans with her twin sister for their joint *quinceañera*, helping her *abuela* make tamales for Christmas dinner, lighting a candle to place next to *Papá*'s picture on the *ofrenda* during *Día de los Muertos*. Mexico was home.

And it was hell.

She'd last seen her homeland over a month ago. Like now, Nacho had driven her there from Phoenix. In chains. She'd begged him to let her go home, but he took her to the Villalobos family compound.

El Lobo had punished Sofia for her sister's betrayal. He'd chosen to carry out the sentence personally, beating her with a leather strap and dragging her to the dungeon. She'd starved for days before Nacho convinced Señor Adolfo he needed her to help him hack into the *Policía Federal Ministerial* server. But before he turned her over to Nacho, Hector Villalobos had branded her with the wolf logo. She would never forget his words as he pressed the metal to her flesh. *"You will always be cartel property. My property."*

And now she was going back. Nacho had always treated her with compassion, but he was not in charge, did not control her fate. What if she had to work on *El Lobo*'s computer? His evil black eyes haunted her nightmares. If she saw him again, she would faint from sheer terror. A tear escaped the corner of her eye and she dashed it away.

The clinking chains drew Nacho's gaze. "Do those hurt?"

She shook her head. "I'm okay."

He swallowed audibly. "This is the last border town before we meet our contacts. We need to talk."

She followed his gaze to a cross street ahead of them. A dingy diner, a dilapidated used tire shop, and a gas station with a convenience store comprised the business district. He pulled into an empty lot surrounded by a rusting chain link fence and cut the engine.

The unfamiliar silence unnerved her. Had she made him angry?

Nacho turned in his seat to face her. "Hector Villalobos is closing a deal on a technology firm in Mexico City. In less than a month, he'll have more than sixty full-time computer experts on board. He'll shut the business down and put them to work for the cartel. Who's going to stop him?"

Señorita Daria's words rushed back to her. She began to tremble. With so many other potential hacking experts around, what could she offer the cartel? Until now, her computer skills had kept her from a horrible fate. Those skills would soon be—the trembling turned into shaking as she recalled the word Señorita Daria had taught her—redundant.

"I think you know what this means," Nacho said.

His solemn expression confirmed her worst fears. She had seen the women who were forced to work as sex slaves. Gaunt, haggard creatures who suffered constant abuse, they were kept in brothels until no client wanted them. And then they were disposed of. She'd heard a coyote describe it as "taking out the garbage."

She looked up at Nacho, tried to speak, and burst into tears. As the sobs wracked her body, she felt Nacho's silent watchful gaze.

He waited for her to collect herself before he continued. "Adolfo called me yesterday to get certain ... information. He said *El Lobo* was asking about you."

She hiccupped, took a deep breath, and spoke around the lump in her throat. "What does he want with me?"

The inkling of an answer edged its way in, setting off her internal alarm system. She'd suffered so much in the past few months. Through it all, she'd managed to keep her faith, her dignity, and her self-respect. She feared she would lose all three when she got to the compound.

"Sofia, I need to ask you a question."

Unable to respond, she simply nodded.

Nacho shifted in his seat and cleared his throat. "Are you a virgin?" A red scald crept up from his collar past his bobbing Adam's apple.

She bowed her head. Of course, he would have his doubts. She spent almost every waking minute with Nacho, but there had been times when one of the coyotes had ordered her to work on a personal computer or tablet. And there had been the days she'd spent in the dungeon, subject to the guards. Yet no one had touched her. And Señorita Daria had explained why.

But *El Lobo* would probably want to be certain. Daria had said virgins fetched a high price. Was he planning to auction her off like cattle?

"Sofia."

Her head snapped up at Nacho's impatient prompting. Should she lie? She did a quick calculation and decided she would almost certainly get caught. Better to go with the truth.

"I am a virgin."

The look of relief on Nacho's face stunned her. Was he about to get some sort of bonus for delivering her untouched? Anger followed quickly. She had believed he cared for her. Thought he was different because he'd never physically harmed anyone. Now he had shown her his true colors. And he was every bit as vile as those he served.

Nacho drew a deep breath as if steeling himself. "When we get to the compound, I have to turn you over to Adolfo. He'll have you checked by a doctor and made presentable."

"Presentable?" She pictured livestock on an auction block. "Presentable for what?"

"For *El Lobo*." Nacho looked away. "He'll want you for himself."

The lump that had been in her throat plummeted down to her stomach, sending up a molten blast of bile in its place.

"No." She shook her head. "No. This can't be happening."

Nacho clasped her hand. "I can't let that happen."

"So you're going to take my virginity?" She blinked. "Now?"

"No." He drew the word out, rolling his eyes. "I thought you knew. Thought you could tell. I ... care about you. A lot."

She could barely keep up with the emotions whirling through her. Instead of threatening her, Nacho was ... what? Trying to help her? She couldn't trust the tiny bud of hope that began to unfurl. Not when so many previous hopes had been crushed. Besides, why would he give a shit what happened to her when he clearly had a future with the cartel? Why would he risk it for a scrawny, beaten-down, underfed girl destined for one of the brothels when *El Lobo* tired of her?

"You care," she whispered, "about me?"

"I know what's in store for you if you go back to the compound." He shook his head. "You're so pretty, so delicate, so sweet." Sorrow filled his eyes. "You won't survive."

Her face flamed. "You think I'm pretty?"

He pulled her into his arms. "I think I've fallen in love with you, Sofia Pacheco." He kissed the top of her head. "But I'm a wanted fugitive and—oh yeah—I work for a ruthless killer who wants you for himself." He gave her a lopsided smile. "No happily ever after for us."

"You could leave the cartel," she said.

He stroked her matted hair. "Then I would be on the run from the law *and* the cartel. I wouldn't last a week. My best hope would be a US jail cell." He snorted. "No thanks."

She leaned against him quietly, aware he spoke the truth.

After holding her a long moment, he broke the embrace. "See that gas station?" He took out the key to her manacles as she nodded. "I'm going to pull in to top off the tank." He laid the key on the console. "Then I'm going to the bathroom in the back and you're going to escape."

"Nacho, they'll kill you if you come back without me. I know too much about their business."

"You don't know as much as you think. I've limited you to hacking. I've never let you work on Villalobos business accounts or handle banking transactions. I'll take my beating. It'll be worth it."

The young man who had been her captor had become her savior. She couldn't bear the idea of him suffering for helping her.

Anguish raised her voice to a shrill shreak. "They won't beat you, they'll butcher you!"

"I've made up my mind. If you won't cooperate, I'll leave you at the gas station unconscious." He slid his knuckles along her cheek. "I'd rather not."

"I'm scared for you, Nacho."

"I only ask one thing." His eyes bored into hers. "When the cops interview you, stick with the story that you escaped. That's why I'm having you go through the motions. Your story will stand up to questioning if you can remember what you actually did rather than try to make shit up." He framed her face with his hands. "*El Lobo* has spies everywhere. If he finds out I let you go, he'll go out of his way to make my death memorable as an example to the others." He brushed her tears away with his thumbs. "This has to stay between us. You cannot tell a single soul. Not even your mother or your sister. No one, understand? My life depends on it."

Her heart broke. "No one can ever know that you saved my life? That you are a good man?"

"I chose this life, *bonita*. This is the price I must pay." A single tear coursed down his cheek as he brought her lips to his for a tender kiss.

44

VERANDA GAVE UP on sleep. Lying awake most of the night in Chuy's bed, her fitful bouts of slumber had all featured Sam crumpling to the ground in slow motion, blood seeping into the dusty earth beneath him.

She tumbled out of bed and staggered to the shower. The hot water failed to wash away images from the day before. She had to see Sam for herself.

Spurred into action by a clear goal, she toweled off and made her way to the stackable washer and dryer tucked behind a partition in the corner. Her hands found the black BDUs and fitted T-shirt she'd stuffed in before flopping onto the bed hours earlier. Working on autopilot, she slid on her clothes and stuffed her feet into scuffed black boots. After pausing to slurp down a K-cup's worth of liquid stimulant, she steered Chuy's custom Harley Fat Boy out of the garage. Still without a city car, her cousin's motorcycle was her only transportation. And her only means of escaping Lieutenant Diaz.

Bright rays of morning sunlight slanted through bent venetian blinds, suffusing the hospital's waiting area with a golden glow. Her head, her body, and her heart ached. Grumbling to herself, Veranda slouched deeper into the worn fabric of the visitor's room chair and checked the wall clock again. Less than a minute until visiting hours began at eight. She recognized her Homicide squad's voices coming from a corridor on her left as they meandered in her direction, and prayed Diaz wasn't with them.

She'd been at Phoenix General for half an hour when her Homicide team arrived. One of the nurses had confirmed what Diaz had told her late last night. Sam had pulled through surgery and his condition had been upgraded to serious but stable.

"There you are," Marci said, interrupting her reverie. "We've all been trying to reach you. Why aren't you taking calls?" The rest of the squad filed in behind Marci, each face registering surprise at her presence.

"I muted my cell last night to get some sleep," she said, getting to her feet. "Not that it worked." Her gaze drifted to the floor. "Must've forgot to turn it back on this morning."

She'd silenced her phone to avoid her boss, but no one called her on the lie. Anxious to change the topic, she asked about the investigation.

"Like you said, I've been out of touch all morning. What's going on at the pit building?"

"Still an active scene," Marci said. "Agent Ortiz is there with the local ATF Field Office working with our bomb squad. They're checking for booby traps, chemicals, or stockpiled explosives. What's left of the structure is unstable, so they're taking it slow."

"How about Agent Rios?"

Everyone turned to Doc, who didn't disappoint. "Agent Rios sustained a linear skull fracture," he said, lifting his hand in a placating gesture at their looks of alarm. "He got off easy. That'll heal on its own in about six weeks. No subdural hematoma or other complications. No need for surgery and the prognosis is excellent. He'll be released tomorrow. The ER doc wants him to wait a couple of days before he gets on an airplane though."

For the first time in days, Veranda laughed. "So, Diaz still has a roomie."

Tony looked perplexed. "I don't get it."

Marci heaved the world-weary sigh of a detective whose partner tried her patience constantly. No one was fooled. Squabbling was their default setting. Neither would have it any other way.

Marci spoke slowly, enunciating each word. "It's funny because they can't stand each other." She turned back to Veranda. "Maybe they'll bond over a tub of Ben and Jerry's while they watch *telenovelas*."

Tony put his hands on his hips. "That's just wrong."

"You're right, it's not fair." Marci nodded vehemently. "But there isn't room for all three of you on that couch, Tony. You guys are all pretty big." She widened her eyes. "I know. Maybe you can take the *federale*'s spot on the sofa when he leaves town. I don't know what the lieutenant likes, but I can tell you're a Chunky Monkey guy."

It felt good to share a lighthearted moment. "Thanks," she said to Marci. "I needed something to smile about."

Frank, usually silent, spoke for the first time. "You can smile about Sofia Pacheco." He waited a beat, then added, "She's been found alive."

"Where?" Veranda sucked in a breath. "Is she okay?"

"The owner of a gas station near the border found her yesterday afternoon," Frank said. "She seems to be doing well under the circumstances. Apparently, she managed to escape from Nacho's van when he stopped for gas. She got loose while he was in the men's room."

Her heart soared. She'd heard Sofia wasn't there when SAU raided the cartel's armory base. Everyone had concluded Nacho had taken her to Mexico. Searches along the borders had come up dry.

"One of our victim specialists is bringing her here." Frank indicated the hospital around them. "She'll get medical treatment and they'll take her statement."

Veranda had met Sofia's mother and twin sister but had never seen her in person. "Has her family been notified?"

"They're flying in to take her back to Mexico," Frank said.

Marci grimaced. "I wouldn't want to be Nacho right now."

"I don't think Hector will kill him," Veranda said. "He's too valuable, especially with Daria and Salazar out of the game."

Tony eyed her. "We've got questions for you too. What did you do to the lieu yesterday?" Having started his career on the NYPD, Tony still peppered in some of their slang. "Diaz went *loco* after your phone call." Tony darted a glance over his shoulder, leaned in, and lowered his voice. "Did you hang up on him?"

Where to start? Diaz had showed up at the pit building in a towering rage. After yanking her off Salazar, he'd scanned her from head to toe, asking if she was okay three separate times. She didn't want to discuss it with her squad. Or anyone. Ever.

The sound of medical clogs on hospital-grade vinyl tile saved her from making an excuse not to answer, driving thoughts of her supervisor into the dark recesses of her mind.

A middle-aged woman whose black hair and dark skin contrasted with her neon green scrubs smiled at them. "Eight o'clock on the dot and he's asking for his squad." Her sweeping glance encompassed the entire group. "But only five minutes. He needs rest."

Mumbling her thanks, Veranda blew past the nurse and headed for the corridor, anxious to lay eyes on her partner. She pushed through the door to the private room, wrinkling her nose at the antiseptic smell. Her gaze followed the sound of beeping monitors to settle on Sam. He sat upright with his back propped against two pillows. His normally ruddy complexion had paled, but his piercing gray eyes were sharp as they met hers.

"Heard you've been busy," he said.

The familiar timbre of his deep voice cracked the dam holding her emotions in check. She rushed to the bedside and grasped both of his hands. Careful of the tubes, she bent down and kissed his cheek. Her squad mates were right behind her, offering greetings as they gathered around the bed.

Veranda drew in a steadying breath and composed herself. "It's good to see you, Sam."

She knew her words fell ridiculously short. Even if she hadn't been surrounded by her fellow officers, wringing her hands and going on about how frightened she'd been at the prospect of losing him wasn't her way.

Sam was old school, where cops weren't supposed to gush to their partners about their innermost feelings, so his response was in kind.

"Good to be seen."

Standing at the foot of the bed, Marci gently placed a hand on the white blanket covering his feet. "How do you feel?"

Before Sam could make up his mind, Doc spoke. "Some of the doctors talked to me off the record. Good news is you'll make a full recovery. Bad news, you'll have residual discomfort for weeks throughout your thoracic area. Also, we'll have to watch you for signs of infection. If you notice any—"

Marci cut him off before he could start listing symptoms. "I'm sure he'll be fine."

Sam groaned. "Last time I got shot, they released me the next day. Now they want to keep me for five days."

"They're not called cop-killer rounds for nothing," Frank said. "And you're lucky you took the hit from the Glock and not the fifty-cal."

Sam's mustache twitched. "Remind me to buy a lottery ticket." He raised a bushy black brow at Veranda. "They told me what you did."

She waved a dismissive hand. "I improvised."

"Tell us more about this improvised plan of yours," Marci said, grinning. "The little I heard sounded completely nuts."

"I'm surprised our lieutenant isn't sharing this room with me," Sam said. "I'm sure you gave him a coronary."

Doc nodded, the fluorescent lights glinting from his glasses. "Judging by his florid coloration and the visible presence of veins in his neck and temple areas, I would say his blood pressure was close to stroke range when he left here yesterday."

She grimaced at the memory. "He was worse by the time he got to me. You should've seen him throwing his weight around like an angry bull, barking orders at everyone in sight. And for a minute I thought he was going to take off Salazar's cuffs and go a few rounds."

"Damn," Tony said, drawing the word out as only a Brooklyn-ite could. "Wouldn't wanna be you right now."

"He ordered me to get Daria's bite wounds cleaned and checked." She held up her fingers, showing off three Band-Aids. "Tried to explain myself while he drove me to the hospital yesterday, but he just gave me a death stare until I stopped talking."

"Damn," Tony repeated.

"After my debriefing last night, he took me to Chuy's apartment. Told me he'd come by this morning to give me a ride to PSB." She shrugged. "Oops. Guess I forgot."

She would put off her trip to the Professional Standards Bureau as long as possible. Dealing with internal affairs always put her on edge, and this time she had a lot to answer for.

Tony gave her a knowing look. "Like you forgot to take your phone off mute?"

"Something like that." She quickly changed the subject. "Does anyone have an update on Salazar?" Veranda assumed Doc would have pumped his hospital contacts for info on everybody.

Doc pushed his glasses up. "Salazar told the ER doc that a pile of cement chunks fell on him before he was pushed into a twelve-foot-deep hole, and then somebody gave him a scalp massage with a Glock." He flicked a glance at Veranda. "Nobody believed him until they saw the radiographs. He sustained multiple contusions to his head consistent with his statement, but only suffered a mild concussion. The radiologist said his skull must be made of titanium and his pain threshold has got to be high enough to enter orbit."

"Is he still here?" She recalled Diaz ordering Salazar transported to Phoenix General under heavy guard.

"In the lock-down ward on the fifth floor," Doc said. "They're keeping him for observation. When the treating physician signs off, he'll go to jail."

"Speaking of Salazar's injuries," Tony said, eyeing Veranda. "I saw photos of him taken in the ER. Are those claw marks on his face your handiwork?"

She snorted. "Daria's the scratching and biting type. I'm the ass-kicking and pistol-whipping type."

A broad grin lit Sam's face. "Nothing but respect."

Marci leaned forward to bump Veranda's fist. "Wish I could've gotten in on that."

"Stop it," Tony said. "You two are gettin' me all hot."

The door creaked open. Sam's wife walked in, red-rimmed eyes surrounded by dark circles bearing witness to her bedside vigil the previous night. The laughter in the room evaporated like raindrops in the desert.

In the deafening silence that followed, Sarah spotted Veranda among the group and headed toward her. Veranda watched her in wary silence, still clutching one of Sam's hands.

Sarah drew in a deep breath, apparently composing herself. "Sam talked to me earlier this morning when he woke up. He explained what really happened yesterday." She smiled down at Sam, who gave Veranda's hand a reassuring squeeze. "He said you pushed him aside and stepped in front of him to return fire," Sarah continued, returning her gaze to Veranda. "You saved his life."

"I just did what—" Veranda began.

"Lieutenant Diaz also spoke to me," Sarah said, lifting her fingers to Veranda's cheek. "You risked your life to protect my husband." Her eyes grew moist. "And in return, I slapped your face and questioned your loyalty." She pulled Veranda into a tight hug. "I was so scared for Sam, so angry he'd been shot." She straightened, tears streaming from her pleading eyes. "Can you ever forgive me?"

"There's nothing to forgive." Veranda's free hand found Sarah's, and she became the middle link in a human chain, bonded to Sam and his wife.

"I told you, Sarah," Sam said, his voice was huskier than usual. "Veranda and I have each other's backs."

Doc took off his glasses and scrubbed his eyes with his knuckles. "This hospital air aggravates my allergies. They should put HEPA filters in every room."

Veranda shared a knowing look with the rest of the squad as the door squeaked again.

The nurse poked her head in the room. "Time's up. Everyone out except Mrs. Stark."

Veranda released her grip and joined the others shuffling toward the door.

"Hold up a minute," Sam called out to her, apparently interested in a private conversation.

"Go ahead," she said to the squad. "I'll catch up later."

When the door closed, he beckoned her closer. "Sarah wanted to give you something." He nodded to his wife, who reached into her purse and pulled out a glossy black box that fit in her palm. "This was Sam's."

Veranda pulled the lid off. "I can't accept this. It's too valuable." She lifted a silver St. Michael pendant dangling from a thick chain.

"Sam hasn't worn it in years," Sarah said. "I bought him a gold one when he made Homicide. You should have it."

She turned the medallion over. "Thank you. It's beautiful."

Sarah dabbed at her tears with a tissue from the box on Sam's bed tray. "Come and visit us while Sam's home recuperating."

"I will," she said, meaning it. She turned and walked through the door.

Lieutenant Diaz waited in the corridor with his arms crossed. He glared down at her like a scowling gargoyle perched on a cathedral. "You've been avoiding me."

45

VERANDA FACED DIAZ, raising her hands as if her outstretched palms could stave off the tidal wave of anger about to break over her. "I forgot you were coming to pick me up this morning."

Diaz gave her a derisive snort. "Save it, Detective." He spun on his heel and marched down the corridor. "Let's go."

"Professional Standards Bureau?" She fell into step beside him.

"You're forty-five minutes late for your appointment." He gestured to a sign on the wall with directions to the various hospital departments. "I'm parked by the ER."

Maybe he thought she had no transportation since he hadn't replaced her fleet car. "I've got my own ride. I can get to PSB." She had no desire to get in a car with Diaz, especially when he was in such a foul mood.

"You're coming with me. I'll drive you back here afterward." His tone brooked no argument.

This was obviously punishment for her escape this morning. The upcoming interview would be the mental equivalent of a body cavity search. She stifled an exasperated sigh and lengthened her strides to keep up as he strode along the maze of corridors leading to the ER exit.

When they passed through the revolving door, she peered up at Diaz. His jaw line sported an uncustomary layer of dark stubble and his thick black hair looked like he'd dragged his hands through it. A lot. He obviously hadn't gotten any more sleep than she had.

In the parking lot, she peeled off to stand by his car's front passenger door. They'd walked through the hospital in awkward silence. Still feeling the weight of his disapproval, she tried to redirect his anger toward a more appropriate target.

She met his gaze across the roof of the car. "Doc said Salazar's on lockdown upstairs waiting for medical clearance to leave."

Diaz glanced up at the rows of windows striping the hospital's exterior, frowning as if he could see into Salazar's fifth-floor room. "That's turning into a diplomatic nightmare." He pressed the key fob.

After the chirp, she opened her door and angled into the front passenger's seat.

"The Mexican government requested expedited extradition," Diaz said, clicking his seatbelt closed. "Salazar's not going to contest it."

She pictured a battalion of Armani-suited cartel lawyers laying siege on the courthouse like an invading army. Salazar would have no reason to fight to stay in the US, despite the outstanding murder warrants in his home country. He could take his chances on trial there and, even if he lost, Mexico had no death penalty.

"But we're going to charge him with murdering Daria, here in the States, right?" she said. "That takes precedence."

"They haven't recovered Daria's remains." Diaz started the car and backed out. "We don't have a homicide warrant yet."

"Only because they're still going through the wreckage. They'll find her body sooner or later."

Diaz had the air of a doctor about to deliver a bad diagnosis. "And the county attorney isn't likely to charge him even when we do." He motioned her to let him finish when she leaned forward in her seat to argue. "Salazar's only giving minimal answers, but he denies throwing Daria into the pit. According to your statement, you never actually saw him do it and he never admitted it to you." He flicked a glance at her. "He claims Daria slipped and fell in."

"Total bullshit." She couldn't believe Salazar was going to use the he-said, she-said defense. And worse, it might work.

Diaz returned his gaze to the road. "Salazar wasn't at their armory building when SAU hit it, and the coyotes we captured aren't talking. The only charges we can bring are the assaults on you and Rios. We're holding him on a prior outstanding abduction warrant right now. Interpol's sending us paperwork from six countries and counting."

She thought about how many people Salazar had assassinated on *El Lobo*'s orders. Public officials, private citizens, and rival criminal leaders across Central and South America.

"So, he does his time here, then makes the rounds to the countries who want him for murder. He'll spend the rest of his life bouncing from one prison to another." She shrugged. "I don't see the problem."

"Except that the Mexicans want him first," he said, maneuvering around a slow-moving cement mixer. "As in, ahead of us."

"That's not the way it works." Agitated, she was back to leaning forward in her seat. "He's in our custody. We get the first bite."

Diaz waved away her comment. "This has gone all the way to *Los Pinos*."

She knew *Los Pinos*, The Pines, was the Mexican equivalent of the White House. The current resident, *Presidente* Miguel Bustamante, was in the final year of his six-year-term. Since Mexican presidents only serve one term, Bustamante wasn't concerned about reelection. He wanted his place in history. Pundits hotly debated whether his campaign pledge to end the reign of terror brought on by the cartels had been fulfilled.

The unexpected connection piqued her interest. "Why does Bustamante care about Salazar?"

"The Villalobos cartel is the largest criminal organization in the country. Salazar is the most feared member of the cartel besides *El Lobo* himself. Bustamante wants to parade Salazar in leg irons to show he's not afraid to take on the biggest bully in the school yard." Diaz stopped at a traffic light. "Remember our conversation with Chuy at Lorena's house?"

"Baz wants to hire my cousin for some sort of op in Mexico City," she said. "And we all thought the timing could be right for the summit meeting between POTUS and Bustamante."

"I did some checking. The meeting is scheduled to happen in two months. They'll renegotiate tariffs and trade agreements, so everything's on the table."

Understanding dawned. "Bustamante thinks the mother-of-all-perp-walks will jack up his popularity. Increase his home field advantage."

The light changed, and Diaz started forward again. "Agent Flag has been in constant contact with the State Department since we took Salazar in. POTUS wants leverage and Bustamante wants Salazar, so we've been ordered to stand by."

"I don't believe this is happening."

He pulled into a weed-choked gravel parking lot in front of an abandoned storefront covered in peeling paint. As she registered that he'd taken a detour on the way to PSB, the tires crunched to a stop under the shade of a palo verde.

He cut the engine and canted his large frame toward her. "What I don't believe is that watered-down story you told in your debriefing last night."

She cursed herself for getting in the car with him where he could corner her. Raising her defenses, she pinned him with an indignant glare. "I answered every question."

"You left things out." He rested his left arm on the steering wheel, his right on the seat back. "You know it. And I know it."

She had no trouble interpreting his body language. He faced her full-on, giving the appearance of openness while taking up more space in the confines of the car. He wanted answers and he would pressure her to get them.

Responding with her own nonverbal signal, she crossed her arms. "About what?"

He studied her reaction when he spoke. "Salazar."

She conjured a confused expression to hide her growing unease. She'd only left one detail out of her after-action debriefing last night. Both involved Salazar. She briefly pressed her eyes closed, remembering her deal with the devil. But Diaz couldn't possibly know about that. Could he?

Still maintaining her puzzled expression, she probed. "Exactly what do you think I didn't report, Lieutenant?"

"You said he pushed you out of the pit," Diaz began, raising his index finger. "Knocked you clear of the building before it exploded"—a second finger went up—"and used his body to shield yours from falling debris." He wiggled three fingers in the air. "A professional killer saved your life three times." His eyes narrowed. "Why?"

No one had been present when she'd made the pact with Salazar. A confession that he'd demanded she kill Daria in exchange for saving her life would work against him. If Salazar hadn't talked, then Diaz was fishing.

She uncrossed her arms to shove his hand away. "Are you accusing me of something, Lieutenant?"

Dropping all pretense at civility, Diaz got up in her face. "Something's going on between you and Salazar." His nostrils flared. "Out with it!"

He was goading her. An interrogation tactic she'd used on suspects. "What makes you say—"

"He put his filthy mouth on yours!"

Absolute silence engulfed the car for several heartbeats.

Diaz pressed his advantage. "I left the hospital right after you hung up on me yesterday. After calling SAU, I intercepted them on the way. Sergeant Grigg wasn't happy about it, but I drove an unmarked fleet car in front of the SAU vehicles. When I got close, I saw Salazar lying on top of you. According to your statement, you pretended to be unconscious to get the drop on him, but you never explained what he did."

Diaz had targeted her like a guided missile. He'd launched his attack, and she had little hope of diverting him, but she gave it a try. "The point is that I arrested him. That's why he's in custody right now."

"You didn't answer my question."

"I didn't hear one."

"Did Salazar's lips touch yours or didn't they?"

She flung her hands up in frustration. "What difference does it make? He tried to kill me."

"That's a yes." Diaz rendered his verdict with the finality of a judge, then jabbed a finger at her. "There's more you're not saying. When we get to PSB, you'd better be prepared to explain why Salazar is acting like you're his ... his ..."

"Like I'm his what?" The words echoed in her ear, jarring loose a fragment of memory.

She stared at Diaz. Her jaw slackened as realization seeped in.

"You just figured something out." He made it a statement.

Her hand flew to her mouth. "Something Salazar said." She spoke through her fingers. "After I arrested him, I asked him why he'd protected me. He said, 'Because you're mine.'"

"He thinks you're his *mujer*?" Diaz said, using the Spanish word for woman.

Her hackles went up. She and Diaz shared the same cultural background. When a man referred to a female as his *mujer*, it implied deep, intimate, protective feelings for her. Mexican men often introduced their wives this way in casual settings, rather than the more formal *esposa* or *señora*. Diaz's use of the term implied that Salazar harbored intense possessive feelings for her.

"No, not like that," she said, her tone sharp enough to cut. "We have the same father! You and Commander Webster were the ones who came up with the theory that *El Lobo* made executing me a requirement for his replacement. If you two are right, Salazar couldn't let me die in the blast—or as a result of it—because, technically, I would be Daria's kill, not his."

Diaz closed his eyes, tilted his head back, and released a long slow breath. "He needed to keep you alive so he could take credit for your death."

"The media would have reported that I died in the explosion. He wouldn't get a do-over."

Apparently swayed by her logic, Diaz relented. "I'm sure it made perfect sense to Salazar's twisted mind."

Twisted, indeed. "Now it's my turn." Borrowing Diaz's tactics, she edged closer and leaned into his personal space. "I saw you whisper in Salazar's ear while you escorted him to the transport vehicle. When he muttered something back, you tweaked his cuffs. What did you two say to each other?"

"That's between us." He regarded her. "I will tell you that his parting words to you were a promise. He's not going to stop."

She rolled her eyes. "He's in custody. He can't get to me."

Diaz wasn't deterred. "Which will infuriate *El Lobo* even more. Three of his children are dead. His organization is like a ship taking on water. He's scrambling to plug the holes while you've sidelined his most valuable asset." He scrubbed a hand over his stubbled chin. "He's going to come after you like never before."

She considered the prospect of Hector's wrath. "I'm not afraid of him."

"Cartels are brought down by dozens of agents in multiple countries," he said, paying back her previous exasperation in full. "It takes years of meticulous planning. You are one police officer. Let Flag and Ortiz and the *federales* handle it."

She looked at him in silence.

He opened his mouth, then closed it. His eyes softened as his lips parted again. He hesitated, as if about to say something against his better judgment. "When I saw Salazar on top of you and you weren't moving, I thought … I thought you were dead. I never want to feel that way again." He gripped her arm. "Please, Veranda, stay out of this."

Her gaze traveled down to his fingers clutching her forearm. "Take your hand off me, Lieutenant."

He didn't move.

She had an overwhelming sense of déjà vu. Five days ago, she'd latched onto Diaz to keep him out of the storage unit. Now he was doing the same to keep her out of her father's crosshairs. If Diaz believed she could just walk away, he didn't know her at all.

She owed her lieutenant the truth. "I can't avoid this any more than *El Lobo* can."

Diaz reacted as if she'd doused him with a bucket of ice water. A fleeting grimace of pain passed over his face before he recovered, reverting to management mode.

"Thank you, Detective. I know what I have to do now." The temperature in the car seemed to plummet. "Your war with the cartel has to stop. In the past, you've had too much leeway. That's about to end."

His grim determination caught her off guard. "How?"

"There will be an investigation into all of your actions," he said. "Followed by a Disciplinary Review Board."

Like their confrontation at the storage unit, this showdown had ended in an explosion. This one, however, had a delayed detonation. Diaz's comment meant her violations of departmental policy were a foregone conclusion. A DRB only convened when the internal investigation sustained allegations against the officer. Its function was to mete out discipline.

"You lost control of your department-issued weapon," he continued. "As a result, a fellow detective was shot. Your cell phone was stolen, providing information allowing a criminal organization to hack into our server. Again."

"But we already discussed that, I was the victim of a crime and—"

He plowed on despite her objection. "The Board will also consider the more serious allegation of disobeying a direct order given by a superior officer."

Her temper flared. "That's not the point."

Diaz reddened. "That's the whole fucking point!"

She felt as if an entire herd of buffalo was thundering straight at her, but she was trapped in a canyon with no way out.

Drawing in a long breath, Diaz composed himself. "I will serve as your adversary and provide testimony against you at the DRB."

Her supervisor would become her prosecutor. Despite everything he knew about the case. About her. Shock warred with hurt, choking off her ability to speak.

All traces of warmth and compassion were gone when Diaz looked down at her. "You'll be held accountable for your actions and forced to stop investigating the cartel. Period." He turned away from her and gripped the steering wheel. "Salazar promised to kill you. I promise to protect you, even if it means taking your badge."

46

Villalobos family compound, Mexico

ADOLFO OPENED HEAVY double doors. Unsure what to expect, he peered inside his father's expansive office.

Hector Villalobos had been secretive all morning. An hour earlier, Adolfo had rapped his knuckles against the polished wood. His father had opened the door, a frown creasing his brow. Before Adolfo could speak, the secure satellite phone signaled an incoming call. Hector had shoved him outside with orders to wait until he was invited in.

Now his father greeted his return with a triumphant expression, gesturing to the ornate mahogany conference table and speaking in his customary elegant Spanish. "Take your seat."

As patriarch and pack leader, *El Lobo* claimed the chair at the head of the rectangular table. Each of his offspring had assigned seats along either side.

As Adolfo padded across the thick Persian rug, his gaze swept the table, drinking in the visual representation of his success. He hid his pleasure at the sight of empty chairs where Bartolo, Carlos, Daria, and Salazar would have been. He was the last man standing. He had won.

His father sank into his plush leather seat. "What have I always taught you about adversity, *mi'jo?*"

Adolfo began to bounce his foot repeatedly. He'd listened to enough of his father's dramatic speeches to recognize one on the launch pad. Grateful Hector hadn't chosen a clear glass tabletop, he crossed his legs to stop his wayward foot and answered by rote. "A true leader turns adversity to his advantage."

Hector offered Adolfo a rare smile. "I have secured the Rook."

That explained the mysterious phone call. Years of cautious overtures had finally paid off. *El Lobo* had scored a particularly well-placed inside man in law enforcement. He wondered if his father would reveal the Rook's identity at last.

"Congratulations." He returned the smile. "I'm sure he will serve us well." He'd deliberately used the Spanish conjugation for *we*, emphasizing his new place as second-in-command. He may have won by default, but he'd take a victory in any color package.

"Forget the Rook. I'll get to him later." Hector stroked the streak of silver hair that ran down the center of his goatee. "Now, we discuss Nacho. What has he told you?"

His father had put him in charge of interrogating their computer expert. A task made more difficult because of his fondness for Nacho. As CFO, Adolfo needed someone with computer skills. Two years ago, he'd hired a tech firm to trace an unauthorized withdrawal from one of the accounts. When an impressive number of false trails eventually led to a teenager, Adolfo recruited him. Others prized Nacho's hacking, but Adolfo saw his potential as a future top lieutenant in the organization. He hoped this mistake hadn't been a fatal one for his protégé.

"Nacho told me Daria went rogue. When Salazar put her in chains, she shanked the coyote assigned to watch her and escaped before the police surrounded the armory. Salazar ordered Nacho to take Sofia Pacheco here and went after Daria himself. He doesn't know what happened to them after that."

"I had plans for that girl." The lines in Hector's face deepened with his scowl. "Elaborate plans."

He'd seen the aftermath of *El Lobo*'s "plans" with young girls. Sofia had no idea how fortunate she was. Suppressing a shudder, Adolfo hurried to do damage control.

"Nacho assured me she has no knowledge of, or access to, any of our accounts or other sensitive information. He only used her for hacking. When the police interview her, they'll only learn how to strengthen their firewalls. Nothing about our operation."

Hector didn't appear mollified. "You might believe his story about the girl's escape, but I do not. He must be disciplined as an example to the others."

"Nacho's in the dungeon." Adolfo spoke quickly. "I've told him he will only have a daily ration of water and nothing else for an entire week." He hoped the punishment would be enough to appease his father.

"His loyalty must be reinforced."

Dread rushed through Adolfo as he waited for his father's verdict.

Hector pronounced his sentence with the casual indifference of a traffic court judge dealing with a jaywalker. "You will use the branding iron to sear our logo directly over Nacho's tattoo. I will supervise." His dark eyes glinted with malice. "And if you pass out this time, Adolfo, you will awaken to the heat of the iron on your own chest."

"Yes, sir." His face flamed with humiliation. He'd ordered many brandings but couldn't carry out the torture himself. Between the shrieks of agony, the scent of burning flesh, and the sight of charred skin, his overwrought brain shut down. More than once, he woke up to the jeers of his siblings and the disapproving glances of his men. Coming out of his reverie, he realized his father had changed the subject and struggled to catch up.

"… a full report from my lead counsel this morning," Hector was saying. "Salazar told him Veranda Cruz is lying. She is the one who pushed Daria into the blast pit just before it detonated. He tried to save Daria when Cruz struck him in the back of his head with her gun. She will pay for that."

He kept his reservations about Salazar's account to himself. "Did the Phoenix legal team provide an update?"

"Salazar has an extradition hearing tomorrow. I don't understand the details, but the lead attorney says the process will take at least six weeks if everything goes smoothly."

He felt his brows climb up his forehead. "Salazar could be in Mexico in six weeks?"

Hector pointed at the floor. "And he will be standing right here less than twenty-four hours after that."

Adolfo clenched his fists as if they could hold onto his fading dreams. He had won. No one else was left. He would be his father's true heir. Except that Hector Villalobos was planning to break his bastard child out of prison to give him what was rightfully Adolfo's. He stared straight ahead in numb disbelief as his father continued.

"The Rook's first assignment is to provide an opportunity for Salazar to escape once they're in Mexico City."

Aware he should say something, he cleared his parched throat. "How will you get word to Salazar?"

Hector looked at him like he was an idiot. "The attorneys have already told Salazar about the plan. He'll be ready when the time comes."

A loud tone interrupted the awkward silence that followed his father's words. Adolfo recognized the incoming call signal from the secure satellite phone. Hector leaned forward to press the intercom on the table.

A male voice penetrated the muffled static in the background. "Señor Villalobos?"

"I am with Adolfo. It's time you two met."

Adolfo tensed. This must be the Rook. He wondered why his father didn't activate the view screen.

"I'm sure we'll have a chance to shake hands at some point." The Rook's tone dismissed Adolfo, then he moved on to more important matters. "As we discussed earlier, I'll stay in Phoenix for the extradition hearings. The politicos are happy to have my regular reports, especially when the two presidents are asking for constant updates." He spoke like someone giving a report to a superior.

Hector's response reinforced their respective roles. "Do you foresee any problems?"

"No, sir. Bustamante has the upper hand since POTUS wants concessions. He'll pay on the back end though."

Clearly, this man had access to sensitive information from the highest offices in both countries. Adolfo detected an unfamiliar accent in the Rook's Spanish. It wasn't the intonation of an American who had learned Spanish in school either. He sounded like a native speaker, but from where?

"I've finally found something Bustamante and I agree on," Hector said. "He wants Salazar back in Mexico as badly as I do, but for different reasons." He chuckled. "I will enjoy watching Bustamante squirm at his own press conference when his prize bull gets out of the pen."

Apparently too excited to remain seated, Hector got to his feet and began pacing. He seemed to be thinking out loud. "After I have Salazar back, I will deal with Veranda Cruz."

"What do you have in mind?" the Rook asked.

Adolfo thought it was a bold question for a new subordinate, but Hector didn't take exception. In fact, he seemed eager to share.

Hector spun to look at the intercom as if it were the Rook sitting on the table. "In the past, I have sent others after her. This time, she will come to me. Let's see how long she survives without an entire police department behind her."

Adolfo couldn't hide his shock. "You're going to drag an American police officer here?"

"No," Hector said. "Salazar is. Which is why I must get him freed before I deal with her." He gave Adolfo an enigmatic smile. "You have a role to play as well."

Adolfo's hands, still concealed under the table, twisted together. None of his father's schemes ever went well for him. He was certain this one would not break with tradition.

Eyes narrowed, Hector resumed pacing. "Detective Cruz has a debt to settle. She will stay in my dungeon. Receive my sentence. Face my justice."

Adolfo wondered if the Rook was familiar with *El Lobo*'s over-blown speeches or if he understood their significance. The more agitated Hector became, the more dramatic the verbiage. In a man who didn't express strong emotions, this was a rare tell.

He gazed at the intercom, thinking about the man it concealed, and decided to prod the Rook. "Why are you helping us?"

"Your father and I have an understanding," the Rook said without hesitation. "I don't need your *chavos*."

Adolfo tilted his head. "You don't need my ... boys?"

The speaker crackled with laughter. "My slang is obviously different from yours," the Rook said. "I mean money. I don't need your money."

Adolfo exchanged a look with his father, who seemed amused by the confusion. He turned back to the table. "To me, *chavos* is a street word for boys. Your Spanish isn't Mexican. Where is your accent from?"

Hector strode back to the table. "Stand by while I connect your video feed." He pushed a button and the image of a man standing in front of a plain white wall filled the flat screen.

Adolfo's first sight of the Rook caught him off guard.

The Rook smiled at his surprise. "Not what you expected?"

Hector stood next to Adolfo, admiring his newest acquisition. "I've never explained why I call him the Rook."

"I thought it was because you love chess, and he's an important piece."

"True, but also because of his name."

Adolfo struggled to make the connection. Spanish-speaking players call the rook *el torre,* the tower. He shook his head, unable to work it out.

The man on the screen laughed. "My mother's maiden name is Torres. I learned Spanish from her side of the family. My looks are inherited from my father. His people are Irish. My great-grandfather immigrated through Ellis Island a hundred years ago. Back then, the Irish faced discrimination like Latinos do today. Nobody would hire a man named Flanagan, so he hid his accent and changed his surname. By dropping four letters, he converted it to a symbol of national pride."

Hector clapped a hand on Adolfo's shoulder. "Meet Special Agent Nicholas Flag of the Department of Homeland Security."

47

VERANDA STOOD IN the eye of the hurricane. That moment of calm in the center of chaos before the other side of the storm buffeted her. A morning spent in the hot seat at PSB had clarified her situation as nothing else could. Lieutenant Diaz and the Phoenix Police Department would use every ounce of their considerable power to control her. After Diaz dropped her back at the hospital, she'd visited with Agent Rios in his room. Satisfied he would recover, she passed by the gift shop on the way to the parking lot. A Navajo dreamcatcher featuring a howling Timber wolf dangled in the window. Her wolf dream rushed back to her, bringing inspiration with it.

Starting today, she would take back control. And she would begin with her own body.

That had been her plan four hours ago. Now, all sense of control deserted her as she gazed up at the burly man looming over her. He was about to inflict serious pain. Gripping the arms of her chair, her eyes traced the jagged scar climbing up his neck to disappear into his dense beard. She couldn't understand how anyone had survived such a grievous wound.

The man clearly lived up to his street name, Oso, the Spanish word for "bear." Intricate body art decorated every inch of his six-foot-five-inch frame not covered by his black leather vest and blue jeans. Even his face bore three dark blue teardrops spilling down from the outer corner of his eye, an obvious prison tatt.

Oso slid a beefy finger, encased in a purple latex glove, under her bra strap. "Take it off."

Her T-shirt was already draped over a hook on the back of the locked door.

He withdrew his hand to pick up a long steel needle from a tray of instruments and grinned down at her, revealing a gold tooth. "I hope you have a high pain tolerance."

Transfixed, she watched him insert the sharp instrument into a machine that looked like a drill and switch it on. The high-pitched sound catapulted her nervous system into overdrive. Her body jolted upright in the chair.

Chuy's voice came from behind her. "Hey *mi'jita*, what's up with you?"

Pulse pounding, she twisted around to look at her cousin. "I got a distorted fragment of memory." She blinked, trying to distinguish between the vision in her mind and the reality around her. "This whole situation ..." She swept out a hand to indicate the back room of the tattoo parlor. "Gave me something like a flashback."

She'd called her favorite cousin before leaving the hospital, finally ready to accept his offer of help with the cartel tattoo over her heart. Once a solution came to her, she couldn't stand the idea of living with the Villalobos family mark another day.

Chuy had taken her to Oso, the best cover-up tattoo artist in Phoenix. Chuy's description of his former cellmate on the way to Tiffany's parents' house hadn't done Oso justice.

After serving their respective sentences, Chuy and Oso had both faced the reality that no one was going to hire them. Unlike many of their fellow former inmates, each had beaten the odds to become small business owners.

Oso talked with her for over an hour about her idea, what was achievable, and what was not. Oso worked strictly freehand, explaining that he would create the artwork as he saw fit based on her vision. He'd showed her his portfolio and asked her to trust him. Unfortunately, her trust hadn't extended to sharing her previous experience regarding tattoos. She should have warned him.

"What kind of flashback did you have?" Chuy asked.

She was far more comfortable baring her skin than her soul. There was no sense hiding either now, and she needed time to collect herself. Chuy knew some of the story, but she was about to confide more than she ever had.

Drawing a deep breath, she pointed at her exposed upper left chest. "A high-ranking member of the Villalobos cartel did this after drugging me. All I have are distorted images and bits of memories. The noise from the machine must have triggered a reaction."

Concern wrinkled Oso's heavy brow. "Are you sure you want to do this?"

"I've never been more certian of anything." She met his eyes, willing him to understand. "People I care about—my former boyfriend, my partner, my family—have been hurt because of me. My department is going to hold a hearing to decide if I should keep my badge." She hesitated before admitting the final part. "And Hector Villalobos wants me dead."

Chuy swore under his breath. "While I'm in Mexico, I should take out that *pendejo* myself."

"You aren't going anywhere near him." She narrowed her eyes. "This is my battle, not yours."

Chuy showed signs of arguing but seemed to think better of it. Oso was there, and Chuy wasn't supposed to discuss his new sideline.

Instead, her cousin settled for a menacing scowl. "We aren't done talking about this, *mi'jita*."

She turned her attention back to Oso, whose expression telegraphed skepticism. She would have to prove her commitment.

She reached around behind her back. "Some things I can't control, but this I can." She unhooked her bra. "Do I want to do this? No." She grasped the lacy material and tossed it aside. "But I *need* to do this."

Chuy and Oso exchanged glances.

"Okay, I hear you," Oso said. "Let's change the ink to make it your own, but are you sure about the design?"

"I had a dream about a gray wolf," she told him. "Today, it finally clicked. I'm not part of the Villalobos clan, but I've been wearing their mark for seven weeks. It's time I did something about it."

She reflected on the effect her unwanted body art had on people, picturing the paramedic's reaction at the storage unit scene when he spotted it. The EMT's expression echoed the one Cole quickly hid the first time he saw it. Finally, she remembered the full-length mirror at her mother's house. Tiffany had to cover the black wolf and letter V with body makeup so she wouldn't mortify the guests or cause her family more pain. She squared her shoulders. After today, the cartel tattoo wouldn't mar her body anymore.

"We've gone over this," Oso said after a long pause. "But I'll remind you one more time. This is a substantial piece of work and the tatt you're changing is black. You'll sit in this chair a lot over the next couple of weeks. It's a process. The first session will take a couple of hours and cover a fair amount of fresh skin in some sensitive areas." He paused to regard her. "I won't lie. It'll hurt." At her nod, he continued. "I'll use a white ink enhancement first. We'll see if that gets you where you want to go. If not, I can blend in some lasering to fade the color more."

The wolf's head would remain over her heart, but Oso planned to lighten it to gray and soften the face with a ruff of fur. She'd opted to add a full body to the newly redesigned head, insisting Oso make it distinctly female. The gray wolf would cover almost half her torso, from its head on her chest to its bushy tail curled over her hip. Oso had warned her the artwork over her rib cage would cause the most pain.

The red V above the original tattoo symbolized her Villalobos bloodline, a scarlet letter forced on her to bring public scorn and humiliation. Instead of lasering it off to deny her father, she would enhance it to honor her mother, adding letters to create the name Lorena had chosen for her. Veranda.

When the transformation was complete, the new creation would evoke her own personal code. Still lupine, deadly, and fierce, but tempered by compassion and full of heart.

"Any last questions?" Oso asked her.

This felt like the final preflight check. Replaying their discussion in her mind, a small but important detail occurred to her. "Can you make the eyes hazel?" She'd inherited her mother's eyes, another special bond she wanted to memorialize.

"I'll match them to yours." Oso leaned in close. "I see shades of green, brown, and gold. Very pretty."

"*Oye cochino*," Chuy said, thumping his fist into Oso's shoulder. "Don't be gazing into my cousin's eyes like that."

"Who you calling dirty?" Oso tried to pull off a wounded expression, but only managed to look like he'd swallowed a jalapeño. "I'm a professional."

Chuy rolled his eyes at Oso before handing her a stick of gum. "You were out of it the last time you got inked, so you don't know what it feels like. Chew on this and squeeze my hand if you need to. You've got to be still no matter how much it hurts."

All transformation involved pain. Serious transformation left scars, visible and hidden. She smiled. This pain, she had chosen. And she would embrace it. Settling back against the chair, she popped the gum into her mouth and slipped her hand into Chuy's before turning to Oso. "Bring it on."

As the needle pierced her skin, she contemplated the forces that had shaped her. Born of her father's brutal crime. Saved by her mother's selfless love. The new body art would represent both aspects of her nature, blending shadow and light.

I am the gray wolf.

Acknowledgments

When I took off my gun and badge for the last time a few years ago, I thought retiring from a career in law enforcement would end my constant background ruminations about crime. Turns out, I had a lot of stories floating around in my head that wanted out. I am blessed and humbled to have the opportunity to share them.

One of the tools both real and fictional detectives use is familial DNA analysis. I am very grateful for the technical expertise of Jody Wissel Wolf, who checked my forensic science for accuracy. Jody is that wonderful combination of scientist and bibliophile that so many of us admire. Any errors regarding DNA evidence are solely mine.

Editors are a crucial part of the book-birthing process. Fresh eyes and a fresh perspective are helpful when my blinders are firmly in place. Huge thanks to Deborah J Ledford, Terri Bischoff, and Nicole Nugent for all you do.

A sincere *muchas gracias* to Liza Fleissig, my phenomenal agent, and Ginger Harris-Dontzin, her sharp-eyed business partner. Liza has unstintingly given her time and talent at every turn and bump in the road. And there have been bumps...

Last, but definitely not least, a special shout-out to a *New York Times* bestselling author who took time from her busy schedule to pay it forward. J.A. Jance is not only an amazing talent but a kind mentor who generously shares her hard-won wisdom garnered from a prolific and successful writing career.

Once the story is written, readers need to hear about it. I am truly grateful for the efforts of booksellers, reviewers, and librarians. In addition, extra thanks go to Dana Kaye and Samantha Lien of Kaye Publicity for their enthusiastic support in spreading the word.

Nothing helped me make the transition from cop to author more than professional writers' organizations. Sisters in Crime, International

Thriller Writers, Mystery Writers of America, and the International Society of Latino Authors have all made an enormous impact.

I am blessed with a wonderful family, whether blood-related or bound by love. Their acceptance of me, with my many foibles, warms my heart as nothing else can. First and foremost are my husband, Michael, who encourages my dreams, and my son, Max, who inspires me every day. In addition to relatives and in-laws, I consider some of my closest friends to be family. Words cannot express my gratitude for your love and support over the years.

Finally, I would like to thank the readers of crime fiction. It's exciting to interact with such smart people at events and speaking engagements. Because of my background, some have asked why I write fiction over true crime. The question made me realize that after years of being forced to watch things turn out the way they do, I wanted to have them turn out the way they should.

SkaiStyle Photography

About the Author

Before her foray into the world of crime fiction, Isabella Maldonado wore a gun and badge in real life. She retired as a captain after twenty-two years on the force and moved to the Phoenix area, where her uniform now consists of tank tops and yoga pants.

During her tenure on the department, she was a patrol officer, hostage negotiator, spokesperson, and recruit instructor at the police academy. After being promoted, she worked as a patrol sergeant and lieutenant before heading the Public Information Office. Finally, as a captain, she served as Gang Council Coordinator and oversaw a patrol district station before her final assignment as the Commander of the Special Investigations and Forensics Division (since renamed the Investigative Support Division).

She graduated from the FBI National Academy in Quantico in 2008 after eleven weeks of physically and mentally challenging study for 220 law enforcement executives from around the world. She is proud to have earned her "yellow brick" for completing the famous FBI obstacle course.

Now her activities involve chasing around her young son and enjoying her family when she's not handcuffed to her computer.

Ms. Maldonado is a member of the FBI National Academy Associates, Fairfax County Police Association, International Thriller Writers, Mystery Writers of America, International Society of Latino Authors, and Sisters in Crime, where she served as president of the Phoenix metro chapter in 2015 and sat on the board until 2019.

WWW.MIDNIGHTINKBOOKS.COM

From the gritty streets of New York City to sacred tombs in the Middle East, it's always midnight somewhere. Join us online at any hour for fresh new voices in mystery fiction.

At midnightinkbooks.com you'll also find our author blog, new and upcoming books, events, book club questions, excerpts, mystery resources, and more.

MIDNIGHT INK ORDERING INFORMATION

Order Online:
• Visit our website www.midnightinkbooks.com, select your books, and order them on our secure server.

Order by Phone:
• Call toll-free within the U.S. at
  1-888-NITE-INK (1-888-648-3465)
• We accept VISA, MasterCard, American Express, and Discover
• Canadian customers must use credit cards

Order by Mail:
Send the full price of your order (MN residents add 6.875% sales tax) in U.S. funds, plus postage & handling to:

> Midnight Ink
> 2143 Wooddale Drive
> Woodbury, MN 55125-2989

Postage & Handling:
Standard (US). If your order is:
> $30.00 and under, add $6.00
> $30.01 and over, FREE STANDARD SHIPPING

AK, HI, PR: $16.00 for one book plus $2.00 for each additional book.

International Orders: Including Canada
> $16.00 for one book plus $3.00 for each additional book

Orders are processed within 12 business days. Please allow for normal shipping time.
Postage and handling rates subject to change.